Sh_____ep
in hi_____ in
warning. She was playing with fire now, but she desperately
wanted to lose herself in his heat. "I know you do."

It was his turn to laugh. "Oh, brat," he drawled in a husky
voice that rumbled through her and set her blood humming.
"I want to do so much more than just kiss you."

With a silent gasp, she stared disbelievingly at him in the
blue-gray light, her pulse pounding in her ears with every
racing heartbeat.

"I want to wrap your naked body in satin sheets and splay
you across my bed, then lick every inch of you. I want to nibble your throat and breasts, stroke your thighs until you spread
yourself open to me and beg to be taken." The gleam in his
eyes was predatory. "And it certainly wouldn't be nice."

* * *

Praise for Anna Harrington and DUKES ARE FOREVER

"A touching and tempestuous romance, with all the ingre-
dients Regency fans adore."
—**Gaelen Foley**, *New York Times* **bestselling author**

"Ripe with drama and sizzling romance...The complex
relationship between Edward and Katherine is intense and
skillfully written, complete with plenty of romantic angst
that propels the novel swiftly forward. This new author is
definitely one to watch."
—*Publishers Weekly* **(starred review)**

"As steamy as it is sweet as it is luscious. My favorite
kind of historical!"
—**Grace Burrowes**, *New York Times* **bestselling author**

Also by Anna Harrington

Dukes Are Forever

ALONG CAME

A

ROGUE

ANNA
HARRINGTON

FOREVER

NEW YORK   BOSTON

Copyright © 2016 by Anna Harrington
Excerpt from *How I Married a Marquess* copyright © 2016 by Anna Harrington
Cover design by Christine Foltzer
Cover illustration by Chris Cocozza
Cover copyright © 2016 by Hachette Book Group, Inc.

Forever
Hachette Book Group
1290 Avenue of the Americas
New York, NY 10104

forever-romance.com
twitter.com/foreverromance

First Edition: February 2016

Forever is an imprint of Grand Central Publishing.
The Forever name and logo are trademarks of Hachette Book Group, Inc.

The publisher is not responsible for websites (or their content) that are not owned by the publisher.

The Hachette Speakers Bureau provides a wide range of authors for speaking events. To find out more, go to www.hachettespeakersbureau.com or call (866) 376-6591.

ISBN 978-1-4555-3405-0 (mass market); 978-1-4555-3404-3 (ebook)

Printed in the United States of America

OPM

10 9 8 7 6 5 4 3 2

Dedicated to Jennifer Smith (and Lilly) for your patient answers to all my questions. And to Allison Fetters for enabling my gardening addiction.

Also, a very special thank-you to Michele Bidelspach and Sarah Younger.

CHAPTER ONE

London, England
March 1816

*I*n the shadows of the private opera box, Nathaniel Grey lowered the glass of whiskey from his lips and smiled down at the beautifully coiffed head bobbing at his crotch.

Oh, Lady Margaret Roquefort was a lovely woman with a deliciously wicked mouth whose company he enjoyed immensely. Luckily, she also shared his interest in opera, finding far more fun in the activities that occurred in the dark boxes than in whatever happened onstage.

The rising notes of the aria drowned her soft moan of pleasure as her lips closed tightly around him. Shutting his eyes, he let himself savor the moment.

He wasn't meant to be here, two boxes down from the Prince Regent, taking pleasure in one of the most beautiful ladies in English society. Not him. Not an orphan so inconsequential to the world that the lie he chose to tell about himself—that he was the runaway son of a blacksmith—was a decided improvement over the truth.

But in his life, he'd more than earned the right to be

among the gentlemen of the *ton*, having killed—and nearly been killed himself—to protect all of them, without a word of thanks. Yet while he could dress like them, gamble with them, drink their best whiskey, and bed their finest ladies, he would never truly be one of them.

And he didn't give a damn if he wasn't.

In fact, he liked it. Living on the periphery of society gave him a freedom he would never have as one of the quality, and freedom meant everything to him.

"Grey," Margaret moaned. He reached down to stroke his knuckles across her cheek.

He smiled at the irony as arousal throbbed hot through his veins. Would Lady Roquefort be pleasuring him right now if she knew the truth about him? He choked back a laugh. Knowing Margaret, she would have been sucking even more eagerly in rebellious glee.

A baroness and an orphan...Wouldn't that juicy bit of *on-dit* send scandal rippling through the *ton* if anyone found out?

But he'd made damned certain no one ever would.

Even at just ten, when he ran away from the orphanage, he knew how to lie about himself and lie well enough to talk his way into a job as a stable boy at Henley Park, where he had a roof over his head, food in his belly, and an education thrust upon him by the Viscountess Henley. When he turned eighteen, he purchased an officer's commission and enlisted with the Scarlet Scoundrels of the First Dragoons.

That was the man Margaret thought she was enjoying tonight. The army officer who led charge after charge on the Peninsula, only for a single bullet to end his cavalry career and force him to once again reinvent himself, this time as a War Office agent. Losing his command had been damned hard, but the end of the wars had created a need for trusted agents, and he was good at spy work. So good, in fact, that he'd been offered a coveted position on the Continent. If all went as planned, he'd be in Spain by next month.

Success was so close now that he could taste it. He *craved* it. Everything in his life had led to this opportunity, and he planned on seizing it for all he was worth.

But for now he was here, with Margaret's eager mouth and hands on him, enjoying himself immensely.

The soprano reached her last trilling notes. Pulling a rasping breath through his clenched teeth, Grey shuddered and released himself. Margaret swallowed around him as her hot mouth milked his cock. When she'd finished, he pulled away and handed her the glass.

As she drank the remaining liquor, he fastened up his trousers. Ah, how much he enjoyed the opera! And one of these nights, he fully intended to watch a performance.

"Ugh—whiskey!" Margaret made a disgusted face as he took her elbow and helped her to her feet. "You know I can't stand the stuff, Grey. Why don't you ever drink port or brandy—something I enjoy?"

"I never drink brandy." His mouth twisted with distaste. "Not anymore." Brandy reminded him of the French, and he'd done everything in his power to put the war behind him and to focus instead on his future.

Applause thundered around them as the audience rose to their feet and filed from their boxes for intermission. The mindless chatter among the blue bloods rose nearly as loud as the opera singers.

"Port, then." She set the glass aside and smoothed her hands down her skirt to press out any telltale wrinkles. His lips twitched in amusement at her expense. Oh, how much he enjoyed women like Lady Roquefort! Those well-bred ladies of the *ton* who were always so proper and fashionable, even when on their knees. He would miss their sort when he was in Spain. "Next time, bring me port."

He gave her a charming smile, this woman who meant absolutely nothing to him except as an evening's entertainment, and stifled a contemptuous laugh because she thought she could order him about.

"Of course, my lady." He reached out to trail his fingers over the top swells of her breasts, revealed by the daringly low neckline. Her breath quickened beneath his fingertips as he purred, "Anything you desire."

She trembled against his exploring hands. "All the ladies were gossiping about you earlier in the retiring room."

"Hmm...and what did they say?" She expected him to ask, so he indulged her, yet he couldn't have cared less about those gossipy hens.

"They wondered what Major Grey was like as a lover, if he'd singled out anyone to be his mistress or if he prefers being promiscuous."

"Promiscuous," he murmured with mock solemnity, dipping his head to trace the tip of his tongue into the valley between her breasts. "Definitely promiscuous."

With a flirtatious laugh, she swatted at his shoulder and forced him to step back as the noise of the milling crowd grew louder. She adjusted her long gloves. "How do I look?"

"Stunning." He raised her hand to his lips. "As always."

The flattery was empty, but it pleased her. Which was all that mattered. He needed to keep her happy only so he could enjoy Mozart again with her next week.

Her eyes shining at the compliment, she leaned back against the wall. "Quite a coup, securing a private box all to yourself. However did you manage?"

"I've always appreciated the privacy of a reserved box," he expertly deflected her question.

He'd long ago grown used to the backhanded compliments leveled at him by her sort. They no more bothered him now than getting caught in a warm summer rain. But he wasn't foolish enough to open himself to further criticism by admitting that the box belonged to Edward Westover, Duke of Strathmore and his former colonel in the Scarlet Scoundrels.

No doubt Margaret thought she'd been utterly scandalous tonight by having her mouth on him. She was right, of course. Even the rank of major wasn't enough to gain status among the quality when he had no fortune or family name to accompany it. Neither did he care. He was free to bed whomever he wanted, whenever he wanted—and in the case of Lady Roquefort, *wherever* he wanted—and answer to no one but himself.

"Now, be a good girl"—he turned her toward the box entrance, happily done with her for the evening—"and return to your husband before the old baron discovers you're missing."

With a satisfied grin and a playful slap to her ass that made her jump, he was gone, stepping through the curtain into the milling crowd in the hallway and leaving her behind without another thought.

The hour was still early. Plenty of time yet for cards at one of the clubs since he no longer had any reason to linger at the opera. After all, he certainly hadn't attended to hear the music.

Maybe he'd rouse Thomas Matteson from whatever dull evening he'd planned and bring him out with him. After all, they'd been best friends since they'd served together in Spain, where they'd saved each other repeatedly from both French soldiers and Spanish husbands.

Grey's brows drew down slightly. Odd to think how much

their lives had changed in the past two years. He had become
an agent while Edward and Thomas had both moved into
the ranks of the peerage, with Edward becoming Duke of
Strathmore and Thomas gaining the courtesy title of marquess when his father unexpectedly inherited a duchy. Yet
their lives were going to change again. Grey was heading
back to Spain, and Edward—God help him—was going to
become a father.

Best to squeeze in as many good nights as possible now,
Grey decided as he made his way downstairs, slipping between groups of operagoers gossiping in the hall and on the
wide stairs curving into the grand lobby below. He nodded at
the handful of acquaintances he knew among the crush, but
they only returned bewildered stares, as if surprised to see
him.

As he skirted a group of pastel-clad debutantes at a safe
distance, a shocked whisper rose from behind a flutter of
fans. "The marquess!"

Lots of marquesses among the quality, Grey dismissed. He
paid the comment no mind as he descended the stairs and
passed a group of gossiping hens with the same shocked ex-
pressions, the same frantic flitting of their fans in agitated
excitement as they stared in his direction. Just as with the debutantes, he gave the hens a wide berth. The last thing he wanted
to sour his mood tonight was those disapproving glances that
society matrons were so skilled at sending rakes like him.

Snippets of conversation wafted up to him as he reached
the lobby. "So terrible...the marquess...dying like that..."

Hmm. A dying marquess. So *that* was what stirred such
excitement tonight. Fresh news about the Marquess of Dunwich. The old man had taken to bed a few days ago with
the same fever that had claimed both his son and grandson,
leaving the title without an heir apparent, and the entire *ton*

buzzed with speculation over what would become of the title when he died. Based on the titillated anxiousness floating through the crowd tonight, the old man must have finally given up the ghost.

He nodded at the Earl of St. James and his mother as he passed, doing his best to catch the eye of Baroness Sydney Rowland, standing next to them. The young widow was beautiful and exactly the kind of woman he preferred—

A man stepped directly in front of him, stopping him abruptly.

Grey couldn't remember the man's name but recognized him as a distant friend of Thomas Matteson's from university. "I say, major," the man said, perplexed. "I'm damnably stunned to see you here tonight."

Grey shrugged. "I enjoy the opera." He grinned with private amusement. "Especially the arias."

The man's face scrunched into a deep frown. "But I thought, with today's events—surely, you'd be at Chatham House tonight."

Ah, of course. That's why everyone was eyeing him so oddly. Alistair Crenshaw, Marquess of Dunwich, had been distantly related to the Matteson family through the marriage of Thomas's sister, and most of Mayfair knew that he and Thomas had served together on the Peninsula. It was Thomas who had shown him the intricacies and potential of a rake's life among the quality once they'd returned to England, and their friendship gave him a grudging acceptance within the *ton*. Everyone must have thought Grey would be giving his condolences to the family tonight.

He shook his head. "Decided on the opera instead. I'll pay my condolences tomorrow."

The man blanched. "But—but the marquess!"

"Dead, apparently. Terrible shame." Then he moved on

through the crush, ignoring the completely astounded look on the man's face.

He neared the door, longing for the coolness of the night outside—

"The marquess was so young."

He stopped instantly, his head snapping up. A *young* marquess?

The man who uttered that news stood only a few feet away with a group of bejeweled ladies and gentlemen. Grey forced a lazy half smile that belied the rising unease inside him as he sauntered over. "Which young marquess?"

"Chesney." The man blinked, surprised that anyone in the opera house could possibly not have heard the news. "Shot in the street at sunset. No one knows—"

Thomas. For a moment he stared in disbelief, his stunned mind unable to comprehend the words falling from the man's mouth. Then his blood turned to ice as panic sped through him and the air squeezed from his lungs. *God no* . . . it couldn't be. Not Thomas—but the expression on the man's face was too certain to be wrong.

Grey ran for the street.

When he reached Chatham House, the townhome was ablaze with candles and lamps, and his heart stuttered with dread. Two saddle horses stood tied in the front, along with the massive black carriage marked with the Duke of Strathmore's coat of arms.

He raced up the front steps of the stone portico and pounded on the door. Jensen, the Chatham butler, opened the door but did not step back to let him pass.

"The house is closed tonight, Major," Jensen told him, his ashen face drawn and his gray brows knitted with worry. "Please return tomorrow."

When he tried to shut the door, Grey shoved his shoulder

against it and pushed his way inside, forcing the butler to stumble backward to make way for him.

Had it been any other night, he never would have caused such an uproar. He would have returned the next day as asked, just to keep peace. But tonight, he refused to stand on politeness.

"Where's Chesney?" Grey demanded. "Is he here?"

"Major, please!" Jensen glowered at him. "The house is closed upon order of His Gr—"

"Jensen." A commanding voice from the upstairs landing cut through the scuffle. "Let him pass."

The butler glanced up at Edward Westover, Duke of Strathmore. With an aggravated *humph!* beneath his breath at having his authority undermined, he stepped back to let Grey into the house.

He raced up the curving marble stairs, his heart pounding with fear. "Thomas?" he rasped out.

"He's here," Edward informed him solemnly, keeping his voice low so he wouldn't be overheard by the servants. "The surgeons are with him."

"He's alive?" Grey gripped the wrought iron banister to steady himself.

A grim solemnity darkened Edward's face. "Barely."

He exhaled a long, shaking breath. "Jesus...what happened?"

With a glance at Jensen still lingering in the foyer, Edward nodded toward the nearby billiards room. Grey followed him inside and accepted the scotch his former colonel poured from a bottle on the table just inside the door, the half-filled glass beside it telling him that Edward had already sought out his own liquid strength.

As he raised the glass, he tried to hide the shaking in his hands. "Was it the French?" he asked quietly.

Edward and Grey were two of a handful of people who knew that Thomas had continued to dedicate himself to his country after leaving the army, signing on to work secretly with the War Office. If the French had discovered he was spying, they might have attempted an assassination.

Edward shook his head. "He'd been visiting at Strathmore House and was on his way home when a footpad shot him." He reached for his glass and took a long swallow. "A groom heard the report and found the man rifling through Thomas's pockets."

Grey steeled himself. "How badly is he wounded?"

Edward's face turned to stone. "Gutshot."

The air rushed from his lungs, and Grey leaned against the wall, squeezing his eyes shut against the mix of fear, dread, and fury swirling inside him, unwilling to believe the worst. *Dear God* . . . not Thomas, not like this. Not after he'd faced down death in Spain, only to be killed two streets from his own home.

"The surgeons are operating now. Thank God that groom came upon him when he did, or he would have bled out right there." Edward studied the amber liquid in his glass. "Jensen sent a messenger to the house. When Kate heard, she insisted on coming with me to attend the surgeons."

New worry spun through him for the duchess. "In her condition?"

Edward's lips pressed together grimly at the reminder that his wife was expecting. "You try stopping her when she's set her mind on something."

Taking careful breaths, concentrating on the air filling his lungs and forcing back his growing grief, Grey tried to steady himself. But his heart kept pounding harder, his stomach roiling. *Gutshot* . . . Thomas was alive, but he'd most likely be dead by dawn.

"Damnation!" Edward slammed down the crystal tumbler so hard the liquor splashed onto the table. He rubbed his thumb and forefinger at his forehead, at that moment appearing as if he'd aged decades. "I sent him away tonight. Kate asked him to stay with us for dinner, but I wanted an evening alone with her." Guilt stiffened his shoulders as he shook his head. "If I hadn't—if I had just invited him to stay, offered another drink…"

"It wasn't your fault, Colonel," Grey assured him.

"I know," he agreed quietly, "but it damned sure feels like it." He shoved his glass away. "I've sent a messenger to his parents at their country estate."

"He has a sister, too, near York—Emily," Grey reminded him as an image from five years ago flashed through his mind of a stick of a girl with blond braids who had adored her doting older brother. She'd want to know, would want to be by Thomas's side… "We need to send a messenger to her, too."

Edward nodded grimly, although both men knew the harsh reality that the news wouldn't reach Thomas's family for days. By then, he would likely be past whatever comfort they could give. "I've hired Bow Street to track down the footpad and ordered Jensen to close the house to visitors. There's nothing else to do but wait."

Grey stared at him, the grief inside him turning into fury. *Wait?* Like hell he would. Downing the rest of the scotch in a single, gasping swallow, he shoved himself away from the wall and charged toward the door.

"Where are you going?" Edward called out after him.

He glanced over his shoulder as he strode from the room, his calm outward appearance belying the white-hot rage burning inside him. "To find the man who did this."

Edward followed him. "Let Bow Street take care of this. They have access to Mayfair."

"I have better contacts. I'll have my men in the streets within an hour."

"Grey." Edward put his hand on Grey's arm as they reached the stairs, and repeated pointedly, "Bow Street has access to Mayfair."

Grey clenched his jaw at the unspoken meaning underlying Edward's comment. The runners would be allowed into any house in Mayfair if they said they were investigating the marquess's shooting, while he and his War Office men wouldn't be allowed past the front door.

His eyes narrowed icily at the reminder that he would never belong to English society, no matter how hard he worked, no matter how many promotions he earned. He'd never cared before tonight, and the truth had never cut more deeply than at this brutally frustrating moment when being an outsider made helping Thomas impossible.

"I will find that man," Grey repeated, wrenching his arm away from Edward's grasp and charging down the stairs toward the front door. "I might not have the same access to Mayfair as a Bow Street runner or a blue blood," he bit out, "but I also have nothing to lose. And if Thomas dies, I'll make that bastard regret the day he was born."

"Grey—"

"I *have* to, Colonel. I have to do something to help, however I can." He paused at the bottom of the stairs to glance back at Edward. His chest tightened with anguish and helpless frustration as the adrenaline coursed through him. "I won't simply stay here and wait for him to die."

Then he strode out the front door into the black night.

* * *

Grey shifted uncomfortably on the chair in Thomas's bedroom as the morning sunlight shone around the closed
drapes. His muscles ached stiffly, and he winced as a sharp
pain stabbed into his lower back.

One week had passed since the shooting, and he'd spent
yet another sleepless night at Thomas's side, keeping watch,
leaving the house only to help Bow Street track down the man
responsible. He'd found the footpad himself in a seedy tavern
in Spitalfields, bragging about how he'd robbed a gentleman in
Mayfair, still possessing the watch he'd stolen from Thomas's
pocket. *Bastard.* Two runners had to pull him off the man to
stop him from beating the son of a bitch to death right there in
the tavern, only for him to stand before the gallows at Tyburn
yesterday morning and mercilessly watch the man swing.

Perhaps war had hardened him too much. Perhaps he had
no compassion left after all the atrocities he'd witnessed in
the wars. Because when he watched the shooter die, he'd felt
glad. And relieved, knowing the man could never harm anyone else.

The door opened quietly, and Edward Westover stepped
into the room. His tired gaze found Grey's and held it in
a moment of shared concern, then drifted to the bed and
to Thomas's weak body lying there as comfortably as they
could make him.

But how comfortable could Thomas be given the hell
he'd been through in the past week? And given that his
arms and legs were bound to the bed to keep him from tossing about in fitful bouts of feverish sleep and ripping open
the sutures. Kate Westover had insisted on that, the young
duchess crying in choking fits as she begged the two men to
tie him down. They had done it without a word, without a
glance at the other, knowing it had to be done even as their
chests filled with guilt.

His gaze swung back to Grey. "You spent the night here again." Not a question, but a grim accusation.

"Yes." And he'd spend tonight here, too. Although, he thought, grimacing as he shoved himself from the chair and rubbed at his stiff neck, the least Jensen could do was offer to bring in a cot for him. But he wouldn't complain, not with Thomas lying so still, so pale in his bed.

"How is he?" Edward asked quietly.

"Better." He'd slept through the night at least, for once not thrashing about in the bed nor crying out in his sleep. That was due to the receding fever and the longer and more frequent stretches of wakeful consciousness that came as he slowly regained his strength. But the color had yet to come back to his sallow cheeks, his face still as pale as a ghost's.

Edward moved slowly to the side of the bed and frowned down at Thomas and the ugly black sutures marring his side. "At least the swelling has gone down. Kate will be glad of that."

"Is the duchess here with you?" Grey stepped up beside him. Together the two men stared solemnly down at their friend, helpless to do anything more than continue to hold their vigil.

Edward shook his head. "She wanted to come, but I made her stay home. She's exhausted and needs to rest, both for her sake and the baby's." Then he frowned. "But most likely she'll be back this afternoon. I doubt I can keep her away for long."

Grey nodded, his chest swelling with appreciation and gratitude for the duchess. She'd insisted on being at Chatham House nearly as many hours as he had, and far more than Dr. Brandon, the official physician tending to Thomas. "Don't keep her away too long, Colonel." He said softly around the knot in his throat, "Thomas is better when she's here."

Edward heaved a heavy breath and nodded. "He likes it when she feeds him."

Despite the heaviness weighing in his gut, Grey crooked a half grin. "He likes looking down her dress when she leans over to put the spoon to his mouth."

"That, too." Edward grimaced. "When he's healed, I plan on pummeling him for it."

Grey's eyes moved slowly over Thomas, his body so still except for the faint, steady rise and fall of his chest. So impossibly pale… "Then I hope you get to beat the hell out of him very soon," Grey said quietly, his teasing words dull with grief.

"Me, too," Edward murmured.

A clatter of noise went up from downstairs and broke the post-dawn silence of the still-sleeping town house. The front door opened loudly. Footsteps rushed in and out of the house as muffled shouts sounded outside. Then an angry voice called through the halls.

Edward slid a sideways glance at Grey. "Chatham's arrived."

"Apparently," Grey muttered, not looking forward to seeing Thomas's parents. They had never approved of his friendship with their son, and certainly not after the incident five years ago when they'd caught him kissing their daughter. They tolerated him now only because they didn't want to alienate Thomas.

Moments later, his mother ran into the room. Mary Matteson, Duchess of Chatham, halted when her eyes landed on her son. A soft sob tore from her throat. She came forward slowly toward the bed, her hand shaking violently as she reached for Thomas's cheek.

"Thomas?" His name was a pleading whisper between choking sobs. "Thomas, can you hear me? Darling, it's Mother...please...please wake up..."

Soft cries poured from her, her already red-rimmed eyes revealing the tears she must have been crying for days, ever since the messenger arrived with news of the shooting and along every mile from Lancashire as they raced back to London.

"He's so cold and pale," she breathed in an anguished whisper, her fingertips stroking his face. "My baby—my poor baby boy..."

The two men looked on helplessly, before Grey had to turn away, his eyes blurring.

Edward placed a hand gently on her shoulder. "He's out of danger now," he assured her, his quiet voice calm and steady. The same timbre Grey remembered from Spain whenever Edward spoke to the wounded men after a battle, to give them whatever comfort and courage he could. "Dr. Brandon confirmed it. Thomas will be just fine."

Then her cries of worry turned to ones of relief. She grabbed Edward's hand and squeezed it tightly. "But—but he's not waking up..."

"He's been sleeping deeply all night," Grey interjected gently, yet keeping his distance. He wasn't welcome here, but he wanted to ease her suffering however he could. "Sleep is a good sign. It means his body is healing."

She glanced over her shoulder at him, and surprise crossed her face, as if she hadn't noticed he was there. Then her lips pressed together tightly, and she nodded to acknowledge his words before turning back to Thomas.

"Thank you, Your Grace," she told Edward. "Your friendship means more than Chatham and I can ever express. Thomas is alive because of you."

"And Major Grey," Edward corrected gently, his gaze glancing over her head to meet Grey's.

Grey could have told him to save his breath. He had no doubt that if Edward hadn't been in the room, she would have already had the footmen toss him out on his ass.

"Thomas!" John Matteson, Duke of Chatham, strode into the room. His face was pale with worry, and his hands clenched helplessly at his sides.

A tall and imposing man with the same military bearing as Thomas, the duke had served in India with the East India Company, acting as a military liaison to the local maharajas for a decade before returning to England with his second wife and infant son, where he served as an administrator until he unexpectedly inherited. What struck Grey every time he saw the man was how much Thomas resembled him physically, but how little in temperament and character.

He took his wife's shoulders and stared down at his son. "Mary, how is he?"

She choked back a cry and whispered, "He's alive." She turned her head and buried her face in her husband's shoulder as she sobbed. "Our boy's alive..."

"Thank God," Chatham breathed out, then his arms slipped around his wife to briefly hold her close. "I told you that all would be fine." He released her and stepped back, ending the uncharacteristic display of emotion. He glanced around the room. "Where's Emily?"

Edward cleared his throat. "I dispatched a messenger to her. He returned three days ago with this." He lifted a letter from the fireplace and handed it to her father. "She plans to come as soon as she's able."

Chatham unfolded the letter and scanned it quickly. His shoulders stiffened, but he nodded at Edward with a stoic expression. "Thank you."

Grey knew what that letter said. Thomas's sister Emily had thanked Edward for the news of the shooting, grateful beyond words that the colonel had thought to contact her, but claimed she was unable to travel to London. Still in mourning over her husband's unexpected death last fall, she was too ill to travel, the roads in the north too treacherous in the spring rains, but she would come as soon as she could. *Tell Thomas I love him, and always will…*

Damned lies, all of it. When he'd met her five years ago, she'd openly adored her older brother, who in turn doted on her and affectionately referred to her as "the brat." That young woman would have done anything to be at her wounded brother's side, not letting sickness nor the weather stop her.

But the recently widowed woman who sent this letter— apparently, Grey didn't know her at all anymore.

"Mother…" The word was little more than a breath on Thomas's lips, but the soft sound pierced the room.

Mary Matteson sobbed and cupped her palm against his cheek as she sat beside him on the bed. "I'm here, Thomas. Father and I are both here."

His eyes remained closed, but he licked his dry lips as he slowly woke. "I'm sorry…I'm so sorry…"

"No, darling, no." She leaned over to kiss his forehead as fresh tears rolled down her cheeks. "It wasn't your fault. It wasn't—"

He tried to move to reach for her, but the ties held him down.

She pulled back and glared accusingly at Grey through tear-glistened eyes. "Get these things off him!"

Anger pierced him at the indictment on her face, mixing with the horrible guilt he already carried for having to tie down his best friend in the first place. But he held his tongue and said nothing, knowing now wasn't the time to defend himself to Thomas's parents. And not in his sickroom.

"Mary," Chatham told her, "he wouldn't be tied down if Dr. Brandon didn't think it necessary."

Instead of reassuring her, his explanation only made her weep harder.

Thomas's eyelids fluttered open heavily, taking all his strength to open them. "Don't cry, Mother," he whispered. Then he rasped out, "Water...please."

Mary nodded and reached for the pitcher and glass on the stand beside the bed, but her hands shook so violently that she nearly spilled it.

"Here, let me." Grey stepped forward and took the glass from her, then carefully slipped his hand beneath Thomas's head to raise it from the pillow. He held the glass to Thomas's parched lips and tipped it just enough that he could take several swallows, then eased his head back down onto the pillow.

Unfocused, Thomas's blue eyes swept around the room. Bewilderment flashed across his pale face. "Emily...?"

"She's coming as soon as she can," Grey assured him with the lie, knowing the truth would only upset him. That most likely she wouldn't come at all. During the past two years, Thomas and Emily had fallen out and rarely communicated, although Thomas had always refused to say why exactly other than that Emily had gotten married. "The weather is bad up north, and she can't travel yet. But soon."

His answer didn't calm the agitation in Thomas's eyes. "I need her, Grey...I need Emily."

Grey stared down at him, his chest ripping open painfully beneath Thomas's soft pleading. He was still so weak, with the loss of blood leaving his skin nearly transparent and his muscles still too fragile to move from bed. Every breath was a struggle.

"Bring the brat to me . . . please . . ."

Grey nodded, not trusting himself to speak. He knew what he had to do.

"We'll send our own coach and escort for our daughter, Major," Chatham interjected. "This is none of your concern."

Grey ignored him and cast a glance at Edward, whose solemn expression signaled his complete understanding of the unspoken question that passed between them. He nodded once.

Turning on his heel, Grey strode from the room, through the house, and out the front door. His jaw was set hard, his mind determined.

"Send a message to Arthur Hedley at the Horse Guards," he ordered the groom who brought out his horse from the stables, then tossed the man a coin to make certain the message was delivered. "Tell him to follow me north to Yorkshire."

Knowing the former sergeant would catch up with him by nightfall, he mounted his horse and set off. Thomas wanted Emily by his side, so that was exactly what he would do. Put her at Thomas's side.

No matter what it took to get her there.

CHAPTER TWO

Yorkshire, England

*S*nowden Hall. *Thank God.*

After three days of hard riding, Grey gratefully turned his horse down the lane toward the large Yorkshire farm where Thomas's sister lived, with Hedley falling into a trot beside him. Three days of near-constant riding through miserable rain and unseasonable cold, stopping only when the night grew too dark to travel on—all because Thomas had asked him to fetch his sister, and Grey would have moved heaven and earth for him.

Although, he thought, grimacing as he glanced up at the thick, darkening clouds that promised more icy rain by nightfall, he hadn't realized that moving heaven and earth meant riding into hell. But he wouldn't rest until he delivered Emily Matteson Crenshaw to the Chatham House doorstep.

Without warning, a bullet tore into the tree trunk inches above his head. The wood splintered with a loud pop.

Christ! Dropping from his horse to the ground, he rolled

behind the stone wall edging the stable yard of the white stone house and reached for the pistol beneath his coat.

"Get down!" he yelled at Hedley.

A well-trained soldier who had served under him with the Scarlet Scoundrels, Hedley dove behind the wall and crawled toward Grey on his stomach. Hedley scowled, drawing his own pistol. "Seems they don't like visitors none, Major."

"Apparently not." Grey took a deep breath to calm his racing heart. The last thing he'd expected this morning was to be pinned down by gunfire. "Where's it coming from?"

"The side garden."

Glancing down the wall just long enough to see that it offered a way to stalk closer to the shooter, he handed his pistol to Hedley. "Keep his attention while I circle behind."

"Aye, sir!" Hedley snatched Grey's hat from his head and tossed it high into the air above them.

A shot rang out as a bullet drove through the crown.

Grey stared incredulously. "What the hell—"

"Drawin' his attention, Major, as ye ordered." Hedley fought back his laughter but not his grin as he immediately tossed up the hat again, but this time drew no fire.

"Just keep him occupied," Grey muttered as he snatched up his dead hat from the ground and started forward to circle behind the garden. His hat was ruined, but Hedley's joke revealed what they needed to know. Whoever was shooting at them had only one gun and needed time to reload.

He moved carefully, half crawling behind the cover of the stones. As he reached the end of the wall, he signaled to Hedley, who pulled the pistol's trigger and sent a ball shattering into the wall near the house's roof.

At the answering gunfire, Grey leapt to his feet and ducked around the corner. Keeping his back toward the wall, he circled behind the house and into the cover of the side garden's overgrown bushes and fruit trees. He crouched low and waited for the next gunshot.

Well, *this* was a surprise. He and Emily hadn't parted under the best of circumstances, he'd admit. But while he hadn't known what to expect this afternoon when he rode up to her door, it sure as hell wasn't gunfire.

When the next shots sounded, he made his way quickly through the garden. Up ahead, obscured by thick bushes, two figures crouched behind a low garden wall, where they took aim up the drive.

Grey hurled himself forward. A scream filled his ears as he tackled the shooter to the ground, discovering in a flash of confusion—

A woman.

A soft, curvaceous woman in dark blue muslin and white lace with golden-blond hair. Her large, sapphire-blue eyes stared up at him with a mix of fear and fury. Right before she sank her teeth into his forearm.

Blasting a sharp curse, he twisted to pin her arms to the ground and keep her mouth out of biting range, slinging a heavy leg over both of hers to prevent her from kicking. "Stop that!"

"Get off her, you brute!"

The handle of a wooden garden rake struck at his shoulders, and he flinched, ducking his head as an older woman in a servant's gray dress and white cap swung the rake repeatedly at his head.

"Get off her before you hurt her!" the maid bellowed.

"Hurt *her*? She shot at *me*!" he growled, holding the blond woman's wrists together with one hand so that he could grab at the swinging rake over his head with the other.

"You deserved it!" the blond woman hissed, futilely trying to wiggle her way out from beneath him. "What kind of gentleman would—"

At the sound of her voice, Grey froze. He searched her face as the memories triggered in his mind. "Brat, is that you?"

She ceased struggling. Those same blue eyes he now remembered so vividly widened in stunned surprise. "Captain Grey?" His name was a breathless whisper, as if she couldn't possibly believe it was him.

He flashed her a crooked grin. "It's a pleasure to see you again."

The rake hit him over the head.

"Damnation, woman!" He made another grab for the handle. "Stop that!"

Hedley pounced on the maid from behind, seizing her by the waist and swinging her around in a circle as he yanked the rake from her hands and threw it out of reach. She kicked her legs and tried to hit him with her fists, but he simply lifted the short woman off her feet and dangled her helplessly in midair until she gave up her struggles with an angry *humph*.

"I got 'er, Major!" the sergeant announced proudly over the top of her head.

"Good," Grey answered, his eyes not leaving Emily's face as she lay beneath him on the ground, now incredibly still except for the shallow rise and fall of her breasts with each breath. "Take her inside and calm her down, will you?" He added wryly, "And try not to let her hurt you."

"Aye, sir." Hedley nodded and set the woman on the ground, then bowed his head politely and motioned toward the house. "After you, ma'am."

The maid stubbornly crossed her arms. "I'm not leaving!"

"It's all right, Yardley. They're old friends of mine,"

Emily explained. With an irritated grimace, she tugged her hands free of Grey's grip and pushed at him to slide away.

Grey complied, although it took him a moment to clear the sudden fog from his brain and release her. Instead of helping her to her feet, however, he leaned back against the wall, his arm resting across his bent knee as he stared at her, utterly bewildered to find her like this. Shooting at him. And beautiful.

The maid glanced warily from Grey to her mistress. "My lady, I don't—"

"I'm fine." She drew her legs beneath her. "Would you please serve refreshments in the drawing room?" A soft pleading crossed her face, a silent communication between the two women that Grey couldn't decipher. About him. *Interesting.* "Captain Grey and I will be along in a moment."

Yardley frowned, still concerned. "All right, but I'll be just right inside in the kitchen." She pointed a long finger at Grey. "If you lay a hand on my lady, be advised, sir, that I keep a drawer full of knives in there, and I know how to use them!"

Grey's lips twitched, wanting desperately to laugh at both the bulldog expression on Yardley's face and the astonishment on Emily's that her maid would dare threaten a man twice her size. "I have no doubt of that, ma'am," he answered with forced solemnity.

With another *humph*, she spun on her heels and stomped toward the house, with Hedley following behind, his hand clamped over his laughing mouth.

Not knowing what to expect after the way they'd last parted, Grey slid his eyes to Emily. She stared back in wonder, one hand pressed against her stomach and her face pale, as if she were seeing a ghost. In a way, he supposed, she was.

"It's good to see you again, Emily," he said quietly.

Although she wasn't just Emily or Miss Matteson anymore. She was Mrs. Crenshaw now, a fact that made her seem far older than her twenty-one years. She was no longer the sweet and innocent young woman he remembered who sat for hours in the garden with her sketchbook and pencils, drawing her world. Or the starry-eyed girl who asked him one afternoon if he would teach her how to kiss.

"Captain Grey," she forced out, as if it took all her strength to acknowledge him.

He grimaced. Oh, she wasn't happy to see him. This was *not* going to be fun. "You remember me, then?" They'd gotten along well five years ago until he'd lost his mind and kissed her, and he hoped they could again. Otherwise, it was going to be a damnably long ride back to London.

"Of course I remember you." Regret flashed in her eyes.

Her reaction pricked at him. Well, he deserved it, he supposed, for his part in the debacle. "It's major now, actually."

She blinked, puzzled. "Pardon?"

"I've been promoted." He didn't know why it mattered, but he felt the undeniable urge to tell her. As if she were still a starry-eyed sixteen-year-old he could impress.

"Oh." She looked away, clearly *not* impressed. "Congratulations."

Well, *that* stung. So the brat was still peeved at him, even after all these years. A *very* long ride back to London . . .

But something else was wrong here. Her pallid face and trembling hands, which she couldn't keep still, how her eyes darted to look everywhere but into his—with a concerned frown, he reached gently for her shoulder. "Are you all right?"

She jerked her hand away from her stomach as if burned. Drawing back, she shifted out of his reach. "I'm fine."

He stared at her curiously. More than lingering regret

and embarrassment over that kiss burned in her sapphire eyes. Something dark lurked there as well, stirring the short hairs on the back of his neck. It was the same look he'd seen on the faces of captured soldiers during the war. He saw *fear*.

Concern tightened his chest. "If something's wrong—"

"Nothing's wrong. But I—I think it would be best if you left," she said frankly, her lips tightening as her face grew pale.

"Don't you even want to know why I'm here?" he asked gently, perplexed at the swirling mix of emotions pouring from her. Good Lord, she practically dripped with them.

For a moment, she said nothing, only staring back grimly, her eyes glistening. Then she lowered her face away as she twisted her skirt in her fingers. "I already know."

His brow furrowed. Surely Chatham hadn't sent another messenger to arrive before he did. "Do you?"

She nodded jerkily, then swallowed. Hard. "If you're here, then…" Choking out so softly that he could barely hear her, she whispered, "Thomas is dead."

A tear of grief slid down her cheek, and she squeezed her eyes shut.

The air rushed painfully from his lungs at the sight of her looking so wretched, so utterly devastated. Despite the rift between them, Thomas loved his sister, and he knew Emily loved Thomas. And Grey's heart melted for them both.

He gently wiped away the tear with his thumb. "No, Emily." His knuckles trailed across her cheek to soothe her. "Your brother's alive."

Her eyes flew open. Watery sapphire pools stared at him, incredulous and vulnerable.

"Thomas is *alive*," he repeated and cupped her face in his hands. "We never expected—but he survived." He grinned at her, unable to hold back his own relief. "He's too damned stubborn to die."

"Oh, thank God," she murmured, her petite body sagging with relief. "Thank God!"

She threw her arms around his shoulders and buried her face against his neck. His hands lifted to her back in a loose embrace to comfort her.

As she shifted into his arms, her breasts pressed against his chest, and his breath hitched—well, she was certainly no longer a stick with blond braids. The brat had grown into a woman, one whose warm lips now brushed against his neck as she murmured over and over her thanks to God for saving her brother, her thanks to him for bringing her the news...and each word shot straight through him to the tip of his tingling cock. *Sweet Lucifer.*

Swallowing hard, he gently took her shoulders and set her away from him.

She wiped at her eyes. "You didn't have to come all this way." But gratitude swelled in her soft voice. "You could have sent word—"

He grinned at her. "I've come to escort you to London."

Her hand paused in mid-swipe as the bright happiness on her face disappeared, replaced once again by that mysterious fear he'd glimpsed earlier. This time stronger than before. For a moment, he thought she might just jump to her feet and flee like a frightened hare.

"Thomas asked for you," he explained. "I promised to bring you to him."

"Thomas asked...?" For a fleeting moment, a desperate longing registered in every inch of her, the overwhelming compassion and grief she felt for her brother palpable. She pressed her hand against her heart.

Then suddenly she stiffened, and the vulnerability he

glimpsed in her vanished as a veil came down over her face. Yet she couldn't hide the fear. *That* still shined in her eyes as brightly as her lingering tears. "Thank you for telling me about Thomas. I truly appreciate your kindness and your devotion to him, more than you know." She hesitated, as if forcing herself to say, "But I'm not going anywhere with you."

He was stunned. "Emily—"

"Mrs. Crenshaw," she corrected, then more softly, "if you please."

He clenched his jaw. What should he care if she preferred formality from him? But inexplicably, it angered him. So did her refusal to see her brother. Had the sweet girl he remembered turned into a coldhearted bitch?

"I can't possibly travel right now, Major." Her voice caught as she gave her apologies, but she hurried on. "So you and your man will have to leave after your tea."

"We're spending the night," he countered.

Her eyes flared, as if she didn't know whether to be furious or terrified at the prospect of having him as a guest. "There's no room for you here."

Skeptically, he raised his eyes to the large country house behind her and silently arched a brow.

"We're not able to accommodate guests at this time," she clarified with an almost desperate impatience to convince him to leave. Averting her eyes, she focused intently on pulling at her skirt with her fingers. "But there's an inn at the village—"

He grabbed her hand, stilling it against her skirt.

With a shocked gasp, she looked up at him, her blue eyes round and huge.

"You really expect me to believe that?" He kept his voice low and his anger checked, but he refused to release her wrist as she attempted to yank her hand away.

"It's true!"

"It's a damned lie," he growled.

"Captain Grey!" Aghast at his accusation, she struggled to free herself, but his grip only tightened. He didn't trust her not to run for the hills. Or for a kitchen knife.

"*Major* Grey," he corrected irritably, wanting no misunderstanding that he might still be the young officer she'd wrapped around her finger five years ago with her sweetness and innocence. He'd fallen for her manipulations then, but he certainly wouldn't fall for them a second time. "This is more than simply not wanting visitors, Mrs. Crenshaw. You *shot* at me!"

She sniffed haughtily. "And you rode up uninvited."

His eyes narrowed. The brat had grown into a woman, but also into one of the worst liars he'd ever met. And certainly the most infuriating. "Since when do society ladies shoot at visitors, uninvited or otherwise?"

"Since they—" Her mouth snapped shut on whatever it was she was about to say, and she stopped struggling. Her gaze dropped to his chest as she pleaded in exasperation, "Please, just go away!"

But the more she demanded he leave, the more determined he was to stay.

Yet this time when she tugged to free herself, he let her go. To give her enough rope to hang herself with her lies.

She scrambled to her feet, her restless hands brushing nervously at the bits of grass clinging to her skirt as she backed away from him. "I'm sorry you came all this way for nothing, Major, but I'm too ill to travel. I'll write to Thomas—"

"The hell you will!" he exploded as the thin thread of his patience snapped, the curse so fierce she flinched. "You are coming with me to London, and we are leaving first thing in the morning."

"No." The damned chit jutted her chin defiantly into the air. "I absolutely refuse!"

Slowly, he rose to his full height and clenched his jaw to keep back the ungentlemanly response about where she could shove her refusal. Her eyes grew big as saucers at the white-hot aggravation she sensed in him. Instinctively, she stepped back.

And he pursued, advancing toward her with each step she retreated. "I'm not leaving without you."

"Please, Grey." Another step back, another advance... until her back hit against the wall of the house, until she raised her hands futilely against his chest to push him away. "You have to go!"

The pleading tone in her voice, the increasing panic in her eyes—she was desperate to make him leave. "Why?" he demanded, refusing to budge.

"Because—because you can't stay—"

"Why did you shoot at us?" He pressed in closer, trapping her between the house and his body. So close that her hands flattened against his chest.

"I didn't know it was you."

"Obviously. Why?"

"Please just go—"

"What's wrong here?"

"Nothing! I swear."

"Tell me."

"Grey, *please!*" Her shoulders slumped, and he felt her hands on him change, no longer pushing him away but now fisting into the lapels of his coat to keep him close. Not that he would have gone anywhere until he had the truth.

In her panic, her breathing faltered, unwittingly drawing his attention to her chest. And that was a mistake. Because it was a very fine chest indeed, the tops of her full breasts rising and falling rapidly against the neckline of her tight bodice with each fast breath.

She's the brat, he reminded himself, tearing his gaze back up to hers. Thomas's sister. The woman who would get him killed at the hands of his best friend if he dared lay a finger on her again. And certainly not a woman he should be looking at as ... well, as a woman.

He locked his eyes on hers and refused to let them stray lower. "You shot at me."

"There have been highwaymen—"

"Brat," he growled in warning at the lie she was about to tell.

"There is nothing of concern here." Then she forced a smile that did nothing to reassure him. "And I promise not to shoot at you when you leave."

Despite her attempt at humor, his eyes narrowed. "If nothing's wrong—"

"There's not," she protested, far too quickly.

"Then answer me this." He lowered his head until his eyes leveled with hers, until his face hovered so close he could feel her trembling breath shadowing his lips. "Where are all your servants, Mrs. Crenshaw?"

She froze, the only movement a momentary widening of her eyes, a deepening of the fear in their wild depths. The look of a caught prisoner.

"I've been here for a while now, and no one could have missed that gunfire when we arrived. Where are your footmen and grooms?" He took her chin in his fingers and held her so she couldn't look away. "And do *not* lie to me."

She stared warily at him, as if trying to decide exactly how much she could trust him. Then she answered, the single word tearing from her in a hoarse whisper—"Gone."

He couldn't possibly have heard her correctly. "Pardon?"

"My husband was killed in a riding accident five months ago," she whispered, as if terrified of being overheard. "But there were other...incidents. The servants feared for their lives. Half departed the night of his death, the others were gone by his burial. A handful remain, and if they hear gun-fire, believe me, they will not come to investigate until it is long over."

Grey stared at her, unable to fathom the creature before him and the situation she described. Was she really spinning ghost stories and expecting him to believe them?

He straightened away from her, yanking her fingers free from his coat. For a moment, her hands stayed in the air, as if still grasping for him, before she lowered her arms to her sides to bury her hands in the pockets of her baggy pelisse.

He shook his head. "Your parents never mentioned any of this. Thomas never said a word."

"My family doesn't know." She drew a ragged breath, her gaze training on his chest. "Andrew died last fall when the weather was too bad for them to travel to his funeral. Then, the time was simply never right to tell them about the ser-vants."

Never right? For God's sake, she'd been widowed and abandoned by her staff, and the time was never right to ask for help? "Mrs. Crenshaw—"

"I was unwell," she interrupted. "Andrew's death was such a shock—I fell ill. And then..." Her voice trailed off, and whatever she had been about to say was lost. "But I'm better now. In fact, I plan on closing up the house and return-ing to London next month, when the roads will be passable and when I'm feeling stronger." But the words came far too smoothly, too practiced, and her eyes lifted to his, as if searching for proof that he believed her. "And now you know everything."

That was a laugh. He'd barely scratched the surface of the secrets being kept here.

"As you can see, there's nothing to concern you, but I cannot accommodate guests. Nor do I feel up to traveling... even as much as I want to see Thomas." An aching grief passed over her face before she averted her eyes, and she drew a shaking breath, her hands wrapping in her skirt. "So when will you be leaving, Major?"

"Tomorrow." He stared at her, grimly noting all the obvious signs of fear and unease she so openly displayed. "First light."

Her shoulders sagged, and a soft sigh of relief escaped her. "I'll have Yardley bring the letter to you at the inn—"

"Oh, no," he interrupted with a forced calmness he didn't feel. "You misunderstand me."

Her eyes darted up to his. Sudden panic made their blue depths resemble a storm-tossed ocean. The tip of her tongue darted out nervously to wet her lips, and he watched, fascinated by the little movement. He placed his hand on the wall beside her shoulder and leaned in closer, close enough to see her pulse racing tantalizingly in the hollow at the base of her throat.

The brat, he reminded himself again. Thomas's sister, which meant she was as good as a sister to him, too... a sister who just happened to have amazingly plump breasts.

"I'm not leaving without you." He drew a deep breath to steady his concentration. "Hedley and I are spending the night here, and in the morning, you're coming with us to—"

With a frustrated groan, she shoved futilely at his shoulders. "Why won't you just trust me?"

His rising frustration matched hers as he ground out, "Because the last time we met, you nearly 'trusted' me straight into a duel."

"Oh, for heaven's sake!" The words poured from her with an angry groan. "How many more times will that kiss ruin my life?"

His head snapped back as if she'd slapped him. "*What?*"

Her hand flew to her mouth as she realized what she'd said, deep regret dancing in her wide eyes. "I'm so sorry," she forced out, muffled between her fingers. "I didn't mean—oh, Grey…"

His eyes narrowed on her. She'd certainly meant it, all right. "The last time I saw you—" He angrily choked off. Lord, how this woman roiled his insides! One moment, the minx had him wanting to strip her naked, the next he wanted to wring her little neck. "Damned stupid of us—of *me*—to let you talk me into…" *Christ!*

He'd been kicked out of Ivy Glen, nearly lost Thomas's friendship—now the damned woman had the nerve to blame *him* for ruining her life?

"Forget it, Emily. Please." He'd certainly done his best to do just that, until Thomas sent him here, apparently straight into hell after all. "I'm still being punished for it by your parents. I don't deserve to be punished by you, too."

She gaped at him. "Punished—*you*? When *I* was sent—" She stopped, her eyes narrowing curiously on the bewildered look he gave her. Remorse darkened her face as she asked quietly, "You truly don't know? Thomas never told you?"

"Told me what?" He sighed heavily, wanting nothing more than to put the past behind them for good, get on the road to London, and leave for Spain, where he already should have been. "He said you went off to school, then got married."

And widowed last fall. Was that what was wrong? His heart skipped. Was all this emotion because she was still grieving her late husband?

"Emily," he pleaded, his voice gentling, "tell me what's wrong so I can help you."

She hesitated, an expression of such grief and fear dashing across her face that he lost his breath. For one moment her lips parted, and she looked pleadingly at him for understanding, as if she wanted to unburden herself—

Then her mouth snapped shut, the veil once more falling over her face.

She arched a brow. "You won't leave here without me?" she asked, veering the conversation back to their standoff.

"No," he answered firmly.

"Then we seem to have a problem, Major." Indignantly, she pushed him back and stepped past. "Because I'm not going anywhere!"

Clenching his jaw so tightly that the muscle twitched in his cheek, he watched her bend over to pick up the hunting gun she'd used to shoot at him. Then she walked away toward the house.

"You don't have a choice," he called out to her retreating back. He'd shove her into a carriage and drive away with her inside if it came to that.

She faced him, holding the gun expertly in the crook of her arm. "Thomas taught me how to shoot. He's a very good shot. The best, in fact." She paused meaningfully, a warning in her voice. "Since my husband's death, I sleep with a loaded pistol next to my bed. And I never miss."

His mouth twisted wryly. "You missed me earlier."

"I hit a foot above your head, exactly where I aimed." She tucked a golden curl behind her ear. "So please keep that in mind should you decide to try kidnapping me in the middle of the night."

With a toss of her head, she opened the door and disappeared inside the house.

Grey stared after her, blowing out an aggravated breath. Where on earth had the adorable brat gone? How had this woman with the temperament of a she-devil and the body of a temptress taken her place, a stubborn minx who refused to leave her home without force and who had just threatened bodily harm to him should he attempt to try?

He rolled his eyes. *Good Lord*. What had he gotten himself into?

* * *

Emily leaned against the wall and squeezed her eyes shut as she struggled to calm both her racing heart and her swirling mind.

Captain Nathaniel Grey ... *Impossible!*

Yet here he was. The man she still remembered so vividly from his visit to Ivy Glen when she was sixteen ... those chocolate eyes that crinkled when he laughed, that mouth that grinned so charmingly, and that thick, unruly blond hair curling at his neck. His body was broader now, the hard muscles of his chest and shoulders much more developed, but those eyes were the same. So were the chiseled lines of his handsome face.

Grey. She could hardly believe it. Thomas had sent him to her after all these years, and he'd appeared like some dashing knight in shining armor. Yet as she fought back a sob of anguish, she knew she had no choice but to chase him away.

With grim resolve, she pushed herself away from the wall and hurried downstairs to the kitchen to find Yardley.

The woman had been with her for the past two years, arriving just after Andrew brought her to Snowden, when he decided the maid who had attended Emily since her debut was disrespectful to him and replaced her. Emily had been devastated. But the older woman was kind and gentle, and now Yardley was the only person in the world she trusted with her secrets.

"My lady." Yardley nodded as Emily entered the kitchen, putting together a tray to take upstairs to the men.

"We're having guests for the night," Emily told her unhappily.

Yardley's hand froze in midair as she placed a saucer on the tray. "Is that wise?"

"I don't believe we have a choice." She frowned as she looked down at the shortbread on the tray. Five years ago, Grey had raved about Cook's cinnamon biscuits. If she had known he was coming, she would have made some for him. Yet perhaps it was better not to make him feel too welcome, not when her primary goal was to drive him away.

"And who are they, my lady?"

"Major Nathaniel Grey and his man." Emily hesitated. How on earth did one describe Grey? "The major is...an old family friend."

But he was far more than that. Even at sixteen, she'd realized how special Grey was. Dashing and kind, he possessed a fierce determination to carve out a brilliant career for himself, and a handsome presence that caught the ladies' attentions. With her, though, he'd simply captured her heart. Yet to her chagrin, he'd paid her no more mind than a piece of furniture...until that one afternoon in the garden.

"A family friend, eh?" The suspicious glance Yardley slid her as she placed a teacup onto the saucer told her that the woman didn't believe her.

"It's not what you think." Yet she couldn't stop the blush of embarrassment heating her cheeks.

The last time she'd seen him, the *very* last time—heavens, she'd been so foolish! She'd asked him to give her a

kissing lesson so she would know what to do with suitors...
or some such silly nonsense she barely remembered now.
Yet her manipulation worked, and he'd kissed her. It had
been the most magical moment of her young life, until her
parents stumbled upon them. Amid angry shouts and accu-
sations, Grey left Ivy Glen, with Thomas riding away after
him. And two days later, she was sent to boarding school,
where her parents hoped to keep her away from "upstarts"
like the captain.

"Major Grey served with my brother in the wars," she explained with more pride than she had a right to feel. Even
after suffering the consequences of what she'd done that
day, she couldn't forget him and followed him the best she
could through Thomas's letters—her heart soaring with his
heroics, laughing at his antics, even crying when he'd been
wounded. She'd been so upset, in fact, that she wrote to his
parents to assure them that he had friends in her family, only
for the letters to return undelivered. "I trust him." *I think...*

Yardley removed the water from the stove and poured it
into the teapot, giving Emily a wary look. "Why do I suspect
there's more you're not telling?"

She bit her lip and divulged with embarrassment, "When
I was a girl, I fancied him."

Yardley paused as she set the teapot onto the tray.

"It's nothing to worry about now," she insisted. She
shrugged it away as the childish infatuation it was.

But it wasn't childish infatuation that had just made her
curl her hands around his lapels and attempt to pull him
closer, that had her pulse racing and her body tingling in the
most intimate places—

Silently, she cursed herself. It wasn't Grey that made her
behave like such a cake. It couldn't possibly be *him*. Certainly, she'd gotten over her fascination with him years ago.

No, it was all the changes she was going through. All the lonely and fear-filled nights she'd endured. All the responsibility for the farm sitting on her shoulders. For the past two years, she'd run the property in Andrew's absence, managed the tenants' leases, and somehow made certain the servants were paid. Then she had to bury her husband and pretend to mourn. No one could go through that and remain unaffected.

So when Grey appeared this afternoon, a kind face from her past offering to help her, it was natural that she should yearn to be comforted, consoled, protected—God help her, she wanted to be *wanted*. Of course, it hadn't helped that Grey had lain on top of her like that, the solid weight of him pressing down deliciously into her, or that the masculine scent of him filled her senses, the heat in his chocolate-brown eyes warming between her thighs...

Well, she thought with chagrin, perhaps she hadn't completely gotten over him, after all. While he'd certainly not given her a thought in five years.

She ignored the twinge of vexation in her chest as she admitted, "He never paid me any mind then, and he won't now."

"Don't be so sure, my lady," Yardley warned as she wrapped a towel around the pot to keep it warm.

No, that was the one thing about which Emily was certain. Clearly, Grey remembered that kiss only for the temporary rift it caused with Thomas and the lingering animosity between him and her parents. But she'd lived with its consequences every day since, in a life of isolation and abandonment that affected her even now...only to discover that he hadn't known any of the hell she'd suffered.

She'd never blamed Grey—well, perhaps she'd blamed him just a *little* bit. But truly, it had all been her fault, a childish stunt to capture the attention of a man with whom she'd been so infatuated that she hadn't considered the consequences. And yet, while she regretted manipulating him and certainly regretted getting caught, she'd never once regretted *kissing* him.

"Why are they here, then?" Yardley asked, reaching for the spoons.

"My family sent him." Emily took a deep breath to steady herself and not let fresh tears fall at the thought of Thomas. "He came to tell me that my . . ." She choked out around the knot in her tightening throat, "My brother is alive."

"Oh, my lady." Her bottom lip quivered, and Emily suspected Yardley might just cry, too. "It's a miracle!"

She nodded slowly, then forced out with a smile, "Thomas has asked the major to escort me to London to see him."

A teacup slipped from Yardley's hand and smashed against the stone floor. Emily startled, jumping back a step, her hand reaching to cover her belly.

"Oh no!" Yardley shook her head adamantly.

Emily knew she wasn't speaking of the broken cup. "Don't worry," she reassured her. "I'm not going with him, and I've told him so."

But her heart tore at not being able to sit at Thomas's side and hold his hand while he recovered. How much she so desperately wanted to do exactly that! But at what cost? To endanger her own life, the lives of her family, possibly even Grey—her father was a duke now, but even a duke and all his money wouldn't be able to stop someone determined to harm them. Her heart ached with grief and fear. *Dear God*, how would she ever bear it if anyone was hurt because of her?

Doubt darkened Yardley's face. "He doesn't seem like the type of man who gives up easily."

No, he certainly wasn't that. In fact, she doubted Grey had ever waved a white flag of surrender in his life. "I'll find a way to convince him to leave."

"How?"

"I don't know yet." She lifted her hand to her mouth and worriedly chewed on her thumbnail. He had seemed so determined to keep his promise to Thomas, but she was just as determined to stay right where she was. "But I will."

Yardley lowered her voice. "Are you going to tell him about your husband?"

"No," Emily answered firmly. "And neither can you. Not one word, not to anyone."

Yardley bent down to sweep up the broken cup. "You can trust me."

At the hurt tone in her voice, Emily immediately felt guilty and murmured apologetically, "I know." But sometimes she wished there was someone else she could confide in and trust besides Yardley. Ironically, someone exactly like Nathaniel Grey.

No. Not even he could know her secrets. Because then he would tell her family, and if her family knew, they would come for her to return her to London themselves, and then it would only be a matter of time until *all* their lives were endangered.

"We're going on to Glasgow, just as we planned," she said quietly. But her chest tightened painfully as she realized that meant she couldn't see Thomas when he needed her most, that she might never see her brother ever again.

As if sensing her doubt, Yardley smiled reassuringly at her. "My sister will be right glad to have us with her. New place, new life...you'll be safe there. No one will think to come looking for you there."

Emily nodded, but she didn't feel reassured. They would

have to leave soon; she wouldn't be able to delay much longer. But lately, as the time drew closer, the dread inside her grew until she thought she might not be able to bear it.

Her shoulders slumped. She was suddenly tired, the energy vanishing from her limbs as a headache pulsed at her temples. Usually at this time of the afternoon she lay down for a nap, partly because she always tired after lunch, but mostly because she was seldom able to sleep well at night. Today, with the surprise of seeing Grey again, the fatigue swept over her in a wave.

Yardley frowned, placing a motherly hand on her shoulder. "Are you all right? You don't look well."

"I'm just tired." She was so *very* tired, in fact. Tired of struggling on her own and not being able to turn to her family for help, tired of being so isolated and alone with only Yardley to confide in, tired of being frightened all the time... "I think I'll go up to my room and lie down. Would you take the tea things into the drawing room for the men and give my apologies to Major Grey? They'll need rooms as well, and please ask Phipps to stable their horses."

"Aye, my lady. I'll take care of everything."

Emily smiled wearily. "I know you will."

Yardley nodded over her shoulder at her as she lifted the tray and carried it from the kitchen. "I always do."

CHAPTER THREE

$\mathcal{W}$ith a muttered curse, Grey gave up all hope of sleeping and rolled out of bed. He couldn't get Emily out of his head.

He grabbed his trousers from the chair and yanked them on. The sweet girl he'd remembered from Ivy Glen was gone, and in her place was a harridan who claimed she was too ill to travel. A delay was possible, he supposed, if she'd been especially distraught over her husband's death. But she certainly wasn't behaving like a grieving widow. And after the way she'd begged off his company this afternoon and evening, he suspected that her bouts of illness were more convenience than convalescence.

Still, he considered as he tugged his shirt over his head, people changed—he certainly had—and he hadn't seen her in five years. His only information about her during that time had been whatever news Thomas thought to share, and Grey didn't dare ask for more. He heaved out a breath as he sat on the chair and reached for his boots. The brat had certainly grown up. The stick with braids had matured into her long legs and golden hair, into those big blue eyes. And he could have sworn she smelled of cinnamon.

Not that it mattered how good she smelled, or looked, or felt—she was completely untouchable. Since his return to England, he'd made a specialty of bedding society widows. They knew how to separate sex from love and posed no threat to his freedom, and rarely were there complications. But *this* widow was an endless complication.

He blew out a harsh breath. He'd been too long without a woman beneath him, that was all. With everything that had happened during the past few weeks, sex had been the last thing on his mind, so naturally, he should feel aroused when he was around a beautiful woman.

That was it. Had to be. Because the alternative, that he actually found the brat desirable, was unthinkable.

He didn't bother buttoning his waistcoat or tucking in his shirt before heading downstairs to find a bottle of liquor to help him sleep. There was no need to finish dressing. After all, no one would see him. The few remaining servants were asleep upstairs, undoubtedly Emily would claim illness all through tomorrow morning and well into the afternoon in order to avoid him, and in his room next door, Hedley snored loudly enough to wake the dead.

But as he passed the upstairs sitting room, he saw light falling softly beneath the closed door. So...someone was awake after all.

He opened the door silently.

Emily sat reading a book on the settee near the small fire. In her lavender satin robe, with her bare feet tucked beneath her and her golden hair falling freely in thick waves around her shoulders, she resembled the carefree young woman he'd known five years ago. Except that a second, more lingering look revealed the truth. Before him sat an experienced and challenging woman with a sensuous and very kissable mouth, long legs perfect for wrapping around a man's waist, and full curves that could provide hours of delightful distraction. And he was achingly aware of every delectable, tempting inch of her.

And *that*, he grudgingly admitted to himself, was the real reason he couldn't get her out of his head tonight. Because for a brief moment in the garden when he'd been lying on top of her and she'd been wiggling beneath him, he'd wanted to be buried inside her.

As if feeling the heat of his gaze, she looked up with a soft gasp and froze. The same horrible fear he saw in her that afternoon gripped her pretty face for just an instant before she realized it was him. Then the fear melted into uncertainty, and she bit her bottom lip indecisively for just a moment before finally sending him a faint smile.

Well. She didn't seem happy to see him, but at least she wasn't firing a gun at him. A decided improvement. And with this woman, he'd gladly take whatever victories he could get.

He leaned against the doorjamb, not daring to step inside the room. "You're awake, Mrs. Crenshaw."

"So are you." She closed the book and set it aside, sliding her legs off the settee as she sat up and unwittingly giving him a fleeting glimpse of smooth, shapely calves.

"Couldn't sleep." He cleared his throat and forced his eyes away from her legs. "Thought I'd look for a whiskey." Although the sight of her was much more intoxicating.

She hesitated, then offered, "Would brandy do?"

His stomach churned at the thought of the stuff, and if he had a lick of sense in his brain, he'd have been running back to his room as fast as he could to get away from the temptation of her. Yet he nodded, knowing the drink would buy him time with her. Alone. "Nicely, thank you."

She rose gracefully from the settee. The last remnants of the awkward girl he remembered vanished beneath the smooth swing of her womanly hips as she crossed to the cabinet in the corner, then bent over and gave him such an inviting view of her round derriere that he inhaled sharply through clenched teeth.

She withdrew a crystal decanter and tumbler and splashed the golden liquid into the glass. With a look of challenge, she held it out to him and waited for him to come to her to claim it.

His lips twitched wryly at the irony that the woman who refused to leave her home was once again holding her ground. And that a strong drink was now the least of what he wanted to claim from her tonight.

Unable to resist her siren song, he stepped inside and closed the door, then slowly crossed the room to her.

"I'm glad we have this chance to talk," she told him.

"Are you?" He didn't believe her for a second.

She gave a jerky nod. "I just—I just wanted to say that what happened—at Ivy Glen—" she began haltingly, her embarrassed voice as soft as the crackling fire beside her. "I don't blame you. It was completely my fault, and I apologize for all the problems it caused." She held out the tumbler in a peace offering. "Truce?"

His lips curled in relief as he took the glass. "Truce."

She was watching him, waiting expectantly, so he forced himself to take a sip. Surprisingly, the brandy went down smoothly.

He nodded toward the decanter. "You keep brandy in your sitting room?" The brat was one surprise after another.

"I have trouble sleeping. Sometimes, a glass helps."

"Like tonight?" He frowned, concern tightening his chest. Perhaps she hadn't been feigning illness after all. "Are you unwell?"

"I'm better, thank you." She folded her hands demurely in front of her. "But I was quite fatigued earlier."

"Yes, I suppose you were." He took another swallow, finding a forgotten taste for brandy, before adding wryly, "After all that shooting."

She nodded. "Nothing tires out a lady quite like hunting."

He choked.

As he struggled to fight back the coughs, he slid a glance at her and caught her eyes gleaming mischievously at his expense. For the first time since he arrived at her doorstep, he saw something in those blue depths besides fear and anger. And it was nice. *Very* nice.

"Thank God you didn't go for the kill," he muttered.

She sighed regretfully. "Next time."

And then, seemingly despite herself, she laughed—not much of one, to be honest. A truncated and nervous little bubble, but still a laugh. And he was damned happy to hear it.

He studied her over the rim of the glass. She wasn't classically beautiful, certainly not the kind of striking woman who usually drew his attention, and despite her natural grace, she lacked the urbanity he found so alluring in society women. But her face was arrestingly pretty, and combined with her challenging willfulness, which had kept him on alert since he arrived, and her curvaceous body, which had kept him half-hard, she intrigued him more than any woman he could remember in ages. If ever.

"Tell me," he asked, wanting to know more about the woman she'd become, "do you still sketch?"

Her breath hitched. "Pardon?"

"You sketched at Ivy Glen." He moved to sit on the settee uninvited, kicking his long legs out in front of him and foolishly settling into the conversation while she wisely—if frustratingly—held her ground on the far side of the room. "Do you still draw?"

"Not since I married." She stared at him in wonder. "You remember that?"

"Of course, I do. You carried that sketchbook with you everywhere you went."

"That was when I still dreamed of being a famous artist. I wanted to paint pictures to hang in museums and palaces." She glanced down shyly at the belt of the robe tied loosely around her waist. A faint smile played at her lips. "I didn't think you'd remember anything about me."

"Of course, I do," he repeated, this time in a low murmur. "Why does that surprise you?"

"Because you didn't—" She censored herself and said instead, "Because it was a very long time ago."

He puzzled, wondering what she'd originally planned to say. But she turned away from him to grasp the fireplace poker and stir up the coals until the flames caught and brightened the room around them.

A playful tone entered her voice. "And because you were an army captain, and I was just Thomas's annoying little sister."

His lips curled. Yes, she had been that, all right.

She hesitated, then admitted, "To be honest, I never thought I'd see you again."

"Nor I you." But he was glad he had. Not only was he enjoying her company now that a truce had been established, but he also suspected she needed him far more than she let on. "You know, Thomas told me stories about when you two were children and all the trouble you caused together."

"It was always his fault." At that, she set the poker aside and smiled conspiratorially at him. "*I* was perfectly innocent in everything."

"Of course," he agreed with mock earnestness. He swirled the brandy in the glass and asked casually, "So what happened that you two aren't close anymore?"

From the corner of his eye, he saw her body stiffen, her smile fade. Pained regret flashed over her face, then disappeared beneath a forced smile. "I got married." She shrugged the question away. "A woman leaves her family and looks to her husband for support and love."

My God, she was the world's worst liar. "But you two were so attached—"

"I heard stories about you, too," she interrupted, and none too smoothly, but he let her, even knowing full well how she'd purposefully changed topics. Apparently, she wasn't good at subterfuge, either. "About your activities in Spain. All kinds of stories."

"All kinds?" He grimaced, remembering his exploits off the battlefield, the drunken fights in the local taverns, the relentless pursuit of the local wenches.

"*All* kinds," she repeated pointedly, slowly approaching him.

"Good Lord," he muttered in embarrassment and gulped down the rest of the brandy.

With another laugh—this one more relaxed than the first—she took the glass from him and refilled it. She arched a disapproving brow at him over her shoulder. "Did you and Thomas really shave a goat?"

"That goat had it coming. He devoured a perfectly good pair of boots," he defended shamelessly, although in retrospect, perhaps leaving the beast bald hadn't been the best of reparations. "Besides, it was Thomas's fault."

"Oh, undoubtedly." Her eyes sparkled disbelievingly. "And the incidents with the hay cart, the casks of wine, the flamenco dancers—"

"Lies, all of it," he warned as he accepted the fresh glass, this time making her come to him. "Don't believe a word. I was always a perfect gentleman."

Clucking her tongue softly, she shook her head. "What a shame, then. The image I had of you in my head as a rake has been shattered. I'll never think of you the same way again."

"Good." He blew out a hard breath.

She laughed, and his chest filled with warmth. He could easily get used to that sound...soft and soothing, like falling rain.

"And who are you these days, Grey?" Her eyes shined mischievously. "A gentleman or a rake?"

"Both," he answered earnestly. And she should be grateful for that. Because tonight, the gentleman was keeping the rake at bay.

Her laughter faded. Her face grew serious, and she hesitated before saying quietly, "Thomas wrote that you'd been wounded."

His gut tightened, unprepared for that swift change in conversation. "Yes."

"What happened?"

"Are you sure you want to know?" He held her gaze, and to her credit, she didn't avert her eyes. "That's not usually a story society ladies want to hear."

She shrugged a shoulder. "I'm not an ordinary society lady, I suppose."

No, you're certainly not. And he couldn't help but wonder exactly how extraordinary she was, how far from the expectations of propriety she'd be willing to stray. With him.

Slowly, he reached over to pat the seat cushion beside him.

But she didn't accept the invitation and only continued to watch him warily through lowered lashes, as if unable to decide how far she could trust him.

"Sit down, Emily," he ordered softly. "There's nothing scandalous about two old friends enjoying a quiet conversation."

Clearly, though, she didn't believe that, her eyes sweeping from her dressing robe to the door, back from the door to his half-undressed appearance as he lounged on the settee... When she didn't move, a stab of unexpected disappointment pierced him that the brat should prove so ordinary after all.

Then, surprising him, she agreed. "I suppose not." Tentatively, she sat down next to him, curling her legs beneath her. Her small surrender pleased him far more than he had a right to feel. "Two old friends," she repeated with a smile.

Oh, he was certainly feeling friendly, all right. But not trusting himself to respond to that without giving her cause to slap him, he said nothing and raised the glass to his lips.

"What happened to you in Spain?" she prompted after a moment. "How were you hurt?"

This certainly wasn't what he wanted to talk about tonight with a half-dressed, beautiful woman sitting next to him. Yet the serious expression on her face told him it was important to her. So, inexplicably, it became important to him. "We were charging the end of a cannon line," he began. He watched the golden liquid with a frown as he swirled it thoughtfully. "We'd made it across the field when I looked down and saw the hole in my breeches, the blood...I knew I'd been hit. The ball had cut through my thigh." Two inches lower, and it would have taken his knee. Two feet higher, his life.

"You didn't know until you saw it?" Confusion darkened her face. "Didn't you feel it?"

He took a large swig of brandy. "No."

Men in battle often didn't know they'd been shot until they saw the wound or lost too much blood to fight on. They were distracted by the noise and action, by the adrenaline pulsing through their muscles, and by a single-minded focus on killing in order to stay alive.

But how could he explain all that to a gently bred lady? He shouldn't be talking about this with her in the first place. Although it was surely safer than what he'd wanted to share with her, he supposed...a detailed explanation of how he wanted to peel away her clothes, lay her bare body in front of the fire, stroke between her thighs until she moaned with pleasure—

He cleared his throat and shifted uncomfortably. "We were in the middle of battle," he said simply, not trusting himself at that moment to say anything more.

His answer seemed to satisfy her, though, because she nodded solemnly as if she understood. And perhaps she did. She'd already known immense grief in her young life, maturing her far beyond other women her age.

Slowly, he held the glass of brandy toward her, daring her to go a step further in proving just how extraordinary she was by sharing the drink with him. The only other women who'd ever done such a thing were those like Lady Roquefort—society women who considered him little more than a titillating way to disrupt the monotony of their lives.

Not Emily. She was there because she wanted to be with *him*. And he liked it. More than he should have. But never before had he experienced having a soft woman in whom to confide the hard details of his life, never before had he experienced the lure of a woman who understood him so well.

She lowered her eyes to the glass. "I don't think…"

"It's your brandy, after all," he tempted.

She hesitated, then acquiesced. "Just a small sip."

With a deep breath, her decision made, she carefully took the glass from his hand and placed her lips to the rim where his had just been. He watched the soft undulation of her elegant throat as she swallowed, the small movement cascading through him.

He went hard. *Sweet Lucifer.* Thank God he'd been enough of a cad not to tuck in his shirt or he would have embarrassed them both. The shy teenage girl had grown into an alluring woman. And not just physically. *Everything* about Emily drew him, right down to her soft laughs and haughty little sniffs.

Good Lord, she was seducing him, and she didn't even realize it.

She handed back the glass. "Was Thomas with you when it happened?"

"Yes," he answered quietly, turning his focus back to the war, which dampened the throbbing at his crotch as effectively as if he'd rolled in snow. "He took me behind the lines and made certain the surgeons tended to the wound."

He'd done far more than that, in fact. When Grey had lost consciousness from the pain caused by the surgeons digging into his thigh after the ball, Thomas stood fast, pistol in hand, and refused to let the bloody leeches amputate his leg.

He took a large swallow of brandy, wishing it could have been something much stronger, and murmured, "He saved my life."

A comfortable silence fell between them, and he was glad for it. There was no need to go further into the gruesomeness he'd experienced during the war. It was in the past. Except for an ugly scar that would never disappear and a slight limp

when he'd been riding too long, there was hardly any mark
that he'd taken a bullet that changed the direction of his life,
sweeping him from Spain back to England.

"I heard you became an agent after that," she said quietly.
"And a good one."

His lips curled with pride at her small compliment. "I'd
like to think so. In fact," he admitted, feeling an irresistible urge to share his good news with her, "I've been
offered a new position on the Continent, an important
one. I'll be overseeing operations in southern Spain." He
paused. "I should have left already, but I delayed because
of Thomas."

And because of you. Which was another reason he had
to convince her to leave tomorrow. He'd already angered
Lord Bathurst, Secretary of War and the Colonies, by delaying these past few weeks since the shooting. He doubted he
could delay much longer and still receive his promotion.

Her hand covered his as it rested on the cushion between
them, and gave his fingers a small squeeze that shot straight
through him. He shifted uncomfortably. The aching returned
to his cock in full force.

"You're a good friend to him," she said quietly.

When she didn't pull her hand away, he dared to stroke
his thumb along hers, and his gut tightened when he elicited
a soft tremble from her in response.

"So," she whispered a bit breathlessly, which pleased him
immensely, "are you happy?"

He smiled at her question. No one had ever asked him
that before, and it would have been an odd question coming
from anyone but Emily. She'd always been perceptive, those
blue eyes undoubtedly noticing far more than she let on.

"I'm very happy with my life." Since he was currently
sharing a brandy with a beautiful woman who didn't realize

that her dressing robe had gaped and given him a tantalizing view of the swell of her breast— "*Exactly* as it is."

As if reading his mind and the wicked thoughts swirling there, she drew her hand away. He resisted the urge to grab after it like some green boy chasing his first woman.

"Thomas never wrote much about his time in the army, at least not about anything important," she told him, her fingers pulling at the hem of her robe. It fell open around her legs and revealed just the tips of her bare toes beneath, but he wished it would open further so he could see exactly how long those legs of hers had become. "He told stories about all the trouble you two got into, what Spain looks like…Sometimes he complained about the food or the weather, but he never mentioned the fighting."

"Real heroes seldom talk about what they do in battle." In his experience, it was the men who saw very little action who told the most stories, their tales always exaggerated and usually lies. Most likely it was because men who had truly seen the fires of battle never wanted to experience them again, not even as memories.

"Thomas was a hero, then?" she asked quietly.

"The bravest of the Scarlet Scoundrels," he assured her. Then he couldn't resist adding with a grin, "Except for me, of course."

But this time she didn't laugh at his teasing. Instead, she kept her eyes lowered as she twisted her fingers in the folds of her robe. "What happened to him, Grey?"

She meant the robbery, of course, but the solemnity in her voice made him wonder if she didn't mean something more. "He was walking in Mayfair," he began reluctantly. Her brother should have been the one to share this with her, but if he wanted to convince her to leave with him tomorrow, then he knew he had to tell her the grisly details tonight.

"He'd been to Strathmore House, and on his way home, he was stopped by a footpad."

Her hand trembled, so he reached slowly to enfold it beneath his. He half expected her to pull away again, but she didn't move except to draw a deep breath to steady herself.

"The man shot him." When he felt her flinch, he tightened his hold on her hand. "The bullet entered his side, right here." He tapped his left side with his free hand. "He lost a lot of blood, so much that he didn't wake for nearly three days, and when he did, he was feverish, delirious . . . None of the doctors thought he would live." In a low voice, he admitted guiltily, "Neither did I."

Her fingers tightened gently around his to reassure and comfort, as if she knew he shared her pain.

"Thomas wants to see you." He squeezed her hand. "Whatever's come between you two, you need to put it aside. For him."

For a moment, she didn't move, didn't respond, only stared at him in the flickering shadows of the dying firelight. Then she stood and slipped her hand from his as she walked away.

* * *

Emily stared down into the fire, this time not finding the energy to stir the flames. She was trembling again, not from the grief of knowing how Thomas had been hurt but from the agony of not being able to see him. And she wanted to—*oh God*, how much she wanted that! But she couldn't see him, not when her presence might very well endanger his life.

She inhaled deeply. Grey was waiting for her to explain. She could feel the heat of his gaze on her back, just as she could still feel the tingling in her fingers where he'd held them. Just holding his hand had given her more comfort than she'd felt since her wedding, and when the warmth and strength of him flowed into her, she'd almost let herself believe that everything could be all right again.

If she'd felt that much comfort from merely holding his hand, then how soothing would it be to be held in his arms, kissed, touched—

"Emily," his deep voice murmured at her shoulder, sending a warm pulse down her spine.

She gasped. He'd moved so silently she hadn't heard him approach.

"Are you all right?" he asked, his voice thick with concern. "I didn't mean to upset you."

"You didn't," she assured him. But he did. Just his presence here upset her, tearing her between lying to keep him safe and wanting desperately to confide in him, between wanting him to leave and wanting him to wrap his arms around her to hold her close.

Now, with his body near enough to heat her back, every inch of her hummed with long-forgotten need to be wanted as a woman. And with the way his head hung low over her shoulder and his lips poised close to her ear, his ragged breath warm against her cheek—could it be possible that Grey wanted her, too?

She could barely dare to believe that, yet the pulsing inside her was simply too electric, too thrilling to be wrong. Her body knew instinctively what his wanted. But would he act on his desire? If she simply leaned back, bringing her body against his hard chest, would the gentleman in him set her away, or would the rake wrap his arms around her, remove her clothes to reveal her to the firelight—

No. Tears of frustration and torment dampened her lashes

because she so desperately wanted what she could never have.

"Come with me to London," he cajoled, his fingers touching hers as her hand dangled at her side.

Anguish sliced at her heart as the enormity of what she was refusing crashed through her—the opportunity to be at her brother's side, the chance to be in Grey's arms. Squeezing her eyes shut, she choked out, "I—I can't."

"Why not?" His hands brushed up her arms now, heating her skin as if the sleeves of her robe didn't exist.

"Because I...I haven't been feeling well." His caresses made it difficult to think, and damn him, he knew it, too! "I need a few more weeks, Grey, please."

"If I come back for you then," he asked quietly, his lips so close to her ear that they brushed her earlobe with each word, "you'll return with me?"

"Yes." Another lie. Because when he returned, she'd be gone.

He took her shoulders and faced her toward him, and his eyes turned hard as they leveled on hers. "Brat, you are trying my patience."

Her lips parted in stunned surprise as the heat he'd flamed between them vanished. "What do you—"

"You're beautiful when you lie." He arched a brow. "But you're still lying."

She desperately shook her head. "Grey, please—"

His hands tightened around her arms. "Are you in trouble?"

She fought back a gasp. Oh God, he knew...somehow, Grey *knew*! And for a heartbeat, she wanted to admit the truth to him and put an end to the lonely nightmare her life had become. But she couldn't.

"No," she lied, the single word barely above a whisper.

The hard flicker in his eyes told her he didn't believe her. In that instant, she had a glimpse of the War Office agent he was, suspicious and wary, catching every detail.

Then he softened, and she glimpsed the man beneath the agent, who gazed on her with concern. He asked gently, "Are you in danger, Emily?" As she stepped back to escape his grasp, he pursued her and cupped her face in both his hands. "Let me help you."

A knot of emotion tightened her throat at the strength and support Grey offered. And God help her, she wanted to take it. She wanted to crawl into his arms, to somehow bury herself inside him and finally be safe—

She groaned softly. "You shouldn't be here."

"If you didn't want me at Snowden Hall," he countered, crooking a half grin, "then you should have aimed lower with your gun."

She didn't laugh at his teasing. Instead, she fisted her hands helplessly at her sides to keep from reaching for him. "That's not what I meant."

He frowned. "Then what exactly did you mean?"

She shook her head, futilely attempting to chase away both the fear and the arousal blossoming inside her. She should never have allowed him into the room with her tonight, or offered him a drink, or let him *ever* get this close. While she wore nothing more than her robe and thin night rail beneath, Grey stood there in the firelight half-dressed himself, with his shirt collar hanging open wide and revealing the place where his neck and shoulder met. That place where she found herself longing to place her lips…

Madness! She would have laughed at herself if frustration weren't grinding razor-sharp inside her.

"I meant—" She swallowed hard. "That you should leave tomorrow. I insist."

He folded his arms across his chest, and the determined gesture frustrated her to infuriation. "I am not leaving unless you—"

"Stubborn man!" she snapped and stalked away.

His brow arched as he countered evenly, "Stubborn woman."

In exasperation, she pressed the heels of her hands against her forehead, not knowing how to feel about him— if she should be furious, disappointed, aroused—or if she should grab her pistol and start shooting at him. Again.

"Why won't you just leave?" she half demanded, half begged.

"I will," he answered earnestly. "As soon as you tell me the truth."

She threw up her hands in aggravation. "I *have* told you—"

A metal click sounded softly at the door, and the words strangled in her throat. She froze, sudden terror ripping the air from her lungs.

But Grey only frowned, staring at her in bewilderment. He hadn't heard it. But *she* knew the sound of fear—she'd lived with it for the past five months, and it slithered through her like a sickening poison.

"Grey," she whispered, so low that his name was nothing more than a terrified breath, "I think someone's trying—"

An explosion boomed through the house, the sound of shattering glass lost beneath her scream.

CHAPTER FOUR

*G*rey rushed to the door and pulled on the handle—
locked. Behind him, he heard Emily gasp as she fought back
a second scream.

"Where's the key?" he asked evenly, forcing his voice to
stay calm for her sake.

"I don't have one—not in here—I never lock it—"

"Someone just did. Hedley!" He pounded his fist against
the wooden panel. "Hedley, wake up!"

The commotion in the house grew louder around them.
More crashes, more shattering glass, followed by the panicked sounds of running feet and muffled shouts.

"Stay back!" Grey ordered. Retreating a stride, he lunged
forward and slammed his shoulder against the door. Then
again. And again. But it didn't budge.

"Grey, stop!" Emily rushed forward, her hand on his arm
to pull him back. "*Stop*—you'll hurt yourself!"

"I have to get us out of here." He pounded at the door
with his fist. "Hedley!"

Then he saw it—the first tendrils of gray smoke curling beneath the door. From the tightening of her fingers on his arm, he knew Emily saw it, too.

"The house is on fire," she whispered, her face white with fear. "They're burning it down around us."

"The hell they will!" he growled.

He broke free of her grasp and ran to the window, tossed it open, and leaned over the sill, hoping for any kind of escape route. But there was no ledge connecting their room to the one beside them, and a two-story drop to the ground waited below. They were trapped. Jump from the window and die, or burn alive inside the room.

"Major!" From the opposite side of the door, Hedley pulled frantically at the handle, but the lock wouldn't give. "It won't open!"

"There's a key downstairs in the kitchen," Emily cried out.

"Forget the key," Grey ordered. "Go fetch an ax from the stable and chop the damned door down!"

"Aye, Major!"

As Hedley's footsteps pounded away, Emily grabbed his hand. Her fingers laced tightly through his as if she were afraid she'd lose him if she let go. "But the key is downstairs."

"Brat." He cupped her face in his free hand to hold her still while he explained as calmly as he could given the chaos unfolding around them, "Whoever is doing this locked us into the room so we couldn't get out before they set the place on fire. They would have thought to take the key from the kitchen so no one could unlock us."

She choked out a terrified sob.

"But Hedley will get us out, count on it," he reassured her, although he didn't feel all that certain himself. "And I will protect you. Do you trust me?"

Sucking in a shaking breath, she nodded jerkily. "With my life."

"Good." Her soft admission stirred a warmth deep inside his chest. Later he would let himself wonder what that meant, but now— "Help me find a way out of this room."

He snatched up the iron fireplace poker and began to pound it against the door handle, hoping to break it free so he could ram the poker inside and twist open the lock. Smoke billowed beneath the door now, the smell acrid and pungent as the wood panels grew warm to the touch.

"Could you shoot the lock open?" she asked desperately.

"If I had my gun." But he'd left it in his room, not thinking he'd need a weapon inside a sleeping house.

He twisted the poker against the handle, trying to force open the lock as he pried at it, all the muscles in his arms and shoulders straining with brute force. But it didn't give. With a curse, he raised the poker to strike the door again.

She waved a gun in front of his face. "Here!"

"What the hell—" He drew back in surprise and stared. A dueling pistol with pearl-inlay handle and acid-etched barrel, elegantly beautiful, and wholly impractical. And so old he wondered if it would even fire.

"Be careful," she warned, "it's loaded."

He blinked. "You keep a loaded pistol in your sitting room?"

"Of course."

For a heartbeat he stared at her incredulously. Then, grinning broadly, he murmured appreciatively, "Good girl." He gestured toward the settee. "Get behind that."

She did as ordered, and standing at an angle to the door, he raised the pistol and fired. The ball hit the lock and shattered it, the metal pieces falling away. Dropping the spent pistol, he kicked hard at the door, and this time, it broke open with a splintering pop.

With a snarling whoosh, smoke and heat poured into the room. Rolling flames curled across the ceiling.

"Emily!" he shouted over the noise of the burning building, calling her to come to him.

But she was frozen in fear, her eyes wide as they stared at the flames. Even from across the room, he could see her shaking violently.

He rushed to her, grabbed her hand, and pulled her toward the door. When she saw the flames engulfing the hallway, she screamed and jerked back with terror. His grip tightened around her wrist so she wouldn't be able to pull away, so tightly that he was certain he bruised her. But he refused to let go.

"Come on—we've got to go. Now!" He dragged her into the hallway and straight into the raw heat of the fire.

Forcing her to crouch low beneath the billowing smoke, he pulled her along behind him as he half crawled down the hallway toward the stairs, moving as quickly as he could beneath the lowering wall of smoke. But she could barely walk and still shook violently with fear, and she coughed and gasped as she struggled to breathe in the thick smoke.

As they reached the stairs, Hedley raced up toward them. A damp cloth was tied around his mouth and nose, an ax gripped in his hands. When he saw Emily, he grabbed for her arm.

"I've got her," Grey yelled. "Get the others out of the house!"

"They're all outside."

"Then get yourself out!"

"I'm not leavin' you, Major."

"Go! Get to the stable and hitch up the team. Quickly! We'll be right after you."

With a worried frown, Hedley nodded and turned to hurry down the stairs and back through the burning house. A good soldier, Hedley would never disobey orders, and Grey was counting on that. He needed to get Emily far away from here as quickly as possible.

"Come on, brat," he coaxed. He slipped his arm around her waist to help her down the stairs, their way nearly black with smoke and lit only by bright flashes of searing flame.

But she was too overcome to follow, and her legs crumpled beneath her. He scooped her into his arms as she fell, her body frighteningly lifeless, her arms unable to cling to him as he cradled her against his chest.

Slipping his hand behind her head to press her face against his shoulder and protect her from the heat and swirling billows of smoke, he carefully descended the stairs, then carried her through the house and out the front door into the cold night.

Around them, everything was confusion and panic. The two male servants had given up on the house, letting it burn to the ground in favor of attempting to dump water on the outbuildings and save whatever they could of the farm. A sobbing Yardley huddled by the garden wall, staring incredulously at the flames now engulfing the roof and spreading down to the ground floor, unable to believe the terrible sight before her. The night sky was alive with flames and sparks, and all of it glowed like the fires of hell.

Forcing back the panic that pulsed through him, Grey laid Emily down on the damp grass. Her body slumped helplessly onto the ground. She coughed violently to clear the smoke from her lungs and inhale fresh air.

"Breathe, Emily," he pleaded between his own coughs, his voice a raw rasp from the smoke as his hands squeezed her arms.

But she couldn't catch her breath. Her mouth gaped open and closed futilely like a fish out of water.

He grabbed her shoulders and shook her hard. "Breathe, damn it!" He wouldn't lose her—he *wouldn't*! "Breathe!"

With a violent, shuddering gasp, she inhaled sharply, her lungs finally finding air. She took rapid breaths now and gulped frantically at the cold air between pain-filled coughs. But she was breathing again, and relief fell through him.

Grey pulled her against his chest to press her close. As she continued to gasp, shaking with an occasional cough yet unable to speak, he rubbed his trembling hands over her back. The emotion that flooded over him with each of her deep breaths overwhelmed him, and his smoke-stung eyes blurred as he buried his face in her hair as she clung to him. A black streak dirtied her face, the hem of her robe was singed, her bare feet most likely burned—but she was alive. *Thank God.*

He rocked her gently in his arms long after her breathing steadied and her shaking calmed, long after her arms rose up weakly to encircle his neck. After coming so close to losing her, he now didn't want to let her go.

"Dear God, brat," he whispered, his voice hoarse with emotion. "I thought I'd lost you."

"Grey," she mumbled against the bare skin of his neck, her voice scratchy and rough, "are you hurt—"

"Major!" The small carriage and two-horse team drove toward them from the stable, with Hedley mounted on the driver's seat and the reins twisted around his hands, expertly controlling the skittish horses.

When the carriage stopped on the lawn beside them, Grey lifted Emily into his arms and carried her to it. He flung open the door and placed her inside, then he leaned out the door and ordered, "Drive!"

As the carriage lurched to a start, Grey swung back inside
and slammed the door closed. He didn't care where they
were headed as long as they left. Sitting on the edge of
the bench across from her, facing backward as the carriage
swayed and rocked down the lane toward the road, he
reached for her hands and held them tightly. She breathed
more easily now as her skin warmed and the color returned
to her cheeks.

Her fingers curled gratefully around his. "Yardley," she
whispered. "I can't leave her behind. We have to go back for
her."

The hell they would. "I'll send for her once we're safe."

Her eyes turned pleading. "Please—"

"We are *not* turning around," he forced out through
clenched teeth.

At the strong resolve in his voice, she wisely stopped
pressing for her maid and nodded. She blinked hard, tears
gathering at her lashes. "What you did back there—"

"It stops," he hissed furiously as he leaned across the
compartment toward her. His fingers clamped down hard
around her wrists so she couldn't pull away. "The lying, the
deceit—you *will* tell me the truth, Emily. *Now.*"

"I can't!" she cried.

He jerked her toward him until she nearly fell into the
space between the benches at his feet. Fury blazed through
him. "For Christ's sake! Someone just tried to burn you
alive!"

Instead of bursting into sobs, an inscrutable mask came
down over her face. She didn't look away, her eyes unwavering from his in the dark shadows as she bravely but silently
held his gaze and refused to give up her secrets.

He stared at her, stunned. *Good God.* What must she
have been through in her life if she could react so calmly,

so stoically, after everything that had happened tonight? He would have given her credit for that if he didn't want to throttle her so badly. If it didn't seem to him that she had...expected it.

A sickening dread rose in his gut. She *had* been expecting it.

"What are you keeping from me?" he demanded, his teeth clenching so hard in his frustration with her that the muscles in his neck worked. "Why is someone trying to kill you?"

She inhaled sharply. In that heartbeat's hesitation, he saw indecision flash in her eyes.

"Emily," he pleaded as he leaned toward her, his anger replaced by core-wrenching concern as he desperately tried to get her to trust him. "Tell me, please, so I can protect you."

A soft, anguished sound tore from her throat, and she shuddered, her eyes squeezing shut. "Andrew."

"What about him?" he demanded. He didn't give a damn about her husband.

"His death wasn't an accident," she admitted in a whisper so low he barely heard it.

"What do you mean?" Confusion pulsed through him.

She opened her eyes and stared at him. The raw fear he saw in her was so intense, so monstrous that it ripped his breath away—

"He was murdered."

Christ. He remained perfectly still, not letting his expression register his shock. He stared at her closely, gauging the emotions on her face, remembering the fear he'd seen in her eyes and the loaded pistols she apparently kept in every room of the house.

For once, she wasn't lying.

"How?" he asked as gently as possible.

"He went out riding, and when he didn't come back,

the grooms went after him. They found him in a field. His skull..." She shook her head, unable to offer more.

His heart tore for her, knowing the pain she suffered but also knowing he had to uncover more in order to help her. "Riding accidents are common." He loosened his hold on her hands, just enough that she could sit back, but he didn't let go. If he gave in now to those soft pleadings of hers, he might never learn the truth. "What makes you think it anything more?"

"Andrew was a solid rider," she explained. "Not as good as you and Thomas, but he never would have fallen off like that. If the horse rolled over on him or broke its leg...but to just fall off an unharmed horse in the middle of a flat field— never."

He squeezed her fingers. Sorrow swelled inside him that she'd lost her husband, that she was so desperate to find a reason for her loss that she clung to the possibility of murder. "It happens sometimes, even to the best riders."

She gave a faint shake of her head, as if she'd pondered that very thing every day since he died. "How does a man fall from a horse hard enough to crush his skull but not get a smudge of dirt on his clothes?"

His heart skipped. He didn't have an answer for that.

"Whoever killed him didn't chase him down, didn't attack him," she continued, her fingers tightening around his. "Whoever it was talked him down from the horse, I'm certain of it. Andrew knew and trusted him. Which means I most likely know and trust him." Then she whispered, so softly he could barely hear her, "Which means I can't trust anyone."

When she raised her eyes to his, the fear was gone, replaced by a deep fatigue and firm resolve, an expression that was almost emotionless now that she'd confessed this secret to him. She was completely drained yet forced herself to endure. He'd seen that same expression on the faces of the war wounded, of civilians forced to flee from their homes, of old soldiers who had served too long in the heat of battle—it was the look of survival.

"I know you must think me an utter bedlamite," she continued, "shooting guns at you, claiming my husband was murdered when I have no real proof...but I'm not mad, Grey." She jutted her chin into the air with grim determination. "I *know* my husband was murdered."

"But why?" He shook his head gently with disbelief. "Emily, what you're saying—"

"Because Andrew became the heir apparent to Alistair Crenshaw, Marquess of Dunwich," she poured out in a rush, yet so softly whispered that he barely heard her over the rolling wheels beneath them. "That's why he was killed."

She pulled away. This time, stunned by that news, he let her go.

He stared across the dimly lit compartment at her. *Impossible.* Of course, stories littered English history of men who committed fratricide and patricide in order to inherit titles and of women who killed to become heiresses. But to murder Andrew Crenshaw, a man few people in London knew existed and even fewer cared about...no. Her grief over losing her husband had made her irrational, that was all.

"At the time your husband died, no one knew who was in line to inherit," he explained gently. "Even the Committee for Privileges didn't know." Or the gossip of that would have poured through London like a spring rain.

"Someone knew," she assured him. "They've known for six months."

"Tell me."

She drew a deep breath. "It started right before Andrew

was killed, strange happenings around the estate...a stray bullet from a hunter hit the carriage, a footman who fell down the stairs swore he'd been pushed, food was poisoned..." She held her arms wrapped against her lower stomach, as if trying to hold and comfort herself. "At the time no one thought they were anything more than just accidents."

"Then your husband died," he murmured, "and you began to suspect they were more than coincidental."

She nodded. "A month later I received a letter from Dunwich's attorney, stating that Andrew was the new heir—they hadn't heard that he'd died. He was a distant cousin, you see, so I never thought to send word to that branch of the Crenshaws. But I knew when I saw that letter what happened to him and why."

"And the accidents?"

"They stopped when he was killed." Her blue eyes glowed bright even in the darkness. "Until tonight."

His blood turned cold. He understood now why she'd pleaded with him so fiercely to leave, why there had been such fear in her eyes when he'd refused. Whoever had caused the accidents and murdered her husband was still there, still watching her, and whoever it was thought Grey was a threat. Enough of a potential risk that he'd set the house on fire to try to kill them both.

"That's why I wanted you to leave," she whispered and looked down at her trembling hands in her lap. "I couldn't bear it if—" The words choked her. Turning her face toward the shadows, she breathed out softly, "I could never forgive myself if anything happened to you because of me."

His chest tightened with wrenching regret. He'd been wrong about her, so very wrong...He'd thought she was simply a coldhearted harridan who couldn't be bothered with her brother when she'd actually been going through hell. Alone and isolated in the countryside, she'd been dealing not only with the grief of her husband's murder but also the terror of knowing that whoever did it might come after her.

No wonder she needed brandy to help her sleep and kept a loaded pistol in her sitting room. No wonder she'd shot at them when they arrived. *Good God.* For the past five months, she must have felt as if she were being hunted.

But now she had him. And he would protect her the same way he'd always protected her brother. With his life.

He held open his arms. "Come here, brat."

* * *

Emily stared at him as he waited for her, his arms wide in invitation, and the emotions churned inside her.

For so long, she'd been alone. First during those long years at school when she'd never fit in and made no friends, then even after her marriage, when she'd lost both her husband and her brother. All alone and isolated...until today, when Thomas sent Grey to her.

Nathaniel Grey. More than loneliness drew her to him. It was *all* of him—the way his grin warmed her insides, how she could talk to him so easily, how he made her laugh even when she was so furious with him that she wanted to throttle him. She admired most of all the fight he possessed, the determination to carve out a better life than fate had given him. She was even attracted to the vulnerability she glimpsed in him, that vulnerability he tried so hard to hide from the world beneath his devil-may-care veneer.

She nearly laughed that the same man who inadvertently caused her loneliness was now the same man offering to rescue her from it by taking her into his arms. And oh, how badly she wanted to let him! Yet she was still keeping secrets, and how furious would he be when he learned the truth? She'd told him about Andrew, but nothing else had changed. And every minute she spent with him only continued to put his life in danger.

But for now, they were safe, and finally, he was hers.

Slowly, she reached out her hand, and he took it to help her across the bouncing carriage to sit beside him. When his strong arms folded around her to draw her close, she melted against his chest and closed her eyes.

So warm and strong, his arms encircling protectively around her—for a moment, she did nothing but let herself *feel*. And sweet heavens, how good he felt! The strong heartbeat beneath her fingertips as her hand rested on his chest and the steady rise and fall of his deep breaths soothed her more than she could ever have imagined, and when he placed a tender kiss at her temple, she trembled.

"Are you chilled?" he murmured against her hair, misreading her reaction.

He released her and moved across the swaying compartment to pull up the other bench seat and reach inside the box for a lap rug. He found one and tucked it around her like a blanket. She couldn't help but smile at that. They were fleeing through the dark night for their lives, but he was worried she might be chilled.

He knelt on the floor and looked up at her, his eyes solemn with concern. "How are your feet?" he asked gently. "Did you burn them?"

She shook her head. "They're just a bit tender, that's all."

Dubious of her assessment, he reached down to her bare foot where it peeked out from beneath the singed hem of her dressing robe, and she caught her breath as his large hand folded warmly around her ankle so he could examine it in the dim light of the carriage lamps. When his fingertips stroked carefully over her sole, soothingly drawing curving circles against her skin, she closed her eyes with a sigh. Having his hands on her, even in such an innocent touch, felt so good that she could barely sit still.

He released her left foot and reached for the right, to again trace his fingers over her. But this time, she would have sworn that his hand reached further up her calf, that his fingers lingered longer against her skin. And this time, the feeling that warmed up her leg was anything but soothing.

He slipped his fingers between her toes.

She caught her breath in a trembling gasp. *Oh, sweet Lord!* He was slowly gliding his fingers *between her toes* in the most delicate caresses she'd ever felt in her life, and every inch of her tingled, electric. How was it possible that a simple foot rub could be so erotic? Or if his hands were all the way down on her toes, how she could feel each slow, slippery slide of his fingers ache all the way up between her thighs?

She swallowed, afraid he might feel her trembling again and wrongly think she was in pain. Or worse, to think that she was some shameless wanton, so easily titillated...even if she was. Because no matter how much she wanted him—and heaven help her, she wanted him desperately—some lines could not be crossed now. Not even with Grey.

"No burns, then?" she forced out, as lightly as she could, yet her voice still sounded husky to her own ears.

"Nothing serious." He caressed his fingertips along the bottom of her foot in soft, slow circles. "But I'll examine them again in the morning to be certain."

If this was how it felt to be examined, she didn't think she could endure it a second time. Not without insisting that he examine all of her with those wonderful fingers of his, just as slowly, just as tantalizingly...She nodded tightly. "If you insist."

He sat next to her and took her back into his arms, angling his long legs across the compartment to give her as much room as possible. Even this small gesture made her eyes sting with gratitude at his thoughtfulness.

He tucked a curl behind her ear. "Close your eyes, brat," he urged, "and try to rest. I'll watch over you."

I'll watch over you... If only it were that simple, she thought sadly. But at least for this night, she could let someone else take care of her.

With a sigh, she laid her head against his chest and closed her eyes. Rocked by the swaying carriage and lulled by his heartbeat in the darkness, she fell asleep in his arms.

CHAPTER FIVE

*T*he next afternoon, Emily lay curled up like a cat on the bench next to Grey, her head resting against his shoulder and his arm lying lazily across her back. Since leaving Snowden, she'd spent the night and most of the next day sleeping. She hadn't realized how exhausted she'd truly been until she had this opportunity to sleep, safe and protected. Yet she'd rested more peacefully than she'd ever imagined possible in such a cramped position in a cold, bouncing carriage while the dark day grew more and more chilly and wet around them.

All thanks to Grey. Whenever he brushed his hand over her back or shoulder, or took the liberty of tucking a stray curl behind her ear, the gentle touches comforted her and nearly lulled her back to sleep. Oh, she could easily grow used to this.

A sigh of contented relaxation escaped her, the soft sound earning her another stroke of his hand down her back. *Very easily.*

The day hadn't been all silence, though. Between naps, they talked comfortably like old friends. He was fascinating,

even more so than she remembered because the years had
tempered his brash personality and given him a maturity she
found intriguing. He told her stories about Spain and the War
Office, but she noticed that he never shared anything from
his childhood or the days before he joined the army. While
that hadn't surprised her, it hurt her more than she wanted to
admit that he didn't trust her with that part of his life.

In her turn, she described childhood adventures with
Thomas, the two of them often ganging up on helpless tutors
and nannies, and how he taught her how to ride and shoot as
well as the boys. She shared her old dream of being an artist
and even described her school days, although hiding most of
the bad incidents and injecting far more happiness into the
telling than she'd ever felt as a pupil. Whenever Grey asked
about her life since she'd married, though, she answered in
such a vague manner that he wouldn't be able to draw any
definite conclusions. She wasn't yet ready to talk about her
marriage. Not even with him.

She sat up and stretched, her muscles stiff from the ride.
A glance outside at the sky confirmed that the weather
hadn't improved.

"Are we going to stop for the night, or are we driving
straight through again?" she asked, concerned both about
being caught in a storm and about highwaymen.

"We'll stop." He slid to the bench across from her to give
her more room. "We're far enough away now to be safe, and
Hedley needs to rest."

"Of course." They'd stopped just before dawn at an inn
to change out teams, to buy food, and apparently, as she
discovered when Grey came back to the carriage with a
greatcoat for himself and a pair of shoes for her, to literally
buy the clothes off the innkeeper's back. Grey sent word
back to Yardley for the maid to travel to London and meet

Emily at Chatham House, and Hedley hired a man to be a second driver so that he and Grey could rest between turns in the driver's seat. After only a short break, they'd driven on, to put as much distance as possible between themselves and whoever tried to burn them alive.

Emily could use a night at an inn, too. Despite the naps, her aching body craved the softness of a mattress, and her belly longed for a hot meal.

She sighed gratefully. "I never suspected the thought of spending the night at a posting inn could be so appealing."

"A hot meal, a warm hearth," he drawled as he arched a sardonic brow, "and a room that doesn't burn down around you in the middle of the night?"

"Heavenly!"

As she laughed softly, he grinned at her, his eyes sparkling even in the dim blue-gray light of the rainy day. His smile cascaded through her, all the way down to the singed tips of her toes. *Oh my.* It warmed her from the inside out, the way no blanket ever could.

She cleared her throat and glanced out the window to distract herself from how appealing he looked, all travel-rumpled and unshaven, but the mud-streaked glass made it impossible to see anything. "Do you think—"

The vehicle lurched, the wheels stopping so suddenly that she sailed off the leather-cushioned seat and across the compartment, straight toward him.

With a fluid motion, he caught her and pulled her down onto his lap. She gasped in surprise and threw her arms around his neck.

They'd stopped. Everything around them came to a sudden halt. Except her heart, which now pounded so fiercely she was certain he could hear it. Or worse. That with her body pressed against his like this that he'd be able to feel it.

His mouth hovered close to hers, their eyes level as she sat perched precariously across his thighs with her arms wrapped around his neck. Her heart began to beat impossibly faster.

"Are you all right?" he murmured, his eyes flicking down to stare at her mouth before glancing back up to hers.

As the heat of his breath fanned her cheek, she nodded jerkily. "I'm the one who landed on you." She forced a nervous smile, as if sitting on the lap of a handsome army major was the most ordinary thing in the world. But she'd die of mortification if he ever suspected the fluttering for him low in her stomach or how her breasts grew heavy as they brushed unintentionally against his chest. "Are *you* all right?"

"Just fine," he answered, although she could have sworn she saw a fleeting grimace of pain on his face. "Perhaps I should check outside to see—"

With another swaying lurch that once again left her clinging to him to keep from falling, the carriage rolled forward.

"What happened?" she whispered.

Her cheek brushed against his. At the delicious sensation of his beard stubble scratching her skin, a tingle swept through her, landing straight between her thighs and blossoming the intimate ache growing there. She squeezed her eyes shut and tried to remember to breathe.

"We're moving again." His voice tickled her ear, making her tremble. "We must have been stuck." But his arms didn't loosen their hold around her, his hands on her back didn't drop away. The warmth of his body seeped through her thin dressing robe and stirred a prickling heat beneath her skin that made her remember how good it felt to be in a man's arms, to have her body pressed hotly against another's.

"Oh." Suddenly her mouth went dry, and she licked her lips to wet them.

"Mrs. Crenshaw," he rasped out hoarsely.

"Yes?"

He cleared his throat. "You're still sitting on my lap."

"Oh!"

Embarrassed, she tried to scoot away, but her off-balance position worked against her. Her feet failed to find purchase on the floor, and she could do nothing more than wiggle her bottom against his thighs.

And he wasn't helping. Instead of setting her on her feet, Grey sucked in a mouthful of air between clenched teeth and just sat there, his body stiffening.

"Emily," he ground out.

"I'm trying, but I can't get my balance to—"

"*Stop* wiggling!"

She froze.

Slowly, she raised her gaze to look at him. And lost her breath. "Oh," she whispered, her swirling mind unable to think of anything else except the raw desire she saw in his eyes. She nervously licked her lips again, and this time, when his gaze fell to her mouth, he didn't look away.

Her heart pounded fiercely now for a whole new reason. Grey wanted her...didn't he?

Oh, she simply didn't know! What she knew about men could fit on the head of a pin, and even that had proved so very wrong before.

But she understood Grey now, knew what kind of man he was and what goodness lay in his heart. If he could make her lips tingle with only his hot gaze, then *surely*...

Or surely *not*. Because he hadn't tried to lay a hand on her, not once during all this time they'd been alone. For heaven's sake! They'd been more intimate five years ago when he'd given her that first kiss. And even now confusion poured through her at the way he stared at her mouth so longingly but made no move to kiss her.

Blast it! Did the infuriating man want her or not?

Unable to bear the uncertainty any longer, she gave a little wiggle. Just a small, teasing movement of her bottom against his hard thighs to test his reaction—

With a curse beneath his breath, he grabbed her waist and forced her to sit still. But she felt him tremble, his breath growing shallow and shaky. And she knew for certain…she *knew*—he wanted her! After all these years, she could barely dare to believe it, but the rush of empowerment was intoxicating, the electric thrill that pulsed through her simply delicious. For the first time in two years she felt alive and feminine, alluring and beautiful, and all because of him.

"Nathaniel," she whispered.

"Mrs. Crenshaw," he forced out between clenched teeth.

She smiled at the contradiction of this man, of the gentleman and the rake warring inside him. So *this* was how it was going to be, was it? The gentleman in him was clinging to some misplaced vow he must have made to Thomas not to touch her or to some code of honor among army comrades. But the rake wanted her, she saw it in his eyes—for God's sake, she felt it pressing hard against her bottom!—but he wouldn't let himself act on that desire.

Perhaps, she admitted to herself with a pang of disappointment, it was better if he didn't. No matter how much she wanted him, she couldn't reveal herself completely. The danger to all of them was still too great.

But that didn't mean she couldn't tease him just a bit and make him finally admit that he'd been wrong to ignore her for the past five years, that she was far more now than just the girl he'd kissed in the garden and so quickly forgot.

And anyway, they were in a carriage, for goodness' sake; it wasn't as if anything truly intimate could happen here.

Oh yes. It was time for another lesson.

"Emily," she corrected, then audaciously slid her fingers through the hair at his nape. Goodness, how soft it felt when the rest of his body was so gloriously hard. "My name is Emily."

"Mrs. Crenshaw," he returned tightly.

Fighting back a smile of amusement, she twirled his hair around her fingers and asked with false innocence, "Am I too heavy for you?"

A pained expression of half desire, half annoyance darkened his face. "No."

"Did I hurt you when I fell on you?" She trailed her fingers along his jaw to his chin.

"No," he repeated, but this time, his voice hitched.

"Hmm." Her eyes stared at his sensuous mouth as she daringly brushed her thumb across his bottom lip, earning her a sharp inhalation of his breath. The ache inside her grew hotter, and all the blood in her body seemed to pool between her thighs. She was doing this to teach him a lesson, but if she wasn't careful, she'd be schooled herself on the lessons of playing with fire. "Is it uncomfortable having me on your lap?"

"Very," he bit out.

Laughing softly at that, she leaned against him to lightly brush her breasts against his chest, and when he shuddered, she thrilled with her newfound power over him. She knew she should stop, knew she was flirting with danger even now, but she'd wanted this moment too much, and for too many years, to stop now.

She pressed her lips to his neck, to that spot she'd longed to kiss since last night when he entered her sitting room with his shirt neck falling open, and rained soft kisses across his skin. He groaned, and she couldn't help but wonder... who would win, the gentleman or the rake?

"If I'm making you uncomfortable," she taunted against his neck in a sultry whisper as she yearned for his kiss, to be in his arms as his lips captured hers, "then perhaps you should do something about it."

"All right."

Without warning, he lifted her from his lap and set her down on the opposite bench with a teeth-jarring thud.

"There." He sat back and folded his arms across his chest, glowering at her. "Now I've done something about it."

Gaping in astonishment, Emily stared at him. She couldn't believe he'd done that!

Then a bubble of laughter escaped her. Her hands flew over her mouth to keep it back. But she was unable to stop it, and soon her shoulders shook with uncontrolled mirth.

She laughed with abandon. It felt good, oh so very good! All the fear and worry of the past five months lifted from her chest. Her body seemed to float with the emotional release, and all the relief made her absolutely giddy. For the first time in two years, she felt happy and free, and she dared to let herself hope that perhaps, just perhaps, the future wouldn't be so bleak after all.

"Brat," he warned, his voice low and angry.

"I'm sorry—I didn't mean—" she choked out between laughs.

Her life was in danger, her future uncertain, and the man she'd adored since she was sixteen just physically rejected her—their situation was so ridiculous, so *ludicrous* that she simply couldn't help laughing! Even with Grey glaring at her from across the compartment.

"But you have to admit that we're quite a pair, aren't

we?" She shook her head as her laughter faded into soft giggles. "You're a rake who won't touch me, while I've been longing to kiss you again since I was sixteen."

"You're not sixteen anymore," he snapped out.

"And you're not my brother. For God's sake, Grey! I know you want to kiss me...so let yourself kiss me. No harm can come of that." She pressed the back of her hand against her lips as the last of the laughter died away, and she admitted quietly, "And it would be nice."

He leaned toward her across the space between the two benches, his elbows resting on his knees. "You think I want to kiss you?"

She froze at the dangerous tone in his voice and the intense flicker deep in his eyes. The little hairs along her arms stood up in warning. Heavens, she was certainly playing with fire now! Yet she so desperately wanted to lose herself in his heat.

She swallowed. Hard. "I know you do."

It was his turn to laugh. "Oh, brat," he drawled in a husky voice that rumbled darkly through her like thunder. "I want to do so much more than just kiss you."

She stared at him in the blue-gray light, her pulse pounding in her ears with every racing heartbeat.

"I want to splay you across my bed and lick every delectable inch of you until I've had my fill. I want to nibble at your throat and breasts until you shiver, stroke my hands between your thighs until you spread yourself open wide and beg to be taken. I want to taste the sweetness of your warmth as I plunge inside you and hear your cries when I've satisfied my hunger." The gleam in his eyes was predatory. "And it certainly wouldn't be *nice*."

With heat shamelessly flushing her cheeks, she momentarily forgot to breathe. She should have been shocked by his words, should have scolded him for saying those things, or slapped him, or... Yet it wasn't shock she felt, but pulsing arousal.

He looked undeniably masculine as he lounged on the bench, his waistcoat half-unbuttoned and his neck rakishly bare to his shirt collar, his long legs kicked out casually in front of him. Shivering even now from the hot need flaming inside her, she craved him. She wanted to perch on his lap again and lick her tongue down into the patch of chest revealed by his open collar, wanted to strip away his shirt and waistcoat completely and let her fingers explore the hard muscles beneath. And God help her, she wanted to offer herself to him just as he described, as a willing and wanton feast.

But she could never have him now. He'd arrived five months too late.

"I'm not a nice man, Emily," he continued. "I use women for my own pleasure. I seduce them, take whatever enjoyment I can in them, and never give a thought to their feelings or needs. If they're satisfied, it's only because it brought me pleasure to make them so."

She shook her head, staring at him defiantly. "I don't believe you."

"You should." He leaned forward to punctuate his words. "And you should know that you'd be no different. The perfect woman, in fact, since you're exactly the kind of woman I prefer... a beautiful society widow, one who would never consider being seen with a rogue like me in public let alone want to leg-shackle me. A woman who cannot complain publicly when I ignore her after I've grown bored of being inside her." He sent her a disdainful look that she might ever think of him as anything more than he was. "Whatever delusions you've been clinging to about me, you need to get them out of your head right now."

Her eyes burned, her vision growing blurry. "I have no delusions about you."

"Good. So don't ever tease me again about kissing you, brat. Because I won't stop with just a taste of you." As he leaned back, his eyes gleamed wolfishly, and she shuddered at the unrepentant hunger she saw in their dark depths. "I'd devour you."

Giving her a last hard look, he turned his face toward the window.

She bit her lip hard, fighting back the knot of wretchedness rising in her throat but unable to stop the trembling that gripped her. Her hands shook as she looked down at them in her lap, overwhelmed by the harshness of what he had just told her about himself and her own shameless arousal to it. He'd laid himself bare, telling her the most horrible things... but she knew from Thomas's letters that they were true.

Shame flooded through her that he was so brutally honest about himself while she still kept secrets that could endanger both their lives. "Grey," she whispered before her courage could leave her, "I need to tell you..."

"What is it?" he growled but didn't look at her.

"The reason I can't—"

The carriage jerked again, and both of them grabbed for the handholds to keep their seats as the vehicle gave a loud creak and groan, then stopped. The wheels dropped, and the carriage settled to a leaning stop toward its side.

After a moment of stillness, Hedley flung open the door and peered inside, his face grim. "We're stuck," he explained succinctly.

Sliding a sideways glance toward Emily, Grey muttered, "You have no idea."

He pushed himself off the seat with a curse, then leaned

out the door and peered around the side of the carriage toward the team and front wheels.

"Dalton, how bad is it?" he demanded, calling up to the newly hired driver, still perched on top of the rig.

"Too bad fer us t' push out, I'd say," Dalton answered in a thick Yorkshire accent. "We'll be needin' a second team t' haul 'er out, seh."

"How far to the next inn?"

"Jus' down th' way a bit, couple o' miles."

Grey glanced down the road. "We can get there on foot?"

"Aye, seh. A' hour's walk o' two, most like."

Grey nodded grimly and dropped to the muddy ground. "We'll walk from here, then."

Emily peered out the door after him. A swamp had replaced the road. Mud came up past the horses' fetlocks, and the entire surface was so slippery that the carriage had slid toward the edge of the road and into a muddy hole that was impossible to drive through. The front left wheel lay buried to the axle.

He gestured for Hedley. "I'll need you to come with Mrs. Crenshaw and me. I want safety in numbers out on the road."

"Aye, Major."

He glanced up at the driver. "Dalton, you'll wait here with the carriage, and Hedley will come back with a second team to pull you out."

The man nodded. "Aye, seh."

"Let's go, then, Major." Hedley glanced glumly at the gray-black sky as he tossed up a pistol to Dalton. "It ain't gettin' any sunnier."

Thinking that Hedley's comment might be the grandest understatement she'd ever heard given the dark storm clouds gathering on the horizon and the increasingly cold wind,

Emily took Grey's proffered hand and let him help her down from the leaning carriage.

When her feet touched the mud, she lost her footing and slipped. His hands instantly encircled her waist to catch her. He lifted her easily into his arms and carried her to the center of the peaked road where the mud was shallower. He released her to the ground, and she shivered as her breath clouded the cold air.

"Only an hour's walk," he assured her. He shrugged out of his greatcoat and held it open for her.

She shook her head. "I don't need—"

"Put the damn thing on," he growled.

Angrily, she shoved her hands into the sleeves. The coat covered her like a tent, from chin to toes.

"Thank you," he muttered sarcastically. With a grimace of frustrated irritation, he buttoned up the coat, then dropped his hands away from her.

She swallowed down her frustration. Apparently, the gentleman had won after all, his restraint still firmly in place as the practical and protective hero set on saving her in spite of herself. Immediately, she missed the other Grey, the rake who'd looked at her as if he wanted to ravish her.

"Can you do this?" he demanded.

"Of course." She jutted up her chin defiantly. She would *never* let this man think her weak, even if she had to crawl to the inn on her hands and knees.

"Come on, then." He took her arm and led her down the road beside him, helping her find her unsteady way in the mud until she yanked her arm away from him and stomped on ahead by herself. He let her go. Driven on by mutual irritation and a desire to escape each other's company when they finally reached the inn, they made good time.

Until the first drops of freezing rain began to fall.

* * *

Grey kicked open the door of the White Stag Inn and carried Emily inside, her body cold and limp in his arms from the freezing rain and cutting wind of the howling storm. Too damned stubborn to admit that the cold was overwhelming her, she'd collapsed, her frozen legs and feet unable to walk, and he'd carried her the last mile in his arms. "A room— *now*!"

Across the crowded common room, travelers who had already sought refuge for the night looked up in startled curiosity from where they gathered around tables laden with steaming bowls of stew and tankards of ale. The innkeeper scowled at the puddle of mud Grey carried into the inn with him and at the driving wind and icy rain blowing through the doorway from the blackness of the storm outside.

The man waved his hand dismissively. "Go piss yourself—"

Hedley lunged across the bar and grabbed him by the throat. "Major Grey has requested a private room for th' daughter of the Duke o' Chatham," he explained slowly in a frighteningly calm voice. "Now, which room will be the lass's?"

The innkeeper's eyes grew wide. "We're full—" he choked out. "The storm—"

"Which room?" Hedley demanded again, his hand tightening. "I'm certain ye saved one."

Gurgling rose from the man's throat, and he pointed up the stairs. "Right side," he gasped, "far end of th' hall."

Hedley released him. The innkeeper jerked back, his hand going to his throat as his eyes narrowed murderously.

"Send up hot stew and ale." Grey glanced down at Emily in his arms. She was so wet and cold that she'd actually stopped shivering. The freezing rain had soaked through to her skin, and she was nearly unconscious. His gut clenched hard with worry. "And buckets of hot water for a bath."

"At this hour? You're fuckin' mad—"

"*Do it*," he growled and rushed her toward the stairs.

Hedley reached into his pocket and slapped a coin onto the bar. "Food and a hot bath for the lady." Then another one. "And a bottle o' whiskey for me." One last coin. "If ye please."

The innkeeper snatched the money into his fist and angrily shook it at him. "Well, you should've said so before!" He jerked his thumb toward three barmaids standing at the side of the bar, gaping in wide-mouthed wonder. "Go on! Get a bath and food upstairs now!"

As the women scurried into action, Grey carried Emily quickly through the inn. His own body was soaked and chilled, and so cold that his fingers barely moved as he shifted her in his arms. But all that mattered now was getting Emily warm. He reached for the door to the room and flung it open, brought her inside, and placed her gently on the bed.

"Grey," she whispered painfully, so softly he could barely hear her. Her eyes were still closed against a face that was shockingly white. Tiny droplets of cold rain clung to her frozen lashes. "I . . . I need . . . to tell . . ."

"Shh, just rest, brat." He leaned over and touched his lips to her forehead. Cold as ice. He tore himself away from her to hurry to the small fireplace.

As he piled up the wood and kindling, he pushed down the sickening guilt that he was to blame for not forcing her back to the carriage when the rain began. For believing her when she adamantly claimed despite chattering teeth that she was fine enough to carry on. For so desperately wanting to put distance between them after that carriage ride that he'd trudged on until the rain turned to sleet and the winds into a hurricane. Until she'd collapsed.

His numb fingers shook hard as he fumbled with the tinderbox. Finally, he struck a spark and set ablaze the pile of kindling. Then he tossed in log after log until the fire blazed.

When he returned to her, she was shaking again. He blew out a sigh of deep relief. *Thank God.* Shaking meant she was reviving, but he had to get her warm. And as long as she stayed in those wet clothes, the material would hold the cold close to her skin, and she would never warm up.

He lifted her into his arms and gently tugged her to her feet, holding on to her to make certain her legs didn't buckle beneath her. Then he unbuttoned the coat and peeled it down her arms and off, leaving her in the ruined satin of the dressing gown she'd been wearing when they fled Snowden Hall.

His still-shaking hands smoothed her wet hair away from her face. "Better?"

She nodded, shivering violently. "So cold…"

"I know." Slipping an arm around her to steady her, he led her to the fireplace and the heat of the fire, then he covered her hands with his, rubbing them to bring feeling back into her numb fingers. "But we're safe now, I promise."

He raised her hands to his mouth and huffed a hot breath against them, feeling her shudder in response. She was stronger now, her skin warming slowly and the color returning to her cheeks. She was out of danger.

His chest lightened with relief. And this time, when he raised her hands to his lips, he tenderly kissed her fingertips in silent apology.

A knock sounded at the door.

"That must be Hedley," he told her. "Stay here by the fire. I'll be right back."

She nodded and raised her shaking hands to the heat of

the flames. With a dubious look over his shoulder to check that she was still on her feet, he answered the door.

"Major." Hedley nodded and handed over the bottle of whiskey, then glanced past him at Emily and lowered his voice. "How is she?"

Grimacing, he shook his head. "Not well. Where's that bath?"

"Right behind me."

Grey stepped aside to let the maids into the room, who set down the small tub and filled it with hot water coming from the kitchen in a bucket brigade. He stood back and watched the sudden flurry of activity. *Good God.* When Hedley carried out orders, he did it well. So did the small fortune he was certain they'd paid for such attentive service. The parade of barmaids finished in just a matter of minutes. Hot stew and warm bread waited on the mantel, extra blankets lay spread over the bed, and the tub sat full and steaming.

The last maid out the door threw Grey a flirtatious smile and an inviting swing of her hips. He knew she would gladly provide very attentive service tonight, too. For the right price.

But his only concern was Emily and his two men. "Send someone to fetch Dalton and the team back here for the night, and leave the carriage until the morning," he instructed Hedley. "We'll deal with it when we're dry and rested. You both deserve a good night's sleep."

"Aye, Major." He tugged at his hat brim in thanks that he wouldn't have to go back out into the storm. His eyes drifted to Emily. "An' the lass?"

"I'll get her settled and make certain she's safe." He felt compelled to add, "Then find someplace downstairs to spend the night."

"All th' other beds are gone. We'll be on benches, looks like."

Grey nodded. "Still better than muddy ground in the middle of a battlefield, eh?"

"Aye," he agreed, heartfelt. "That 'tis."

"Save me a bench, will you? And see if the innkeeper has a wife or daughter with a dress and coat they'd be willing to sell." Grey raked his gaze over the man's muddy clothes. "And a fresh set of clothes for you, too."

"What 'bout you, Major?"

"Me? Barely caught a drop." Even as he said that, water puddled around his boots. "I'll be fine."

With a disbelieving arch of his brow, Hedley tugged at his hat again, then nodded toward Emily. "G' night, missus."

"Good night." Emily returned a jerky nod. "And Hedley," she added, her voice shuddering as fiercely as the rest of her, "thank you."

"'Twas nothin', ma'am."

"You saved my life," she whispered.

The sergeant's grizzled cheeks reddened. "'Tweren't no effort."

Grey clenched his jaw at the way Emily sent Hedley a grateful smile. He'd saved her life, too—twice now, in fact—and the brat had yet to thank *him*. Then again, he thought with chagrin, Hedley also hadn't admitted that he wanted to ravish her and then leave her.

With a long sigh brought on by fatigue, cold, and immense frustration, he shoved Hedley out the door, then locked it tight in case anyone decided to try to take the rest of their money. He turned around. Emily stood before the fire where he'd left her, still shaking but less violently now, with her hands outstretched to the heat. She was going to be fine.

And now he desperately needed to get warm himself. He frowned at her as he crossed to a wooden chair in the corner and sat to remove his boots. "Better take off that robe, I think."

"I can't."

"Why not?" With a fierce pull, he tugged off the first boot, the leather clinging stubbornly to his wet foot. "You're wearing your night rail beneath, aren't you?"

"But it's wet, too."

"It will dry faster without the robe over it." He scowled in growing frustration, both with her and with the ruined state of his favorite pair of Hessians. He tipped over his boot and frowned as a stream of water poured out of it.

Dropping it to the floor, he made a mental note to make Thomas purchase him a new pair of Hoby's finest, then reached down for the other boot.

"All right," she acquiesced hesitantly. "But that's all I'm wearing, just so you know."

Damned stubborn woman. She'd nearly died twice in two days, and she was worried about propriety? "Don't fret, brat." He tugged off the other boot and glanced up at her. "You don't have anything I haven't seen be—"

The boot slipped from his hand and fell to the floor.

He stared at her, his lips parting in stunned surprise.

She stood in front of the fire wearing only the wet night-gown, turned sheer from the rain and clinging to her like a second skin, the robe in a pile of wet satin around her feet. In an instant, he took in the full length of her. Wet blond hair hanging down her back, nipples straining like dark pebbles through the white cotton, long legs stretching down from the triangle of curls between her thighs...

...and the small but distinct bump at her lower belly.

"Christ," he whispered.

The brat was pregnant.

CHAPTER SIX

*W*hen he didn't say anything, only stared at her from across the room, Emily swallowed. She now shook more from nervousness than the cold.

"Grey," she said softly, folding one arm modestly over her breasts and the other protectively over her belly against the incredulous stare he leveled on her. "I couldn't tell you when we were at Snowden. I tried in the carriage, but...please understand."

He straightened on the chair, his shoulders stiffening.

"I found out after Andrew died," she continued uneasily. Her gaze lowered to the floor because she wasn't able to bear the stunned surprise on his face, the betrayal in his eyes. "That's why I couldn't tell anyone. When the letter arrived from Dunwich's attorney, then I knew—I *knew* I had to keep this baby a secret. I had to protect it however I could."

As he rose slowly from the chair and approached, she drew a deep breath, but her shaking only grew worse.

He stopped in front of her, towering over her by almost

a foot, yet she didn't raise her gaze to meet his, not wanting to see the cold accusation darkening his face. Instead, she trained her eyes on his chest, not daring to raise them. Whatever he thought of her for hiding this secret from him and putting his life at risk, she was certain that it wasn't charitable.

"If someone was willing to kill Andrew because he was the heir—if they knew I was carrying his child and possibly the next heir, then—" She choked on the words, unable to make herself utter her worst fears aloud. "I love this baby, Grey, more than I've ever loved anything in my life. I know that sounds silly. It's barely a bump, really, and not even visible with my clothes on. But I wanted this baby with every ounce of my heart and soul." Even now her chest burned with the same fierce love and determination to be a mother as when the baby was conceived. "And I will do anything to protect it. *Anything.*"

Slowly, he placed his large hand over hers as it rested against her belly, the small bump nearly hidden beneath his outstretched fingers. "Me, too," he assured her.

Her breath hitched as her eyes flew up to his face. *Dear Lord*, had he really just said... "Pardon?"

His eyes never lifted from their joined hands. "I swore to protect you, Emily." Each quiet word blossomed inside her like a spring rose. "And this baby is part of you."

Warmth radiated through her from his palm down to the tips of her toes. Goodness, she hadn't expected *that*! She'd anticipated yelling and cursing, threats of telling her family and the Crenshaws... even returning her straight back to the burned-down house to leave her there amid the smoldering timbers and ashes.

Oh, he was furious with her, despite his outward appearance of calm; she could see in his dark eyes the anger and betrayal that she'd kept this from him, this secret of all secrets. But for some reason she couldn't fathom, he kept his anger in check. For the moment anyway. And that, at least, was a hopeful sign. The first one she'd had in months.

"Is that it, then?" he asked pointedly, this time unable to keep the hint of angry accusation from his voice. "Anything else you're keeping from me?"

She was unprepared for the overwhelming relief that cascaded through her at finally being able to share news of the baby with him, and she shook her head, unable to speak around the knot in her throat.

"Good," he murmured. Slowly, he reached for the neckline of the nightgown plastered to her skin. "Then let's get you undressed and warm."

She gasped, her hands flying up to stop his. "Grey, you can't!"

"In addition to protecting you, I also promised to take care of you." His deep voice softened, yet the resolve lacing through it told her that he'd brook no argument. "So let me take care of you tonight."

With a hesitant nod, she dropped her hands away. She held her breath, not daring to breathe as he unfastened the handful of buttons, then slowly peeled the wet material down her body and off, until she stood naked and trembling in front of him. Oddly, she felt no shame, not even when he lifted her into his arms and carried her across the room to the bathtub. After all, she'd just entrusted him with the biggest secret of her life, and she didn't think it was possible to be any more exposed, any more vulnerable than by admitting she was with child.

He lowered her gently into the warm water of the waiting tub, and she sank into its steamy heat up to her breasts. Sliding down beneath the water with a grateful sigh, she felt her skin prickle as the heat soaked into her and warmed away the bitter cold.

He frowned down at her, a new concern furrowing his brow. "Earlier, at Snowden—you said you were ill...the baby?" Each word came awkward and slow.

She smiled at that. Her fearless hero was befuddled by a simple pregnancy. "Yes, in the mornings. Yardley says it's common when a woman's increasing."

As if relieved that he had nothing more to worry about than that, he nodded and stepped back. She watched, mesmerized, as he unbuttoned his wet waistcoat and removed it, hanging it over the wooden chair. His shirt lay plastered over his chest, outlining each hard, well-defined muscle beneath.

He paused as he pulled his shirt free from his trousers. "A baby and illness on top of Crenshaw's murder and fleeing servants." Surprised admiration tinged his voice. "You dealt with all that alone?"

"I had Yardley." She smiled in gratitude at the maid's devotion to her. "I don't think I could have survived without her."

His deep voice purred huskily, "And I think you're much braver than you believe."

Her eyes darted up toward his at the quiet compliment. But he'd already lifted his shirt over his head, leaving her to rake her gaze shamelessly over his bare chest and the muscles in his shoulders, the sculpted ridges of his abdomen, the dusting of golden hair that led down beneath the lean waist of his trousers—

Oh my! She averted her eyes, thanking God that the hot water hid the flush in her cheeks. She *was* a proper lady, after all.

Then her very improper eyes slid slowly back to him, to steal a very unladylike peek at his physique. And what a wonderful figure it was, too. Tall and lean with every muscle hard and well defined across his chest, broad shoulders that narrowed to his waist, muscular arms... When he turned around to throw the shirt over the chair with the waistcoat, the view from the back was just as fine. Muscles rippled across his back as he reached down to toss another log into the already blazing fire.

Stripped down to only his damp trousers—for a moment, Emily wondered if he planned to remove even those, given her own naked state—he picked up the soap from the washbasin and carried it over to the tub, knelt beside her, and began to lather the soap in the bathwater.

Her breath choked. He planned to... *wash* her?

She swallowed nervously even as the idea tempted her so much that her thighs clenched. "You don't have to—"

"Lean up," he commanded gently.

She hesitated. No one had *ever* washed her before, certainly not a man. Yet knowing she had no choice but to do as he ordered, and not wanting another argument, especially when they were finally getting along, she fought back her uneasiness, closed her eyes, and leaned forward. Besides, it was only a bath. He most likely washed his horse once a week.

When his hands touched her shoulders and spread the soap across her bare skin in slow, soft caresses—*oh, lucky, lucky horse!*

She bit back a soft moan of pleasure. Everywhere his fingers brushed over her skin, heat radiated and chased away the last of the cold until she pulsed hot and tingling, the ache of the chill replaced by a far more electric one. As his hands slipped lower to languidly roam up and down her spine, a contradiction of sensations skittered through her. The slippery-smooth soap beneath his rough hands, not washing so much as massaging, the soothing warmth of the water against the exciting caresses of his fingers—she trembled.

"Are you cold?" he asked, mistaking the reason for her shiver, and poured warm water down her back. "Better?"

"Oh yes," she sighed in a long exhalation, no longer bothering to hide her enjoyment. Her head sagged forward, and with his thumbs, he massaged the back of her neck and rubbed out the tension. Oh, this was nice...*very* nice.

He took her shoulders and eased her back against the tub, then reached for her arms to leisurely wash each one. Despite the heat of the steam drifting up from the water, she shivered as his soapy hands rubbed down her arm to her hand, then tantalizingly along each finger.

"You're barely showing at all now, but you wouldn't have been able to hide the baby much longer." He gently lowered her left arm into the water and reached for the right, then started all over with the delightfully slippery caresses. Everywhere he touched, goose bumps dotted across her skin in his wake. "If someone was watching you, they'd have soon known."

Her soft admission came as a breathless sigh. "I had a plan."

"Of course, you did," he murmured.

She thought she heard a touch of amused admiration in his voice, but all logical thought was driven from her mind at the wickedly scandalous feel of his hands slipping down under the water to reach for her leg, to begin the sweet torture of washing down her thigh and calf to her foot. She bit her tongue to keep back another soft sigh of pleasure, not wanting him to think her a complete wanton for enjoying a simple bath this much. But that was *exactly* how she felt, and she liked it immensely.

"Yardley has a sister in Glasgow who owns a dress shop. I was planning to go there, change my name—" She caught her breath when he ran his fingers between her toes. Oh, how much she liked that! If he kept that up... She licked her lips and forced out, "She was going to take care of me until the baby arrived. If it was a girl, I would have gone back to London to be with my family."

"But if it was a boy," he murmured, his hands moving to her other leg, his fingers gently kneading along her calf to her knee, "he'd be the heir to a marquessate."

"Then we'd have stayed in Scotland, and no one would ever have known."

His hands paused in their caresses. "You would have denied him his birthright?"

"Yes." If it meant saving her son's life, she would have done exactly that. This baby meant the world to her, and she would sacrifice everything to keep him safe.

"You would have had to live a lifetime of secrets," he mumbled. "Could you have done that?"

"You have." She opened her eyes to find him staring at her, his chocolate-brown depths warm and arousing in the firelight. "Your entire life has been a lie."

* * *

Grey froze, his heart stopping for a fearful beat. His hand stilled against her body beneath the water.

What she implied was impossible for her to know. *Impossible.* He'd covered his tracks too well over the years for anyone to figure out the truth. Not even Edward Westover and Thomas Matteson. And especially not some society chit living in Yorkshire whom he hadn't seen in five years.

Yet somehow, she knew. In the stormy blue pools of her

eyes, as she waited patiently for him to let down his pretenses so they could truly be themselves with each other, he could see the truth. But there was no judgment on her face, no disdain, no pity—he thanked God for that, because he didn't think he'd have been able to bear any condemnation for the way he'd chosen to live his life. Not from her. For some reason he couldn't name, what Emily thought of him mattered.

He sat back on his heels, drawing his hand out of the water. "I'm just an army officer. No secret there."

"Perhaps not," she said quietly. "But what were you before?"

"Younger," he quipped. Ignoring the sudden tightening of unease in his chest, he curled his lips into a half grin, the smile he used whenever he wanted to get his way with a woman.

But when she frowned like a governess, his grin faded. He should have known charm wouldn't work on this one, not that he needed any more proof that Emily Crenshaw wasn't an ordinary woman.

"Who I was doesn't signify," he stalled, hoping she would let the matter drop.

But of course, she didn't. "It does to me." She reached for his hand, and the warmth of her touch shivered through him. "Who are you, Nathaniel Grey?"

A forced shrug of his shoulders. "Just the runaway son of a blacksmith."

"From Trovesbury Village," she added flatly.

"Yes."

Her eyes saddened, and he felt the force of her disappointment as fiercely as if she'd slapped him. "There is no blacksmith in Trovesbury named Grey. There never has been." She laced her fingers through his, as if she could sense in him an urge to flee. "When Thomas told us you'd been wounded, I tried to write to your parents, to assure them that you had friends in our family and that we would do whatever we could to help."

Oh God. His world began to rock beneath him.

"Even though the letters were franked, they weren't received, so I contacted the local constable for help." Her eyes fell to their two hands, her soft fingers interlocked with his rough ones, and humiliation curled through him. "He told me that there were no blacksmiths named Grey, not in Trovesbury, not in the entire county." She took a deep breath. "Thomas doesn't know. I haven't told anyone. It's your secret, after all—"

"Yes, it is," he snapped.

Outwardly, she ignored that, but he felt her fingers tighten against his. "But I've told you all my secrets."

His jaw tightened at her unspoken challenge as he asked sarcastically, "You show me yours, I'll show you mine? Is that it?"

"I think," she offered shyly, biting her lip, "I've already shown you all of mine."

Sweet Lucifer, she had indeed, and a stolen glance confirmed it.

In the flickering shadows of the firelight, the water just tickled at her breasts, her nipples puckering from its warmth, while beneath the surface, her round hips gave way to impossibly long legs on a woman so petite that the top of her head barely reached his shoulder. And if he looked hard enough, he would see the tiny baby bump, barely visible.

In his life, he'd seen so many naked women that he couldn't remember them all, stunning women who commanded the attention of every room they entered. But

Emily...well, Emily was different. Quietly beautiful, alluring without trying. Simply lovely.

"I trust you, Grey." She slipped her hand away from his and closed her eyes, and even though she sat within his reach, she suddenly seemed a world away. "I only wish you knew how much you can trust me."

He stifled the bitter laugh that rose to his lips. She had the body of a woman, but still clung to the innocence of a child if she believed in trust. She, of all people, should have known that there were some secrets that were meant to be hidden away, secrets that weren't safe to reveal to the light of day.

Trust me. She had no idea how much she was asking of him, to trust her not only with his secrets but also with his life. If anyone found out the truth, his reputation would be ruined; his position in Spain would be repealed, and possibly his entire career at the War Office ended. Everything would be stripped away, and he'd be back in the streets. He'd fought too hard for too long to lose everything.

But if he didn't tell her the truth, nothing would be the same between them. This fragile friendship they'd managed to carve out would shatter, and he'd never be able to confide in her again. If it had been any other woman asking this of him, he would have flat-out refused. But not Emily. The brat had gotten under his skin since he saw her standing in the garden with such fear in her eyes—no, perhaps this pull toward her had always been there, even when he'd kissed her all those years ago at Ivy Glen.

He muttered a curse of surrender under his breath. "All right, you win."

Of course, she'd won. Truly, could there have been any other outcome, even knowing the admission she wanted would endanger his future? She trusted him with her life. He only hoped he could do the same.

"You're right," he admitted grudgingly. "My father wasn't a blacksmith. Or if he was, I didn't know it." He paused. "I was an orphan."

Slowly, she opened her eyes, and he steeled himself against what he expected to see in those sapphire depths—pity, contempt, disdain. Instead, all he saw was understanding and compassion. "Tell me."

"Are you certain?" He'd never told anyone before about his childhood, nor did he plan on speaking of it ever again, so he needed to make certain she understood from the beginning the importance of this moment and the depth of the trust he placed in her hands.

"Yes," she whispered.

Slowly nodding, his expression carefully stoic, he reached for the soap. "Then lean back."

Emily stared at him warily for a moment, sensing that something had just irrevocably changed between them and that there would be no going back now.

She eased herself down against the tub. Until that moment, she'd felt no self-consciousness in front of him, and nothing about the bath had changed—she was still just as naked beneath the water now as she'd been five minutes ago. But this time when he lathered the soap between his hands and brushed it over her shoulders in long, caressing strokes, she trembled with vulnerability. There were no more secrets between them now, no more barriers of any kind. They'd both laid themselves bare, her with her body and him with his past.

"My earliest memory is from the orphanage when I was around three," he began quietly. "I don't how I got there or when. But it was either stay there or live on the street, and at least there, I had shelter from the rain and an occasional meal."

"What was it like?" she asked breathlessly as he slowly reached for her leg, to massage down her thigh to her knee and calf.

His fingers lingered against her skin, drawing slow and delicate patterns against her wet flesh. "Exactly as you think...cold, dank, filth everywhere." Delicious heat flared up her leg to the ache blossoming between her thighs. "We were left to run wild."

"Wasn't there—"

Her voice hitched as he stroked his hand up her inner thigh and nearly to the wet curls at her center, making her squirm in the warm water and distracting her from the details of his past. He wasn't even bothering to pretend now that he was washing her. Sweet Lord, he was *exploring* her! It was scintillating. Scandalous. Wickedly sinful. And oh, she didn't want him to stop.

But she *needed* the truth.

As his hand retreated back down her leg, she took a deep breath and tried again. "Wasn't there a matron to oversee you?"

"Yes. But since she beat us, I doubt she cared what we did."

"Grey—" He swept his hand up her leg again, this time letting his fingertips graze against her feminine folds before retreating, and a shiver tore through her. That time, he successfully distracted her, and whatever she was about to say fell lost forever.

"I never knew my parents. I made inquiries a few months ago, but nothing came of them."

She tried to concentrate on what he was telling her, but she was rapidly losing her ability to breathe, caught between arousal and relaxation, swept away by his erotic caresses.

"I ran away when I was ten," he continued, both with his story and with his tender assault on her body as his fingers closed around her toes and gently squeezed. "That was when I made up the story about having a blacksmith for a father and lied about being a runaway apprentice. Lots of apprentices run away, so I became just another. Eventually, I found a job as a stable boy for Viscount Henley."

"Henley?" Closing her eyes, she licked her lips as he decadently rubbed soap between her toes, one by one. Oh, how much she liked *that*...and she suspected he knew, too, and was using her own body against her in distraction. "I know him—I mean, his family."

Another long stroke up her leg to her thigh. "You know the dowager viscountess, I'm sure."

"Lady Henley is a friend of my parents. She's very..." Her voice trailed off into a soft whimper of disappointment at the retreating strokes back down her thigh to her knee, moving his hand away from the part of her that craved his touch the most and now pulsed hard in aching syncopation with her heart.

"Formidable," he finished.

If his hands hadn't been on her body, she might have heard the affection for the viscountess in his voice. But she was only aware of the way his fingers continued to erotically lather the soap against her skin and knead her muscles, sore and stiff from the long carriage ride. With a deep sigh, she melted beneath his seeking hands.

"So I grew up in the Henley stables and discovered I had a gift for working with horses." He gently scratched his fingernails seductively along her inner thigh. "As soon as I could, I joined the army."

"As a Scarlet Scoundrel." Squirming as he drew slow circles against her skin, unable to sit still beneath the delicious torture the bath had become, she fought back a whimper. Well, he was certainly a scoundrel for bathing her like—

Her breath caught as she suddenly realized where the regiment's nickname had come from. Little to do with battle, more to do with women. And if Grey were one of its most scoundrel-minded officers...God help her.

"Then you became a hero," she breathed, unable to speak above a whisper.

"No," he corrected, "I became a lurker."

She opened her eyes, her lips parting. *A lurker?* She couldn't have heard him correctly. "Pardon?"

With a devilish smile, he took her surprised reaction as an invitation to brush soap bubbles over her bottom lip with his fingertip.

"That's what I do, brat. I lurk." He traced the outline of her mouth, and the tingling of tiny bubbles bursting against her lips reverberated with the force of fireworks and made her tremble. "I live on the fringe of society, never completely part of that world." His eyes slowly followed his hand as he trailed his fingers away from her mouth and down her neck. "*Your* world."

But he was wrong. It wasn't her world, and it never had been. As the daughter of an East India Company official, an exiled schoolgirl, then a widow, she'd spent her life exactly as he had...on the outside looking in. They were two of a kind, and knowing that made her feel even closer to him.

His hand paused at the hollow at the base of her throat. She forced herself to breathe calmly beneath his touch, but her heart beat so hard and fast at the realization of how much they shared that the blood pounded through her ears in a loud rush. He was the one she'd been searching for since she was sixteen, the man who understood how it felt to be an outsider, to be surrounded by people yet feel so terribly alone. And any doubts she had about him disappeared beneath the soft strumming of his thumb against her racing pulse. The same soft stroking that now throbbed through every inch of her.

"I'll never have their respect nor their confidences." His fingers traveled lower, down into the water-beaded hollow between her breasts. She gasped as he began to draw small, tantalizing circles against the inside swells in the lather clinging to her skin. "I'll never be welcomed into their drawing rooms or to their soirees."

But he would be, and she'd make certain of it. Even as she bit her lip to keep back the soft whimper that rose inside her when his hand drifted lower, she promised herself that she would somehow find a way to make that happen.

His fingers slipped over her breast in a flutteringly light touch, barely grazing against her nipple, but the unexpected sensation jolted her with the force of a lightning bolt. She shuddered and bit her lip to keep from moaning, to keep from begging for more because she feared that if she did, then he would stop, the same way he'd stopped in the carriage. Yet between her thighs the pulsing ache continued to grow, and she shifted her hips against the side of the tub to keep her legs from shaking so hard they splashed the water.

"But it's never bothered me." Thoughtful reflection tinged his voice, oddly contemplative considering that he was drawing slow circles across his palm with her hard nipple. "In fact, it's given me the freedom to move between social classes as I wish, belonging to whichever is most useful. I have the best of both worlds."

When his hand closed over her breast, the low moan she'd been holding back fell helplessly from her lips. Shamelessly, she arched herself to press his hand even harder against her. Shivering, aching, yearning for more...only Grey did this to her. He aroused her in a way her husband never had, and when he gazed at her with heated desire, she knew what it meant to be wanted as a woman.

Every terrible minute of his life had brought him to this night. With her. Even as her mind fogged from his touch until she could barely think, she instinctively knew that if one piece of him were different she wouldn't crave him like this nor feel the arousal he radiated through her. It was all of him that did this to her, and she wanted *all* of him.

"I have the freedom to enjoy those parts of society I want and never bother with obligations nor consequences. I gamble in their clubs, hire their tailors, and enjoy their finest entertainments, including their widows and their wives." His thumbs circled her nipples as they poked achingly out of the lather, drawn into hard points. "But I've never wanted any of their daughters." His voice was husky and oddly strained. "Until now."

Her eyes flew open. "Grey—"

He dipped his head to capture her wet nipple in his mouth. He relentlessly suckled and licked and nipped until she panted helplessly beneath him, her words lost beneath a throaty moan of sheer delight. Struggling for breath, she ran her fingers through his still-damp hair, wanting to feel him, *needing* to feel all of him.

"The daughter of a duke," he murmured as his tongue laved her nipple. "Graceful and kind." He took the bud between his teeth and worried at it until her fingers dug against his skull with arousal, and he chuckled against her flesh. "A bit devilish." Then he shifted to begin the sweet torture anew with the other nipple, coaxing another shivering moan from her. "So damned seductive." As his mouth suckled at her breast, his hands reached beneath the water to stroke down her body. "Simply beautiful."

Arousal flashed through her like a wildfire, tickling at her toes and burning the ends of her hair, tightening hard between her thighs. Barely able to breathe beneath his heated attack against her senses by his mouth and his words, she felt herself running toward something she couldn't name, something only Grey could reveal to her. Something she desperately needed.

She'd never felt this way with Andrew. Her body had never craved possession and surrender the way it did now with Grey, who seemed to want to touch and taste all of her, slowly and torturously, because he knew she would find pleasure in it. Even now, as he lifted his mouth to take delicate nips up her throat to the underside of her chin, the thought curled through her like a ribbon zigzagging through a stay that he'd lied to her in the carriage. He would never see her as one of his merry widows to ravish and leave. She knew better. Any man who touched her this gently, this affectionately, could never be the coldhearted rake he described.

"Kiss me," she begged, having waited far too many years to have his lips on hers again.

"I told you, it won't be nice," he warned as his teeth scraped along her jaw.

She tilted back her head to give him access to her throat. "God, I hope not!"

He laughed as his lips captured hers, and she drank in the sound. Hot, forceful, and insistent, his mouth blistered as it took possession of hers. He kissed her as if he couldn't get enough of her, couldn't taste her deeply enough, couldn't kiss her thoroughly enough—with a low groan, he shoved his tongue between her lips and plundered her mouth until he left her frantic to have his hands all over her body.

She shamelessly opened her thighs in invitation to touch her *there*, the one place he'd yet to explore, the place that ached so desperately for him that it left her panting and shaking with need. "Grey, please."

Another groan tore from him, this time of frustration as he pulled away from her.

"I can't." He rocked back onto his heels and stood unsteadily, running a shaking hand through his damp hair. "I should never have let it get this far—*Christ!*"

As he looked down at her, she saw the battle raging inside him, the raw desire for her warring with his control. "Yes," she urged, desperately wanting his touch, "you can. I want you to."

He rasped out hoarsely with a regretful shake of his head, "We've already been through this, Mrs. Crenshaw."

"Emily," she insisted, cringing at her married name. She sickened to hear it when his hands and mouth had been on her only moments ago. "I'm just Emily."

"No." He gave a short, bitter laugh. "You're not."

"Because of Andrew? If that's what stopping you…" Drawing a deep breath for strength, hoping he would understand, she admitted, "I didn't love him."

His eyes flickered down disbelievingly toward her belly, and her hand reflexively covered the bump, which was barely visible beneath the water.

"I wanted a baby. He was my husband, and I—" Her voice choked. "But I never loved him, not like a wife should. And he certainly never loved me."

Slowly, she rose from the tub and stood, letting the droplets of warm water rain down her naked body. Goose bumps dotted her skin, not from the cold air but from the nearness of him, even now wanting him so badly she shook with it.

But the stubborn man refused to touch her. His fists clenched at his sides to physically restrain himself from reaching for her, and his eyes determinedly fixed on her face as if it would shatter him to glance down at her body.

Aching harder with each passing heartbeat that he kept himself from her, she whispered, "Touch me, Nathaniel."

He didn't move, yet his eyes filled with a hungry heat at her plea. "I shouldn't."

"But you want to."

The single word tore in a rasping groan from his throat. "Desperately."

"Good." Unable to endure the lack of contact with him a moment more, she touched his cheek. The stubble of his two-day beard scratched beneath her fingertips, and he inhaled sharply through gritted teeth as if her touch pained him. "So do I."

"Damnation!" Knocking her hand away, he grabbed her shoulders. "What you're asking of me—I have to stay away from you. Can't you see that?" Despite his words, his hands tightened their grip, and she felt him shift her closer, felt the heat of his bare chest next to hers, so close but not yet touching. "I'm a rake, Emily, a perfect scoundrel—"

"Stop saying that! You are not." Tears of angry frustration blurred his handsome face. "Not to me."

He shook his head. "I use women, Emily, and you don't deserve that. Because that's what it would be—only physical, no matter how much we both enjoyed it." A soft groan tore from him as he dropped his gaze to roam lasciviously down her front, leaving her trembling and aching even harder for him. "And I suspect I would very much enjoy it," he murmured, and the deep purr of his words fell through her like liquid fire. He tore his eyes back up to hers. "But you deserve a man who will marry you, give you a home, a family—I can't give you that."

"I don't want that." *Not anymore.* Once, she'd dreamed

of having exactly that, only to discover that the price of her dream was too dear. Now she wanted only this moment, this night...this man. When she leaned forward and placed a kiss in the middle of his bare chest, his entire body stiffened. "All I want is you. *You*, Grey, for however long I can have you, in whatever way."

"Emily." His husky voice cracked. She knew his resolve was melting, knew from the way his hands now curled over her shoulders to draw her near rather than push her away that he was breaking.

Her lips whispered kisses across the planes of his chest to his shoulder. "You said in the carriage that I was your perfect woman."

"You are," he bit out grudgingly. His hands slid down to her back, and his arms tightened around her despite his determination to refuse her.

"Then let me be perfect for you tonight." She touched her lips to his and shivered at the need she tasted in him. She'd waited years for this night, and she refused to wait any longer.

"And the baby?" His conflicted desire to both protect her and ravish her showed in his frustrated grimace. "I don't want to hurt you."

Her heart skittered deliriously at his concern. Smiling joyously against the sting of tears, she whispered, "You won't."

With a groan of surrender, his hand swept down her body, then up between her thighs to capture her folds against his palm. The swiftness of his touch ripped her breath away.

Emily closed her eyes and clung helplessly to him. One of his arms snaked like an iron band around her lower back to keep her hips in place against him as he boldly stroked his fingers into her cleft, seeking out the softness and heat he had almost denied himself, although with her arms now locked around his neck, nothing could have torn her away.

"Is this what you want?" he murmured against her temple.

She nodded her forehead against his chest and panted hard, unable to recapture the breath he'd stolen. His fingers relentlessly teased at her, stroking back and forth against her folds and making her wet beneath his touch. The depth and pressure of each shivering caress increased until he slipped two fingers into her warmth.

She gasped at the sensation of having him inside her like this, at the deep slide of his fingers and the teasing curl of his fingertips for just a beat before retreating slowly, as if he couldn't bear to release her. Her heart raced, her blood began to boil. And when he twirled his fingers wickedly with each deep plunge—a moan tore from her.

"Is this the way you like it, brat?"

Is this the way... She nodded wordlessly as her throat tightened with emotion. He thought she'd been touched like this before, that she was experienced enough to know what pleasures to ask for, what touches to demand. But she'd never done this, not even with Andrew. Grey was the first to share this wonderful new intimacy with her, making this night even more special.

"Or this?"

As his fingers continued their slow rhythm of plunge and retreat, his thumb delved into the top of her cleft and flicked against the sensitive bead buried there.

Her hips bucked against his hand. "Yes—oh yes!"

"Jesus," he murmured at her violent reaction to so small a touch. "You're so responsive..."

"Grey," she whimpered pleadingly, although she wasn't certain what she was begging him to do, except that her body craved more...more wanton caresses, more deep plunges, more of *him*.

He pressed his thumb against the pulsing nub again, but this time he didn't relent, not when her hips jerked nor when she shuddered against him. Not even when her knees buckled beneath her and the only thing keeping her from slipping back into the bath was his strong, unyielding arm around her waist. He rolled the sensitive point beneath his thumb until her entire body shook uncontrollably, until her sex tightened around his fingers—

The cry tore loose from deep inside her as she collapsed beneath the waves of delicious pleasure spreading out to envelop all of her. The exquisite clench and release inside her was more than she could bear, and she sank limply down his chest.

*   *   *

Catching her as she sank away, Grey lifted her into his arms. He carried her across the room and placed her gently onto the bed.

He stared down at her, and his breath caught at the glorious sight of her, lying naked and trembling with nervous anticipation for him to make love to her. Her red lips were swollen from his, and her breasts rose and fell tantalizingly with each panting breath. Emily, sweet Emily—she was beautiful, brilliant, strong...and tonight, she belonged to him.

He kissed her one more time, then moved away to stand at the edge of the bed and unfasten his trousers. Her gaze drifted down his body to linger beneath his waist, and she swallowed nervously. Evidence of his need for her already bulged against the fabric, only to stiffen more beneath the heat of her curious eyes. He knew she'd seen at least one naked man before, but she'd never seen him. Watching her face to witness her reaction to her first glimpse of him, he unfastened his trousers and pushed them down his legs to kick them off—

Her eyes darted up to his and stayed there, glued to his face.

Unmoving, he grinned with unabashed amusement at her sudden shyness. "Look at me, brat," he ordered quietly.

"I am looking at you," she returned, her eyes never leaving his.

Stubborn chit. He almost laughed that his little seductress should suddenly turn so timid.

But when he saw how fiercely her body trembled, his amusement fled. "Emily," he said gently, "please look at me. I want you to."

Taking a deep breath, she tore her gaze away from his and down his body. Across his chest, along his front to his hips, then lower still... Her big blue eyes widened as her lips formed a silent *oh* of surprise. The honesty of the small reaction pleased him immeasurably. So did the way she shifted to lean toward him to get a better view and how the tip of her tongue darted out unconsciously to lick her lips.

Slowly, he stalked forward and crawled up the length of her. Possessive and predatory, he knelt over her on all fours, trapping her between his hands and knees and preparing to take the pleasures she offered. He'd warned her. He'd told her what kind of man he was and how he didn't plan on stopping with only a taste.

And now he planned on devouring her.

He dipped his head to sweep his tongue across her lips, to part them and plunge deeply inside, to taste the moist sweetness within and touch his tongue seductively to hers.

She gasped at his bold plunder of her mouth and the rough domination of his lips and tongue. His mouth molded hotly against hers as his hands found her breasts to cup and squeeze her fullness, to roll her taut nipples between his fingers and thumb.

A soft whimper fell from her lips. It coursed hotly through him, straight down to the tip of his hard cock as it flexed between his thighs.

Leaving her gasping for breath, he tore his mouth away to nip and lick his way down her elegant throat to her collarbone, reveling in the sweetness of her skin and the heat of her flesh against his lips. Even now, he thought he smelled the sweet scent of cinnamon clinging to her, mixing with the musky scent of her arousal. A delectable perfume that only made him crave her more.

"You taste good," he murmured as his mouth moved lower to take her nipple between his lips and suck. "Spicy and sweet...," he whispered against her flesh. "Cinnamon and sugar."

Then he laved her berry-ripe nipple like a boy licking sugar from a strawberry. With a moan, she breathed a wordless plea for him to bring his mouth harder against her. He gladly obliged, suckling at her as he fluttered his hand lightly across her other breast, tickling her nipple seductively with his palm.

As he worshipped at her breasts, she traced her hands hesitantly over his shoulders and down his chest. He groaned and took a deep breath to steady himself as her hands swept further downward, her fingertips fluttering over the ridges of his stomach. Then lower still...

She whispered, "Can I touch you?"

"Yes." A thrill raced through him. *God yes.*

When her fingertips brushed against the base of his cock,

his entire body stiffened, tense and waiting, holding his breath. Her fingers gently traced down his hard length, tentative with light caresses, and he relaxed against her soft touch with a sigh.

But when her hand closed around him and gently squeezed— "Like this?"

He couldn't hold back the shudder that jolted through him or the growl that tore from his throat as she began to stroke up and down his shaft. "Emily, that's . . . Yes, just like that."

Her touch was unlike any he'd felt before with any other woman. She sought out his erection in half-innocent exploration, half-wicked seduction, and all of it was maddeningly arousing, leaving him rock-hard and aching to claim her.

He squeezed his eyes shut and fought to maintain control. Every muscle in his body screamed with need to plunge into her warmth and drive to release. But he had to make this good for her, he absolutely *had* to. Tonight was all for Emily, and whatever pleasure he found was simply because she granted it.

Emboldened, she rolled her palm over his tip, and the hot friction combined with the ongoing stroking of her other hand along his shaft to drive him out of his mind. "Does it hurt?"

He gave a jerky nod, unable to move in any way else lest he lose himself against her fingers like an untried green pup and embarrass himself. "It hurts good. So damnably good . . ."

She gave a throaty laugh of pleased delight, and as his cock jumped in her hands, he sucked in a panting mouthful of air. He wanted to pleasure her longer, to kiss and lick his way over every inch of her enticing body until she squirmed, whimpering and begging for him, but he simply couldn't hold back long enough now. Good Lord, he was on the verge of bursting! And from only a few strokes of her hand.

Nudging her legs apart with his knee, he settled between her thighs as he kissed her hard, ravishing her mouth the way he planned on taking her body. She moaned against his lips, and he'd never heard a more erotic, more thrilling sound in his life.

He carefully shifted forward onto one arm to keep his weight off her belly, then reached with his other hand to position his rigid cock against her entrance and nestle down into the first layer of her wet folds. Holding himself there, he felt her tiny muscles tighten around his tip, as if her body were trying to draw him inside of its own volition.

Yet he waited, delaying the sweetest movement and reveling in the anticipation. He would never again have this moment of sliding inside her for the first time, and he wanted to make it last just a few heartbeats longer.

He brushed his lips against her temple. "Emily." Her name was a prayer for absolution, a plea for redemption—

Lowering his hips, he sank smoothly inside her in a single stroke, sheathing himself fully to the hilt in her gloriously tight warmth. He pressed down until his hips seated against hers, unable to plunge any deeper, then he groaned as her softness enveloped him. He squeezed his eyes shut, for a moment doing nothing but lying still inside her and enjoying the wonderful sensation of having her surrounding him.

A soft whimper rose from her lips in an incoherent plea of need. Granting her wish, he rocked himself against her. With slow, shallow beats of his hips against hers, he set himself to growing the arousal inside her. But soon, unable to keep himself in check, he deepened his thrusts until each plunge brought a moan to her lips, each retreat a whimpering sigh of loss.

"Move with me, darling." His hands slid down to clasp her hips and show her how to rise from the mattress to meet each thrust. "Show me that you want me."

When she raised her hips tentatively to meet his, he groaned her name and lifted her against him, again and again, until she found the natural rhythm of their joined bodies, until her hips instinctively strained against his, until she writhed eagerly and uncontrollably beneath him.

Her arms clasping around his shoulders, Emily closed her eyes as she shivered with joy. She'd never known that being with a man could be this wonderful, this good. And oh, how good it felt! Not once during her marriage had intimacy been like this...this special, this perfect as it was right now. Grey wanted her; the raw need she saw in his desire-hooded eyes thrilled her immeasurably, and surely, *this* was how it was meant to be between a man and a woman. Aching. Raw. Hot and sweaty. Absolute perfection.

But even this wasn't enough. Something was happening to her, something she desperately *wanted* to happen. Without warning, flames flared through her from the inside out—she knew then how intimacy was supposed to be between a man and woman. Oh, dear God, she *knew*!

The cry ripped from her throat as all the muscles in her body clenched tightly. Her sex flexed around him, then released in a shattering shiver of exquisite pleasure that exploded out like a million stars from her center where he lay buried. She fell limp beneath him, unable to do anything more than gasp for breath.

Grey pumped his hips hard against her, all restraint gone as he now sought his own climax. "Never—never this good," he groaned incoherently. "Only you, Emily...God, brat, only this with you..."

She felt the first small squirt of his release inside her, and without a trace of shame, she tilted her hips to receive him. There was no need to be careful, no need to deny herself this last pleasure and most precious gift from him. With a shuddering groan, he plunged deep inside her and poured himself into her, his thighs and buttocks straining to empty every last drop. Then he collapsed onto his side beside her.

Her eyes still closed, she lay with one hand resting against his chest, the exact same spot she'd been touching when she shattered around him. His heart.

"Emily, are you all right?" His raspy voice came thick with concern. He placed his hand over her lower belly. "The baby?"

"We're both fine." She slipped her hand over his, entwining their fingers. Then she opened her eyes, and at the look of happiness on his face, sheer joy danced inside her. Yet she bit her bottom lip. "But..."

"But?" He tensed with sudden apprehension.

She hesitated, then blurted out, "Oh, Thomas can never know about *this*!"

He laughed and pulled her tightly into his arms.

CHAPTER SEVEN

$\mathcal{A}$ knock at the door cut through her sleep, and Emily woke with a start.

Her eyes darted around the strange room, lit brightly by the morning sun pouring in through the window. She blinked, taking a moment to remember where she was and how she'd gotten here, why she was naked...and what happened last night. Her chest warmed with happiness. For once, being in Grey's arms hadn't been only a dream.

With a smile, she turned over to reach for him—

The bed was empty.

Her smile faded with a sharp pang of disappointment. He was gone, having left while she'd been asleep. And judging from the cold mattress beneath her fingers, most likely before dawn.

The knock came again, and her heart skipped hopefully—foolishly—even as she knew it wasn't Grey. It *couldn't* be. After all, the man who'd laid bare all her secrets last night and ravished her so thoroughly wouldn't have knocked.

Crawling out of the bed, she reached for the greatcoat he'd left tossed over the chair and scrambled into it to cover her still-naked body, her fingers buttoning it closed to her neck. Then she opened the door.

A young woman stood in the hallway, the same buxom maid from last night who had so blatantly offered herself to Grey.

"Yes?" Emily asked stiffly, unprepared for the jealous stab in her chest.

"G'mornin', missus." She smiled and lifted up a small tray. "The major ordered breakfast. Said ya prefer t' take it in yer room this mornin'."

"Of course," she mumbled politely, stepping back to let the woman pass. Once again she was struck by the contradiction Grey embodied. The gentleman in him was thoughtful enough to make certain she had breakfast, yet the rake couldn't bring himself to stay until morning.

The maid placed the tray on a little table beneath the window. "Cook made it special fer ye."

Emily lowered her gaze, feeling guilty that the cook went out of her way, especially since she had no appetite. "I'm certain it will be delicious." She forced a grateful smile. "Please thank her for me."

The maid answered with a nod, then sashayed toward the door. Emily followed, thinking the woman was leaving, but then the maid stopped and reached into the hall to retrieve the bundle of fabric and bucket of hot water she'd left there.

"The major asked m' t' give ye this, too." She set the bucket by the washbasin, then handed her the bundle of fabric.

Emily unfolded it and held it up. A blue-print gingham dress with long sleeves and a high waist that would serve well enough to keep her dressed for the rest of the ride to London. And just baggy enough to hide her belly.

Her throat tightened. Leave it to Grey to think of that, too.

"The major said 'e 'ad to see t' th' team an' carriage," the maid told her over her shoulder as she retreated toward the door, "but that 'e'll see ye downstairs once yer dressed."

Her heart sank with disappointment. So Grey wasn't coming back. She stonily forced out a polite, "Thank you."

The door shut behind the maid with a gentle click.

Closing her eyes tightly, Emily sank onto the edge of the bed and tried to clear the riot of emotions fogging her mind and painfully tightening her chest. If Grey thought less of her this morning because she'd given herself so freely last night, she didn't know how she'd bear it. Or worse... what if he thought nothing of her at all?

His scent still clung to the sheets and covers, that masculine smell she loved of leather and soap now swirled together with the musky odor of sex. It clung to her body, too, like an invisible imprint branding her as his, and she resisted the urge to crawl back beneath the covers and wrap herself in it, to fall back into the dream of being in his arms.

But she couldn't. He was waiting downstairs, and although she had no idea what she would say to him this morning or what kind of emotions—if any—she would see in him, she had no choice but to face him.

With a deep sigh of resolve, she pushed herself off the bed. She might not have a choice in how he felt about her, but she was determined not to let him see how confused she was about *him*. But what was there to be confused about? She scolded herself. Last night was only physical intimacy, after all. It wasn't as if she had fallen in love with him, for goodness' sake!

Yet an hour later, after she'd bathed, dressed, and fixed her appearance as best she could, her heart still beat anxiously as she made her way downstairs to the courtyard where Grey would be waiting. She dreaded seeing the disdainful or disinterested way he might look at her now, and heavens, how would she keep from crying when he did?

The morning was beautiful. The sun shined clear and bright with the kind of slight chill in the air that often followed a violent storm, and the day promised nothing but white clouds and warming breezes. Except for scattered mud puddles, there was no sign of the storm that had been unleashed on them yesterday. Yet she barely noticed any of it, her mind too distracted by last night's events and what she would say to Grey when she first saw him.

The team was already hitched to the battered carriage when she entered the stable yard, and Grey and Hedley stood beside it, their brows furrowed in concentration as they assessed its condition. At the front of the team, Dalton finished checking the harness buckles to make certain everything was in place before they set out for another long day of travel, one that would bring them to within a half-day's ride of London.

Hedley gave her a polite doff of his hat as she approached. "G' mornin', missus."

Frowning at the carriage, Grey looked up distractedly at Hedley's greeting and saw her. For a beat, he froze. Then a slow and knowing grin tugged at the corners of his sensuous mouth, and he politely bowed his head. "Lady Emily."

Just like that, all the anxious dread fretting away inside her vanished, replaced by a wanton heat as his gaze drifted leisurely down her front. A gaze that was anything but disinterested. Her chest lightened. Grey might very well end up loving her and leaving her, but it wouldn't be this morning.

"Major Grey," she returned, staring at him a bit shyly through lowered lashes.

"I trust you slept well," he drawled, his deep voice carefully emotionless even as his eyes shined wickedly.

"Very well, thank you." As her face heated beneath the intensity of his gaze, she knew she was in danger of giving away without a single word what had happened between them. "And you?"

"Not a wink," Hedley interjected with a grimace, reaching to rub the small of his back. "Those damned hard benches made it impossible—"

"Sergeant, your language," Grey admonished quietly, nodding toward Emily. "There's a lady present."

Hedley's face pinched with embarrassment. "Beggin' yer pardon, missus." He took a breath and began again, "Those *darn* hard benches made it bloody well impossible for me an' the major to sleep!"

Grey rolled his eyes in exasperated amusement, his lips twitching but not saying anything. Likewise, Emily bit back her own laughter at the faithful sergeant's expense.

"I am sorry to hear that, Mr. Hedley." She placed a hand briefly on his arm and smiled at him with genuine affection. "Tonight when we stop, we'll make certain you have a proper bed."

"That would be lovely, missus."

The idle chatter with Hedley continued for a few more minutes as he politely asked her about her breakfast and if she had everything she needed for the day's travel, although she had no idea how she managed to participate coherently in their conversation with Grey's eyes watching her so intensely. The raw desire inside him was transparently obvious to her. How on earth could no one else see it? Her mouth went dry at the devilish thought of what awaited her tonight in the darkness if he looked at her that heatedly in the bright light of morning.

She cleared her throat and forced away the thought before she turned scarlet and embarrassed all of them. "Are we departing, then?"

"If you're ready," Grey put in.

"I'm ready for anything," she answered without thinking.

And at that, the expression on his face turned positively predatory. Like a wolf delighting in finding its prey. "Well, then." He grinned. "Dalton!"

He turned to signal to the driver that they were ready to start. She wondered if he also did it to give himself a moment to wipe that sinful look from his face before Hedley noticed and suspected there was more between them than an old acquaintanceship, because when he turned back toward her, his face was once again composed.

"I'm taking the first turn up top at the reins," he told her. "That way, Hedley can catch a few more hours of sleep inside with you, if you don't mind."

Disappointment stabbed through her, but she didn't let it show. "I don't mind at all."

Hedley smiled gratefully. "My thanks to you, ma'am." Another doff of his hat, another hand to his back. "An' me spine thanks you, too."

"Help Dalton with the team while I settle Lady Emily, will you?" Grey ordered. "The harness might have stretched from pulling through the mud yesterday."

"Aye, sir."

As Hedley hurried to the front of the carriage, the realization struck Emily that Grey no longer referred to her as Mrs. Crenshaw, and a happy warmth stirred low inside her.

"Are you all right?" he asked in a quiet voice, one surprisingly soft and intimate even as his eyes remained fixed straight ahead on Hedley and Dalton as they worked the harness. "You looked a bit uneasy when you approached."

"I didn't know what to think." She gently accused, her own voice helplessly overflowing with emotion, "You left in the middle of the night."

His shoulders sagged almost imperceptibly, but she noticed. Lord help her, she noticed everything about this man. "I had no choice."

"You didn't have to sleep on a bench with Hedley." Knowing how well he could read her, she didn't bother trying to hide the hurt she'd felt when she woke to find him gone. Or her confusion now to know that he'd chosen a hard bench over her bed. "You could have stayed with me."

"No," he corrected in a rueful murmur, "I won't risk your reputation."

"I don't care."

"I do," he answered firmly.

Then she felt his fingers brush hers as her hand rested against the folds of her skirt, and her breath hitched. Just as suddenly as his hand had touched hers, he shifted away before anyone could see. At the loss of his warmth, she bunched her skirt into her hand, twisting the material around her fingers.

He hesitated, his eyes still staring straight ahead as if he was afraid to look at her. "I've never spent the entire night in a woman's bed. I've never wanted to stay around long enough afterward to actually sleep with her. But with you," he admitted tenderly, "for once I wanted to stay."

Her throat knotted, yet she didn't dare let herself hope that he might care about her beyond friendship. "Did you truly?"

"Yes." His brows raised slightly as if the answer surprised him as well. "Apparently, brat, you bring out all kinds of new desires in me."

Her lips parted in surprise. "What do you—"

"All done, sir!" Hedley called out.

"Good," Grey answered. He moved to open the carriage door and put down the step to help her inside. "Let's depart, then."

He held out his hand to her. As she slipped hers into his to step up into the compartment, his mouth lowered close to her ear and murmured, "Can the baby handle another long day's ride?"

Her chest tightened at his concern. "Yes," she returned in the same low voice. "Grey, thank you for—"

But there was no time to say anything more because Hedley appeared immediately at his side, ready to join her in the carriage. Grey squeezed her fingers tenderly with a gleam in his eyes before releasing her hand, as if he knew she planned to thank him for saving her life. More times than he realized.

As she turned to take her seat, she stopped. A small package wrapped in plain paper and twine sat on the bench. She looked up at the two men who stood waiting by the open door. "What's this?"

"Nothing important." Grey shrugged. "Thought you might like something to chase away the boredom during today's ride."

Then he moved aside to let Hedley step up into the compartment and settle onto the bench across from her, before securely closing the door and climbing up to the driver's seat. With a lurch, the carriage started off.

Once they were under way, she curiously turned the package over in her hands. She glanced up at Hedley. "Sergeant, what is this?"

"We stopped in th' village on the way back from fetchin' the carriage so we could buy you a dress. 'Tweren't no seamstress in the village, though, so the major requested th' shopkeeper open his mercantile for us."

She dubiously arched a brow. "Requested?"

"Strongly suggested," he amended with a grin. "When we was buyin' the dress, the major got that for you, too. Like he said, ma'am, ain't nothing much."

Muttering something beneath his breath about benches, sore spines, and the devil, he leaned back against the squabs, closed his eyes, and fell asleep before they were more than two miles from the inn.

"Something to chase away the boredom?" she murmured softly. Unable to bear the curiosity any longer, she pulled at the twine and worked the knot away until the paper fell open on her lap.

Her eyes widened. A sketchbook and set of pencils—she could scarcely believe it! Her fingertips trembled as they traced affectionately over the book and touched each of the four pencils bound with a pink ribbon, all of them thoughtfully sharpened and ready for use.

She smiled with happiness even as a tear dropped onto the book in her lap. Because it was the most wonderful gift anyone had ever given her. Because Grey remembered the girl she used to be, which meant she would never be just another widow for him to bed.

And because she knew she loved him.

* * *

"You're moving again," Emily chastised as she traced a line carefully across the sketch she was making of him.

"The whole damned carriage is moving," Grey grumbled and folded his arms irritably across his chest.

"You're fidgeting, then."

He crooked an exasperated brow. "I'm bored."

"I'm not." A smile tugged at the corners of her mouth. Her eyes shined brightly in the early-afternoon sunlight as she slid him a seductive look. "Perhaps this evening we might consider...nude sketches?"

He leaned forward on his seat. "Believe me, darling." His

voice dropped to a husky purr. "The last thing I want you stroking with your hand tonight is that pencil."

She blushed instantly scarlet, the color fanning out from the back of her neck and flushing down below her neckline. She pretended to not hear his comment and focused all her attention on her sketch, her eyes not lifting from the page as if her life depended upon it.

He chuckled. *Little minx.*

His turn on top had ended an hour ago, and he'd gladly joined her inside, where she'd thanked him for her gift with a kiss that left his blood humming and his cock half-hard. Then she promptly set about drawing his portrait when what he wanted to do was introduce her to the pleasures of a rocking carriage. But since he'd used the excuse of wanting to prevent her boredom when he'd purchased the set for her, he couldn't very well refuse.

Truly, he was glad he hadn't. Sitting there across from him, she was lovely, as warm and golden as the sunlight slanting onto her shoulders though the window. The slight frown of concentration on her face as she carefully traced out his profile and the way she bit her bottom lip at particularly tricky lines only made her more appealing.

His chest lightened. When was the last time, if ever, that he'd felt this relaxed and satisfied? For once, he was perfectly content. And judging from the way she hummed softly as she sketched, so was she. And *that* pleased him more than he wanted to admit. He'd never cared before about a woman's feelings the day after he'd bedded her, but with Emily, he did care. A great deal.

She looked up and beamed. Her glowing smile swept through him, and his gut clenched. Two days ago, she'd been living in terror and hunted in her own home, but now, she was safe and in high spirits, alive and free...The change in her was nothing short of an answer to his prayers. Her nightmare wasn't over yet, he wasn't that naïve. Once they reached London, he would have to ensure her protection however he could and hunt down the man who killed her husband and set fire to the house, but for now, she was happy. And Emily's happiness was simply infectious.

"You know," he commented, "people aren't usually so happy to be bounced across the countryside for hours in a carriage with worn springs."

She peered at him shyly through lowered lashes. "I know it sounds silly," she began tentatively, as if testing the newly forged trust between them, "but I keep thinking that this is how it is with ordinary couples taking long trips together. Quiet conversations, stretches of silence that aren't the least bit awkward, and…" Her lips sheepishly tugged upward.

And anticipating another night in each other's arms. She'd left that bit unsaid, but he caught the underlying implication in her words and in the way her eyes sparkled wickedly at him. Clearly, she was looking forward to stopping at some filthy, cramped, rat-infested inn with scratchy bedding and lumpy mattresses as much as he was.

He didn't understand it. He should have been tired of her by now, as he would have been with any other woman in whose company he'd been for this long. But he wasn't. Puzzlingly, being with Emily only attracted him more. In fact, when he'd been on top of the carriage during his turn at the reins, all he could think about was how much he wanted to be inside the compartment with her. How much it irked him that on this morning of all mornings it was Hedley who rode with her instead.

When they reached London tomorrow, he would deliver her to her family, and everything would change between them. But he had today. Why waste a moment of it?

He reached up idly to brush his fingers against the window curtain, watching her slyly from the corner of his eye. "Do you know what else couples do in carriages when traveling long distances?"

"No," she answered naïvely. "What else do they do?"

With a devilish grin, he pulled closed the curtain. "Oh, play little games to pass the time."

"Games?" The disappearance of her smile indicated that she'd followed the sudden turn of conversation and suspected where he was headed. "What kind of games?"

"The best kind." He reached across to close the other curtain, leaving them ensconced in the muted light filtering inside the compartment. He lowered his voice seductively. "Would you like to play with me, brat?"

At the obvious innuendo, her eyes locked onto his, and her cheeks pinked irresistibly. "Oh yes," she breathed out quickly. When he crooked a brow at her eagerness, her cheeks deepened to a rosy red. "I mean—naturally, I wouldn't want you to be bored."

"Very thoughtful of you," he murmured with earnest gratitude. Stripping off her clothes and licking his tongue over every luscious inch of her would certainly keep away the boredom.

As if sensing the wicked thoughts swirling through his mind, she inhaled tremulously in anticipation. "What shall we play, then?"

"I have an idea." He flipped the lock on the door.

"Somehow I knew you would," she muttered, which only made him smile more wickedly.

"The game is simple. We take turns giving commands to the other, and no matter what the command, you must do it. You cannot refuse, or you lose."

Her breath came faster now. Arousal tantalizingly flushed her skin at her neckline. "How do I know if I've won?"

"Trust me," he murmured. "You'll know."

Despite the heat of his gaze, or perhaps because of it, Emily shivered.

Games... They were playing games, and she had the titillating suspicion that the game he proposed was going to be scandalous, or he would never have drawn the curtains; intimate, or he wouldn't be looking at her as if he wanted to ravish her; and oh so very wicked, or he wouldn't have used that low, husky voice that wrapped around her like a spell. Already her heart pounded, and an ache flared between her legs just at the hint of doing something sinful.

And that was exactly what she wanted to do. Be very, *very* sinful with this man.

"You'll go first, I presume?" she asked, suddenly nervous beneath his wolfish stare.

"Of course," he answered, and a bit too gleefully, she thought, although she couldn't help the responding goose bumps dotting her arms.

"Of course," she echoed wryly. "However did I guess?"

His eyes gleamed at her sarcasm. "Remember, you have to do everything I say."

"Until my turn, when you have to do whatever *I* say," she reminded him. And how she was looking forward to *that*! To having this strong, powerful man under her command. "When will it be my turn?"

"When I command it." He grinned deviously, then gave a teasing cluck of his tongue, scolding her. "Haven't you been paying attention?"

She scowled. "That doesn't sound fair to—"

"Put down the sketchbook and pencil."

Her heart skipped. His first order sounded more like a request than a command, but she did as he bade her and set them aside. "What next, then?"

His gaze fell to her mouth. "Lick your lips."

"Lick my—" She stopped. Then softer, not quite believing... "You want me to... seriously?"

The grin faded from his face, and a dark, intense expression replaced it. He repeated quietly but firmly, "Lick your lips for me, brat."

Her blood began to hum. She slowly did as he ordered and traced the tip of her tongue over her lips. An ordinary movement, one she did several times each day without a thought, but now, with him watching her, the gesture felt undeniably erotic.

"Like that?" Her voice came much huskier than intended.

"Exactly like that," he murmured. His eyes fixed on her mouth for a heated moment before traveling slowly down her body. "Now lift your skirt."

Her skittering heart completely somersaulted. He'd already seen her naked—for God's sake, he'd *washed* her!—but now, with both of them fully clothed in the carriage, revealing even the smallest bit of skin seemed somehow more intimate. Vulnerable. And wantonly exciting.

With a shaky breath, trying to hide the trembling in her hands as she ran them down her legs to her knees and grasped the muslin in her fingers, she pulled her hands back and drew her skirt upward. The lace-edged hem rose slowly up her legs, scandalously stockingless, to reveal inch after slow inch of bare calf. Everywhere his gaze grazed her legs, she felt a shiver of heat as real as if he were actually stroking his fingers over her skin.

The hem reached her knees, and she stopped.

"Higher," he rasped.

Her heart pounded fiercely, joined by the throbbing ache between her legs, as his desire-hooded eyes fastened on her skirt. Despite the casual way he continued to lean back in his seat, she could see the arousal in him and hear his breathing turn rapid and shallow in anticipation.

Emboldened by his reaction, she nudged the hem higher to teasingly reveal legs closed together at the knees and a short stretch of bare thighs above. The skirt bunched modestly across her lap and hid from his view the triangle of curls beneath. Her own breath came short and quick now, her mouth suddenly so dry that she had no choice but to lick her lips again beneath the heat of his stare, which slowly caressed up one naked thigh and down the other.

"Higher, brat."

"Higher?" Instead of the surprised squeak she expected, the word came as a throaty moan.

He gave a single, jerking nod, his gaze lingering wickedly at her lap. "I want to see all of you."

For a moment, she didn't move—she *couldn't* move! She'd never even undressed in front of a man in the daylight before, and now, to reveal herself in a such a wanton way, in a rolling carriage in the afternoon sunlight, no less... But his eyes stayed on her, patiently waiting and wanting, making heat and moisture gather between her legs, and she knew she couldn't stop. She was helpless to his commands, because as much as he wanted to see her revealed, she wanted equally as much to bare herself to him.

"Is this what you want?" she whispered. She placed her hands just above her knees and slid her fingers back along her thighs, pulling up the skirt until it reached her hips and bared her from the waist down.

The air ripped loudly from his lungs. Her eyes flew up to his face, but his gaze was fixed on her legs, on the long stretch of nakedness beneath the waist of her dress and the little patch of curls just peeking out from between her closed thighs. His expression burned, filled with such raw desire that she shivered beneath its heat.

"Jesus, brat." He shifted uncomfortably in the seat. "You've got me hard already."

"Good," she purred, running her hands up and down her bare thighs, drawing his attention to her core. "Then I'm winning."

He drew a shaky breath and mumbled, "I think we're both winning."

As she stared at him, a devilish realization fell through her, and she suddenly understood how to play this game. Even though he was giving her commands, she was the one in control because she held the power to grant his wicked wishes. And she liked it. *Very* much.

With a seductive smile, she ordered softly, "Then command me again."

It was his turn to lick his lips. "Open your legs."

Raw excitement jolted through her. With her thighs trembling, she slowly parted her knees a few inches, just enough to teasingly reveal a small glimpse of what lay between her legs but not wide enough for his seeking eyes to have a good look. A frustrated sound tore from his throat. A thrill pulsed through her at the power she possessed over him, with the mutual control he held over her.

"Wider," he growled, his eyes fixed on the spot between her legs. "You know what I want. Open your legs to me."

With a soft whimper, she closed her eyes, placed her hands on her knees, and pushed, spreading herself wide to his hot gaze.

A masculine groan of satisfaction filled the tiny compartment, the deep sound rumbling through her straight down to her aching core. The cool air tickled against her bare womanhood, exposed in the muted sunlight filtering in through the curtains, but her skin prickled with heat. Not daring to move until he'd looked his fill of her, she took soft, shallow pants of breath as her frenzied heart raced, and as she waited in sweet anticipation for the next command, she prayed he liked what he saw.

"Dear God, you're beautiful…" Then, so softly she almost missed it, "Touch yourself."

Her eyes flew open.

He leaned forward in his seat, his elbows over his knees as he stared at her with the greedy hunger of a starving man. Desire gleamed in the chocolate depths of his eyes, with so much arousal pulsing through him that his erection prominently tented his trousers. Emily shivered with her own growing need. This wasn't the patient tenderness with which he made love to her last night; this was raw, primal, predatory. The feast he'd promised to make of her. And all of her shook with the desire to be devoured.

"Touch yourself, Emily," he repeated with an intensity that swirled down her spine. "I want to watch you pleasure yourself."

She froze. Had the game gone too far? In fact, were they still playing games? She was torn between knowing she should stop before she crossed a line from which she might never be able to retreat, and the wicked desire to seduce him without laying a finger on him.

A soft sigh fell from her trembling lips, and she slipped her hand down between her thighs.

He didn't make a sound as he watched her brush her fingertips through the curls guarding her womanhood, his attention rapt on her seeking fingers. She felt deliciously wanton, brazen, and wholly unashamed beneath his intense gaze. Oh, *sweet heavens*—she felt alive!

Closing her eyes, she leaned back against the squabs with

her legs spread as wide as the narrow carriage allowed, then she stroked her fingers down into her cleft and across her hot folds, to touch herself the way he wanted. To explore herself as she'd never dared do before, not even alone in her bath.

He groaned, the sound as close as if he were leaning over her on the seat, yet she couldn't bear to open her eyes to look at him. "You have no idea how delectable you are," he whispered, his deep purr swirling through her head and increasing the rapid tattoo of her pulse, "how innocently seductive...how many times in the past two days I've fantasized about watching you do exactly this."

Emboldened by his words, she mimicked the way he caressed her last night, with teasing little swirls and strokes against her folds. An animal-like groan tore from him, and the primal sound aroused her to a throbbing frenzy. She'd never heard a man groan with desire like that before, never with so much raw passion and unbearable need. And he wasn't even touching her!

Exciting her to gasping shivers, the thrilling desire that pulsed through her now drove her to find the same release he'd given her last night. She abandoned herself to the throbbing ache beneath her fingertips and sank her fingers deep into her wet softness just as he had done, to caress herself, explore, arouse...She whimpered plaintively, reaching the edge of release but unable to plunge over the cliff without him.

"Kiss me," she ordered, her voice a throaty plea of desperate need and unbridled arousal. "Now—I need to be kissed."

His mouth captured hers, hard and demanding and greedy, and he shoved his tongue between her lips to claim both the kiss and all of her as his. He continued to thrust his tongue deep inside her mouth, to taste and plunder, even as he lowered himself slowly to the floor between her thighs. Tearing his mouth away from hers, he nibbled his way down her front, over her breasts and belly, to place a tender kiss on the inside of her bare thigh.

Her eyes flew open. "What—" Her hands gripped his shoulders. "What are you doing?"

"Exactly as you commanded," he murmured wickedly against her flesh as he turned his head to reverently place a delicate kiss on her other thigh. "I am kissing you."

She squirmed, her heated body yearning to have his mouth on her. But surely, he couldn't mean kissing her there—

He licked his tongue against her. *There.*

"Oh, sweet heavens!" The moan poured from her as her head rolled back in helpless submission.

"It's your turn," he breathed devilishly against her, his lips tickling over the throbbing center of her spread thighs, "and I must do as you command."

Her fingers dug through his thick hair to find some purchase to keep from falling away as the tip of his tongue slowly circled her. Kissing and tasting, licking and nibbling, his mouth was utterly wicked...and oh, so divine! She'd never imagined she could ever feel both as wanton and wonderful as she did at that moment, with her body writhing shamelessly against his lips.

He nibbled down her cleft, only to drag a long lick back up the length of her to the pulsating nub— She gasped at the electrifying jolt of pleasure as his lips grazed against the sensitive point, her legs slamming closed against his shoulders but for his hands on her inner thighs, torturously holding her open wide to his greedy mouth.

"You taste heavenly," he murmured against her. "So sweet and delicious...and all mine."

She gasped as his tongue plunged deep to invade her body, then moaned as he thrust in and out of her in a quick, stabbing motion that left her lungs breathless and her sex quivering against his mouth.

"Grey," she begged, uncertain if she was pleading for him to stop or to keep fanning the ache inside her.

He laughed at her confusion, and the deep sound rumbled tantalizingly against her womanhood. What a wicked, wicked game he'd picked! That even when he was losing he was winning. She was helpless against him, shuddering and weak. And hotly craving more.

She whimpered as a primal yearning spilled through her, and she lifted her hips to force his mouth even harder against her, his tongue even deeper. So close, so *very* close to release... but he expertly kept her dangling at the cliff's edge without letting her plunge over.

"My turn again," he rasped. "Do as I command, brat."

"Yes—anything! Anything you want," she whined helplessly as he placed one last, impossibly tender kiss against her throbbing center.

He sat back and pulled her across the compartment to him, lifting her to straddle her legs wide across his thighs. "What I want is *you*." His eyes gleamed like the devil's own. "Right here."

"Here?" Instead of the squeak she expected, her question came as a throaty purr. "Like this?"

His hand dove wickedly between her thighs to fondle her heated folds and wear down her resistance by heightening the ache pounding away inside her. "Just like this."

"But—but we're in a carriage!" she protested, even as evidence of her desire wetted his oh-so clever fingers as they teased mercilessly against her.

"I know." He grinned devilishly at her, then leaned up to

kiss away the moan threatening at her lips. "We won't hurt the baby, I promise."

Her heart softened that even now he was concerned about her unborn child. But to make love in a moving carriage, with her sitting on him like this—she'd never thought it possible, never even *considered*...She squirmed over his large erection pressing hard against her bottom and instantly became amenable to new considerations.

"Yes," she whispered and leaned forward to kiss him, gladly willing to do whatever he commanded.

Grey made quick work of unfastening his trousers, then freed himself from the tight fabric and yanked her skirt up high around her waist and out of his way. She'd aroused him to the breaking point, and he needed to possess her. *Now.*

His hands slipped beneath her to grasp her bare buttocks, and with a soft growl, he yanked her toward him, impaling her on his cock in one swift thrust. He smothered her cry of surprise with his mouth and thrilled at the shudder of wanton pleasure that sped through her at having him inside her, steel-hard and primed to please her.

"Shh," he warned. His teeth nipped at her earlobe as he rocked her gently against him, grinding his hips up against hers until she'd taken his large cock completely inside her and was fully seated over him. Her arms wrapped around his shoulders as she panted breathlessly, and her body trembled in hot anticipation of the climax to come, one he gleefully looked forward to giving her. "They'll hear you outside."

She eased away from him just far enough to look into his eyes as his hands squeezed her buttocks, cupping her in his palms as he raised and lowered her, sliding her tight warmth smoothly up and down his length. *Good Lord*, how glorious she felt! How wonderfully slick and sweet. How unbelievably luscious with all those little muscles inside her clenching tightly around him. And he knew she enjoyed it, too, because she couldn't stop the soft mewling sounds that escaped her.

"Ride me, brat." He pulled her legs up onto the seat on either side of him so that she could balance on her knees over him, then tilted his hips straight up into hers. "Ride me hard."

As he'd commanded, she moved against him, thrusting and retreating as she galloped over him. The sensation was exquisite. He groaned as she leaned back, dug her fingers into his shoulders for leverage, and pumped him hard and fast with her body, as if his cock were a wicked toy created solely for her to take whatever wanton pleasures she desired. Her hips bucked ferociously over his as she drove toward her release.

"Grey!" A helpless shudder raced through her.

Her body gripped down hard around his cock as she tossed back her head and arched her back. The catch of her breath, the quivering of her thighs against his hips as her tight warmth flexed around him—

His arms grasped around her like steel bands as his mouth clamped hard over hers to swallow the helpless cry as she climaxed. Growling his need, he thrust into her from beneath, his hands at her hips keeping her tight against him, then he exploded inside her with so much intensity that a second cry tore from her lips. She collapsed against him, utterly spent.

He held her there with his arms clasped tightly around her and his limp cock still inside her. Her hot sex quivered tantalizingly around him with each residual wave of pleasure that pulsed through her. He didn't want to move, preferring to keep her perched right there over him on his lap the way he'd wanted to have her since she so boldly taunted him in the carriage about kissing her. He hadn't lied to her. He'd not stopped with a taste. *Sweet Lucifer*, what a meal he'd made of her!

"Grey?" she asked softly.

"Hmm?"

"I win."

Laughing, he buried his face against her neck. He'd never been happier in his life than he was at that moment.

The little minx had changed him. For the first time, he found himself enjoying not just a woman's body but also the woman herself. *All* of her. And he had no idea how he'd be able to let her go once they reached London, when she returned to her family and he left for Spain.

CHAPTER EIGHT

*E*mily paused in the doorway of the inn where they'd stopped for the night. Fellow travelers gathered inside around tables and on the tall-backed settles pulled up close to the massive stone hearth. The room smelled of smoke and ale, but its stone walls were freshly whitewashed, its floors clean, and its lamps brightly lit. Her stomach fluttered as she took it all in. Clean, well lit, safe...and Grey, once again, all to herself.

She sighed. *Heaven.*

After they had spent themselves in each other's arms in that wonderfully wicked new game she hoped they'd play again tomorrow, Grey rode for the rest of the afternoon on top of the rig, taking turns at the reins. The silence was just fine with her. It gave her time to finish her sketch of him, to smooth the lines lovingly with her fingertips, and replay in her mind every delicious kiss and caress he'd given her. He didn't mind that she was with child, desiring her despite that, and he seemed to like it when she took the initiative to please him. So tonight she planned on showing him all the various ways she could do just that.

As if reading her mind, he came up behind her. "Will this place do?"

She nodded. A barn and a pile of hay would have served as long as Grey was with her.

"And it's safe. Whoever set fire to Snowden couldn't have followed us here." He squeezed her elbow to reassure her. "You can rest easy tonight."

Her lips twitched as she stifled a smile. Resting was the last thing she wanted to do tonight.

"Let's get settled, shall we?" He took her arm and led her across the room to the bar.

Her heart raced with anticipation. There was nothing sexual about what he'd said, not even an innuendo, yet a shiver raced through her at the tantalizing thought of settling in for the night. With him.

Grey reached for the quill to sign the register and nodded curtly at the bald innkeeper, who finished wiping down the bar and tossed the towel over his stocky shoulder. "We'll need stalls for the horses and two private rooms for the night, preferably on opposite ends of the hall."

At that, Emily's heart somersaulted, and a faint blush heated her cheeks. Oh yes, they were definitely settling in for the night.

"Upstairs to the right." The innkeeper slid two keys across the bar to Grey. "Payment in advance. Have your driver speak with the stable manager outside regarding your team."

Grey nodded and handed over enough money to cover the bill. "And a bucket of hot water in the room for the lady, both tonight and in the morning."

"Aye, sir. And will you and your wife be needin' anything else?"

And at *that*, Emily's heart stopped completely. *Your wife.* The innkeeper thought they were married, that she and Grey were—*oh no.*

Or... oh yes? Was it so wrong for the man to think they were married, especially after they'd been intimate, both with their bodies and their secrets? With the affectionate way she was certain she looked at Grey even now and how Grey kept her so possessively close by his side, could she fault anyone for making that assumption when they'd just strolled inside together at sunset?

It meant nothing, she told herself. Just a mistake on the innkeeper's part.

Still, Grey didn't correct him, and Emily found herself not wanting him to. A small part of her thrilled at the possibility that Grey might finally think of her as someone other than Thomas's little sister, as something more than a friend. And her heart wished with all its might that he could somehow find a way to delay his departure to Spain so he could remain with her in London through the rest of her pregnancy, to be with her when her baby was born... if not beyond.

And for goodness' sake, what harm was there in wondering what it might have been like to have Grey for a husband, for him to be the father of her baby? What sin was she committing to let anyone assume that tonight he truly did belong to her? Surely, even fate couldn't fault her for wanting that.

"We have everything we need," Grey answered with an indecipherable glance at Emily.

Mumbling his thanks to the innkeeper, he tossed the second key to Hedley and gestured him outside toward the stable yard to tend to the team. He placed his hand against the small of her back and steered her toward the dining room and the hot meal waiting within.

He lowered his mouth to her ear. "It meant nothing."

"Whatever do you mean?" She feigned ignorance, although the sinking pinch in her stomach told her exactly what he'd meant.

"A man and woman traveling together—he doesn't want trouble, so he turns a blind eye and addresses everyone as if they're wed."

Her throat tightened as foolish embarrassment swelled inside her, yet she forced her face to remain blank so he wouldn't see the pain squeezing her chest. "Well, it's good to know that the innkeeper will help keep my reputation intact."

"Not just yours. This inn is on the route to Gretna Green. He makes a fine pound off Scottish weddings, I'll bet."

Even though she felt the heat of his gaze slide sideways onto her, she kept her eyes straight ahead and nodded, unable to look at him.

Oh, she was such a fool! While she had been wondering what it would be like to truly be his, Grey had been thinking only of the economics of elopement. She'd gone and done exactly what he'd warned her not to do—she'd confused sex with affection, wanting more from him than just his body.

"I see." She allowed herself to blink just once. Very hard.

He stopped, his hands on her shoulders turning her to face him. He puzzled down at her. "You see what, exactly?"

She gave a small shrug, hoping the simple physical movement could somehow force back the stinging heat behind her eyes. She saw it clearly now, the different ways they lived their lives and the very different goals they had for their futures. That he wanted adventure and intrigue, while she wanted nothing more daring than to be an artist. That he was perfectly content as a rake and a bachelor, while she wanted the chance again for a loving husband and a family, despite her past. That he wanted freedom, and she wanted... *him*.

"How very different we are," she whispered simply.

The quiet words hung in the air between them. For a moment, neither of them moved, neither spoke. Then his eyes narrowed with cold accusation, and his hands fell away from her. His jaw worked hard.

"How do you mean?" he demanded.

She shook her head, knowing she could never make him understand. "That you're who you are, and I'm—"

"That you're a lady, and I'm a rogue," he bit out in a voice so low and cutting it stabbed through her. "I warned you about that, if you'll remember."

"I didn't mean that!" Her heart thudded painfully in her chest with sudden panic. Oh God, she was losing him already— "No! I would never think that."

Mindless of the crowded room around her, she reached a hand for him. But he stepped back, leaving her to grasp at empty air.

Her hand fell to her side. As she stared at him, knowing he could see the tears glistening in her eyes yet helpless to prevent them, the words rested on her lips to tell him how much he meant to her, how desperate she was to keep tonight from being the last time she would be alone with him.

And if she did tell him? If she admitted that she loved him, that perhaps she'd always loved him, then he would know exactly how she felt, and... *Nothing.*

Nothing would change. She would still be a duke's widowed daughter who might very well be carrying a future marquess, and he would still be a rake and spy. He would never be willing to love her the way she wanted, not when his true love was the War Office.

"I'm sorry," she apologized in a strangled voice, somehow finding the inner strength to retreat from him. "I didn't—" She inhaled a jerky breath and shook her head. "I am suddenly not hungry. If you'll excuse me."

He blew out a muttered curse and reached for her hand. "Brat, I'm sorry. Please listen—"

"Lady Emily!"

Emily startled at the shriek of her name across the common room. An older woman in a hunter-green traveling costume and matching hat, complete with billowing ostrich feathers and ermine stole, stood up from one of the tables. She waved a handkerchief excitedly in the air to capture her attention.

"Lady Emily—that *is* you, is it not?"

Emily cringed. *No, please, God, no! Not her, not now!* But it was too late for prayers, and dread curled inside her stomach. Of all the places to be recognized, of all the people to spot her...

Fate had no mercy, apparently. Not even for love.

Lady Gantry was one of the most gossip-mongering women in the *ton*, and to cut her in any way would be to foolishly risk the woman's sharp-tongued wrath across the drawing rooms of London. Steeling herself, Emily forced a smile and bobbed a shallow curtsy as the insufferable woman quickly approached.

"Baroness," she said tightly, "how unexpected to see you... and here, of all places."

"Why, Lady Emily, it *is* you!" The woman squeezed both of Emily's hands, completely oblivious to her distress and the way her watery eyes glanced heart-wrenchingly at Grey. "I knew it! I said as much to my George and his dear wife, Alice, when you walked inside. I said, 'There is Emily Matteson! There can be no doubt of it.' And, indeed, there was not!"

Her temples throbbed already at the woman's grating voice and at Grey's fixed gaze, which never left her face, as if wanting to gauge her reaction to meeting the baroness with him at her side. "You have been well, I hope?" she forced herself to ask.

At that moment, Emily couldn't have cared less how the gossipy old hen was doing, or her son George, a former classmate of Thomas's at Eton, who crossed the room toward them much more slowly than had his mother. A demure and plain woman held on to his arm.

"Oh yes, quite well," Lady Gantry chirped, "now that my George has wed. We expect an heir before next summer, don't we, George?"

Her son answered weakly in the affirmative and looked away, as if bored already with the conversation. His bride's cheeks pinked delicately with embarrassment.

"Congratulations." Emily dropped another shallow curtsy to the pair.

"*Good luck* would be more appropriate, I daresay," Lady Gantry mumbled, shooting her daughter-in-law a peevish glance, but the woman never lifted her eyes from the floor to see it. "How is your family, my dear? I saw Her Grace just last month at Lady St. James's garden party. And now, to run into you, and at a posting inn, no less—what a coincidence! Why, wherever are you traveling?"

Emily swallowed hard, feeling like a caged bird at the Tower Menagerie under Grey's unwavering attention. "My brother was injured. I'm traveling to London to see him."

"Oh yes." Lady Gantry shook her head, clucking her tongue sympathetically. "Such tragic news! Shocked us all. After all, if such a thing could happen to him, then how safe are any of us? But we were all so pleased to hear that Chesney survived."

"Not nearly as pleased as Chesney, I'm sure," Grey muttered acerbically, unable to keep his silence.

Emily gave him a pleading look to behave himself, biting her bottom lip anxiously. Lady Gantry and her son looked at him then and blinked in unison, as if they'd just now realized that he existed.

Apparently finding him lacking or uninteresting, or both, George turned back to his wife, who still had not raised her bashful eyes from the floor.

But the baroness smiled broadly and extended her hand. "You must be Lady Emily's husband. I had heard she married—"

"He's not my husband," Emily interjected quickly. Realizing how emphatically she denied the woman's wrong assumption and unwittingly drew Lady Gantry's puzzled curiosity, she added in explanation, "Mr. Crenshaw passed away five months ago."

"Oh." A perplexed expression flitted across the baroness's face as she unabashedly studied Grey, then swung her eyes to note Emily's lack of proper mourning attire. With a stab of rueful dread, Emily wondered if she'd just made a mistake. A *terrible* mistake. "I am sorely aggrieved to hear that," Lady Gantry purred, in a voice that told Emily she wasn't sad at all at the news. "My condolences."

The baroness's gaze settled knowingly on Grey, her lips curving upward in private amusement, as if she'd just caught the proverbial fox in the henhouse. Then her eyes slid back to Emily, and her smile grew chillingly deeper. She arched a brow, waiting to be introduced.

Oh God, what the woman must think of the two of them! But with no choice, Emily cleared her throat and introduced them. "Lady Gantry, may I present Major Nathaniel Grey?" she spilled out in a flood. "Major Grey is a longtime family friend. He served with my brother in Spain and is now one of Lord Bathurst's most trusted men at the War Office. My family sent him to escort me safely from Yorkshire to be at my brother's side while he recovers."

As the rapid—and well-overdone—explanation fell from her lips for why she would be alone at an inn with one of London's most notorious rakes, Emily realized with horror that she was only digging herself deeper. She wasn't alleviating Lady Gantry's suspicions but furthering them.

The baroness stiffened at Grey's name. Her eyes narrowed sharply, clearly recognizing his rakish reputation if not his face, and she snatched away her hand before he could take it.

Oh God... "Major Grey," Emily forced out despite the tightening knot of panic in her throat, "may I introduce Baroness Gantry?"

With a cool and knowing smile, Grey bowed politely. Then the blasted devil sent the baroness his most rakish, most wickedly wolfish grin. "My lady, a pleasure indeed."

Emily shot him an appalled look of chastisement, which he wholly ignored. He was her escort, truly sent by her family to fetch her, and she couldn't have asked for a better guard to deliver her safely to them. But heavens! Why did the man have to feed into the gossip that was certain to come by behaving like... well, *himself*.

With a haughty sniff at his reputation, Lady Gantry turned her back to him completely.

Emily stared, her eyes narrowing to slits. The nerve of the woman! She'd never before witnessed so rude a cut, and her heart ached with embarrassment for him. Was this what his life was like in London, being subjected to such open disdain? Was this why he preferred to lurk on the fringes of society rather than try to become a true part of it?

Doubt hit her like a slap—is that what he thought of *her* now after their conversation from moments before, that

she was no better than snooty, judgmental women like Lady
Gantry?

How very different we are… Her stomach sickened.

"We've reserved a private dining room for the evening,
Lady Emily." The baroness took her arm and smiled at her.
"So you simply *must* have dinner with us."

Her chest sank with painful desolation. Trapped into dinner with Lady Gantry was the last place she wanted to be.
Not when she needed to thoroughly explain herself to Grey,
to make him believe her no matter how much groveling it
took. And certainly not when all day she'd looked forward
to being alone with him for one more precious night of feeling happy and safe in his arms.

"Thank you for the kind invitation, but I'm afraid I cannot. I have nothing appropriate to wear for dinner." Emily
latched on to the flimsy excuse. "We had to leave Snowden
Hall rather quickly."

Grey muffled a disdainful snort at her dissembling, but
Lady Gantry was oblivious, trying her best to simply will the
scoundrel from her presence altogether. "I will not let you
refuse, my dear! After all, it wouldn't do to have the daughter of a duke eating among riffraff and rogues."

Riffraff and rogues. She meant Grey. But when Emily
looked at him, the indifference in his returning gaze stole her
breath away. Her pleading eyes offered a silent apology, but
he only stared back inscrutably and folded his arms across
his chest.

"Yes, Lady Emily," he agreed, mockingly repeating the
baroness's overly dramatic words, "you simply *must* have
dinner with them. We wouldn't want you with the riffraff. Or
the rogues."

Emily stared at him, knowing the gulf between them
had never been greater than at that moment. Although

he stood there at her side, he already seemed a thousand miles away.

"Very well," Emily agreed quietly, knowing she had no choice but to accept. The words echoed hollow in her empty chest. "I would be happy to dine with you, baroness."

With a tightening of his jaw so imperceptible that Emily would have missed it had she not become so attuned to him, Grey politely nodded to the baroness before his eyes settled on her. "Enjoy your dinner, then. Good night, my lady." He gave her a mockingly deep bow. "I shall see you in the morning."

The hurt of fresh abandonment rushed through her. *In the morning.* He had no intention of coming to her tonight. Oh God, she'd ruined everything! "Grey, wait—"

But he spun on his heel and stalked away, his shoulders unyielding. As she watched him leave, her heart shattered.

* * *

"But Lady Emily, truly—Nathaniel Grey of all people!" Lady Gantry tsked at her and gave a shake of her head. "Whatever was your family thinking?"

Another dinner course, another attack on Grey. With a sigh, Emily pushed her plate away and waved off the pudding the barmaid placed in front of her.

The evening was dragging on unbearably, with dinner lingering through three previous courses and now pudding. Yet neither Lady Gantry nor her son George seemed close to calling an end to the ordeal and retiring to their rooms, although his bride had shyly excused herself after the second course, claiming fatigue after a long day's travel.

Emily longingly wished she could have excused herself as well. But Lady Gantry had insisted she remain, so she stayed, despite the boredom of their stilted conversation and the continued prying into Grey's presence on her trip. Although she'd initially enjoyed hearing about common acquaintances and the events in London during the past two seasons, she'd soon lost interest—

"Don't they realize what a scandalous reputation that man possesses?"

—and hated the relentless attacks on his character. Lady Gantry seemed titillated by relating to her the stories of what Grey was rumored to have done since his return from the war, and with whom. Especially with some woman named Lady Margaret Roquefort. Emily didn't want to hear any of it, but her disapproving frowns served only to encourage the old busybody.

At least George hadn't joined in on the skewering. Her son didn't bother to hide his boredom as he leaned back in his chair at the head of the table and sipped at a glass of port, making a disgusted face at each sip.

"Major Grey is a war hero who was wounded while serving his country," Emily defended, her patience growing thin.

"Be that as it may," Lady Gantry dismissed with a wave of her hand in the air, "the man is still a scoundrel with the reputation of a rake. He has no family—"

"He has *my* family," she interrupted. But even as she said the words, she doubted them. He and Thomas were best friends, but while Thomas trusted him enough to send him to retrieve her home, she also knew how her parents felt about him. Would he ever be welcome at Chatham House for anything more than a game of billiards with Thomas?

Lady Gantry shook her head. "That is not the kind of family to which I refer." She lowered her voice secretively. "The man is the son of a *blacksmith*, everyone knows that."

"Not everyone," she mumbled, thinking of the trust he'd placed in her when he'd told her about his past.

"And the women he associates with—disgraceful! For that alone, you should not be traveling with the man."

George made yet another face into his glass but this time did not take a sip, and Emily wondered briefly if the disgusted look was meant for Grey or for his mother for frowning on the same activities in which George gleefully engaged.

"Guilt by association?" Emily chided. Her patience grew *very* thin now.

Lady Gantry sighed heavily. "It certainly is unfair, I grant you, but that is the way of the world, my dear. Now, *I* shall not utter a word to anyone, of course—"

Emily rolled her eyes. The blasted woman was certain to blab every detail to the London gossips as soon as her carriage rolled to a stop in Mayfair.

"—but you really must be more careful. As the daughter of a duke, you have a responsibility to your position and to your family."

Hot anger flared inside her. Well, she certainly didn't need to be lectured on *that*! She knew full well how dear the price of that responsibility. Her sense of responsibility had sent her without protest into exile at school. It had forced her to give up her dream of being an artist because proper ladies didn't pursue such potentially scandalous careers. Or any career, for that matter. Responsibility to her family had also forced her to remain with Andrew. Even now her shoulders sagged under the weight of it all.

During this whole trip, she had purposefully avoided thinking about that responsibility and what lay ahead for her in London—more smothering responsibility to family, more merciless devotion to position—when all she wanted was to be a good mother and to protect her baby and the people she loved. Which now included Grey.

"Nathaniel Grey...my, my!" Lady Gantry shook her head once again. "Whatever was your family thinking?"

Enough!

"What my family was thinking," Emily ground out, the last thread of patience snapping, "was that my brother was fighting for his life and that they wanted someone they could trust to deliver me safely to them from Yorkshire. Nothing more. And certainly not the scandalous, disreputable arrangement you've implied." She slapped her serviette aside and rose from her chair. "So go ahead and spread your vicious gossip. To disparage a duke's daughter for being escorted to her dying brother's side—you'll only make yourself look like a fool."

Lady Gantry had the nerve to look offended. "Well, I certainly *never*—"

"Major Grey is a good man, and I am so very fortunate to have him with me, protecting me—" Her voice choked with anger, and she said a silent prayer that she'd be able to flee the room before she came completely undone. "Good night!"

Deaf to Lady Gantry's pleas for her to stay and finish the evening, Emily hurried from the private dining room and made her way through the inn. She had to find Grey and apologize for what she'd said earlier, had to kiss him and touch him—

She halted in the doorway of the common room and stared, not wanting to believe her eyes.

Grey sat on a settle in front of the fireplace, his long legs stretched out casually, with a tankard of ale in one hand and a cigar clamped between his teeth. Between his *smiling* teeth, because a barmaid stood in front of him, her large bosom nearly spilling out of her scoop-necked bodice as she leaned over him. She whispered into his ear with an inviting smile as her hand slid along his shoulder to trace her finger-tips through the soft hair at his nape before pulling away.

Emily stared, too stunned to look away. An agonizing stab of jealous pain shot through her, and she swallowed convulsively. Her eyes fixed on Grey as she fought to breathe, watching and waiting to see what his reaction would be to the woman's blatant offer.

He tossed his cigar stub into the fire, pushed himself off the settle, and grinned charmingly down at the buxom woman as he tossed her a coin and said something that made her laugh. He gestured toward the door, the barmaid nodded—

Then he glanced up and saw Emily.

His eyes locked with hers for just a heartbeat before she fled for the stairs.

CHAPTER NINE

$\mathscr{L}$ying on her side in bed, Emily faced the wall and tried to fall into the numbing sleep that refused to come. Her lashes still lay damp from tears as an occasional sob escaped her.

She'd barely reached her room before the hot tears began to flow like water from a broken dam, the anguish inside her chest unbearable. For several minutes she did nothing more than lean back against the closed door, cover her face with her hands, and weep inconsolably. Surely, Grey would follow upstairs after her... But as the minutes dragged on, she realized that he wasn't coming, that most likely he already lay in the arms of the barmaid. With her body and mind both numb from the blinding pain of her heartbreak, she'd somehow managed to undress, pull on her night rail, and crawl into bed.

She had no idea how long she'd been lying here, unable to sleep. An hour, perhaps two. Long enough that the inn grew quiet around her, and the small fire died away and left the room dark.

Oh God, how much it hurt! She'd pressed her hands to her chest, squeezed her eyes shut against the images in her mind of Grey touching that woman, kissing her, enjoying her... She shuddered at each fresh slice to her heart.

In truth, she had no claims to him. No matter how much happiness she'd felt in his arms, he didn't belong to her. And he never would. But Grey knew that. He'd tried to warn her away before he'd ever laid the first hand on her, and never once had he shown any kind of feelings for her beyond the lust of physical attraction and the loyalty of friendship. But she'd foolishly ignored the warnings and yielded her heart along with her body.

Now, teetering on the verge of fuzzy consciousness, her head swirled and her body ached, and she was unable to find the sweet oblivion of sleep. So her troubled mind didn't register the muted click of the door or the soft rustle of fabric in the darkness.

But she felt the quilts lift and the mattress give beneath the weight of his tall body sliding into bed behind hers.

"Emily," Grey murmured. He lay close enough that his body warmed her back but not yet daring to touch her. "What I said earlier...I regret it. I never meant to hurt you."

A hot tear escaped her closed eyes and sank down onto the pillow. Anguish tore inside her too fiercely for her to turn toward him, or even say anything at all.

"I keep expecting you to be like those other ladies I know, women who care only about appearances and their own selfish desires." His warm breath tickled at her neck. "But you're nothing like them. I am so sorry, brat."

She inhaled a tremulous gasp, her lungs burning. He was apologizing, and she suspected he rarely apologized for anything. Yet she couldn't bring herself to open her eyes or face him. The pain of betrayal inside her chest was still too fierce, still cutting as sharp as shards of glass.

"Grey," she whispered painfully, so softly the words barely sounded at all, "that woman…"

"She's a war widow with a young son at home."

"She offered herself to you," she forced out, trying to keep from crying loudly enough that he might hear even as the tears continued to wet the pillow beneath her. "I saw her…and you."

"She did offer." He placed his palm against her back, and she shivered beneath his touch. "I did not accept."

Her sobs caught in her throat. "But you gave her money."

"For her son." His hand caressed her back in slow, tender circles. "Nothing more."

For her son. She was too overcome with heartbreak and its sudden reversal to speak and instead buried her face in the pillow.

But the pain still pulsed dully though her body. She suspected that the heartache she felt tonight would be nothing compared to what she'd feel tomorrow when they finally reached London and had to part, her to her family and him to Spain. She should push him away now; she should ask him to leave, save what little piece of her heart she still possessed, and cry out her pain in private. It was the right thing for both of them, she *knew* it.

But she couldn't bring herself to send him away.

His slow, steady caresses soothed away her jealousy and the last of her hot tears. "You are so sweet and kind, so lovely…" His voice ached. "I can't give you what you deserve, Emily, I know that."

The warmth of his caressing hand seeped through the thin cotton of the night rail and deep into her back, radiating through her until her breasts grew heavy and her thighs ached. Beneath his gentle caresses, her breathing turned labored with quick arousal. God help her—even with her heart breaking, she desired him.

"Yet I still want you." His hand brushed lovingly along the curve of her hip, and whatever fleeting thoughts she had of refusing him melted away. "And I don't want to be without you tonight." He admitted tentatively, his voice rasping as if it cost him a great deal to divulge his feelings, "I need you, brat."

Her heart ached. Grey needed her, but he had no idea how much she needed him. How much she needed him enveloping her and giving her his strength, his body making her whole.

"Nathaniel," she whispered in both forgiveness and soft permission, unable to say anything more.

With a deep sigh of relief, he tenderly kissed the back of her neck. His hands slipped lower to caress her legs, then brushed slowly up her body and pushed her night rail along as he went, bunching it at her shoulders. He traced soft circles against the backs of her thighs, and when his hand dipped into the hollow where her legs met, to stroke against her folds from behind, a low moan of desire replaced her sobs.

"Sweet Emily," he whispered. "You have no idea what you do to me."

His hands traveled on, moving slowly up over her bottom as he took his time to stroke his rough palms over her round curves, to cup her fullness and squeeze gently with each circling sweep of his fingers. The now-familiar ache began to throb low and hot inside her, pulsing in time with each squeeze of his hands on her buttocks, with each shared heartbeat.

He shifted her back against him until her bottom nestled

perfectly into the cradle of his hips. She shivered from the heated arousal that instantly coursed through her, and her breathing became soft, little pants. She wanted him, and she wanted most of all to show him with her body how much she loved him.

Softly sighing out her need, she arched her back against his chest, then reached up to wrap her arm around his neck.

"You feel so good in my arms," he murmured as his hand fluttered across her bared breasts in so light, so tender a caress that she shuddered from the intensity of it. "Unbelievably warm and soft. As if you were made to be here."

Unable to remain still beneath his bewitching words, she pressed her bottom invitingly into his hips and wantonly wiggled against his erection. He groaned, and his hand left her breasts to stray down her front, over the small bump at her lower belly to sift his fingertips through the curls nestled between her legs.

Everything about him tonight was so tantalizingly tender, so enticingly gentle as his hands worshipped her that she felt herself begin to unravel. She whispered his name as her body hummed electric with need to be touched and filled, to be brought to completion. Tonight, she belonged to him and he to her, and she knew as his mouth rained moist kisses down the side of her neck to her shoulder that this wasn't about physical release—tonight, they were making love.

"Please," she breathed, barely able to form the words beneath the intensity of the sensations that swirled through her and captured her as their willing prisoner. "Please, Grey, make love to me . . ." Her voice choked with emotion. "Love me."

Whispering her name, he gently lifted her top leg to hook it over both of his and drew her over him at an angle until she was almost lying on top of him, with only her bottom hip

still resting against the mattress for support. Draped decadently across him, her naked body lay wantonly displayed to
his seeking hands. She ached to please him and parted her
thighs wider in invitation. Tonight, she was all his to touch
and caress however he desired. Without a trace of shame.

He placed his erection between her legs from behind. Her
hips angled upward as his long shaft pressed flat against her
folds and caressed against her as he slowly rubbed it back
and forth across her. With each stroke forward, his hot tip
sent a jolt of electricity through her, and with each retreat,
the creamy drops of her wetness smeared against his length
and made him slippery, letting him slide smoothly against
her intimate flesh in a wonderfully erotic tickle.

"Grey, please," she panted, unable to bear this heated
teasing any longer. She wanted him inside her, joining together not just their bodies but their breaths and heartbeats.
If possible, their souls. "I want you . . . so much . . ."

"Yes, darling," he murmured hotly against her ear. "Anything you desire."

Once again he slid himself slowly forward from behind,
but this time, he guided his tip tight along her cleft and down
into the hollow at her center. A gentle thrust of his hips
pushed him through her soft resistance. She gasped a tremulous breath at the pleasure sweeping through her at being
draped so wantonly across him with his manhood inside her.

"Don't move, love," he pleaded softly. "I just want to
feel you . . . just for a moment." He groaned and tightened his
strong arms around her, and his steely-hard erection shivered
achingly as it lay buried between her thighs.

In that moment of stillness, the world stopped and fell
away. Only the two of them existed, and all she knew was
the heavenly sensation of his strong body encircling hers
as if he never wanted to let go. His fierce heartbeat pulsed

into her back and joined with hers as they beat as one. Each breath blended together until she couldn't tell where she ended and he began.

Unbridled joy flooded her heart. Never, *never* in her life had she imagined that making love to a man could be like this...so beautiful yet shamelessly erotic, vulnerable yet so immensely freeing. Only because of Grey.

Then he began to stroke inside her, soft and slow and nothing like the fierce plunges of that afternoon in the carriage that left her helpless against the intensity of him. In this new position, without fear of putting weight on her belly and harming the baby, he held himself deeper inside her than he'd ever been, but there was no discomfort, only the sinfully exquisite sensation of his large manhood filling her completely. The gentle rocking of his body inside hers was impossibly more intimate than ever before, so much that her hands clenched at the sheet beneath her to keep herself from floating away as fresh tears gathered in her eyes.

"You have no idea how good it feels to be inside you like this." He whispered, his mouth hot against the back of her neck, "My little minx, surrendering herself so vulnerably, so wantonly...so damned perfect."

While one hand cupped her breast and massaged her fullness lovingly against his palm, he stroked down her body with the other to spread his fingers wide and possessively across her mound. Two fingers burrowed down to seek out the place where his body joined with hers. When he stroked his fingertips over the feminine lips that stretched tight around his shaft, she moaned for him, for the wholly wicked thrill of him sliding in and out of her womanhood between his fingers.

No doubt remained that she belonged to him now, in every way. And oh, how much she wanted to be just that—*his*, tonight and forever. She arched her back and dug her finger-tips into the hard muscles of his thighs as they clenched with each impossibly deep plunge inside her, wanting him to for-ever mark her body as his the way he'd already branded her heart.

His middle finger delved down through her folds to find the secret nub buried there. When he touched it, her hips bucked.

"Come with me, love." His urgent whisper sent a water-fall of fiery shivers cascading through her.

She whimpered as the tightening ache in her belly began to spread out to her fingers and toes, as her thighs began to shake uncontrollably.

He rubbed harder against her as he thrust steadily beneath her. "Come with me—now, love!"

She shattered, crying out his name into the darkness.

His hand clamped down hard over her mound to keep her pressed tightly against him, and he shuddered with a groan as he released himself. She gasped at the raw sensation of his hot seed flowing deep inside her, and a new sob tore from her throat at the exquisite intimacy of this moment.

"Emily," he whispered, his voice now shaking as much as his body as he slowly withdrew from her. He shifted her onto her side and pulled her against him to fold himself around her. His feverish body lay covered with sweat, his hair damp against his forehead as he nuzzled the back of her neck. "My beautiful Emily ... you are perfect."

As he held her tenderly in his arms, she blinked away the tears that now fell not in pleasure but wretched sad-ness. She wasn't perfect, far from it, because she'd com-mitted the ultimate sin of falling in love. And when they reached London tomorrow, how on earth would she ever be able to let him go?

* * *

Grey pulled Emily closer in the darkness. The room had grown cold as the fire died, but he hadn't wanted to leave the bed in order to add more coal. Instead, he pulled the quilts higher around her neck and tucked her into the hollow between his shoulder and chest to keep her warm.

She placed a kiss on his chest, and the small contact made his cock flex with desire. Again. He was far from satiated, his body still craving hers, but if he had his way, she'd be too sore and stiff in the morning to even walk let alone ride the remaining distance to London.

But their time together was short, growing shorter with each passing minute, and he didn't want to waste a moment of it. So he tipped her face up and gently but thoroughly worshipped her mouth with his until she trembled.

With a sigh, she nuzzled her cheek against his chest, her fingertips sketching little shapes against his abdomen beneath the quilt. "I never knew being with a man could be like this." Her lips tickled against his skin. "You are amazing, Grey."

His chest swelled. A man could get used to hearing such things, especially coming from a beautiful creature like Emily, whose naked body was soft, warm, supple...Between his thighs, his cock came alert, and he knew he would have her again. And soon. But for now, he simply wanted to hold her.

"When I'm with you," she confessed, her forefinger tracing along the ridges of his stomach, "it feels like I'm exploding from the inside out...but in a good way." She gave an embarrassed laugh. "You must think me an utter nodcock for saying that."

"Not at all." Because he felt the same way. Yet something about her words struck him as odd, and he frowned. "Brat, have you never"—he felt a bit silly using her word to describe the pleasures of orgasm, but he didn't want to embarrass her by being cruder—"*exploded* before?"

"No." Her face lowered in the darkness so he couldn't see whatever emotions played there, but her fingers shyly froze for just a beat before continuing their gentle exploration of his body. "I think it's only because of you."

Yes, a man could certainly get used to hearing such things.

She shrugged. "You give me enough time to enjoy it."

Enough time? Giving a woman time to find her pleasure required only restraint. Of course, some men were incapable of holding back their release—for God's sake, he found it difficult himself to hold back when he was inside Emily. But even men who were incapable of prolonging sex until the woman reached her own climax could bring her pleasure in other ways afterward. Unless the man was so selfish that he cared for nothing but his own pleasure.

His gut tightened with self-recrimination. Until Emily, he had been one of those men.

But the little minx had changed him, in ways he could never have fathomed. He enjoyed her company, her laughter and smiles, all those amusing stories she told and the way she teased him. During the past few days, she had become a trusted friend in whom he could confide secrets he'd never been able to tell even Edward and Thomas.

And in bed, he cared more about her satisfaction than his own. He took exquisite joy in hearing her soft mewlings of desire and in feeling her body quiver with satiated pleasure, and nothing made his own climax sweeter than knowing how much she enjoyed it herself. Never had he felt that way with any woman before, just as he'd never wanted to remain in a woman's bed afterward. He'd always wanted to flee as

soon as he could scramble back into his clothes. *If* he'd bothered to take them off in the first place. Inexplicably, though,
with Emily, fleeing was the last urge he felt.

But what kind of husband was Andrew Crenshaw if she'd
never enjoyed herself with him? Emily enjoyed sex; the past
few days—and nights—had certainly proven that. Had Crenshaw been so selfish and cared so little for his wife that he'd
never attempted to coax her to finish, not once?

He kept his voice gentle as he dared to ask, "Emily, how
was your marriage?"

She stiffened. Instantly, her happiness vanished.

Dread filled his chest. *Good God.* What did that man do
to her? He pressed, "Emily?"

When she hesitated, he suspected she wouldn't tell him.
They'd shared a physical union, but he had no other claims
on her, nor ever would. There was no reason for her to reveal
this part of her past to him.

But then she whispered, "It was a good marriage match
for me at the time."

Grey said nothing, not moving a single muscle for fear
she might stop.

"Father hadn't inherited the title yet when the contract
was made—truly, no one ever thought he would." Her fingers began to move again in slow circles over his chest,
but he suspected she wasn't aware she was doing it. "I was
merely the daughter of an East India Company official, and
Andrew was as high as I dared reach. But he came from a
distinguished family and seemingly had enough money to
keep us comfortable."

"You knew him before you married?" Not such an odd
question to put to her, given the arranged marriages between
society sons and daughters.

She nodded, her cheek rubbing against his chest. "He

courted me." A wistful smile pulled at her lips at the memory. "He brought me posies, took me driving in the park and on picnics, paid me all kinds of attention and flattery... It was nice. *He* was nice."

His gut clenched, and he steeled himself as he asked, "Did you love him?"

"No," she breathed, the single word bringing him an immense relief he didn't deserve to feel. "But I'd thought—I'd *hoped*—that love would come in time."

"What did Thomas think of the match?" Grey vaguely remembered that Thomas had gotten leave to travel to England for the wedding, but when he returned, he said little about it.

"He didn't trust Andrew. He was suspicious of him from the beginning, thought him a fortune hunter and a scoundrel. Mama and Papa didn't believe him, neither did I. He wanted me to break off the engagement, but I couldn't. My parents wanted the marriage, and Andrew seemed like a good man. He even told me that he loved me." Her lips twisted ruefully. "I thought Thomas was just being an overly protective brother."

Grey's chest sank like lead. "That was why you and Thomas had your falling-out, wasn't it?"

She nodded, not raising her eyes. "We had a terrible row, right there in the vestibule of the church on my wedding day, when he asked me one last time to call off the wedding. But I couldn't—the church was filled, everyone was waiting. To call it off then..." She drew a deep, shaking breath. "I was in tears as I took my vows."

He placed a kiss on the top of her head, his heart breaking for her. "Emily, I'm so sorry."

"But Thomas was right after all," she whispered.

"He usually is when it comes to reading people." Her brother had a peculiar gift for it, in fact, one that made him very effective both within the War Office and at bedding women. Certainly, he would have been able to see right through Crenshaw, even if Emily and their parents hadn't.

She nodded and whispered so softly that he barely heard her, "Although for once I wish he'd been wrong."

"What happened?" he asked gently, preparing himself for the worst to come.

"Andrew and I left for Yorkshire right after the wedding. That afternoon, in fact. He said he needed to get back to the farm, that he preferred to oversee it himself rather than keep an agent. I didn't want to leave London so soon. It was my first season after being away at school, and I wanted to rent a house in Mayfair to enjoy it. But he insisted." Her fingers combed absently at the hair sprinkled across his chest. "I found out later that we didn't leave London so much as flee his creditors, his gambling debts, the unpaid rent..."

Grey stared down at her, expecting to see a fury on her face that matched the one boiling inside him. Instead, he saw the resignation of someone who had lived with heartbreak for far too long and no longer possessed the emotional strength to waste on anger.

"Most of my dowry went to pay off his debts, and a month into our marriage, Andrew took the rest with him when he left for York, where he continued to gamble and drink and..." Her voice trailed off.

Bed whores, Grey finished silently, a bitter taste forming in his mouth. She must have been devastated to be a bride unwanted by her husband. The betrayal she must have felt, how utterly destroyed to know he'd lied about loving her—if the bastard wasn't already dead, Grey would have killed him himself.

"I rarely saw him after that," she admitted with chagrin,

"unless he needed money or a place to hide from his creditors." She paused, taking a deep breath. "Even then I thought I might still be able to turn my marriage around, make it work, but it only got worse. Truly, if Andrew hadn't been killed when he was, most likely he would have ended up in debtor's prison."

His gut ached for her. "You could have told your family. They would have helped you."

She smiled sadly. "My father had just inherited a duchy. How would it have looked to society if his daughter returned as a failed wife?"

The pain in her voice was heart-wrenching, and he couldn't help but tighten his arms around her. Nor could he argue with her, knowing her parents as well as he did. Firsthand experience had taught him how much position and influence meant to them.

"You could have told Thomas," he said quietly, tucking a silky strand of hair behind her ear. "Your brother would always help you, you know that."

She shook her head. "I couldn't. At first, I didn't want him to know. I was still hoping that Andrew would come back, that we might yet be able to make a loving home. So I pretended everything was fine." She paused and drew a deep breath. "Thomas rode all the way to Yorkshire when he left the army, did you know that? Just to see me."

He shook his head. He hadn't known. Thomas had never mentioned it. Not once.

"I think he suspected... But I was too proud to admit I'd made such a terrible mistake. So I lied and said that Andrew was only away for a few days. I told Thomas to stop worrying about me, that I was married now and that it was my husband's responsibility to take care of me. Not his. And that he needed to leave me alone." Her voice ached with desolation as she admitted tearfully, "He rode away, and I haven't seen him since."

"You will—tomorrow," he reassured her.

"But I sent him away..." A look of grief marred her beautiful face so wretchedly that his breath ripped from his lungs. "How can he ever forgive me for that?"

He pulled her closer, briefly closing his eyes at the pain. "He loves you, Emily. He'll forgive everything."

She nodded silently, but he wasn't certain she believed him.

He traced his fingertips across her bare back beneath the quilt as another question pricked at his gut. "But you're carrying Crenshaw's child." If there was one thing about which he was certain, it was that Emily would never cuckold her husband, no matter how lonely she was. "He must have come back to you," he said with great tenderness, choosing his words carefully, "and into your bed."

Her hand covered her belly protectively. She turned away but not before he saw her face darken with shame. "Because I tricked him," she confessed in a whisper.

Grey kept his expression stoic, not allowing himself to reveal any expression of pity for her. Quietly and tenderly, without a trace of judgment, he asked, "How?"

She took several rapid breaths, as if forcing the air into her lungs could fend off the pain of the memory. "I wanted a family so much that I was willing to do whatever I had to. I convinced Andrew that my father would increase my dowry if we had children. It was the only way I could get him to return. I'd tracked my courses so I knew what days were best for getting with a child, and..." Her voice trailed off guiltily. "And two months later, I was increasing, and my husband was dead."

Grey knew the rest, how she hid the pregnancy from everyone and resolved to run away. If he had arrived just one week later, she would have already disappeared, most likely hiding herself so well that no one would have been able to find her. Not even him. To think how close he came to never having this chance to be with her...He lowered his head and scattered gentle kisses across her lips, her cheeks, her eyelids—she trembled, and the vulnerability he felt in her sliced into his heart.

"Emily." He nuzzled her neck, willing her to open her eyes and look at him so he could reassure them both that she would heal and be stronger than before. "You did nothing wrong in your marriage or in creating this baby." He took her chin and tipped up her face. "Look at me."

Her eyes opened slowly, the blue depths watery in the shadows.

Even in the short time they'd spent together, he'd come to know this woman better than any other person in his life. He knew what made her happy, what made her laugh and cry, just as he knew exactly what she needed to hear at that moment to drive away her fears. "This baby is a precious gift, the one good thing that came out of your marriage. You deserve to have this child and its love. And you are going to be a wonderful mother."

At his comforting words, the pain and fear in her eyes softened. She self-consciously lowered her gaze to his chest, but not before he glimpsed a brightness in her face. A flicker of hope. The first such look he'd seen in her since he arrived at Snowden Hall.

A soft smile teased at her lips. "I know it's silly—the baby's still only a little bump, after all," she confided, "but I keep thinking of all the time we're going to spend together, all the songs and games I'm going to teach him, all the stories I'll tell him."

"Him?" Grey grinned at that.

She nodded with resolve. "He's going to be a boy, I know it. And I'm going to teach him to sail little boats on ponds, to draw and paint pictures, to conjugate his Latin verbs—"

Grey laughed and tightened his arms around her. Only Emily could see Latin lessons as a precious childhood memory.

Faint worry darkened her face. "Although now that I'm headed to London and he'll be born a marquess, that might all have to change."

"It won't," he assured her, touching his lips to hers. "Except that now you'll have your brother to help you."

She nodded at that, but her worry didn't fade even as she said with resolve, "Then I'll buy him a pony, and Thomas can teach him to ride and shoot better than any little boy in Mayfair." Her blue eyes rose to meet his, an affection in their depths that made him shiver. "And he'll have you to protect him."

"And his mother," he murmured. His heart swelled with emotion for her and her unborn baby. Never...*never* had he cared this much about any woman before. Yet instead of terrifying him, the thought made him ache with longing. For the first time, he wished his life could have been different. For her.

She looked up at him through lowered lashes, a seductively innocent look that stole his breath away. "Make love to me, Nathaniel."

Her words were spoken hesitantly against the darkness, as if she was afraid he might refuse her. But he would never refuse her anything, and certainly not this.

Slipping his arms around her, he rolled onto his back and brought her up on top of him, her legs straddling his waist. He curled his hand behind her neck and tugged her down onto his chest to kiss her.

*   *   *

As the blue light of dawn crept inside the room, Grey reluctantly slipped from the warmth of the bed and quietly dressed. His body was sore and stiff in all kinds of unusual places, an aching reminder of the abuse—and delicious pleasures—he'd put himself through since finding Emily. Even the old bullet wound in his thigh ached painfully from exertion. But he hadn't wanted to waste one precious minute of the time he had left with her.

He paused to watch her sleep as he buttoned up his waistcoat, her naked body still lying soft and satiated beneath the covers from when he woke her just before dawn to claim her a third time. *Sweet Lucifer*, he couldn't get enough of her. And he didn't know how he'd be able to give her up, once he'd delivered her to her family today and he left for Spain.

Yet he had no choice but to leave, no matter how appealing having a future with Emily was becoming. And it *was* appealing, damnably so. Enough that he was beginning to rethink his future plans and wonder if he was making the right decision by never attaching himself to any sort of commitment beyond his career, or if the freedom he'd come to enjoy so much in his life couldn't be replaced by something better. Like Emily.

No. She belonged with her family, where they could help her raise her child, and he belonged in Spain. Breaking off with her would hurt, he held no illusions about that, but it was for the best. His life would continue on its path with the War Office, and she would step easily back into society. Soon, she'd be too caught up with raising her baby to even think of him, and he'd move on from her the way he'd moved on from all the other women he'd known. Without regrets or second thoughts.

Somehow.

She stirred. "Grey?"

"I'm here, brat." He sat on the edge of the bed and leaned over to place a kiss on her bare shoulder.

With a smiling sigh, she stretched like a cat, then reached for his shoulders to bring him down to her for a proper kiss.

"Mmm," she murmured happily against his lips as she trailed her hand down his chest, fingering the buttons of his waistcoat as if considering undressing him. "You spent the entire night with me. You didn't leave."

"I suppose I should have." He touched his lips to hers before straightening. "Especially with Lady Gantry haunting the inn."

"I don't think Lady Gantry will be bothering us."

He frowned faintly. "Oh?"

"She and I came to an understanding last evening." Her drowsy eyes drifted lasciviously over him, taking in his half-dressed state, and his cock flexed eagerly through a yearning will of its own as she offered seductively, "So come back to bed."

He groaned at the temptation she presented, wanting to do just that. "I wish I could, but I need to rouse Hedley and Dalton so they can get the team ready. We're due in London today." *And I'm due in Spain…* The unspoken words hovered in the silence of the room as clearly as if he'd shouted them.

She dropped her hand away from him and sat up, bringing her knees to her chest and wrapping her arms around her legs. "Can't we just run off together instead, somewhere we'll never be found?"

She was teasing, but *Lord*, how tempting that sounded. So tempting he almost let himself consider doing just that. But fantasies about fleeing could never become reality, not for them. Remembering her initial plan to run away, he trailed a finger along the curve of her calf. "Like Glasgow?"

She trembled beneath his caress. "I know a dress shop where we could secure positions."

"Hmm, stocking inspector," he pondered with mock solemnity, stroking a slow circle over her inner thigh. "I think I could learn to appreciate the benefits of Glasgow."

With a laugh, she swatted at his shoulder.

He caught her hand and raised it to his mouth to kiss it. Her fingertips brushed over his cheek as his lips lingered against her palm. "Thomas wants to see you, and he deserves an explanation about the past two years. You owe him that."

She nodded, but her eyes lowered to the quilt. He could feel the fear and dread swelling inside her, so well did he know this woman now.

"You have to tell them about the baby, too," he said solemnly but firmly. "You can't hide it any longer."

Her eyes glistened as she raised her gaze to his. "But I'll also be placing all of them in danger. Someone burned down my house to try to kill me, and they nearly killed you, too. I couldn't bear it if anything happened to them because of me." Her hand slipped over her belly. "Or this baby."

He took her chin and tilted up her face to kiss her softly, trying to reassure her that everything would be all right. "You'll be safe in London. Your family will protect you, and so will I."

She shifted away and arched a disbelieving brow. "All the way from Spain?"

Giving that sardonic comment only a passing glance, yet feeling the biting sting of it in his gut, he slid off the bed and stomped into his boots, then slipped on his coat and pulled his shirt cuffs into place. Her gaze never left him, and he found it oddly intriguing that for once he didn't want to dress and leave a woman's bed. Instead, he found himself wondering what it would be like to wake up next to Emily every morning, and he decided that it would be nice. Very nice, indeed.

"You really have to leave?" she asked regretfully.

He sent her a rueful smile. "Have to."

"But you don't."

He stared down at her, momentarily stunned as her quiet assurance swirled through him. She meant leave the room, of course, but her soft words underlying so much more about his life than she realized.

Good God, could she be correct? Did he really have to leave for Spain, or was the future he now wanted sitting right there all deliciously sleep-rumpled and welcoming before him? The enormity of it made him tremble. Would he ever be ready for something like that?

He shook away the sudden confusion gripping his chest. "We'll leave whenever you're ready. Go back to sleep if you'd like." He leaned over her and kissed her, plundering her mouth as his hand tugged down the quilt to bare a single plump breast. "After all, you had a thoroughly exhausting night." He placed a delicate kiss on her nipple, and it pebbled enticingly against his lips. "And morning."

She moaned softly and lifted her arms around his neck to pull him back into bed with her. But he resisted her siren song and slipped from the room. As he closed the door, he looked up and stopped.

Hedley stood in the hallway outside the room where he and Dalton had slept. From the expression on the sergeant's face, he knew Grey had spent the night with Emily.

Bloody hell.

Grey blew out a harsh breath at being caught but said nothing. What was the point? There was no use denying the truth or attempting to lie his way out of this. Nor, for once, did he want to.

"Be careful, lad," Hedley warned grimly. "I'd surely hate to see either of ye get hurt."

Then he walked down the stairs and left Grey standing in the hallway, cursing himself beneath his breath.

CHAPTER TEN

"You can do this," Grey encouraged quietly as he stood beside Emily at the bottom of the front steps of Chatham House.

She stared at the massive door, her feet refusing to take another step. *This* was the moment she'd dreaded since leaving Snowden Hall, when she'd have to face her family, explain about the baby...and say good-bye to Grey, uncertain when she would be able to see him or be alone with him again. If ever. Now that it was happening, it was just as gutwrenching as she imagined.

None of it was helped by Grey's contemplative quietness today, ever since he left the room that morning. But if he was as troubled by this moment as she was, he chose not to confide in her, instead keeping to himself the heavy thoughts furrowing his brow.

"After all, what's the worst your parents can do?" he asked wryly as he placed her arm reassuringly around his. "Marry you off to an indebted gambler in Yorkshire?"

Jittery laughter bubbled from her, and his teasing proved enough of a distraction to allow him to lead her forward and knock at the door.

"Don't leave me," she whispered, her hand tightening on his arm.

"You'll be fine. Thomas will be happy to see you."

Her throat tightened. "That's not what I—"

The door opened, and Jensen, the family's longtime butler, scowled down his nose at them, not recognizing her. "Major Grey." He bowed stiffly in greeting with all the arrogance of a man who ran a duke's household and brought to his position a solemn responsibility befitting his employer's rank. "Miss."

Emily took a deep breath and forced a nervous smile at the old butler. "Hello, Jensen. How have you been?"

The butler swung his startled gaze from Grey to Emily, staring at her blankly for a moment. Then recognition sank in, and an old affection replaced his scowl. He was so surprised that he actually smiled. "Miss Emily ... my goodness! I mean Lady Emily—I mean, Mrs. Crenshaw." The normally imperturbable butler stammered in stunned surprise. "My apologies, miss—ma'am—my lady."

"Quite all right." She smiled reassuringly, surprisingly touched by his befuddlement. "The last time I saw you I was still just a miss."

Immediately, he collected himself, and his shoulders shifted back, his chin returning to its normal, haughty position. "If I might say so, my lady, you have been missed." His voice choked with emotion. "*Greatly* missed."

"Thank you, Jensen." She rested her hand briefly on the butler's arm, her eyes misting. She hadn't realized until then how much she'd missed him and the other servants. At least someone in London was happy to see her.

With a low bow, Jensen stepped back and opened the door wide to allow her to pass. Emily drew a deep breath for courage and, letting her hand slip away from Grey's arm, entered the grand house.

She glanced nervously around the entrance hall and up the wide stairs to the first-floor landing. "Where is my family, Jensen?"

"The duke is at the Lords, and the duchess is in the drawing room," he informed them as he took Grey's coat and gloves from him. "And Lord Thomas is resting in his room."

Grey remained at her side, but in his peculiar distraction today, he seemed a hundred miles away. Already, she sensed the impending loss of him, and her eyes stung at the heavy emptiness in her chest. For the past several days, she'd come to rely on him, confide in him...love him. How would she be able to go on now without him when he left for Spain?

"Would you please tell them that Lady Emily has arrived home?" Grey asked, his expression grim.

Jensen bowed and retreated quickly down the hall.

Blinking at his unexpected exit, she mumbled with bewilderment, "He just left us here...standing in the foyer."

"Yes, he did." Grey chuckled. "I don't think he quite knew what to do with us."

She frowned. "What do you mean?"

"Well, you are family and shouldn't have to wait in your own home." He averted his eyes to glance down the hall, searching for any sign of her family coming to greet her. "While I should never have been let through the front door."

Her chest tightened with quick regret over the dismissive way her parents had regarded him over the years. "Don't say that."

He shrugged, as if no more bothered by that than a buzzing gnat. "It's true."

Regrettably, it *was* true. If not for his friendship with Thomas, he would never have been let inside at all. But Emily planned on changing that. She didn't know how she'd manage it, but she would make certain that Grey never again felt unwelcome at Chatham House.

"It's not really my home, though," she said quietly, changing topics to move away from the embarrassment she felt over her parents' concern with status. "I never lived here. My family moved here after I married." She shook her head, not knowing whether to laugh or cry at the irony of it all. "I'm coming home to a house where I never lived from one that's now a pile of ashes!"

He squeezed her fingers reassuringly. "You'll be welcomed here," he said quietly, with that same contemplative demeanor that had shadowed him all day. So much so that he'd sat in the carriage with her for most of the long ride today staring thoughtfully out the window, saying nothing. He hadn't even attempted to kiss her, let alone make love to her again, which bothered her more than she wanted to admit.

"Grey." She frowned, suspecting that whatever clouded his mind today had little to do with simply delivering her home. "Is something—"

"Hello, brat."

She looked up at the stairway landing, and her heart skipped. *Thomas.*

He was on his feet, although from the way his hand gripped the banister he was still unsteady, but his color was normal, his eyes shining bright with happiness to see her. Her throat tightened. He was a glorious vision, despite the half-dressed state of his shirt hanging untucked to cover the bandages he wore around his waist and the growth of beard that gave him a devilish air, and she had never been happier in her life to see him.

But emotion overwhelmed her. All she could do was stand there, staring up at him, while her eyes blurred with tears.

He smiled warmly as he carefully descended the stairs. When he drew nearer, she noticed the stiffness in his movements, the dark circles beneath his eyes, his tired and drawn face. He'd lost at least two stone in weight, and through the unshaven growth of beard, she easily glimpsed the sallow paleness of his cheeks. Her heart ached for him, and her grief for the hell he'd suffered stole her breath away.

But he was alive. *Thank God!*

He stopped at the bottom of the stairs, his eyes never leaving her face.

"Thomas," she whispered, his name a plea for forgiveness.

Silently, he held out his hand to her, and she ran to him, throwing her arms around his shoulders.

She pressed him close, feeling the warmth in him and the steady beating of his heart. Thank God, he was alive! And he was going to be all right. To think how close she'd come to losing him, to never seeing him again—to risk that he would go to his grave believing she'd stopped needing him...But she would always need him, and she would never again let her own foolish pride come between them.

Thomas winced, inhaling sharply through clenched teeth.

Quickly, she stepped back, her hand flying to her mouth. "Oh! I've hurt you."

"It's all right." He placed a hand over the wound in his side and reached for the banister with the other to steady himself before giving her a weak smile, but one beaming full of love. "I'm just glad you're here." He slipped his arm around her to carefully hug her to him, then he looked over her head at Grey. His voice choked with emotion. "Thank you for bringing her home to me."

"You said you needed her," Grey replied softly, and Emily thought she saw his eyes glisten just as much as Thomas's. Clearing his throat, he glanced down at Thomas's side with concern. "Should you be out of bed?"

"I'm fine." Despite his assurance, she thought she saw him tremble as he scratched at his wrists, only to drop his hands to his side when he caught her watching him. "Can't stand another damnable minute in that bed. Besides, there'll be plenty of time to rest later." Grinning at Emily, he swept his gaze over her, taking her all in. "I wouldn't have missed my sister's homecoming for the world."

New guilt swept through her, and Emily bit her bottom lip. Grey was certain Thomas would forgive her, but so much had happened... Would he truly forgive her for all the mistakes she'd made?

She drew a deep breath. "Thomas, I need to speak with—"

"Emily!" Mary Matteson, Duchess of Chatham, glided down the hall and into the foyer. "Thank goodness you're finally here!" Her mother turned a commanding gaze at the butler, who followed behind. "Jensen, send a footman to the Lords right away. Tell Chatham that his daughter has returned and is waiting to see him."

The butler nodded and signaled to a uniformed footman standing by the front door who hurried from the house, most likely with a prepared message already waiting in hand for her arrival.

Mary hugged Emily to her briefly, then pulled back and squeezed both of Emily's hands in hers. "We've been beside ourselves with worry about you traveling alone, all the way from Yorkshire."

"I wasn't alone." Emily cast a grateful smile at Grey as he moved to stand beside Thomas. "I had Major Grey to protect me."

Mary glowered briefly in Grey's direction, as if displeased that he, of all people, had been sent to Yorkshire to fetch her daughter, before smiling again at Emily. "Nevertheless, we were worried. An uneventful trip, I hope?"

She lowered her eyes, unable to answer in a way that wouldn't make her mother faint.

"Well, thank God you've arrived safely. We were so upset when we received your letter, stating that you couldn't travel. Of course, it was perfectly understandable, but—" Her mother broke off suddenly and frowned in bewilderment. "Whatever are you wearing?"

Emily shot a pleading glance at Grey to keep his silence. Knowing her family might be in danger even now from whoever killed Andrew, she hesitated over how much of the truth to tell them, wanting to reveal all her secrets in her own way, in her own time.

Grey's eyes met hers, and although he didn't say a word, she now knew him well enough to know that he understood. But there was something else there in the warm chocolate depths of his eyes that caught her attention, something that had been there all day through his distraction and that she couldn't quite fathom—

"Emily?" her mother pressed, interrupting her reverie.

"My apologies," she mumbled and turned away from Grey to force a smile for her mother. "We left Snowden quickly, so I wasn't able to properly pack."

Mary's frown only deepened. "But surely Yardley—"

"So quickly that Yardley had to follow behind," she added, carefully avoiding Thomas's eyes as she dissembled and resisting the urge to place her hand protectively over her baby. Her brother had an uncanny ability to read people, and he'd always been able to see right through her, even when they were children. "I had to buy a dress along the way, and we didn't have time for it to be altered."

"Well, no matter." Her mother looped her arm through Emily's and led her from the foyer toward the drawing room. "You are here now, and that is all that matters. Tomorrow, we shall go to Madame Bernaise and have you measured for a new wardrobe."

Measured by a modiste, who would see her without her clothes—Emily cast a panicked look over her shoulder at Grey, who only stared silently back as her mother led her away, leaving it up to her to tell her family the truth.

"Thomas?" his mother called out to him. "You'll join us in the drawing room?"

With amusement, Grey noted that her question was actually a command, and one that predictably ignored him. Just as he noted that Thomas stood his ground and didn't move from Grey's side.

"In a moment, Mother. I want to properly thank Grey for bringing Emily to us." With a smile, and surprising strength for a man still convalescing, Thomas slapped his hand onto Grey's shoulder and turned him toward the stairs. "Come up to the billiards room. Have a drink with me before you go."

A warning knotted in Grey's gut at Thomas's sudden cheerfulness. "I should be going—"

"I insist." Thomas's smile deepened.

And so did the warning in his gut to flee. But there was no way out of it. It was time to pay the piper. He nodded and smiled grimly, knowing what was coming. "I'd love a whiskey."

As Thomas slowly started up the stairs ahead of him and Mary Matteson led Emily into the drawing room, Grey caught a last glimpse of her as she raised her hand to swipe at her eyes. He halted. Emily was crying—Lord, how he hated when she cried! His hands fisted at his sides as he fought the urge to return to her, sweep her into his arms, carry her from the house, and then—

And then *nothing*. He was still going to Spain, and with all the planning for the baby's arrival and her sudden return to her family and society, Emily would soon forget him. It was the right ending for both of them.

But damnation, the right ending certainly hurt like hell.

He bit back a curse and spun on his heel to follow after Thomas, up the stairs and into the billiards room. Distracted by Emily's tears, he stepped into the room where the two men usually spent most of their time—

Thomas's fist plowed hard into his face. The force of the unexpected punch propelled him back against the wall.

"*Christ!*" He glared at Thomas, not even considering returning the punch. Because Thomas was so weak that a single push could send him sprawling onto the floor. And because he knew he deserved it. Instead, he met his friend's angry gaze and blew out a hard breath, arching a wry brow. "Feel better now?"

Thomas gave a curt nod even as he panted hard for breath after the exertion of the punch. "Much."

Leaving Grey to rub his throbbing cheek, Thomas crossed to the liquor cabinet in the corner. He retrieved a bottle, splashed whiskey into two tumblers, then held one out in a belated peace offering.

Satisfied at the tenuous truce between them, Grey accepted the proffered glass. He couldn't help but notice the irony that this was the room where they'd always ended up on past evenings when he'd come to visit. And the same room filled with hard sticks perfect for beating him senseless should Thomas still carry a grudge about Emily that the punch hadn't satisfied.

"You're doing better since I left," Grey commented as Thomas sank into one of the red leather chairs lining the wall. Choosing to stay out of punching distance, he leaned back against the billiards table, rubbed his cheek, and winced at the bruise already forming there at the corner of his eye. He muttered, "Obviously."

"Strong enough to get out of bed now, but my side still hurts like hell." His eyes—as sapphire blue as his sister's—stared at Grey over the rim of his glass as he took a sip. He shook his head with incredulous disbelief. "You and the brat, for God's sake…" There was more curiosity in Thomas's voice than anger, and Grey took that as a hopeful sign, despite the throbbing at his cheek. "What in the hell were you thinking?"

His fingers clenched against the rail of the billiards table as he stared down into the whiskey. He *hadn't* been thinking, that was the problem. When he was with Emily, she chased all rational, logical thought from his mind, and all he knew was the joy of being with her. She made him feel dashing, brave, strong…worthy of someone like her. She was the most beautiful woman he'd ever known, inside and out.

But he answered simply, "I've never met another woman like her." And as he took a gasping swallow of whiskey, he knew he never would again.

Grey glanced at his best friend, not surprised to find the look of a protective bulldog on his face, because he was certain he wore the same look on his. Emily was wrong to think that Thomas had ever stopping caring about her. The bruise he'd be sporting for the next week certainly proved that.

Thomas leveled his gaze on Grey. "Do you plan on marrying her?"

The unexpected question pierced him like an arrow to the heart. *Marry the brat?*

He'd never thought of marriage as a possibility for his life. Marriage was a fine institution, perfectly noble for other men, but for him it had always meant the end of his freedom. Yet for once, the thought of domestication didn't terrify the daylights out of him. And he'd even considered it briefly that morning at the inn when he'd watched Emily sleeping in the bed they'd shared, dreading the moment when he would have to leave her.

But marriage, even to Emily, would be impossible.

She wasn't wrong when she'd acknowledged how different they were. Within days, she'd be welcomed back into the bosom of society, invited to lavish dinners and soirees, and feted as the center of attention in drawing rooms across Mayfair. His reputation, both as an army officer and a rake, would only interfere with that.

Further, he was due in Spain. Past due, in fact, and he was already wearing Bathurst's patience thin with his delays. He couldn't let this opportunity pass by when it was everything he'd spent his life working to achieve. If he proved himself in Spain, he could expect another promotion and reassignment, this time perhaps back in London at Whitehall itself, an administrative role instead of fieldwork. And with that, he would reach the pinnacle of his career.

Choosing Emily meant having to give up those dreams, and he couldn't bring himself to do that, especially when he had no guarantee that she'd choose him in return. He'd seen how much she'd enjoyed being with him, and he'd felt the way she'd given herself so completely when she lay naked in his arms. But he'd also seen the panic on her face when Lady Gantry saw them together at the inn. Emily might need him now, but what would she do when the immediate need disappeared? Or if the baby she delivered was a boy, born into a marquessate? Which would she choose then—her proper position in society or the rake she couldn't be seen with in public?

Need was a far cry from love. If choosing Emily meant giving up the War Office when she might yet choose society over him, then need simply wasn't enough.

"No, I cannot marry her," he admitted soberly. "And she knows that."

"Then I suggest you two keep your hands to yourselves from now on." Thomas swirled the whiskey in his glass, the force of his warning masked by a trace of sarcasm as he added, "It's damnably dull having this same conversation with you every five years."

With a chagrined grimace, Grey took his words to heart. Thomas might have been joking, but the underlying message was wholly serious. "At least this time you didn't threaten to shoot me."

He dryly arched a brow. "I knew I'd forgotten something."

And at that, Grey knew his friendship with Thomas was still intact, if slightly fractured, although how he'd managed not to find himself at the end of Thomas's pistol this time he hadn't a clue. Unless that was because of the other truth he also knew—that Thomas loved Emily and would never do anything to hurt her, including hurting *him* with anything more than a punch. Even the past two years apart hadn't dulled the special bond between them. Grey only hoped she realized that, as well as how much she could trust her brother. Because the niggling instinct in his gut that had kept him alive as a soldier and a spy told him that the worst was yet to come.

Grey set down his empty glass and pushed himself away from the billiards table. "You need to talk to Emily. She has quite a bit to share with you."

Thomas rose carefully to his feet, his hand over his side. "About what?"

Grey shook his head. "She has to be the one to tell you." And hopefully, resolve the rift between them. "And I've lingered here too long as it is. I need to check in at Whitehall, now that I'm back."

"You're still leaving for Spain, then?" Thomas's face darkened at the possibility.

Grey hated seeing that look after all Thomas had gone through, but leaving was for the best. Emily had her brother again, and he had his new position waiting for him. He nodded. "Within the fortnight."

"Stay, Grey," Thomas urged quietly, placing a brotherly hand on his shoulder. "Just a few weeks more." Then he added a bit grudgingly, and Grey knew it cost him a great deal to say it, "In case she needs you."

A hard tug pulled from deep in his chest, and rashly, he yielded to it. "All right," he agreed soberly, hoping he hadn't just made the biggest mistake of his life.

Although after seeing Emily appear so utterly desolate and wretched when he left her, how could he have done otherwise? But the War Office certainly wouldn't like this new delay, and as Thomas walked him slowly downstairs, he was already trying to think up a new excuse for Bathurst.

As they reached the foyer, Jensen opened the front door, and the Duke of Chatham strode into the house. He handed his coat, hat, and gloves to the footman.

His eyes landed on Grey, then slid dismissingly away to his son. "Where's your sister?"

"Chatham?" Mary Matteson scurried into the foyer, with Emily treading more slowly behind. The duchess saw her husband's face, and her smile faded. "What's wrong?"

Emily looked up and saw Grey, her eyes widening with

surprise to see him still there. Taking the distraction of her father's entrance to slip away, she moved to stand between him and Thomas.

Grey's chest panged painfully for her, hating to see her looking so alone, even when surrounded by family. He didn't know much about her relationship with her parents, but he knew they'd never been close, a rift that his kissing lesson from five years ago certainly hadn't helped. Yet he surreptitiously brushed his fingers against hers as her hand dangled at her side, to reassure her as much as possible.

"Emily, there you are." Her father turned to her, and Grey felt her stiffen next to him as her hand jerked away from his. "I've just heard the news and came as quickly as I could to tell you, since it directly affects your dower at Snowden Hall."

"What news?" she half whispered, holding her breath.

"Word was announced on the floor of the Lords this afternoon." Her father's face turned grim. "The Marquess of Dunwich is dead."

*   *   *

The words echoed through Emily, her body flashing numb as the room pitched around her. The familiar metallic taste returned to her mouth, the numbness behind her knees, the uncontrollable shaking in her hands...all the signs of suffocating fear rushed back in a drowning flood. *Dear God, no—* it was happening again!

And she'd unwittingly placed her baby right in the heart of the lion's den.

Terror churned inside her. As soon as her pregnancy was revealed, all of London would know, and she would never be safe. The murderers would come after her again—*oh God, not my baby!* Her breath ripped from her lungs, leaving her gasping for air and her head spinning with panic. The world plunged away beneath her.

"Emily!" Grey's strong arms swept around her as her legs buckled, catching her as she fell.

He lifted her off her feet and gathered her against his chest. With the strength to do nothing more than cling to him, she buried her face against his shoulder, her hand protectively folded over her belly. Over the innocent baby she loved more than life itself.

"No," she whispered over and over between sobs, "please, God, no..."

"What's wrong?" Mary Matteson demanded with an accusing glare at Grey, then laid a hand against her daughter's cheek as she cried inconsolably. "Emily—Emily, dear, why are you crying? You barely knew the man."

"Give her air," Grey ordered sharply, his deep voice edged with worry, as he turned her away from her mother. When Thomas pressed in with concern, his pale face drawn, Grey explained reluctantly, "She's with child."

Her mother beamed with happiness. "A baby?" Then a beat later she realized its significance and gasped. "An heir!"

Her father's stunned eyes darted to Emily's hand as it lay over her belly, then he took his wife's arm and gently led her back. "Major Grey is right, Mary. She needs space and calm."

Thomas stood beside them, saying nothing. With one arm wrapped tightly around Grey's neck and the other still guarding her baby, Emily closed her eyes, unable to bear the bewildered look of betrayal on Thomas's face for not telling him before now.

"Grey," she whispered, his name a breathless plea.

"She's overwrought," he told them, protecting her once

again. "Give her time to rest, and then she can explain. Where is her room?"

"Bring her this way," Thomas ordered without hesitation, then started quickly up the stairs, grimacing in pain at the effort. "Mother, have Jensen bring up a tea tray."

The duchess nodded and hurried away.

"I'll send for Dr. Brandon," the duke offered helpfully.

"Thank you." For just a beat, Grey met the man's eyes, for once united in their concern for her. Then he carried her upstairs.

Thomas led them to the second floor and down the hall to the bedrooms in the west wing, then pushed open one of the doors and stepped back. As Grey carried her inside, Thomas leaned against the doorway like a tired sentinel, standing guard but giving them privacy.

Grey gently placed her on the bed and reached for her hand as he sat beside her. Her face was ashen, her body trembling, but at least she had stopped sobbing and was breathing steadily now.

He frowned down at her as deep concern pinched his gut. "Well, that was quite a homecoming," he muttered, brushing a golden curl away from her cheek.

"You should experience a Matteson family holiday sometime," she assured him with a weak attempt at a smile, despite a hitch in her voice. "One could confuse it for a stay at Bedlam."

For her sake, he forced a small smile he didn't feel. He was deeply worried about her and now also incredibly uneasy about leaving her here, knowing it would only be a matter of hours—days, if they were lucky—before news of the baby flowed through London like the Thames. The house wasn't well protected from anyone who might want to break in, with old window sashes and easily picked locks, and it was staffed with men like Jensen who were too old and too portly to stop anyone who tried. Even though Thomas was healing, he wasn't well enough to protect Emily and the baby.

His brows knit together. "Do you have other family in London, any place else you can stay?"

She shook her head. "I'll be fine here." Her fingers tightened against his. "The surprises are over now. It wasn't the way I wanted to tell them about the baby, but now that they know, the worst is over. And I want to be close to Thomas."

She'd misunderstood his concern, but he didn't correct her, not wanting to upset her further. Deciding instead to place men on guard around the clock to watch the house, he acquiesced to her wishes and nodded. "Thomas needs you."

Her eyes glistened. "And I need *you*, Grey."

The soft words tore at him, a raw wound opening in his chest as he stared down at her beautiful face, the paralyzing fear once again showing in her sapphire eyes. He *hated* that fear and never wanted to see it in her eyes again.

But what were his choices? If he left her—

His heart stopped. *If* he left her…He knew then what he had to do, and the decision hit him with the force of a lightning bolt.

"I told you, brat," he answered quietly but with deep resolve, "that I would always protect you and your baby." He couldn't resist stroking her cheek in an attempt to soothe her, even as a knot of emotion lodged in his throat. "And that's exactly what I plan to do."

"Grey, a word with you," Thomas called from the doorway with a glance into the hall. "*Now*, please."

Nodding, he stood and squeezed her hand reassuringly. "You're not alone anymore, Emily."

He hadn't quite reached the door of the room when her

mother bustled inside. The look of recrimination the duchess gave him to find him in the bedroom stunned him for a moment, and he glanced past her at Thomas, who mouthed a silent *You're welcome.* Thank God Thomas was on his side, or her mother would have come in to find him sitting on the bed with her daughter, stroking her cheek. And army life had certainly never prepared him for a battle like that.

"Major Grey," the duchess snapped, "a lady's bedroom—"

"—is no place for a gentleman. Thank goodness you're here now, Your Grace." He sketched her a bow and sent her what he hoped she'd believe to be a grateful smile of relief. "I was just leaving to find you." Behind her, he saw Thomas roll his eyes. "Lady Emily needs her mother to care for her, especially at this delicate time."

That took the wind from the woman's sails, and she blinked with momentary confusion, uncertain whether to continue her berating or thank him for his concern. "Well...yes," she sputtered instead. "Yes, of course." She paused, grudgingly forcing out, "I'm certain Thomas has thanked you for bringing Emily safely to us. We...appreciate all you've done."

That was as close to gratitude as he would ever get from her. "I was happy to help, Your Grace."

He glanced back at Emily. Even from this distance, he could see the tears glistening in her eyes, and fresh anguish sliced through his chest. This parting couldn't be helped, but he would be back. And he would make it his personal mission to never see her cry again.

With a polite bow to the duchess, and a deeper bow to Emily, he said his good-byes and strode from the room, each step filled with resolute determination.

"Where are you going?" Thomas demanded, falling into step beside him, his hand covering his wounded side.

"To make arrangements," he answered, pausing at the top of the stairs to glance back at her room. "I've changed my mind."

Thomas shook his head grimly. "If you leave her to go to Spain now, in her condition—"

"No," Grey corrected with unyielding resolve. "I meant about marrying her."

For a moment, Thomas only gaped at him incredulously. "When I asked earlier..." He shook his head. "My parents won't allow it, you know that. And certainly not if that child's a boy."

He blew out a weary breath, not looking forward to *that* battle. But it couldn't be helped. "It's the only way I can protect her."

"Protect her?" Thomas's brows drew down sharply. "Why would—"

"Do I have *your* permission to marry her, Thomas?" he asked solemnly. Emily was over twenty-one and didn't need anyone's permission, but Thomas's opinion mattered. A great deal.

Thomas stared at him for a moment as if his best friend had lost his mind, then grinned slowly. "Welcome to the family."

"Thank you," he sighed with relief, resting his hand briefly on Thomas's shoulder. "Not a word to Emily yet. I want to do this right." He started down the stairs. "I'll be back tomorrow with a ring and posies for a proper proposal."

"And a smelling bottle to resuscitate my parents," Thomas called grimly after him.

Grey ignored that. He'd deal with her parents later. For now, his only concern was protecting Emily. And he *would* protect her. With his life.

CHAPTER ELEVEN

"Tea, Emily?"

Ignoring her mother in her distraction, Emily nervously paced to the end of the drawing room and paused only long enough to pull back the gauzy curtain that filtered out the afternoon sunlight and glance through the large window at the front entrance—empty. No saddle horse. No carriage.

No Grey.

With a sigh of mounting agitation, she turned and headed back across the room, wringing her hands. Even after tossing and turning all night, she wasn't able to sit still today and rest. She'd remained too upset over the news of Dunwich's death, and she'd missed the warmth of Grey's protective arms around her as she slept. Nothing eased her worry and nervousness today, either. Not the book she'd tried to read, not sitting in the gardens, not even her sketchbook and pencils—and certainly not the letter her father insisted she write to the Committee for Privileges, informing them that she was with child. The same letter he delivered himself this afternoon. By tomorrow, all of London would know that she might be carrying the Dunwich heir, and then, *oh God*, what would she do to protect her baby?

Which was why she was pacing now. No—not pacing so much as simply wandering between the two windows, the door, and back, because in her anxious distraction she couldn't have managed a straight line if her life depended upon it.

The long case clock struck, and she jumped. Her heart thumped with the ringing of the hour...one, two, three, four...Her chest fell. Five o'clock, and still no Grey. Surely, he should have returned by now, to see how she'd managed through the night and if she were feeling better. Or at least to reassure her of Yardley's whereabouts, knowing how much the woman meant to her. Or if he'd started the investigation into Andrew's murder and the arson at Snowden. But...nothing.

Her mother held up a teacup as she wandered past, her brow furrowing with concern, and tried again. "Would you like some tea, dear?"

Emily waved it away and kept pacing, raising her thumb to her mouth to bite at her nail.

Thomas was also absent this afternoon, almost as if he was avoiding her, which pained her more than she wanted to admit. She'd told him about Andrew's death and the fire when she told her father that morning. At least the stunned look on her brother's face showed his concern and that he believed she wasn't lying, although most likely he thought her slightly mad. Even if she'd wanted to dissemble, Thomas was the one who taught her how to lie, and she was certain not one of hers would slip past him now. Which was going to make it very difficult when she finally told him the truth about her marriage and how she'd gotten with child, just as Grey had urged her to do.

But she couldn't. Not yet. Not on top of everything else. Right now, all she could think about was keeping her baby safe... and why, oh why, was Grey not here?

With a patient but determined sigh, her mother stood up and thrust the teacup in front of her as she circled the room again, nearly knocking Emily backward with surprise.

"Emily, your tea." This time, the offer was not a request.

"Yes, Mama." With a sigh, she sat on the gold-striped settee across the tea table from her mother and accepted the cup. Her mother meant well, making certain she ate even this tiny bit, but she had no taste for the stuff.

In fact, she'd had no appetite at all since leaving the inn yesterday morning. She'd swallowed only a few bites at lunch today and then mostly because she didn't want to offend Cook, who had been so worried about her lack of appetite after returning her breakfast tray completely untouched that the woman had come upstairs herself to inquire after her. A quick look now at the tray loaded with cinnamon biscuits specially made for her told Emily that Cook didn't believe her protests that she was fine. Her eyes misted at the generosity and concern of the household staff when they hadn't seen her in two years.

"You need to eat, my dear, especially now that you are increasing." Her mother held up a small plate of tiny cucumber sandwiches—also her favorites, and her eyes blurred even more that Cook remembered a detail that small about her. Her mother's voice was soft with concern as she added, "I know you are still tired from traveling, but you must think of your baby's well-being."

His *well-being*? Emily nearly laughed. That was nearly all she'd been thinking about for the past five months. Oh, her mother genuinely worried about her, she supposed, but the irony grated—the same woman who now fretted over her unborn grandchild had banished her own daughter for one foolish kiss.

Emily reached past the sandwiches for one of the biscuits, hoping to find some comfort there, if not her appetite.

A noise sounded from the street. She jumped to her feet so quickly that she nearly spilled her tea, only for her hopeful heart to plummet when she heard the singsong refrain of the rag-and-bone man.

She slowly sank back down onto the settee and raised the cup to her lips.

Her mother drew a deep breath and asked quietly, "Does Major Grey know that you are in love with him?"

The teacup tipped in her surprised hand and splashed a puddle onto the Turkish rug. "Pardon?" she squeaked.

"Major Grey," her mother repeated with a long-suffering sigh, only adding to Emily's mortification that her mother would raise this topic, of all topics, with her. "You are in love with that man, and most likely have been since you were sixteen and saw him riding up to Ivy Glen in his scarlet uniform." With a faint, wistful smile, her mother shook her head as if she knew herself what it felt like to lose her heart to a young officer the way Emily had lost hers so long ago to Grey. "A young lady would have to be blind not to find that sight dashing."

Emily's heart skittered uncontrollably. *Good Lord*, how was it possible that her mother knew what she felt for Grey? Carefully keeping her reaction as even as possible so she could deny it, she slowly returned the cup to its saucer, only to be given away by her trembling hands and the soft clinking of the china.

"But that is all it is, my dear," her mother assured her firmly yet not unkindly. "Only a dashing sight, nothing more. And a lady must always remember to look past the uniform to the man beneath."

A blush heated her cheeks. Oh, she'd certainly seen the man beneath! She set her tea aside before she spilled it again. "Major Grey is a fine man, Mama," she defended. There was no point in attempting to hide her feelings.

"Yes, by all accounts, Major Grey is a good man." A slight chagrin darkened her face as she clarified, "Although his reputation with the ladies leaves much to be desired in the sort of companion I would have chosen for my son."

Her eyes flew up to meet her mother's, and Emily stared at her, wide-eyed and speechless. There was a compliment buried in there somewhere, under many layers, yet still a compliment...for Grey. *Heavens*, she couldn't have been more surprised if Mama had just declared pigs capable of flying!

"And from what I have personally seen," her mother continued grudgingly, carefully pronouncing each word as if it cost her great pain to admit it, "he is devoted to Thomas, and his loyalty to this family and to his country is beyond measure."

Oh, that was definitely a compliment! Yet hearing it come from her mother's lips did nothing to soothe the unease rising inside her. Not when she knew how little her parents liked Grey and would gladly toss him completely from Chatham House if not for fear of losing Thomas's favor.

Mama raised her cup to her lips. "However—"

There! There it was, the shift she'd expected. Emily steeled herself against the insults certain to be unfurled against Grey now.

"He is also an army officer and War Office agent."

Emily forced down her rising ire. "I know exactly what he is," she corrected softly. And what he was...was magnificent. Kind and caring, protective and brave, determined to secure a better life for himself—everything she could ever want in the man she took into her arms...and in a husband, should she ever dare let herself hope for that. "I also am quite aware of his faults." *And happily willing to overlook them.* "So please do not attempt to turn my heart against him."

Her mother's face softened with remorse. "That is not my intention, but you must remember who he is." She lowered her cup to the saucer perched precariously upon her knee. Her eyes never raised from her tea as she said, "No matter what rank he achieves, he will never be a gentleman."

Frustrated anger simmered low inside her that her mother should denigrate him so, the man who saved her life and her baby's. The same kind, caring man who made her feel loved and special. "Is that why you and Papa dislike him so much, because that's how you see him?" she demanded bluntly. "As nothing more than a blacksmith's son who dared to kiss your daughter?"

"Yes, we dislike him," her mother acknowledged quietly but sincerely, her eyes softening as they lifted to meet hers. "But not for the reason you think."

"Because you caught him kissing me in the garden," Emily accused coldly. She remembered what Grey had said to her at Snowden. "Wasn't it enough to punish me by sending me away to school? Why must you continue to punish him as well?"

A flash of shock sped across her mother's face, and she shook her head. "Your father and I didn't send you to school as punishment." Sadness laced her voice. "We were trying to save you in the only way we knew how."

"*Save* me?" The question came out as an incredulous gasp, and Emily could only gape, stunned. The years of loneliness and isolation, of being treated as an outsider by the other young ladies among whom she never belonged, missing her brother and her home so badly that she cried herself to sleep night after night—*Good Lord*, if that was salvation, then..."What on earth did you think you were saving me from?"

Her mother's shoulders slumped, as if defeated. "From dashing young men in their scarlet uniforms," she answered ruefully. She reached for the teapot to refill her cup, although her cup was still full, as if she needed to keep her hands busy and seized on the comfort of pouring tea. "My father was an army man, you know, a lieutenant in India, and I saw first-hand how hard army life can be, both for the men and for the women who marry them. Never enough money, being sent God knows where to live like natives, always the constant fear of attack and death...Later, when I married your father, I suffered through that same life. And I didn't want that for my daughter."

"But—but it was only one kiss!" Emily exclaimed incredulously.

"And I would have done anything necessary to keep it from becoming more, for your sake, with any man who wasn't a gentleman. It wasn't Nathaniel Grey we were worried about but any man who saw you as an opportunity for social advancement." She shook her head and set the pot down, her hand lingering on it regretfully as if remembering her own harsh childhood in India and her marriage before Papa inherited. "I wanted more for you than the life I had—an army officer's wife depending upon the kindness of relatives for a livable allowance."

"It was a good life," Emily argued, rising to her feet. "We had a wonderful home at Ivy Glen."

"Thanks only to your father's brother and nephew," she interjected, bitterness lacing her voice. "Without their kindness in letting us live there, we would have been crammed into rented rooms with barely enough money to feed and clothe us. Nearly every penny we had was because of them. Even then I worried constantly about how to settle the accounts and felt ashamed every time I had to ask for our allowance, through all of it suffering the embarrassment of being beholden to them."

Emily stared at her with astonishment. But that—that wasn't possible! She remembered her childhood at Ivy Glen, how wonderful it had been...but she also remembered the visits by her uncle and cousin, the tension that descended upon the country house, how on edge her mother had seemed. Yet she'd had no idea of their circumstances or her mother's worry. Her parents had always been so careful with appearances, always conscious of social rank and connections. She'd assumed it was because they were social climbers themselves, set on achieving higher positions than they were born to. Never had any other alternative occurred to her.

"I wanted a better life for you, Emily, and when your father and I stumbled upon you two that day in the garden..." A pleading look for understanding swept across her mother's face. "Well, it was obvious to me that you might never get that life. So we asked your cousin for the tuition money to send you to school." Her mother drew a deep breath and admitted, "You needed a better education than I was able to provide for you at Ivy Glen, one that would teach you how to become a gentleman's wife. We also hoped that you would make friends among the other young ladies and acquire their tastes and standards." She paused. "Especially in suitors."

Andrew. The realization hit her like a slap. That was why they'd urged her to marry him, because they thought he would provide the best life possible for her. A gentleman with a decent allowance and a small country estate of his own, relatives in a well-respected family, even a distant connection to a title...They must have thought they'd been blessed by fate to have such a man offer for her. No wonder they didn't believe Thomas's doubts about him—Andrew had been everything they'd ever dreamed of for their daughter.

Emily knew then that she could never tell them about the full misery of her marriage, that the man they thought would be her salvation turned out to be exactly the kind of fortune hunter from whom they'd tried so desperately to protect her. Their concern and love was misguided, oh, terribly so! But it was love, nonetheless, in its own way.

"And you might now be carrying a marquess, which means all those dashing young men will once again be clamoring for your attention." Her mother set her tea aside, as if she, too, had lost her appetite. She added softly, "You might once again be in danger of losing your heart."

Not losing, Emily thought, pressing her hand against her chest. *Lost.* Her heart was already gone, although in truth she'd lost it five years ago, and only finding Grey again had brought it back to her. "Grey isn't one of those men, Mama. He's not a fortune hunter."

"No, I do not believe that he is." Her mother's brow furrowed.

Confusion pulsed through her. "Then why do you—"

"Does he know that you are in love with him?" she asked again, with more tenderness and concern than Emily expected, so much that it took her breath away.

Her face flushed, and she averted her eyes, even as her mother's gaze watched her closely, waiting for an answer. "No," she admitted in a whisper. "I haven't told him yet."

Her mother's voice softened. "And does he love you?"

Her chest tightened with a painful clench. She didn't have the strength—yet possessed far too much pride—to admit that her mother had no worries there, that Grey didn't care about her, at least not the way she wanted. So she deflected the question. "I would consider myself lucky to have his love. He's a war hero and patriot, a man who carved out a decent life for himself against all odds." She added pointedly, "He saved my life."

Her mother shook her head sadly. "You know the reputation he has, Emily."

"As a rake, you mean," she snapped out irritably. *Why* must Mama persist in disparaging him like this?

"No, not that," her mother corrected softly. "His reputation as a man who craves adventure and action, who loves the chase and the hunt." She paused, as if searching for the right words. "I know Major Grey well, given his friendship with your brother," she told her gently, "and you are not the first woman to fall for his dashing nature, nor the first who has wanted to wed him."

Her chest tightened with a hot rush of jealousy. It was true, certainly—if she loved Grey so deeply, then surely other women had also lost their hearts to him just as she had. She couldn't imagine anyone *not* falling in love with him, so completely did she love him. But coming from Mama, the observation was heartbreaking.

Her mother's eyes glistened with sympathy. "And it is a mistake for you to want marriage with a man like him."

"Grey would be a wonderful husband and father," Emily protested, blinking back the stinging in her eyes. Why was Mama torturing her like this? "The best I could ever hope for."

"I'm certain he would," she conceded, surprising Emily so much with her compliment that she gaped at her mother.

Yet her mother's eyes filled with regret and sadness. "But my sweet daughter, what makes you think you would be the right wife for him?"

Emily blinked, stunned. Of all the things for Mama to say—she certainly hadn't expected that! Her heart skipped, and the air left her lungs in one anguished breath. *Because I love him. Because I know his secrets and he knows mine, yet we still care for each other. Because we're perfect together* . . . But nothing came from her lips, because with each skittering beat of her thumping heart, she feared her mother might be right.

"I know both of you, perhaps better than you know yourselves. Even if you somehow managed to change his tiger's stripes and convinced him to marry, even if he became accepted by society . . ." Her mother paused, an expression of grim knowing crossing her face. "A man like him would never be happy leading a respectable life in English society, and you wouldn't be happy with anything else."

"That's not true," Emily whispered defensively, but even as she spoke, tears burned in her eyes.

With a soft expression of knowing pity, her mother folded her hands in her lap and gently shook her head. "To give up his freedom, to leave behind the excitement of battles and chasing enemies for a life of domesticity, babies, social outings— could you imagine a man like him, retired to a life of leisure on a country estate? He would go mad within a fortnight."

Emily lowered her gaze to the floor as she began to tremble. *No.* Grey wasn't like that. He might consider himself a lurker who belonged between worlds, but he knew society and its benefits and would fit into that life as well as any gentleman. She knew it! He'd hurt his own cause in the past by cultivating his reputation as a rake and an outsider, but surely, he could overcome that . . . couldn't he?

"I knew men like him in India," her mother continued quietly, "those men who had a taste for adventure. They were never happy leading an ordinary life, and your Major Grey is the same. I see it every time I look at him."

Emily glanced away as uncertainty swirled through her and mixed with the roiling pain knotting her insides. She had seen the same look in him herself.

"For a man like him," her mother said softly as she rose to her feet and stepped slowly toward her, "even the best marriage would be... well, it would be like trapping a tiger in a cage."

A tiger in a cage. Pain tore through her chest as she squeezed her eyes shut and tried to force away the heartbreak of her mother's words. Because she was right. Grey valued his freedom more than anything else. Good God, he'd told her so! The freedom to shape his own life, to come and go between worlds as he pleased... to accept a promotion in Spain.

"In time," her mother assured her, placing her hand on Emily's arm and gently squeezing, "he would regret choosing a wife over the War Office, and whatever love he holds for you now would only turn to resentment."

"He would never..." Yet even as Emily whispered the words, she doubted them.

Pity swam in her mother's eyes. She reached up to tuck a stray curl behind Emily's ear, the same motherly gesture she used to do when Emily was just a little girl, still in braids in the nursery at Ivy Glen. "Please understand. I do not tell you this to hurt you, my darling, but to keep you from being hurt."

The air tore from her lungs. Oh, it was too late for that! Already the pain and loss reverberated inside her.

A soft scratch sounded at the door, and Jensen entered.

"Your Grace." He bowed to the duchess, then turned to Emily with a nod. "There is a caller downstairs for Lady Emily. Major Grey, ma'am."

Pressing her hand hard against her chest and the heart that pounded so achingly within, Emily drew a sharp breath to gather her strength and find the resolve to face him. All day she'd paced and hoped he'd come see her, but now that he was here, dread fell coldly through her.

The butler paused, waiting for a response. When she didn't answer, he pressed gently, "What would you like me to do with him, ma'am?"

For the first time concerning Grey, she hesitated. Then, drawing a deep breath, she answered nervously, "Would you please show the major upstairs?"

"Yes, ma'am." Jensen inclined his head and retreated.

"I shall leave you two to talk," her mother offered soberly. "But please remember all I've said. It would break my heart to see you hurt."

Her mother kissed her softly on the cheek, then silently left.

With her mother gone, Emily looked down at her hands. They were shaking, with no way to stop them.

She turned away and once again set to pacing the room, this time in desperation to collect herself before Grey saw the anguish on her face and the pain of her shattered heart. Her mother was right. He wasn't the sort of man who could tolerate a normal society marriage, but he knew it, too. Which was why he'd never made any promises to her for a future or any kind of commitment beyond delivering her to London, why he'd never even hinted about marriage. Oh, she was such a fool! While she was falling in love, he had been planning his relocation to Spain.

Even if he changed his mind and decided he wanted

her—*a tiger in a cage*. She closed her eyes against the pain of the truth. Her mother was right; Grey loved being an agent and the life of excitement that accompanied it, the possibility for an even better future it might yet bring him. All she could do was take that away.

And what would become of her if she did and if he grew to resent her for it? She knew what hell it was to be married to a man who hated his wife, who blamed her for turning his life into something he never wanted—who would only end up abandoning her. Oh God, she couldn't bear that again! And certainly not from Grey, of all men. The only man she'd ever loved, and the only man she ever would.

"Emily."

His deep voice shivered through her. She opened her eyes and watched him saunter into the room. The sight of him stole her breath away.

Dressed in formal afternoon attire of a silk maroon waistcoat, tan trousers, and a black superfine jacket, he could have put Beau Brummell's dandies to shame, certainly outshining them all with his golden hair and handsome face. His man had spent hours on the intricately knotted cravat at his neck, his close shave, and the shine of his polished boots. He'd taken her breath away before, even half-dressed and sporting two days' growth of beard. But this...*sweet Lord*, she hadn't been prepared for this! Every inch proclaimed him the gentleman he was born to be instead of the orphan fate had made him.

But when he smiled at her, a look so full of affection that his eyes shined, the tug at her heart told her that nothing from his past signified. What mattered was his future. And she would do whatever she had to in order to ensure that.

Even if it meant a future without her.

* * *

Grey stared at her, unable to tear his gaze away. He'd spent all last night pacing and practicing what he would say to her. Now that the moment had arrived, however, he couldn't remember a blasted word. Of course, the ferocious pounding of his heart didn't help alleviate his nervousness, or how his palms had grown so sweaty that he didn't dare remove his gloves. Or by the weight of the ring box in his breast pocket, acting as a constant reminder that his life was about to change forever.

And it certainly wasn't helped by the way Emily simply stood there on the far side of the room, making no move to rush to him as he'd hoped.

He frowned, a soft pang of uncertainty rising inside him. "Emily." He came forward. "Are you all right?"

"I'm fine." But instead of stepping into his arms as he wanted, she moved away.

He froze. A warning prickled low in his gut. No, she wasn't fine. Not at all.

She averted her eyes as she took another step away from him, and he saw her hands tremble before she twisted them into her skirt to hide them. She was nervous, anxious—

Damnation! His jaw clenched with anger. If Thomas had told her of his proposal plans, he'd pummel him senseless for it, bullet wound or not.

When she moved back yet again as he stepped forward, he halted. His eyes narrowed on her. Bewilderment instantly replaced the anger. Had he completely misread her? From the way she'd clung to him yesterday when he had to leave her, as if her heart would break to part from him, he'd been certain she'd sparked an affection for him. Yet he didn't dare hope for love. That would make this moment far too easy, and he'd never been a friend to fate.

But to behave like this now, as if she'd flee from the room—and him—if she could sidle herself closer to the door...

"Did Thomas speak to you?" he half demanded, not knowing whether to be furious at Thomas or worried about her.

She shook her head. "I haven't told him yet about my marriage," she answered quietly, her gaze pinned to the floor. As if she couldn't find the courage to look at him. "With everything else he's had to deal with, I thought it best to wait a few days."

He clenched his jaw. "That's not what I meant."

"Oh," she breathed out knowingly, still not daring to look at him. "That."

Yes, *that*. Even now ire at her brother prickled in his chest, right beneath the ring box.

"Of course I haven't," she blurted out, blushing scarlet with embarrassment. "But I think he suspects what happened between us."

He gaped at her. She thought he meant about the journey from Yorkshire. She didn't know about the wedding proposal, Thomas hadn't told her—so why on earth was she acting so strangely?

Then her eyes raised slowly, and he heard her catch her breath when she noticed the ugly bruise at his eye. Her mouth fell open as she stated breathlessly, "But *you* had a talk with him about it."

"Yes."

She bit her bottom lip, her concern for him warming his chest. "He hit you?"

"*Oh* yes." He crooked a chagrined brow.

"I'm so sorry."

With an expression of concern darkening her face, she

began to reach a trembling hand toward the bruise, then stopped suddenly and pulled back. As if she'd momentarily forgotten herself. Or was afraid of being burned.

She cleared her throat, her gaze returning to the floor, but not before he saw a flash of pain in her eyes. And guilt. The niggling voice inside his head that she wasn't behaving like herself grew louder.

"Have you seen him yet today?" She nervously twisted her hand in her skirt to prevent herself from reaching for him again. "I'm certain he'll apologize."

He drew a deep breath, determined to ignore whatever was upsetting her—for now—and get through the proposal. Then, once he was certain of his place in her life, he would take her away from here and whatever had happened to make her so nervous, so...pained. "I'm not here to see Thomas." His gut flip-flopped with fresh nervousness. *Dear Lord*—he was about to propose, something he'd never thought he'd do. "I'm here to see you."

"Oh?" She'd forced a casual lightness into her voice, but nothing about the nervous way she stood there, trembling and pale, was at all casual. "I'm fine. A good night's sleep and some of Cook's delicious food did me wonders."

His eyes narrowed, the bewilderment and nervousness pulsing through him turning to irritation. She was lying. Again.

"You were right." She forced an unsteady smile. "Being home with my family is where I belong."

Good Lord, was she lying! But why?

He took a slow step toward her, tamping down his growing frustration. "I came to a decision yesterday," he told her calmly, despite the hard tattoo of his pulse, "and I wanted to speak with you about it."

She shifted away to move behind a chair, placing the

piece of furniture between them as if she were afraid he might pounce on her. He smiled at that, knowing he just might.

"I'm glad you came by." Yet her voice trembled with anything but gladness at seeing him. "I never had the chance to properly thank you for—"

"Emily," he interrupted quietly. The time for games was over. "Marry me."

Her wide eyes flew up to his, so full of raw emotion in their blue depths that he caught his breath. For a moment, all she did was stare back, her lips parted in stunned disbelief, her breathing coming in shallow, little pants... Then she began to shake, so hard he feared she might fall to the floor.

"Darling, sit." In a single stride, he closed the distance to her and took her arm to help her sink down onto the chair. Then he knelt beside her and took both her hands in his. Lord, how she shook! Grinning up at her, he raised her trembling hands to his lips and kissed them. "Stunned you, did I?"

"More than you know," she breathed, so softly he barely heard her.

He chuckled. Her eyes glistened, and his chest tugged at the sight of her tears. At least this time, they were tears of happiness.

She desperately searched his face. "Why?" She choked out the words in breathless astonishment. "Why would you want to marry me?"

He reached inside his jacket—dear God, his own hands were shaking now!—and withdrew the ring box. "I swore to protect you and the baby, and that's exactly what I plan to do."

She remained perfectly still and silent as he opened the box and slipped onto her finger the sapphire and diamond ring he'd purchased because the stone was the same color as her eyes. Her hand trembled even more as she stared down at it, as if she couldn't believe it was real.

"Marry me, brat," he repeated, his own voice catching on the words as a knot tightened in his throat. "Make an honest man of me."

Instead of laughing at his teasing words as he'd hoped, she soberly shook her head. "But—but you were going to Spain—your promotion—"

"I'm going to decline it." Even now, the decision tore at him. It was what he'd been working for since that day he left the orphanage when he was ten and set out to gnaw and claw his way into a better life. But he knew this choice was the right one. Because he would now have Emily. "You were right, brat. I can't protect you all the way from Spain." Hell, he couldn't protect her from the other side of Mayfair. Which is why he needed to marry her, so he could keep her and the baby close.

"Is that why, then?" she whispered, her eyes never leaving the ring on her finger. "The reason you want to marry me—only to protect me?"

His smile faded. "I think it's a damned good reason." Had she really expected love? Admitting he loved her was certainly not one of the speeches he'd practiced last night. He'd barely gotten used to the idea of getting married. To throw love into the mix ... *Good Lord.* Yet he drew a deep breath, held it a moment, and admitted, "Emily, I lo—"

"No!" She shook her head and yanked the ring off her hand with fingers shaking so violently he wondered if she might drop it. She shoved it back at him. "I won't, Grey. I won't marry you!"

Her words stabbed like a knife into his heart. He stared at her, his breath gone from his lungs, utterly bewildered.

During their time together, he'd seen her affection for him—he *knew* it! No woman could fake the caring with which she touched him, the vulnerability when she gave herself to him so tenderly, or the passion when she seized her pleasure from him. Two days ago, lying in the bed still warm from their lovemaking, the little minx had wanted to marry him, he'd been certain of it.

But now…

"Emily." Her whispered name was filled with pain and uncertainty.

His hand closed over hers as she pushed the ring against his chest, to keep her fingers wrapped securely around it. Because if she gave it back—*Christ!*

Each beat of his heart pounded with the grim force of a death knell. Her rejection left him just as stunned as she had been when he'd proposed, just as shaken with disbelief. And filled with confusion. The world had tilted beneath him until he no longer knew which way was up.

He shook his head, not wanting to believe… "Don't you want to be with me?"

She stilled, and the anguished pain in her eyes answered truthfully even as she lied, "No, Grey—no, I don't."

"Why the hell not?" he growled. He was angry— *furious!*—that she'd lie to him now, of all times, and the burning anger mixed with the pain of rejection in his chest. "I care about you, Emily, more than you know. Enough that I am willing to lay down my life to protect you and the baby."

She shook her head. "That isn't—"

"Then what is it?" he demanded.

When she didn't answer, he cupped her face in his free hand. She closed her eyes as if his touch pained her. The sinking feeling seeped through him that she was once again keeping secrets from him. And that this secret might just destroy him.

"We're good together, brat," he murmured, touching his lips to hers and feeling her inhale jerkily. "So very, *very* good...and not just intimately, you know that." He kissed her again. If she wouldn't confess the truth on her own, then he'd seduce it from her if he had to, one torturous kiss at a time. He nibbled at the corner of her mouth, and his tongue slid over the seam of her lips to coax her to open to him. "I've never met another woman like you."

When she parted her lips hesitantly beneath his soft cajoling, he swept his tongue tenderly inside, increasing the intimacy of the kiss until she trembled, until the hand at his chest stopped pushing him away and instead clung to him. A pang of victory pulsed through him, followed by an immense wave of relief. A heavy sigh heaved from him. She was his...*finally*.

"If I had known five years ago the woman you would become," he whispered as he swept his mouth along her jaw to her ear, "I never would have let you go. Not even then." He smiled against her ear as she shivered from the soft flick of his tongue against her earlobe. "Although my career would have definitely suffered." He laughed at himself as he took her earlobe between his teeth and sucked gently. At the shivering response he elicited from her, warmth blossomed in his chest. The warmth of possession. "With you to distract me, I never would have become a major."

She froze, her body stiffening against his with a catch of her breath. Then she shifted away. He leaned in, following her like the pull of a magnet, but she turned her head and pushed at his chest once more. Hard enough this time that she slid out from underneath him and out of the chair, putting half the room between them before his surprised mind thought to reach for her.

He looked down at his palm in utter bewilderment. A fresh wound ripped through his chest, and he flinched with pain. In his hand, she'd left the ring.

"You're wrong about us, Grey," she told him, shaking her head adamantly. "What we shared was amazing. You made me feel so feminine, desirable...," she admitted in a whisper. "You made me feel wanted."

His eyes narrowed in white-hot anger as the niggling voice warning inside his head turned into a scream. This wasn't a list of the reasons for why she wanted him; it was a rationale for rejection.

"But we're not the same people we were five years ago. You have your career, your future plans—" She choked, and he thought he heard a sob in her voice. "We're from different worlds."

His heart stopped, and in that moment's tiny death, he prayed he hadn't heard her correctly. Surely, she didn't mean...But she did. He wasn't stupid enough to lie to himself. And when his heart started again, the pain of it stole his breath away.

He knew this woman better than anyone else in the world, yet for Emily to be so cruel as to say something like that, and directly to his face—the warmth inside him vanished instantly, replaced by an icy bitterness.

"Please understand. I have to think of my baby now." Her hands slid down to her belly, but her eyes never lifted to meet his. "And no matter how much we care for each other, no matter if there's love—" Another rasping choke as the words caught in her throat, another sob. She drew a deep breath and hurried on. "If we marry, you can't protect me and my child, not from society. I'll be cut direct at every opportunity, whispered and gossiped about in front of my face, no longer welcome anywhere in Mayfair . . . I've seen it happen to women for indiscretions far less serious than the lo—than the closeness you and I shared."

Love. She was going to say *love.* His chest burned with betrayal, with the same pain as if she'd slapped him.

She shook her head. "I can't allow that to happen, not when my baby's future is so important."

His eyes hardened on her. "So that's it?" he drawled resentfully, his hands fisted at his sides to keep from shaking her. "You want me to believe that you're refusing marriage so that you can keep waltzing at balls."

A blush of guilt colored her otherwise pale face. "This isn't as inconsequential as you make it out to be."

"Damn you," he said softly.

A soft gasp tore from her. "Grey!"

"Damn you for lying to me again." He saw her flinch beneath his words— *Good.* She deserved to know the piercing pain she'd sent spiraling through him. "Even now, after all we've been through together."

She swallowed. Hard enough that he could see the undulation of her throat even from so far away. "I-I'm not—"

"I know you, brat." He took slow steps toward her, more to keep his own anger in check than from fear of chasing her away again. "You don't give a damn what society thinks of you."

Through tear-blurred eyes, she stared at him silently, her lips falling open—every inch of her so blatantly showing that she knew he'd caught her in her lie yet still desperately clinging to it. But the tears were real, and so was the anguish behind them. He'd come here, engagement ring in hand, because he wanted to protect her and stop her from ever crying again, only to end up putting her into tears himself. But he had no intention of leaving her un-protected, even if he had to toss her over his shoulder and drive away to Gretna Green.

"Why are you refusing me—the *real* reason?" he de-manded. He cupped her face in his hands so she couldn't retreat from him again. "What is it that you want? Tell me. I'll make it happen."

"I want you to do what you planned all along," she forced out through trembling lips, "what you told me you would do that first day in the carriage...love me and leave me."

His heart tore at the anguish he saw on her face. When he'd told her that, he'd believed it of himself. But she'd changed him, and he no longer wanted that life. What he wanted now was her. "I am not leaving you, do you under-stand? Not now, not ever."

"I want you to go to Spain."

"I am *not* leaving—"

"Just go!" she cried, tears streaming down her face. "Please, just leave!"

Pain surged through him, mixing with anger and rising betrayal. To blatantly lie to him once again, and to offer *that*, of all reasons, as her excuse— "I'm not going anywhere," he ground out through clenched teeth.

Her hand darted up to swipe at her eyes as she whispered, "Then I will."

Without a glance backward, she fled from the room.

* * *

Grey angrily slammed shut the front door of his rented town house, stopping his man Hulston in his tracks in the foyer as he scrambled to open the door for him.

"Major, you're back," Hulston said with flustered surprise, knowing the purpose of Grey's afternoon mission and having put much care into dressing him for it. "And so soon."

Muttering a string of curses, Grey yanked off his coat, hat, and gloves and shoved them all into Hulston's waiting arms. Then he slapped the ring box down on top of the lot of them. "Get rid of this!"

"Sir?" Hulston blinked in surprise, not daring to press for more explanation.

"And tell Mrs. Smith to take the night off," Grey ordered, stalking toward the stairs. "I'm going out for dinner."

"But, sir—"

"And then I plan on spending the rest of the night at the clubs."

"Which club?" Hulston's face reddened, even more flustered than before as he held the ring box at arm's length in a futile attempt to hand it back.

"Whichever one lets me through the door," he grumbled, the words too true to be amusing.

"But, sir!"

He snapped out another curse, this one aimed at Hulston's ancestry. "I don't care what you do with that ring. Pawn the goddamned thing and spend the money on drink and whores for all I—"

"Major, you have a visitor waiting," Hulston blurted out before Grey could interrupt him again. "I told her you wouldn't be back for hours, but she insisted."

Damnation! The last thing he wanted to deal with right now was a visitor, especially a female one. After this afternoon, he certainly wasn't in the mood for anything regarding women and had no other goal for the evening than getting blindingly drunk.

"I'm not receiving visitors." He headed up the stairs.

"And you can tell whoever is waiting that she can take her parasol and shove it up her—"

"Nathaniel."

The mature female voice stopped him in mid-step, his foot hovering above the stair. He knew before he turned around—

"Lady Henley," he said curtly but politely, facing her as she stood in the doorway to the drawing room.

The last person he wanted to see right now was the stern old woman from his youth. Emily had damned him to hell with her rejection, only now for the devil herself to appear in the flesh.

But with no other choice, he shoved down his anger and descended the stairs. He bowed stiffly to her. "Viscountess."

She nodded her head regally. "Major Grey."

He motioned toward the drawing room. She had always been inexplicably generous toward him, when the stiff-spined dowager was rarely kind to anyone outside her own family. He wouldn't insult that generosity by asking her to leave, even if at that moment he'd rather shoot himself than entertain a visitor. "Shall I ask Hulston to prepare tea for—"

"I shan't be here long enough for tea." Her old but sharp eyes swept over him critically, and he had the odd impression that she was sizing him up. Like an opponent before a fight. *Good.* He could use a fight right now, the anger over Emily's rejection still burning hot inside him.

With the help of her cane, which he suspected served more as a weapon than a walking support, she spun on her heel and charged into the drawing room.

He followed after, gritting his teeth. The *very* last person he wanted to see right now... when he wanted nothing more than to be making his way to the bottom of a whiskey bottle.

Not taking a seat—apparently, she didn't plan on staying

even long enough to bother with sitting—she stopped in the middle of the room and faced him, thumping her cane firmly against the floor.

"To what do I owe the pleasure, ma'am?" Although no pleasure rang in his voice as he ground out the question, getting right to the point. There was nothing to be gained in attempting polite conversation, not with her.

Her brow rose haughtily. The viscountess had always possessed an intimidating air, even when he first met her twenty years ago. Her crusty imperialness was one of the traits he'd liked best about her, and very few people had the arrogance—or bravery—to defy her. "Your name was mentioned at Lady Agnes Sinclair's garden party."

Well. *That* was a damned lie. Lady Agnes Sinclair was the spinster sister to the late Earl of St. James, aunt to the current earl, and if rumors could be believed, a particular favorite of Wellington's. No one who would have given a scoundrel like Grey a second thought. While he could imagine several scenarios in which his name might arise amid a group of society women, it certainly wouldn't have been at Lady Agnes's garden party. And certainly not in a context to which Lady Henley would have been privy.

"Was it?" He kept his face carefully blank, not giving a damn what those tea party biddies had said about him, yet he felt compelled to ask. Because she expected it. "In what context?"

"Oh, just the usual gossip." She dismissed that with a wave of her gloved hand, which confirmed the falsehood for him and frustrated him even more.

He folded his arms impatiently across his chest. God knew, with the way he was feeling right now, he might just throttle her if she didn't soon get to the reason for her visit. "And?"

"I remembered that you used to work in the stables at Henley Park. I wanted to see you again for myself, to discover with my own eyes what kind of man you had become."

Another lie. He knew from contacts within the War Office that the old woman had been keeping an eye on him since he left Henley Park for the Peninsula. *Odd.* Why would Lady Henley call on him at his home, then lie about her motives? She'd given him a job when he'd been starving and homeless, and later, she was the reason he was commissioned into the First Dragoons. He would always be grateful to her. But being grateful didn't mean he trusted her. Or wanted her nosing around in his life.

He'd had enough of lying society women today. His lips curled sardonically as he held his arms out from his sides, insolently putting himself on display for her. "Have you satisfied your curiosity, then, my lady?"

Ignoring his sarcasm, her eyes narrowed on his face. "You've been punched."

Reflexively, his hand went to his eye, bruised but no longer aching. "I have."

"Well, I certainly hope you deserved it."

He grimaced. "I did."

"And did you return the favor?" she demanded.

"No."

She *humph*ed with disappointment.

He inclined his head, his patience with her visit growing thin. "In the future, ma'am, I will endeavor to please you by pulping at every opportunity any man who disagrees with me."

"Impertinent," she scolded, yet he had the strangest feeling that she approved of his angry sentiment. With a lift of her chin, she pulled at the long sleeves of her old-fashioned dress and swiftly changed topics. "I was pleased to hear you were promoted to major. It was the least Arthur could do for you."

"Arthur?" *Good Lord*, the woman was frustrating!

"Wellesley." She blinked, visibly confused that he didn't know whom she meant. "Why, Wellington, of course."

"Of course," he echoed wryly, as if everyone referred to Wellington by his Christian name.

"And now you work for the War Office." A flicker of amused pride crossed her face, which stunned the hell out of him.

He answered warily, "Yes." *For now.* When Bathurst heard of his plans to marry Emily and decline Spain, he might not be employed there much longer. Wouldn't that just be the icing on this cake of a day? No wife *and* no more career.

"A fine life you've made for yourself for a stable boy."

"Thank you." *I think…* He didn't know whether to take her comment as a compliment or an insult. And at that moment, he was too damned frustrated to care which. He blew out an irritated sigh, no longer able to tamp down his impatience. "My lady, *why* are you—"

"Major Grey." Her steely eyes pinned him. "I have been told that you inquired around Trovesbury Village as to your parentage."

He drew up straight. So *this* was why the dowager deigned to pay him a visit.

But why should it matter to her if he'd written to the constable and to the old parish vicar, asking for any information they might have about a pregnant, unwed woman from nearly thirty years ago? Or that he'd bothered to look through the church's record books when he'd been in Surrey last winter? A wild-goose chase. And none of her business. He'd been curious, that was all, then dropped the matter and not given it a second thought.

Until now. *Now* he was surprised. "Why would you care—"

"You must stop this, Nathaniel." An order? A plea? Or a warning? He couldn't tell from the odd intensity in her voice, the firm resolve on her wrinkled face. "There is nothing there for you to find."

His eyes narrowed. He'd had enough today of society ladies telling him what his life should be. "You don't know that," he snapped.

"But I do. I had you fully investigated when you first arrived at Henley Park, just as I did all the servants employed there." Her gray brow rose slightly. "Your father was not a blacksmith. You were left on the doorstep of the parish vicarage when you were only days old, and the vicar gave you to the orphanage. The name of your mother remains unknown, as it always will."

He forced his face to remain impassive, but he couldn't help the unseen clenching of his jaw, the tightening in his chest as anger rose inside him. She knew—*she knew* about his past. And he suspected she knew a great deal more that she wasn't telling.

"Lady Henley," he growled, "if you know—"

"The past is dead, Nathaniel. Leave it alone." She hooked her cane over her arm. "You have made a good life for yourself, better than even I had hoped. There is no point in dredging up harm and heartache now."

Better than even I had hoped...Confusion surged through him. "Why the hell should you care?"

She didn't even blink at the biting profanity. Instead, her head raised indignantly, and for a fleeting moment, he had a glimpse of the strong woman she must have been in her youth, the woman who ran Henley Park without any help from her philandering husband and eldest son. The woman who still made even the most imposing gentleman quake in his boots and most likely would have referred to the Prince Regent as Little Georgie if His Royal Highness had somehow entered the conversation. A more formidable opponent he'd rarely met.

But he'd already lost one battle today with a willful woman, and he sure as hell didn't plan on losing another.

"Because Henley Park *is* Trovesbury Village," she announced. "Everyone who lives there either works at the main house or possesses a tenancy. Asking questions will only raise speculation, and I will not tolerate rumors of illegitimacy attached to Henley."

Illegitimacy? Anger flared through him. After Emily's lie this afternoon that he wasn't good enough for her, he had no patience left for anyone implying that he'd overstepped his station. His eyes narrowed icily. "I *never* attached—"

"Let me be clear." Her chin raised impossibly higher, her eyes sharp. "I have always held a special affection for you, Nathaniel, and I have always wanted the best for you, including using my influence to make your way easier."

He glared at her, not knowing what to say to that. Not knowing whether he should thank her or toss her out on her bony, aristocratic ass.

"But I will not let anyone ruin my family's name and reputation by unleashing spurious gossip. Not even you, Nathaniel."

He forced through clenched teeth, "I am *not* unleashing—"

She slammed her cane against the floor. "The Henley family name is unsullied, and I intend to keep it that way until my last breath!" Spinning on her heel, she stomped from the room, pausing in the doorway to glance back at him with a final warning. "Leave the past alone, and be happy with what you have."

He stared daggers after her, hearing the thump of her cane into the foyer and out the front door as Hulston scurried to open it.

What the *hell* was that about? He let loose a curse that would have sent the dowager's head spinning. One that did, in fact, make Hulston gasp in the hallway.

He stormed from the drawing room and charged up the stairs three at a time. Blasted aristocrats and their pretentiousness! Damn their arrogance! And for what reason were they special, except to be squeezed from the right woman's womb in the right birth order? Wealth and position unearned. Wholly undeserved. Yet thinking they had the right to reign over everyone else, bending them to their will.

He tore at the buttons of his waistcoat, ripping away two as he hurriedly peeled it off and then set to removing his shirt. The viscountess had always been generous to him. But he'd be damned before he allowed anyone to hold his life hostage, to tell him what he could or could not have.

Including Emily.

She *would* marry him, and he *would* protect her. No matter what he had to do to convince her, no matter how long it took, he wasn't giving up without a fight.

CHAPTER TWELVE

June 1816
Three Months Later

Reynard Crenshaw raised the teacup to his lips. "I must say, I was quite surprised by recent events."

So was I, Emily thought wryly, balancing her own untasted cup of tea on her knees as she sat across from him in the drawing room of Chatham House. Although shocked and terrified would have been a more accurate description. Even now, eight months pregnant, she wasn't used to the idea that she might be carrying a marquess.

As if reading her daughter's worried mind, her mother reached a hand across the settee and squeezed her elbow reassuringly. But the gesture did little to comfort her.

Emily hadn't wanted to attend tea with Mr. Crenshaw, who was Andrew's second cousin and for now the heir presumptive to the late Marquess of Dunwich. The last thing she wanted to do was dredge up bad memories of what happened at Snowden Hall or remind herself of how much danger she and her baby were still in, even though no additional attacks had been made since she arrived in London.

But her mother insisted, reminding her that she would need all the help and support she could get from the Crenshaws once her baby was born, especially if it was a boy.

Although, truly, she found the man surprisingly pleasant, given the awkward circumstances.

"I am only a banker," he explained unassumingly, a faint smile of self-deprecation on his lips. "I find all this a bit overwhelming."

Emily couldn't help but smile faintly at that, because she'd been just as overwhelmed herself. And certainly, he'd led a quiet existence until he was notified seven months ago that Andrew Crenshaw was dead and that his entire life would be changing forever, only to be told again when she arrived in London that an unborn baby might now stand between him and the inheritance.

"And so," he continued, "I hope that you will excuse any confusion or misunderstanding on my part as we go forward."

Her mother smiled. "Only if you excuse any from us."

He chuckled softly at that, and Emily found herself liking him a great deal, this distinguished man in his late forties, with gray at his temples and a humble bearing. "I very much doubt I will have to do so, Your Grace."

Despite having a future as uncertain as Emily's, he gave no impression of malice toward her, just as she saw nothing in him to suspect he was responsible for Andrew's murder or the attack against her and Grey.

His son Harold, however, was harder to read. The young man sat quietly at the side of the room and spent most of the afternoon staring out the window. Bored.

An only son in his last year at Cambridge, Harold had yet to determine a career for himself. A few questions asked by her mother at the beginning of the tea to make him feel welcome revealed that he was not interested in a military commission nor a living in the Church. Nor did he seem thrilled to pursue banking with his father, which appeared to be the only choice left to him should Reynard not inherit.

Overall, he appeared sullen and distant, resentful of having to attend the tea instead of spending the day with friends on St. James's Street, and Emily had been relieved when he withdrew to the side of the room to be by himself.

"And now, Lady Emily—" Reynard sent her a warm, friendly smile and pulled her attention back from his son. "We wait for your baby to arrive. In the meantime, I shall enjoy getting to know you and your family better."

"Yes," her mother agreed with a soft sigh of relief, her shoulders relaxing slightly to hear that. "After all, there is no reason we cannot be amicable, whatever should follow."

Whatever should follow...Her mother meant contesting the inheritance should she deliver a boy. Even now her mother worried over securing her daughter's future. Emily looked away, embarrassed—

And caught Harold staring at her coldly. Then he turned back toward the window, once again bored with the conversation.

"I agree, Your Grace." Reynard set his cup aside. "I want to assure you, Lady Emily, that I will not petition the Privileges for the title should you have a son. No good would come of it."

"That is very kind of you." Her mother relaxed, visibly glad not to have a fight on her hands. "Isn't it, Emily?"

"Yes," she agreed, although she was more relieved at having even this small bit of certainty regarding her baby's birth than at any concern over titles or fortunes. "Very kind."

A prickle tingled at the back of her neck. She looked up,

and this time when she caught Harold's gaze on her, his eyes narrowed icily. And this time, he didn't turn away.

"Further, Lady Emily," Reynard continued, once more drawing her attention back, "if the child is a girl and the inheritance does come to me, I shall provide her an ample allowance for a comfortable living, tuition for a good education, and eventually a dowry."

Emily blinked in surprise at the man's unexpected kindness. "That is very generous of you, Mr. Crenshaw."

"Indeed," her mother interjected, nearly as surprised as Emily.

"But—" Emily frowned, noticing this time how Harold's cold gaze pinned on his father. "Why would you do such a thing? You're under no obligation."

"You and your child are family." He smiled gently at her. "Now, with Andrew's passing, your family should be even more dedicated to helping you."

"Thank you," she whispered, her throat tightening with emotion.

He rose to his feet. "It's time for Harold and me to take our leave. Thank you for a most enjoyable tea, Your Grace." Reynard bowed to her mother, then to Emily. At his father's signal, Harold stood and sketched a single, shallow bow in her direction that seemed to Emily more mocking than polite. "And my gratitude to you as well, Lady Emily, for a most pleasant afternoon. I hope we shall see each other again soon."

Easing herself belly-first onto her feet as gracefully as possible, Emily smiled genuinely. "I very much look forward to it."

"Shall I walk you out, Mr. Crenshaw?" her mother asked.

"Thank you, Your Grace." He offered his arm to her.

When the two men and her mother exited the drawing

room, Emily exhaled a heavy sigh of relief that all had gone well, and she reached for the bell pull to summon Jensen to clear away the tea things. Then she began to pace restlessly as she often did of late, her hand going to her round belly.

And it had gotten quite round, in fact, during the past three months since she'd arrived in London. The small bump that had been barely visible at five months even when she was naked had blossomed. No—*blossom* implied something delicate, like a flower. This was...

Good Lord, she felt as big as a house!

Oh, she wasn't, of course, and Yardley, who had arrived in London two days after her and Grey, commented frequently that she should have been much larger, in fact. That she was carrying small. But to Emily, all the changes to her body, the restlessness, and mood swings only magnified one hundredfold as she grew closer to her confinement, and she simply couldn't imagine being even bigger.

Pausing in her pacing, she forced herself to breathe, trying to ease her racing heart. *Smothered*—that's how she felt. Which was most likely why she felt the restless need to move, because if she moved, then she didn't feel so oppressed by the news of her pregnancy, which had sped through London society like a storm, and by the inundation of callers who wanted to see for themselves if the rumors were true. Society matrons, curious old fops, giggling cakes of young ladies—they'd descended upon her like locusts since her return. Worst of all were those old acquaintances she hadn't seen in years who suddenly wanted to strike up new and dear friendships, not one of whom she trusted. After all, Andrew knew the person who had murdered him. The murderer might very well be in London with her now, someone who had even been invited inside her home.

Nor did she like leaving the house these days, which

only compounded the smothering oppression weighing upon her shoulders. The bigger her belly grew, the more aware she became of the attention people paid her. And the more vulnerable she felt. Even during something as simple as a walk through Hyde Park, she didn't feel safe unless she had Thomas at her side, because even now she still worried that someone would try to hurt her baby.

Then came the men from the Committee for Privileges. Wanting to assess her situation themselves, they set her down in the library and subjected her to all sorts of indelicate and prying questions about her baby, her marriage, her marital relations...until she'd been beside herself with mortification. Until Thomas nearly threw them out of the house himself.

Thank God for Thomas. What would she have done without him? Although she often wondered who was helping whom recover from the ordeals of the past few months.

"My lady." Jensen bowed his head to her as he entered the room.

Taking a deep breath, she composed herself quickly and forced a smile, as if she hadn't a care in the world. "Jensen."

"The afternoon post, ma'am." He held a silver salver toward her with yet another letter in Grey's familiar handwriting.

Her chest tightened with anguished frustration. Oh, *why* wouldn't the blasted man simply leave her alone?

He hadn't gone to Spain as she'd asked. Oh no—he'd remained right in London, devil take him. And he'd refused to leave her alone. Nearly every day during the past three months, he'd sent flowers and gifts she was forced to return and written notes she refused to answer. Worse, several times each week, he arrived at Chatham House not to visit with Thomas but to ask for her, only to force her to refuse to see him. It was a bittersweet torture, as if he could make her change her mind by simply wearing her down. The only concession she allowed herself was to keep one rose from every bouquet before she returned it, knowing he would never notice that small keepsake missing among the dozens he sent her.

But she couldn't see him. If she saw him, she'd beg to be held, and if he held her—

She pressed the heel of her hand against her chest. *Dear God*, how it hurt!

Even during the ride from Yorkshire, even as she lay in his arms that first night, she knew she'd have to give him up when they reached London. But she'd never imagined the pain would be this wretched. Or that she'd not only have to let him go but be forced to drive him away by making up that horrible excuse that she believed him not good enough for her. Oh, the furthest thing from the truth! Yet she would gladly let him believe the worst of her, taking the full brunt of his anger if it meant securing his future.

And given the choice, she'd rather he hate her now than later, when he realized all he'd lost by marrying her.

"Ma'am?" Jensen prompted gently. Worry darkened his brow.

"Thank you," she whispered. Drawing a deep breath of resolve, she took the letter and placed it onto the tea table, not having the strength to read it now. Later, when she could lock herself into her room and cry over it, just as she'd done with the others . . . Her shoulders sagged heavily, exhausted. She rubbed at her forehead as a sharp pain throbbed behind her eyes.

"Are you all right, ma'am?" Jensen frowned. "Should I send for Yardley?"

She smiled weakly, touched by Jensen's concern. "No need. I'm only a little tired."

Worry crossed his gray brow, but he let the matter drop. "You also have a caller, ma'am."

"A caller?" *Grey*. Again. Her chest sank, her fatigue growing to the point of tears. Sweet heavens, how much more of this was she expected to bear? She didn't know which one of them would survive the longest in this standoff of wills they'd entered.

She sighed and issued the same order she'd given nearly every day for the past three months. "Please tell Major Grey that I'm not receiving callers."

"Apologies, ma'am, but it's Her Grace, the Duchess of Strathmore."

Kate! Emily smiled. For the first time that day, her spirits lifted, and the weight eased from her shoulders. "Please show Her Grace upstairs."

He nodded and retreated from the room.

Katherine Westover, Duchess of Strathmore, had been the first visitor to Chatham House after Emily arrived in London. Although Kate and her husband, Edward, were there to call on Thomas, the redheaded duchess with the welcoming smile and bright green eyes greeted her warmly, and the two had become fast friends. Of course, it helped that they were both with child. Kate was three months behind, but they'd bonded over their mutual pregnancies, and Emily found Kate's advice about babies, her friendship, and her loyalty to be a godsend. Just as she'd come to admire the duke. From the way he doted on his wife, Edward dearly loved her, and Emily couldn't help the niggling envy inside her whenever she saw the couple together. It was the same loving marriage she'd wanted with Grey but now could never have.

"Emily!" Kate Westover glided into the room, waving away Jensen's attempt to announce her. She took Emily's hands and squeezed them warmly as she leaned in to kiss her cheek, but when Emily pulled back, the young duchess frowned. "Are you feeling all right?"

"I'm fine," she assured her. "Just a little tired, that's all."

But her assurance didn't lessen Kate's concern. "I should go and let you rest—"

"No! Please stay." Her hands tightened on Kate's as she led her toward the settee, as if to physically stop her from leaving if need be. Kate had no idea how much she needed this visit. "Talking with you will raise my spirits more than anything else."

"All right," Kate agreed, but the dubious look on her face told Emily she wasn't convinced. "Perhaps for just a short stay, then."

"Good." Relieved at having Kate to distract her from thoughts of Grey, Emily sent her an overly bright smile. "Have you seen Thomas this afternoon? He's almost completely recovered now. He'll be back to his normal life soon, I'm certain."

Kate hesitated, as if she didn't quite agree with Emily's optimistic prognosis, but then nodded. "He and Edward went for a ride in the park, leaving us ladies to our gossip." She reached into her reticule and withdrew a small jar. "I brought this for you. An herbal cream. Rub it over your belly twice a day, and it will help keep your skin firm and soft."

"Thank you." Emily's eyes glanced at Kate's own belly, which already showed quite roundly and twice as much as Emily had been at six months. "And how are you?"

"Every part of me is swollen and bloated, sickness has kept me locked in my room every morning until well past noon, and I am twice as huge as I was just a month ago." A glowing smile spread across her face as her hand reached to lovingly rub her belly. "And I've never been happier!"

Emily hugged her, despite the stab of envy in her chest. Kate had Edward to share in all the happiness of this wonderful time of her life, but Emily had lost the one man with whom she wanted to share it most.

"I keep warning Edward that I must be carrying twins— and girls!" Kate laughed, her eyes gleaming mischievously. "It would serve the colonel right to be surrounded by a houseful of women who won't be ordered about."

Emily forced a smile, while inside she was miserable. Edward was going to be a wonderful father, she had no doubt of that. But her baby would have no father, and that thought both saddened and worried her immeasurably.

"Emily, I'm concerned about you." With a troubled frown, Kate took both her hands and held them on the cushion between them.

She shook her head, doing her best to alleviate Kate's worries. "I'm fine, truly. I know I'm carrying small, but I promise to eat more. Cook and Yardley will make certain of it. And I'll be able to rest more because I'm refusing all social invitations now." She forced a smile. "Except for an occasional stroll through the park, I plan on doing nothing but resting, reading, and gorging myself on biscuits."

But Kate's frown only deepened. "I meant that you look so . . . sad."

At that, Emily averted her eyes. What a ninny she was! How silly to think she could fool Kate into believing she was happy when inside she was miserable.

Kate hesitated, then lowered her voice. "It's Major Grey, isn't it?"

Her tear-blurred eyes flew up to Kate's as her heart skipped painfully. "What do you know about Grey?"

"Edward and Thomas talk," she explained gently. "Don't let them fool you—those men are as bad as gossipy old hens when they get together." As Emily's eyes grew wide with mortification, Kate squeezed her hand reassuringly. "They're only worried about you, and about Grey. I don't know everything, and it's truly none of my business, but...well, apparently, the man's tied himself into knots over you. Edward claims he's never seen Grey so worked up over a woman before." Her eyes softened sympathetically. "And I don't think he's the only one who's suffering."

Emily stared down at her hands as a single tear slid down her cheek.

"Oh, Emily." Her face dark with sympathy, Kate pulled a handkerchief from her reticule and placed it into her hand. "If this is making you so miserable, why did you refuse him?"

She dabbed at her eyes with the handkerchief and launched into the same practiced speech she'd given to Thomas. "Because I'm only now finding my way back into society, and if I married him, I would be cut. I don't want that, not for me nor my child, especially since he's going to be born a marquess. Life will be hard enough for him. He doesn't need any more problems haunting him."

With an excited thrill lighting her eyes, Kate beamed at her and glanced down at her belly. "You think it's going to be a boy, then?"

"I know so." Emily blew out a long-suffering sigh as the baby moved and a sharp kick punched into her ribs. Only a man could cause her this much trouble while yet to be born.

"Grey would never do anything to hurt you, Emily, you know that. He'll protect your child—"

"I know," she whispered, once more glancing away. Lying to Kate was as unbearable as lying to Grey and Thomas. "But I have Thomas now. I don't need his protection any longer."

"Maybe it's not only protection. Maybe…Grey loves you."

Emily shook her head as her chest ached with fresh anguish. Grey wanted to marry her because he wanted to protect her, because of his friendship with Thomas, because of the intimacies they'd shared on the journey…A dozen reasons, except love.

"You need to speak to him, Emily," Kate urged. "Give him another chance."

But what was there to say? She knew the desolation and suffering that came when the man she wanted to love her only ended up resenting her, and she would *never* go through that again. Of course, Grey would claim he'd never do that. He might even believe himself that he'd be able to give up his work…but she knew the truth. What kind of future could they possibly have once he realized how much he missed the excitement of his bachelor life?

"No," she said firmly, wiping away the last of her tears. "I refused him. I won't change my mind."

Kate shook her head. "You two cannot go on like this. It's not good for him, and it's certainly not good for you or the baby."

"That's why I told him to leave for Spain, to go on with his plans." But the frustrating man had refused to budge, devil take him! And as long as he lingered in London, he kept the wounds to her heart fresh and raw. Because she still loved him. And always would.

Kate squeezed her hand. "Let me ask Edward to intercede with Grey—"

"No, please!" Kate was trying to help, and Emily loved her for it, but her involvement would only make things worse. "If Grey thought you were meddling— No, Kate, I won't put you into the middle of this."

"All right, I won't meddle," Kate promised reluctantly, although when she bit her lip, Emily would have sworn she looked...guilty. "However, I won't let you stay all miserable like this, either. Come shopping with me this afternoon," she implored with exaggerated enthusiasm that Emily knew was only for her sake. "An excursion outside will do us both good. Let's go to Bond Street and buy a new bonnet or two. Or six!"

Emily hesitated. "I don't think—"

"Please. Why waste a perfectly lovely afternoon by staying cooped up inside?" Kate squeezed her hands, concern falling over her face. "For me?"

With a sigh, Emily agreed.

An hour later, the two women walked arm in arm along Bond Street, gazing through the shop windows at the displays and taking in all the sights and sounds of the busy street. Emily had to admit that this was a wonderful idea. Certainly the walk was good for her legs, even if she managed less of a walk than a waddle, and the air and sunshine lifted her spirits.

In her two years away, she'd forgotten how much fun it could be to simply meander along the street and peek into shop windows to see all the new fabrics and fashions, the display of shoes and boots at the cobbler's shop, even the rows of jars at the tobacconist. And none of what was shown in the windows could compare to the sight of the dandies strolling in their finery, the flamboyant colors and patterns of their waistcoats, and the arrogance with which they sneered at the world through their monocles.

She suppressed a giggle. Thank God Grey wasn't one of those!

"Oh, look at that!" Kate pointed to a bonnet displayed in the window of a milliner's shop and drew Emily's attention.

Bright red and orange ostrich feathers streamed into the air like poufs of flames over the bonnet's purple brim, decorated with yellow spangles. "Isn't it interesting?"

"Very." She slid a sly glance sideways at her dear friend. "But I know you, Kate Westover, and you couldn't care a fig about hats."

Kate flashed her a brilliant smile and linked her arm through hers, then started them slowly down the street again. "True," she conceded, "but a bonnet like *that*—that's not just a hat. That's a force of nature!"

Emily gave a bubble of laughter. She appreciated beyond measure Kate's attempts to distract her with shopping, because so far, the distraction had been working. She was enjoying herself today more than she had in the past three months.

"You should buy that hat," Kate urged.

"Me?" she squeaked, appalled. "That hat with this belly? Goodness, I'd look like the ostrich egg beneath the nesting feathers!"

"You're beautiful, Emily," Kate chastised. Then she added gently, "And Grey loves you just as you are."

She shook her head sadly. "He's never said so."

"Perhaps not. But when I confronted him, he didn't deny it."

"Kate!" Emily halted in her steps with a gasp, mortified. "You didn't!"

"I promised no meddling," the duchess clarified. "I didn't swear off direct confrontations."

Emily groaned but kept her eyes straight ahead, despite the pain of disappointment thumping in her chest with each heartbeat. "Is that where I'm supposed to pin my hopes, then? That he didn't deny he loves me?"

Kate squeezed her arm. "With these men of ours,

Emily, that's as good as saying it." She added more softly, "For now."

They walked on, with Kate pointing out various items in the windows and Emily feigning interest, her troubled mind once more focused on Grey.

"Look!" Kate gestured at the window, her first show of genuine excitement at anything in the storefronts. "The bookshop. Let's linger a bit, shall we?"

"So we've found your weakness." Emily smiled knowingly and let Kate lead her to the window to see the displayed books.

"An addiction," she sighed deeply. "I am an unapologetic bluestocking, I'm afraid, especially when it comes to science books. I devoured the library at Hartsfield Park last winter." She frowned at the passing shoppers around them and muttered beneath her breath, "Of course, Grey wouldn't pick this store."

Emily frowned, a warning prickling at the backs of her knees. "What do you mean?"

"I promised no meddling," she repeated, a self-pleased smile at her lips. "I never promised not to arrange meetings that might force you two to talk."

"Oh, you didn't!" Emily stared at her, horrified, as she realized why Kate was so insistent about going shopping this afternoon.

Kate slid her a hard, knowing look. "Are you still unwilling to receive him at Chatham House?"

Emily began to answer, then closed her mouth. She couldn't deny it.

"Then I had no choice, for both your sakes. And just to talk, that's all. Whatever happens is completely between you two." Kate lowered her voice, as secretively as if she were carrying out an espionage mission for the War Office.

"We are to pretend to shop, then we'll accidentally run into Grey in front of one of the stores. Since he and Edward are old friends, he'll have a ready-made excuse to stop us to chat. Anyone watching will think nothing of the meeting. At just the right moment, I'll notice a hat in a window, shoes, ribbons—a book, if I'm lucky—and wander off to look at it, far enough away that you two can have a moment of privacy." She sighed the sigh of a thwarted romantic. "It's not ideal, but short of kidnapping you to Strathmore House and risking the gossip of servants, it was the best I could arrange on such short notice."

"For someone who's sworn off meddling," Emily grumbled dryly, knowing she had no choice now unless she wanted to run fleeing back to the carriage, and she didn't think she could waddle quickly enough to escape, "you're certainly very good at it."

Instead of the laugh she expected, or even a scowl of pique, Kate's eyes softened sympathetically. "You are miserable without that man, Emily. And I know that feeling, because I was miserable without Edward. I only want you to be as happy as I am."

Her eyes stinging at her friend's concern, Emily squeezed Kate's hand. Nodding, unable to say anything around the knot in her throat, she looked away—and her heart stopped.

On the other side of the street, Grey sauntered slowly toward them. Dressed casually as if he'd planned nothing more for his day than a ride through the park, in his dusty boots and buckskin breeches, tan waistcoat, and maroon riding jacket, he stood out among the decorated dandies. A hawk among the peacocks. He tugged at the wrists of his leather riding gloves, the only outward sign that he was as nervous as she was about this wholly planned accidental meeting.

And he'd never looked more dashing.

Emily released Kate's arm and stepped toward the street so she could claim a better view of him as he approached, despite knowing that she should run. Her hands shook, a nervous trembling that soon spread to the rest of her, right down to her toes, and worsened with each stride he drew nearer. Dear God, what would she say to him? And he to her? Her heart raced as she fought to breathe. Could she get through this at all without throwing herself into his arms like a complete cake?

With an uneasy smile, more happy to see him again than she would ever admit, Emily stopped at the edge of the street and waited for him to look up and see her. Her eyes focused intently on him. He gave no outward sign that he knew she was there, yet his stride quickened, just barely, almost imperceptibly.

The thundering sound of pounding hooves exploded behind her. Angry male shouts and fearful female screams split the air. She turned—

A phaeton raced toward them down the street. Perched on his high seat, the driver flicked his whip mercilessly and sent the team veering directly at her.

"Look out!" she screamed. With a fierce shove, she pushed Kate away just as the phaeton bore down on them. The duchess staggered backward, missing being struck by mere inches.

But Emily was too close. The wheel snagged her skirt as the rig flew past, tangling her dress around the axle and yanking her off her feet. She spun in a circle, pulled back toward the crushing wheel. She heard the scream tear from her throat as she fell away, saw the ground rush toward her, felt the sharp pain as she hit the cobblestones—

Then everything went instantly still.

Her eyes closed. Muffled screams and shouts reverberated through the fuzzy whirling inside her head, and pain radiating from her bruised body. Then she felt hands gently stroking her face, strong arms lifting her...Through the darkness, she heard her name.

Her eyes fluttered open for a moment, just long enough to see Grey's terrified face.

Then she fainted away.

CHAPTER THIRTEEN

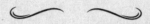

$\mathcal{L}$ess than an hour later, Grey bounded up the front steps of Chatham House and into the foyer.

"Where's Lady Emily?" he asked Jensen, glancing beyond the butler and down the hall.

Jensen's eyes flickered up the stairs. "If you'll wait in the drawing room, Major, I shall inquire if she is—"

"The hell I will," he snarled, and Jensen's face drained to white.

Emily was here, he knew it. He'd put her into the Strathmore carriage himself and barked out orders for the driver to bring her and the duchess directly here, then sent the tiger to fetch Dr. Brandon. He had no intention of being forced to wait in the drawing room for an hour, only to be turned away. Not this afternoon.

No—Emily was here, so was Thomas. And he wasn't leaving until he'd spoken to both of them.

"Grey." Thomas sauntered down the stairs, then dryly arched an eyebrow at the commotion he was making. "Please don't frighten the butler to death."

"Where's Emily?" Grey demanded, his chest tight with worry. "How is she?"

Thomas dismissed Jensen with a nod, and the butler scurried away gratefully. "She's upstairs with Kate Westover and Dr. Brandon right now." When Grey turned toward the stairs, Thomas grabbed his arm and stopped him. "She's fine. Join me for a drink."

"I don't want a damned drink," he bit out, yanking his arm free. What he wanted was to see Emily and find out for himself if she was truly all right, if she needed him. *Christ!* His heart pounded so hard with worry that each beat was like a sledgehammer to his chest.

"Good." Imperturbably, Thomas pushed him toward the drawing room off the foyer. "More for me, then."

Despite the desperate need in his gut to see Emily, Grey went grudgingly, knowing both that he wouldn't be let upstairs until her brother gave him permission and that Thomas was just well enough now to be able to stop him if he tried to force his way upstairs anyway.

Thomas poured two glasses of whiskey and handed one over, then flopped down onto the settee and kicked his boots onto the tea table. Grey sank onto the chair opposite him.

"Emily's fine. Just shaken up a bit and bruised," Thomas assured him, a sympathetic timbre underlying his voice. "She needs to rest, but I'll tell her you stopped by."

Grey took a swallow of whiskey. He was glad he hadn't refused the drink after all, especially now that it was clear Thomas had no intention of letting him anywhere near his sister this afternoon. "She told you what happened?"

"The duchess said there was an accident while they were shopping. A runaway phaeton. That Emily fell and fainted." He pinned Grey's gaze over the rim of the glass. "It wasn't an accident, though, was it?"

"No," he answered gravely, his throat tightening. "Someone tried to kill her."

Thomas's expression never changed, but Grey sensed him freeze. He had lived—and nearly died—with this man, and he knew him better than anyone else in the world, save Emily, well enough to know what emotions he felt even as he worked to hide them. And what he felt was a heartbeat of incredulousness, followed by a flash of white-hot anger. Grey knew that because he'd felt the same thing himself. The sight of the phaeton bearing down on her, that heart-stopping moment when the wheel struck her and sent her reeling to the ground, the sound of her scream slicing through him—and all he could do was look on helplessly. He'd never felt so powerless in his life.

He stared down at his hands. They shook so badly even now that the whiskey bounced in his glass.

"You were right about Andrew Crenshaw," Grey told him reluctantly. Emily should have been the one to tell Thomas this, but the time for keeping secrets was over. "The man was a bastard who left her a month after their wedding, to gamble and whore away her dowry. She lied to you—to everyone—putting up the appearance that her marriage was just fine."

Thomas's eyes flicked to Grey, landing hard on him. His face darkened as he tried to absorb all that Grey was telling him, all the secrets Emily had kept from him. Even Thomas's careful control wasn't enough to stop an expression of betrayal and hurt from flashing across his face, or prevent him from rubbing at his wrists in that nervous habit he'd developed since the shooting.

"And you think that perhaps Crenshaw got in over his head, owed too much money or cheated someone at cards?" Thomas asked quietly, his jaw clenched. He didn't mention Emily's lack of trust in him, and Grey knew he wouldn't.

Not until he spoke to Emily. "That whoever is doing this wants retribution?"

Grey shook his head. "Why attack Emily?" He looked down into his whiskey. "She believes that whoever killed Crenshaw is coming after her baby."

"She told me about the fire, all the incidents surrounding Andrew's death…" Thomas let loose a harsh curse of self-recrimination. "I thought it was someone within her household at Snowden Hall. I thought she'd be safe in London."

"I thought so, too." He frowned into his glass. "But the only one who knew about the baby was Yardley, and Emily trusts the woman with her life. She even offered to help Emily run away to Glasgow."

"You think Reynard Crenshaw is responsible, then?"

He looked hard at Thomas. "Yes."

But Thomas frowned at that. "Reynard has nothing against the baby. He's already stated that he won't challenge the inheritance if she has a son." He leaned forward, resting his elbows on his knees. "He didn't even know she was with child until she arrived in London."

Grey felt the familiar frustration rising inside him again. They were back at the beginning, with no answers and with Emily still in danger. He shoved himself to his feet and began to pace, unable any longer to sit still and do nothing. "Then who?"

Thomas shook his head silently as his eyes followed Grey back and forth across the room in his pacing.

"I'll find him and stop him, whoever he is. I've got Hedley investigating the phaeton driver, and I'm still hoping to hear something from my contacts in Yorkshire." But even as he said that, a frustrated powerlessness gripped him. He'd spent the past hour with Hedley questioning witnesses about the phaeton, and all the conflicting information came to nothing. So had all the leads from Yorkshire. "In the meantime, my men will keep guarding her. If she's right, then the attempts against her should cease with the birth. If it's a girl, they'll stop completely."

"If it's a boy," Thomas agreed gravely, "he inherits at birth. It would be too obvious, then, if someone attempted to murder him in order to inherit."

"And if it *is* someone after revenge for any of Crenshaw's debts"—Grey forced a casual shrug, doing his best to hide the fury he felt toward her dead husband—"then the inheritance will pay off whatever he owes, and there will be no reason to come after either of them anymore." God help the bastard if he did, because Grey would kill him before he let Emily or her baby be harmed. "I don't want her alone for a moment until the baby arrives."

Although if the damned stubborn woman had agreed to marry him by now, she wouldn't be alone.

"I'll make certain Yardley's with her," Thomas assured him.

Yardley, when it should have been him. The sting of fresh rejection coursed through him. "I'm going to check in with Hedley, do some more investigating," he informed Thomas as he moved toward the door. "Tell her I stopped by and that I'll be back." He shot Thomas a determined look. "And this time, she won't be able to avoid me."

"You know, a lesser man would have given up by now."

"Emily doesn't deserve a lesser man." Grey turned on his heel and stalked out the door.

* * *

"In my opinion," Dr. Brandon told Emily as he patted her hand, "you have some nasty bruises along your backside, my dear, but nothing more."

Emily gave a relieved sigh. She'd been terrified for her baby when she regained consciousness in the carriage as Kate rushed her back to Chatham House, the accident now little more than a blurry memory. And a throbbing bruise on her bottom.

Beside her on the bed, Kate Westover squeezed her arm reassuringly around Emily's shoulders. "No other injuries?"

"None that I see." Bushy gray brows lifted at Emily. "I think your backside took the brunt of the fall."

She grimaced painfully and rubbed at her hip. "I *know* so."

"And the baby?" a deep voice interjected from across the room.

Emily looked up at Thomas. He leaned back against the wall beside the open door, arms folded across his chest, his head lowered. Despite the lingering pain in his side, he'd carried her up the stairs from the carriage and gently laid her on the bed, leaving only when Kate shooed him out so that Dr. Brandon could examine her. And now he'd returned to his post, as immovable as a mountain.

Emily's throat tightened at the expression etched onto his face—one of worry and fear. His eyes fixed on the doctor. "Was the baby injured?"

"Not at all that I can assess," Dr. Brandon assured them as he closed his bag and lifted it from the bed. "But you should watch her closely for a few days."

"Yes, thank you, Dr. Brandon." Kate slid from the bed with a grateful smile and placed her hand on the physician's arm. "I'll walk you down."

Thomas nodded to the doctor as Kate escorted him from the room and closed the door behind them, keeping his gaze focused unmoving on his sister as she lay propped up against the pillows on the bed. "Are you truly all right, Emily?"

Where there should have been warmth inside her at his

concern, there was only unease. The little hairs on her arms stood on end, and she could feel a tension spring up between them as thick as water. Something had changed during the few minutes he'd been gone.

"Yes." She forced a nod.

He paused for a moment before informing her solemnly, "Grey stopped by."

"Oh?" She bit her lip in trepidation. "What did he want?"

"To see you, of course."

Her heart slammed hard against her ribs. Seeing him today had shocked her more than the accident. "Is he still here?"

"No." Thomas pushed himself away from the door and came slowly toward her. "He's gone to track down the driver of the phaeton."

Her breath choked as her nervousness turned to fear. "It wasn't an accident, was it?"

"No," he answered quietly.

Oh God, it was happening again! As she pressed the heel of her hand against her forehead, she felt the familiar fear stir inside her chest, the same fear Grey had once chased away by holding her in his arms. "Whoever killed Andrew and set the house on fire...He thinks—he thinks they're coming after me here?"

"We don't know that for certain," he tried to reassure her, but the grim expression darkening his face told her otherwise. "We'll know more soon. No need to worry."

No need to worry? She swallowed back a laugh at that. Oh, there was so much to worry about! But she put on a brave face for her brother, the same one he was showing for her, and nodded.

He sat down beside her on the bed, just as he did when they were little, and his eyes filled with emotion. "But Grey also told me what happened with your marriage."

Quick anger flashed through her. "He had *no* right to tell you—"

"Brat," he whispered pleadingly, unable to find his voice beneath the betrayal and hurt revealed on his face.

Cut by the pain she saw in him for both himself and her, tears of regret swelled up in her eyes. "I'm so sorry, Thomas," she choked out, barely above a whisper as the emotions overtook her. "Please...please forgive me."

With a sob, she fell into his arms and clung to him as she cried, and all the pain, guilt, and regret she'd been carrying inside her finally released. She'd dreaded this moment for so long, so afraid of what he would think of her when she finally told him the truth, how ashamed she would be to admit that she'd been so wrong about Andrew...but there was no recrimination in him, no blame. Only forgiveness.

He held her tightly, rocking her in his arms until her sobs died away into soft sniffs. When she finally stopped crying, he pulled back from her and looked down into her face.

"I love you, Emily." He cupped her face between his hands. "I'd do anything to help you, you know that."

She nodded, unable to speak through the emotions swirling within her.

"You can always count on me for help, brat, no matter what happens." Frowning down at her, he brushed away the last of her tears with his thumbs. "Don't ever hide from me again. I couldn't bear to lose you twice." He forced a crooked grin as he looked down at her big belly. "Or to be kept away from the bulge."

She smiled at him, all her doubts fleeing. Thomas was a wonderful brother, and he was going to be a terrific uncle. "Want to feel the baby?"

Sudden panic flashed through his eyes. "I—I don't—I mean—really?"

She laughed. Her heroic brother who had fought his way across the Peninsula was squeamish about this! She took his hand and laid it over her belly. "Can you feel him?" She smiled lovingly at him. "He's moving."

With his breath held, he gently pressed his palm against her. She stared up at him expectantly, waiting for him to feel…

There!—a movement inside her, a flutter beneath their hands. He gasped, his wide eyes flying up to hers.

The sensation came again, and he laughed with wonder. "Amazing," he murmured, his eyes shining.

"Isn't it, though?" she whispered, smiling down at her belly.

Finally, her dreams were coming true. She was going to be a mother and have the family she'd always wanted. She'd mended her rift with both Thomas and her parents now, making peace with her past and coming to understand them better than she ever had in her life. She'd even begun to draw and paint again, during the past few weeks creating some of the best pieces she'd ever made.

The only thing missing was Grey.

Her chest ached. Dear God, how much she missed him! She thought she'd be able to move on and mend her heart, but she hadn't realized until she saw him again today how much she still longed for him. And he hadn't given up, even after three months of her rejections. Perhaps—just *perhaps*—might he truly love her? Or if not love, then at least care for her enough not to regret marrying her if she accepted his proposal after all?

"Thomas?" she asked quietly, doubt niggling at her. If Grey could persist in his pursuit this long, in the face of consistent refusal…had she misread what truly mattered to him?

"Hmm?" Her brother's attention was still captivated by the baby's movements.

She lowered her voice. "What would you do if you had to give up your work with the War Office? If you couldn't be a spy anymore?"

He laughed as the baby kicked again. "My life would end."

* * *

Reynard Crenshaw strolled into the sitting room of his modest Holborn residence and greeted the unexpected visitor. "Major Grey, a pleasure to meet you."

"And you." Grey shook his hand, immediately struck by how affable he was. And nothing at all as he'd expect from a man willing to commit murder.

"I am rather surprised, however." A perplexed expression furrowed his brows as he gestured toward the chairs in front of the fireplace. "To what do I owe your visit this afternoon?"

Grey waved off his offer to sit. He didn't plan on staying long, nor did he have the patience to engage in pleasantries. Not when he was still too agitated over Emily, still too worried about her and damnably frustrated not to have been able to see her. "There was an accident today involving Lady Emily."

"An accident?" Crenshaw repeated, his bushy eyebrows shooting upward. "Was she injured?"

"She's unharmed." Grey's eyes narrowed as he watched the man's reaction closely, noting that he seemed truly surprised to hear the news and genuinely concerned about Emily. Not a trace of guilt showed on his face.

"And the baby?" he asked quickly.

"Also unharmed." Again, no guilty expression on the man's face, no nervous flicker of his eyes or tic of his facial muscles.

"Please." Crenshaw motioned again toward a chair and then took his own seat, looking aggrieved. "What happened?"

Reluctantly, Grey obliged and sat down, his forearms resting on his knees as he leaned forward, much too on edge to relax. "Someone tried to run her down on Bond Street. She stepped aside at the last moment but was knocked to the ground. Nothing more than bruises, thank God." Yet his heart pounded with fear and worry for her even now. Just as he was certain it always would. Grey leveled his gaze hard on Crenshaw. "But she could have been murdered."

"Murdered?" he echoed incredulously.

"As was her husband."

Crenshaw's face blanched, his lips falling open in stunned surprise. "Andrew? You—you think he was *murdered*?" When Grey nodded curtly, Crenshaw's mouth snapped shut. But the anger Grey expected didn't darken the man's face. Instead, he gazed at Grey with solemn indignation. "And that is why you are here, is it not? You believe I am responsible."

Grey accused, "You had motive. With Andrew Crenshaw dead, you were next in line to inherit Dunwich."

"Of which I was unaware until a full month after Andrew died," he informed him, bewildered annoyance lacing his voice. He shook his head. "I am a banker, Major, not a fortune teller. Neither am I a murderer. I did not want that young man dead."

"Someone did," Grey muttered. He clenched his hands to prevent them from shaking as he added, "And now they want Lady Emily dead."

Crenshaw paled further and leaned back in his chair, overwhelmed by all that Grey had just told him.

Judging from his guileless reaction and the genuine horror in his eyes that someone wanted to hurt Emily, Grey knew this man wasn't Andrew Crenshaw's murderer, nor was he capable of striking down a pregnant woman. The tension in his chest eased, but not the frustration.

Which meant he'd come to another dead end. *Damnation.*

Crenshaw shook his head, stunned. "Who would do such a horrible thing?"

"I don't know." But when he found the bastard, he'd make him pay for every harm he'd committed against Emily, every trace of fear he'd put into her sapphire eyes. Grey laced his fingers together and leaned forward. "I'd hoped that you might be able to tell me."

Crenshaw shook his head, bewildered.

"Did Andrew Crenshaw or your family have any enemies?" Grey pressed, unable to keep down his mounting frustration. "Anyone who would want to see him and his child dead from personal vengeance?"

"I wouldn't know," he answered earnestly, running a trembling hand through his graying hair. "I had not seen Andrew in years, not since he was at school in Winchester, then briefly and only once. I've always known about the other cousins in the family, those connected to the marquessate, but my father was a different line. We were"— he shrugged—"inconsequential to the title. I cannot imagine why anyone connected to our family would want to hurt either Andrew or Lady Emily."

His gut tightened. Without Crenshaw to provide any insight, he had no more leads to follow. But he'd be damned if all he did was sit back and wait for another attempt on Emily's life.

Grey rose to his feet and extended his hand. "Thank you for your time. If you think of anything—anything at all that might reveal more information—you can send for me at Chatham House. Chesney knows how to reach me."

"Of course, Major." He walked Grey to the front foyer, which was barely big enough for both men and the butler, who arrived with Grey's coat and hat. "Please give Lady Emily my regards."

"Certainly." Grey paused, hesitant to insult Crenshaw by bringing up the inheritance, yet Emily was certain it was the motive for her husband's murder and the attempts on her life. "She's convinced she's carrying a son."

Crenshaw's eyes softened knowingly. "I only hope that her baby is born healthy, Major."

So do I... If anything happened to the baby, Emily would never survive it. He trembled at the thought of how much love she carried for her child, even though it had yet to be born. And he would do everything in his power to make certain that baby arrived into her arms unharmed. "Chesney told me that you don't plan to contest the inheritance."

He confirmed that with a nod and a faint smile. "I was never meant to be the heir and certainly would not be now if not for a few cruel twists of fate. If she has a son, then so be it."

Grateful for the man's magnanimity, knowing it would make the coming months much easier for Emily, Grey shrugged into his coat. "Lady Emily is remaining at home now until her confinement. I'm certain she'd welcome visits from you." He paused, adding around the knot in his throat, "Family means everything to her."

"Of course. I would be honored to call on her." Crenshaw paused, his face saddening. "It pains me to think she might be in danger. How could anyone want to harm that sweet young woman?"

Pulling on his leather gloves, Grey answered with a voice so full of raw determination that it was little more than a low growl, "I intend to make certain no one has that opportunity again."

* * *

On the other side of the door connecting the sitting room to the dining room, Harold Crenshaw placed his ear near the crack and listened to the conversation between his father and the man who brought the woman back from Yorkshire. His hands clenched into tight fists at his sides.

So, the little bitch was convinced she was going to have a boy, was she? A little bastard to pop between his father and the title, to steal away his own future fortune.

He should have dealt with her in Yorkshire, just as he'd removed that peacock of a husband of hers. Killing him had been so easy, hardly any effort at all. All he'd had to do was approach Crenshaw while he was riding along a stretch of empty field, charm the man down from his horse by pretending his own horse had thrown a shoe—the same shoe he had ripped off himself only minutes before—and then, while Crenshaw was bent over and examining the horse's hoof, pick up a rock and bash in his head. He left him where he fell.

It wasn't until two months later that he found out she'd been bred, like some kennel bitch in heat. But he'd let himself be convinced that she'd disappear to Glasgow once her stomach grew grotesque with her spawn, that she was too frightened *not* to flee for her life.

And she should have been frightened. *Very* frightened.

Her husband was dead, but news of the baby had never been sent back to London. No one knew. All he had to do was wait for the old marquess to die and his father to inherit, and the frightened little bunny with her unborn litter would have hopped away to Scotland, to disappear without a peep. He'd only have to arrange for an accident or two every few months to keep her frightened enough to remain in hiding, and in a few years, even if she squeezed out a boy, no one would have believed the child to be her husband's if she tried to petition for the title. She'd have been labeled a whore, gotten with a bastard by rutting with some other man while her husband lived apart from her in York.

His father would have become a marquess, and when he died, the fortune and title would have all been his.

He'd planned it all so carefully. Everything had gone smoothly...until that damned footpad shot Chesney, and the major was sent to bring that woman back to London.

His plans were unraveling quickly now, with no time to lose. The bitch was due to whelp soon. A girl child would be completely forgotten, although he was furious at his father for pledging an allowance and dowry from money that should have been all his. But a son would ruin everything.

It was one thing to murder the baby while still in its womb; it would be far too suspicious to kill it after it was born, after having also murdered the father.

No—he had to make certain the baby was never born, and the only way to ensure that was to kill the mother. The driver he'd paid to run her down this afternoon ruined his last opportunity for a believable accident. Now he'd have to take matters into his own hands.

It was time to put an end to her once and for all.

CHAPTER FOURTEEN

$\mathcal{T}$hat night, unable to sleep, Emily sat in the chair in her room and stared into the fireplace at the dying fire and layer of coals that gave off little light and even less warmth. Around her, the house was dark and quiet, with her parents sleeping in their separate suites in the other wing and Thomas in his on the far end of the hall. Outside the house, the city was just as quiet, just as dark and still.

Her troubled thoughts returned to Grey. He was out there somewhere amid the shadowed streets and gaslights. Was he awake as well, too troubled to surrender to sleep? Or was he relieved now that Thomas would take over protecting her and he no longer had to be bothered with her, sleeping deeply without a thought of her? Or, heaven help her, was he even now lying in the arms of another woman? One who made no claims to him, who would never impinge upon his freedom or his future—

A shadow moved at her window.

Her heart stopped. She jerked up her head as a cold pang

of fear slithered down her spine. *Oh God!* Someone was there.

Scrambling up belly-first from the chair as fast as she could, she grabbed her hairbrush from the dressing table and held it up like a knife as the sash of her window jiggled and swung open with a creak. A dark figure slipped inside her room. As he turned to pull the window closed behind him, she raised the brush to throw it—

"Emily, it's me."

Grey. Her heart panged painfully, partially from thinking he was an intruder, partially from *him*.

She shook the hairbrush at him. "You can't be here," she pleaded angrily, careful to keep her voice low as she approached him. "I don't know how you got up here, but you—"

He grinned. "I lowered myself from the roof by a rope."

Her lips parted at that, stunned, and she stared at him incredulously. He'd risked his neck scaling down the house to sneak into her room? Her heart now pounded for a whole new reason.

But no matter how daring his entry, he had no right to be here.

"Then you can just leave the same way." She glowered at him. Arrogant, egotistical, stubborn...oh, the devil take him! Giving an irritated sigh, she placed her hands on her hips and turned toward the door. "And quickly. Before I call for Thomas—"

Grey's hand clamped over her mouth from behind, his lips at her ear. "I need to see you, brat." When she hesitated, his hand covered hers and tenderly squeezed her fingers. He slowly caressed up her arm, and goose bumps sprang across her skin. "Please."

His deep voice seeped into her back and straight through to her breasts. Her nipples tightened traitorously beneath her night rail, and she couldn't bring herself to step away from his warmth. She nodded, and his hand slid away from her mouth.

"What do you want?" she demanded, but her voice sounded not at all threatening as she let him take the hairbrush from her hand and set it on the vanity, most likely to keep her from brandishing it at him again.

"I wanted to make certain you were all right after this afternoon," he answered gently. Then he turned her to face him. "Are you all right?"

She swallowed hard. "You need to leave—"

"Emily." He brushed her hair over her shoulder, tenderly tucking a stray strand behind her ear, then repeated with grave concern, "Are you all right?" They both knew he wasn't referring to the accident.

Her chest sank. How was she supposed to answer that? If she told the truth, that her heart had shattered from having to reject his marriage proposal, he would only pity her. She couldn't bear that. And if she lied, he'd leave, and God help her but she didn't want him to go.

Exhaling slowly, she demanded, "Why are you really here, Grey?" She tried to move back, but he stepped forward, closing the distance between them and taking her shoulders in both his hands to keep her close. "You were here earlier. I'm certain Thomas told you that I wasn't harmed by the phaeton. As for the other..." She raised her hands to push at his chest, but instead of moving him away, her fickle hands clasped his lapels. "I was very clear with my refusal. There's nothing more to be said."

"There are volumes left unsaid between us," he drawled, lifting a disbelieving brow.

"No, you—"

"Damnation, brat!" His hands slid up to cup her face,

drawing her toward him even as he stepped her backward across the room. "I can't lose you. Don't you understand that?"

He kissed her, openmouthed, hard, and hungry, like a starving man wanting to devour her. She shuddered from the intensity of him even as she wrapped her arms around his neck and welcomed his kiss.

"I *won't* lose you," he promised, his words frustrated and fervent as his mouth slid away from her lips to caress along her jaw and down her neck.

"But I don't want to hurt you, Grey." Her fingertips dug into the hard muscles of his shoulders and back as she sought to pull him closer even as she knew she had to let him go. "And that's exactly what will happen if I marry you."

"How could you ever hurt me, Emily," he groaned as his tongue darted out to lick at the throbbing pulse at the base of her neck, "when being with you brings me such joy?"

She rolled her head to give his mouth access to her throat, then bit back the whimper of pleasure rising on her lips when he pulled loose the bow at the scooped neckline of her nightgown and pushed the material aside to trail his lips across her bare shoulder. Heat swirled through her and landed with a shiver between her thighs.

A soft shudder of arousal swept through her. It had been so long since she'd touched him and kissed him, so *very* long…How did she survive the past weeks without him? Dear God, how would she carry on when he left?

"Grey," she whispered pleadingly, unable to find the willpower to step away.

"Only you, Emily." His words tickled against her throat, her ear, her cheek as he swept his mouth back to capture her lips with an aching groan. "I haven't been with another woman since you." He kissed her so tenderly, so lovingly that she sighed against his lips. "And I don't want there to be anyone but you ever again."

A soft sob tore from her, and she knew she was lost.

Her body pressed hard against his, welcoming his hands stroking over her as the two of them carefully moved backward across the room toward the bed. His palms fluttered over her breasts and across her hips. Everywhere he touched, heat prickled beneath her skin and left her yearning for his body to invade hers, for his heart to love her.

He lifted her into his arms and placed her on the bed. As he knelt over her, he stroked his fingertips across her cheek and down her throat to the hollow between her breasts. "No matter how hard I try, I can't quit you, brat." A shiver fell through her, a soft mewling of arousal and need passing over her lips as his fingertips drew tantalizing circles against the inside swells of her breasts. He smiled at her reaction. "And neither can you."

Her heart pounded with equal parts desire and bittersweet pain. She knew she should push him away and end this now, but she needed him too much. Tonight, she wanted him—*all* of him…his laughter and his smile, his strong arms holding her close, his body moving so satisfyingly inside hers. She would deal with the pain tomorrow.

Somehow.

She reached down between them to unfasten his trousers and free him to her seeking eyes and hands. A shiver swept through her at the sight of him. Already he was hard for her, thick and hot, and tonight, for this last time, he was hers. When her fingers closed around him, a guttural sound of pure need tore from the back of his throat.

Without a trace of shame, she began to work at him as he held himself poised over her, one hand sliding up and down his shaft while the other circled the flat of her palm

over his enlarged head. Drops of his essence gathered at his
tip. With her thumbs, she rubbed them over his skin until
he was slick in her hands and easier to stroke as boldly as
she knew he craved. She tightened her grip on him, squeezing his thick girth and sliding the soft skin against her palms
over the steely hardness beneath until his body stiffened and
he shook.

He was ready for her, and with her hot wetness gathered
between her clenching thighs, the sweet ache of arousal
pulsing inside her, she was more than ready for him.

"Grey, please," she whispered as her hand grabbed her
night rail and pulled it up to her hips, baring her trembling
thighs to the cool night air. "I need you."

"The baby—" He shook his head. "I don't want to hurt
you."

Her chest tightened hard with emotion. He didn't want
to hurt her, but he had no idea the pain he'd cause her if he
didn't give her this last night together. "It's all right," she
assured him, running her hands over his chest to quickly unfasten the buttons of his waistcoat and strip it down over his
shoulders and off.

He glanced down at her with uncertainty.

"Unless—" Her fingers stilled, and she swallowed hard to
free the knot in her throat and whispered, "Unless you don't
find me...attractive...like this."

"Oh, brat." He cupped her face and kissed her, hard and
deep, as if trying to prove to her how much he desired her.
"When I said you were beautiful, I meant it." His mouth caressed her lips, her cheek, her jaw, her neck. "You're the
loveliest woman I've ever met, Emily, inside and out. This
baby is part of you, and it only makes you more beautiful."

Hot tears stung at her lashes. If it were possible, she fell
in love with him all over again.

With a gentle push of her hands against his shoulders, she rolled him onto his back. Her body may have wanted his, but her heart *needed* him.

Her hands found his manhood again, and this time, she followed down with her mouth, to pleasure him the way she'd fantasized about since that day in the carriage when he gave her that wicked, wanton kiss between her thighs. If kissing her there brought her that much pleasure, then surely, if she kissed him *here* . . . Her hand closed around him to hold him still as she placed a delicate kiss on his tip.

A low groan rose from him, which emboldened her even more. Her lips closed around him to pull him into the moist heat of her mouth and suck gently. When he shuddered, shivering against her tongue, her chest soared that he liked what she was doing to him as much as she enjoyed the pleasure she gave. She tightened her grip and pumped harder up and down his length even as her mouth drew him deeper, savoring the salty-sweet taste of him on her tongue, the essence that was life and love and pure man. Pure Grey.

"Emily," he rasped, his teeth bared in a strained half-smile of restraint.

His erection jerked in her mouth, and she moaned around him. In response, her body dripped wet for him, all the muscles inside her folds clenching in a hard spasm that made her gasp, with nearly the same intensity as if he were inside her, stroking her with his body.

"Come here, love." With trembling hands, all of him tense and shaking now, he took her hips in his hands and shifted her carefully over on top of him. "I need to be inside you. Now."

Not bothering to remove any more of their clothing, with her night rail gathered at her waist and his trousers only halfway down, she straddled him. His strong hands on her hips guided her as she lowered herself, sliding him inside her inch by wonderful inch, until he was fully sheathed by her body.

She sighed and closed her eyes. With one hand beneath her belly for support, her other hand resting on his chest so she could feel his racing heartbeat, she began to slowly move her hips over him. There was no urgency, no hurry to end this and rush into the dawn, and she wanted to savor this moment as long as possible.

He thrust up gently beneath her, and she rocked herself back and forth along his length to meet each thrust, to withdraw at each retreat before he slid deep inside her again. As the arousal inside her grew toward climax, her hand on his chest fisted his shirt between her fingers, and her thighs clenched tighter against his sides. Her lips parted in a soft gasp, her body tensing around him—

Release rose inside her not as the desperate desire she'd experienced with him before but as a billow of warmth, radiating out from her core to fill all of her with his strength and heat. She rolled back her head as her sex quivered around him, his name a soft whisper on her lips in the darkness.

"Emily...my sweet Emily," he groaned as he released himself, and she sighed again as his life's essence flowed into her, claiming her as his once more.

When he'd recaptured his breath, he eased back against the pillows and drew her possessively into his arms as she slowly slid off him and nestled against his side. His large body trembled around hers, and she thrilled to think that she did this to him, that she was able to bring him such shuddering pleasure.

She closed her eyes beneath his loving caresses as he gently stroked his hand across her back, her hip, even tenderly across her belly. The moment had been so special, so overwhelming that she hadn't realized tears had gathered at her lashes until he kissed them away.

"You have no idea how hard it's been to stay away from you, brat," he murmured against her feverish lips, "when what I wanted to do was break down the front door, storm up here to your room, and...well, do *that.*"

When he grinned wickedly at her, she laughed. A peaceful warmth filled her, from the tips of her fingers to her toes, and she slipped her hand beneath his shirt to feel his heartbeat beneath her fingertips. *This* was how she wanted to stay, to somehow find a way to stop the dawn from coming so she could remain here with him like this forever.

He placed a delicate kiss at her temple. "I also wanted to just hold you in my arms and tell you that I missed you. That I missed your laugh and that radiant smile of yours. That I care about you and that little baby inside you." His voice came as a trembling murmur. "That somewhere along the road from Yorkshire I fell in love with you."

Her heart stopped. Grey *loved* her? She stared at him through wide eyes, not daring to believe...and when her heart began beating again, the foolish thing didn't know whether to leap for joy or shatter into a million pieces.

"Grey," she choked out painfully, her traitorous fingers curling into his chest as his heart raced beneath her fingertips. "You can't..."

"But I do. I lie awake every night fantasizing about you, Emily, and not just how good it feels to be inside you—but dreams of escorting you to the opera on my arm, waltzing with you at balls, and walking with you through the park." He cupped her face between his hands and kissed her so tenderly, so lovingly that he stole her breath away. "I want to create a respectable home and a life with you, and I want to put children of my own in your womb." He drew a shaking breath, taking a moment to steady himself. "I'll admit—this terrifies the daylights out of me. I'd never considered marriage to anyone before, but now..." He caressed a finger-tip over her bottom lip and smiled faintly when it trembled. "Now I can't imagine not being married to you."

She froze for just a heartbeat as his words cascaded through her, leaving her trembling and pulsating with love, her heart somersaulting with joy. But the pain came crashing back just as fiercely a few heartbeats later, because nothing had truly changed.

Yet the temptation of what he was offering was too strong, and if she didn't put distance between them right now, she'd lose whatever thin thread of willpower she had left when it came to him. So she slipped from his arms and stood, her hands shaking so much that she could barely straighten her disheveled night rail. "But I have nothing to offer you..." *Except heartache and regret.*

"Emily, you are everything I want," he assured her.

She shook her head as the anguish rose inside her. If only it were that simple, they'd be back on the road right now, this time driving furiously for Scotland. The wedding would be easy, but the marriage would be brutal.

"Marry me, Emily," he cajoled.

Oh, how much she wanted to do exactly that! She wanted to marry him, give him a family and a home, grow old to-gether surrounded by children and grandchildren...But at what cost to the future he deserved? And to her heart? She'd survived being abandoned once by a husband who grew to hate her; she would never survive it by Grey.

"I can't," she breathed, her hand pressing hard against her chest, as if she could physically prevent her heart from breaking.

"Because I'm not good enough for you," he said quietly, his voice carefully even.

She nodded, unable to put words to her deceit.

"That same old lie again, brat?" With a tired sigh, he pushed himself out of bed and walked slowly toward her. "I didn't believe it the first time you told me, and I don't believe it now."

"It's true! We *are* different." She pushed at him to put him away, but the blasted man only shifted closer, until he held her once more within the circle of his arms. "You weren't born into society—"

He shrugged. "I've achieved it."

"Not completely."

"Close enough." His eyes gleamed with resolve.

She shuddered with dread, knowing he was fully prepared for battle this time. "You're an army officer—"

"I'm a major."

"But everyone believes you're the son of a blacksmith who has the audacity to climb into their ranks."

"And you're a widow who can have the audacity to do as she pleases. Including marrying the son of a blacksmith who became a major."

Her heart wrenched in aggravation at his arguments. "You're a born adventurer. For heaven's sake!" She pointed adamantly at the window. "You came through my window on a rope! Any normal person would have come announced through the front door."

With a wolfish grin, he lowered his head and brushed his lips along the side of her neck. "I couldn't have made love to you if I'd come announced through the front door."

A groan of frustration rose from her as he looped a finger over her neckline and tugged it down to run his lips over the top swells of her breasts.

"Grey," she pleaded, knowing she was losing the battle. And if he kept touching her like this—she gasped as his tongue slipped beneath her night rail to lick across her nipple—oh, dear heavens, she'd lose the war!

"Who wants normal, anyway?" he purred. He gave another tug at her gown and freed a single breast completely to his greedy eyes and seeking lips, and his tongue teased at her nipple as much as his words teased at her heart. "Normal is boring. Normal is for county squires and society dullards who have nothing better to do with their days than waltz at balls and—"

He froze, his lips stilling against her.

When he lifted his head to stare down into her eyes in the dark shadows, she caught her breath at the accusation on his face. He'd figured out the truth, this man who had always been able to read her so easily—God help her, he *knew*!

"Emily?" he asked, a mix of incredulity and dread underlying his deep voice. "Please tell me I'm wrong. Tell me your refusal isn't why I think."

Shamefully averting her eyes, she shook her head as she stepped back from the warmth of his arms. Despite the anguish burning inside her, she was unable to deny it. "I won't trap you, Grey."

"*Trap* me? You wouldn't be trapping me into marriage. I proposed to you because I wanted to marry you, and no other reason." Then his eyes narrowed suspiciously, and he asked quietly, "But that's not the kind of entrapment you mean, is it? You mean the marriage itself."

She nodded, knowing that she wasn't simply burning bridges between them now; she was blowing them up, shattering them into a million splinters that she'd never be able to put back together. "You'll regret marrying me. Not the first year, perhaps not the second . . . but you will once you finally realize all you had to give up."

He stared at her, stunned. "I'm not giving up anything to marry—"

"You'll have to give up your promotion in Spain and your work with the War Office." Her words were not a question. "You can't be a field agent and have a wife, can you?"

He hesitated, and in that heartbeat's pause, she saw the solemn realization darken his face before he could stop it. "I can do other work for them besides fieldwork."

She shook her head as the sadness rushed through her in a breathless shudder. "Even if they let you continue on, you'd be put into an administrative position, completing reports and papers and stripped from all you love about your work, all you've fought so hard to achieve." Tears blurred her vision until she could no longer see the mix of emotions on his face, and she was glad for it, because she didn't think she could bear the heartache and disbelief she saw there. "You told me so yourself that your freedom and your work mean everything to you. And if I take that away—oh God, Grey, you'll hate me for it!"

"I would never hate you, brat," he promised with fierce resolve. "I love you."

She inhaled a sharp, jagged breath at the bold declaration. The pain was blinding. This should have been the happiest moment of her life, the words she'd been waiting to hear since she was sixteen and gave her first kiss to him. Instead, they sliced at her already-raw heart. She shook her head. "You'll hate me, and I couldn't bear to go through that again."

"Again?" His eyes narrowed, piercing accusation flaring in their depths. "*Again*? Is that why you're refusing, because you think I'll be the same kind of husband to you as Crenshaw?"

Closing her eyes, she shook her head. "Grey, please—"

He grabbed her shoulders. "I am not Andrew Crenshaw! I am *not* that bastard," he ground out, his jaw clenched so fiercely that the muscles jumped in his neck. "I would never use you the way he did, and I will *never* abandon you."

With a soft cry of anguish, she shook her head. "You can't promise that... You don't know..."

"Emily, my love—" The grief-stricken words tore from him. He cupped her cheeks in his hands and gently tilted her face to kiss her, a sympathetic touch of his lips that left her aching and anguished. He murmured the promise against her mouth, "I would never hurt you nor abandon you—I would give my life for you."

Her body flashed numb from the wave of pain and grief that swept over her. "Then give it," she whispered, so softly that her words were silent on her lips. But she knew from the subtle stiffening of his body against hers that he heard, that they shivered through him to his soul. "Give up the life we could have had together and go to Spain." A single tear trailed down her cheek. "If you love me, Grey, you'll let me go."

CHAPTER FIFTEEN

"Again," Grey ordered the bartender for another glass of whiskey. He wasn't drunk enough to push thoughts of Emily from his mind, yet that was exactly where he planned on getting. And soon.

Damned stubborn woman! In his life, he'd never encountered a woman so frustrating and challenging yet so undeniably alluring, so gut-achingly lovely—it was enough to call himself a bedlamite for continuing to chase after her all these weeks when he could have simply given up, believed her lie, and headed for Spain. He might have done just that, too, if he hadn't realized after the first fortnight of courting her in absentia that whenever he sent her a dozen roses, only eleven returned.

Then, two nights ago after making love to her, he discovered the true reason why she'd lied to him—the little minx *did* love him... loved him so much, in fact, that she was convinced he'd be better off without her. That she'd foolishly believed he wanted adventure and the War Office more than he wanted her.

He clenched his hands against the bar to fight back the frustration rising inside him again. *Damnation!* He would never hurt her, never use her or resent her the way that bastard Crenshaw had done. And if forced into making a choice, he would gladly give up his career if it meant having a life with Emily. How could the frustrating chit not realize that? Dear God, he would *never* leave her.

But she wouldn't listen, wouldn't believe him. She loved him, all right...loved him straight into hell.

And now, he found himself in some filthy tavern near Drury Lane in the bright morning well before noon, attempting to drink himself into oblivion and wondering what on earth to do to make her believe him.

The bartender placed the whiskey in front of him, and he tossed it back in a single, gasping swallow. As the burn slid down his throat, he signaled for the man's attention and rasped out, "Again."

"Two," a deep voice ordered from beside him.

Christ. Of all people..."Go away, Colonel," he growled.

"Not after I spent all night looking for you."

He slid his gaze sideways at Edward Westover. Even here, in a smoke-filled hell surrounded by thieves, drunks, and whores, he looked regal, every inch a duke, right down to the irritated look of disdain on his imperial brow. No one would ever mistake him for not being a blue blood, nor a battle-hardened army officer. "Then say your piece and leave."

"All right. Kate sent me after you with a message."

"The duchess?" That bit of unexpected information pierced through his drink-fogged brain. What message would the duchess have for—

Edward slapped his hand against the back of his head.

"What the *hell*?" He glared at his old colonel, who stood

there staring evenly at him, his arms folded calmly over his chest.

"She wanted me to be delicate with the delivery," Edward confessed dryly.

Grey rubbed the back of his head. "*That* was delicate?"

"I took a liberal interpretation."

Edward sat next to him and mumbled his thanks as the bartender set two glasses of whiskey in front of them.

"What did I do to offend the duchess?" he grumbled. *Good Lord*, wasn't it enough to have one woman upset at him?

"I don't know exactly. Something about being too much of a nodcock to see the truth. But you've concerned my wife, Grey, which concerns me." He took a sip of the rotgut whiskey, too well trained to make a face at its disgusting taste. He paused, his voice lowering grimly. "She's worried about Lady Emily."

So was he. But Grey said nothing and instead gulped down half the whiskey.

"She's been in tears for the past two days."

His gut wrenched at the thought of Emily in tears. Every tear he saw in her eyes felt like a knife slicing into his heart. But he also couldn't help the anger and frustration that made him bite out, "Tell your wife to talk to Emily, then. She's the one who refuses to marry me." He raised the glass in a mocking toast. "Said the War Office is more important to me than she is."

"That's not true," Edward said quietly. "I've seen how much you care for her."

"I know." His fingers tightened around the glass as he returned to hunching over the bar. "But for the life of me, I can't make her believe me."

"Emily's refusing all visitors now, including Kate. I suppose that was what prompted her admonishment to be delicate with tonight's message. That," Edward muttered, "and the fact that she can't swing into Emily's room on a rope herself."

Grey grimaced. How the hell did the duchess find out about that? "The War Office is wasting its time with Thomas and me." He scowled into his glass. The cheap whiskey was too watered down to get him as drunk as he wanted to be, and as quick. "They should have hired the duchess."

"Please don't give her any ideas." Edward grimaced as he pushed the unwanted whiskey away. "There has to be some way to convince Emily to marry you."

He shook his head at the futility of it. He'd been through this over and over in his mind since the words left her lips, since she begged him to leave her and go to Spain. He'd racked his brain searching for any way to prove her wrong about him. But there was no way to demonstrate his love for her or how much he was willing to give up to be with her— there was no answer except decades of a loving marriage.

And she refused to marry him.

Edward said quietly, "Emily loves you."

He *thought* she did, but... "She's never said it," he grudgingly admitted, staring down into his whiskey. Not even the last time they'd made love, not even after he admitted to loving her.

"She loves you," Edward repeated, just as assuredly as before. "But years with that bastard of a husband compared to a few months with you..." He shook his head. "There hasn't been enough time yet for her to see the truth. Trust me, I know."

Grey was certain he did, given what he'd gone through to marry Kate.

But time was the one thing he didn't have. Already

Bathurst had threatened to rescind the position in Spain if he didn't get himself to Seville soon. If he waited for Emily to realize how much he truly loved her, only for it never to happen, he'd lose both his career and his heart. And then where would he be?

"But if I give her time, if she never believes me—" *If I lose her...* He gave a shake of his whiskey-clouded head. His voice was almost lost beneath the noise of the rabble around them as he ground out, "What difference does love make then?"

"In my experience," Edward answered quietly, "everything."

He briefly rested his hand on Grey's shoulder, then walked out.

The bartender collected the coin Edward had left on the bar, then motioned questioningly toward his empty glass. Grey waved the man away. There wasn't enough whiskey in the world to dull his pain.

*   *   *

"Tea, my lady?" Yardley carried a tray into Emily's room and set it on the table beside her reading chair. "I thought you might like some refreshments."

"Thank you," Emily mumbled numbly, not bothering to move her gaze from the window.

She stood at the glass and stared out at the little garden below, the afternoon sunshine casting lengthening shadows across the rose bushes and sculpted trees edging the walls and walkways, as if watching there could somehow make Grey magically appear. But he wasn't coming to her. And after the way they'd last parted, she doubted if she would ever see him again.

Her shoulders sagged with misery. No more tears could come now; she'd cried them all out after he left, when she lay alone in the bed that still smelled of him. Her chest ached hollow. There was nothing left inside her to give to him now, except the love that she would always carry within her even as she found a way to move on without him.

And she *had* to move on. She had no choice, not with a baby to care for. Even now, she felt a foot kicking against her ribs—he was just as restless today as she was. But this baby was her life now, and everything she did would be for his protection and care. She had her baby to love and the love he would return to her, and she'd depend upon that to somehow find strength in the days to come. All those long, lonely days without Grey.

Yardley poured her tea, adding the exact measure of milk and sugar Emily liked, then took her arm and gently helped her to sit in her chair. With an affectionate smile, she handed her the cup. "Did you enjoy your morning walk?"

She nodded absently and sipped at the tea when Yardley urged her to do so.

Despite her not wanting to leave her bed that morning, Thomas had insisted she dress and accompany him on a stroll through the park. The day was beautiful and bright, the air gentle and warm, but she saw none of it. Her face remained tilted toward the ground, and her troubled thoughts of Grey never cleared. As they'd walked, Thomas had asked about her plans for the baby, but now she could hardly remember a word she'd said. She wasn't even certain how she'd been able to put one foot in front of the other to keep moving.

She pressed her hand against her forehead. *Oh God!* How would she be able to keep moving, breathing, living without him? She would find a way—of course she would find a way, but she doubted the misery would ever leave her.

"Is something wrong with your tea?" Yardley interrupted her thoughts.

"What?" Her distraction must have been evident on her face because Yardley frowned at her. "Oh—it's fine, thank you."

"Better drink up, then. Tea is good for a baby."

"Truly?" She forced a weak smile as Yardley gestured for her to quickly drink up half the cup, then refilled it from the pot. Thank God for Yardley. Whatever would she have done without the woman's help during the past two years?

Her maid nodded with a sly wink. "Makes him English, my lady."

Emily took a long sip of tea. It tasted different from usual, with hints of a faint licorice flavor. But it was still pleasant and warm, and she wouldn't dare refuse it and risk yet another argument about how she needed to eat more. Yardley smiled at her reassuringly, waiting for her to drink the tea and nibble at one of the biscuits, even though it tasted like sawdust on her tongue.

"The house is quiet this afternoon," she commented as Yardley moved around the sitting room, straightening the pillows and curios, putting away the stack of books and the set of paints Grey had sent her several weeks ago as part of his attempt to wear down her resistance and win her heart. It had been the one gift she'd selfishly allowed herself to keep.

"Everyone's gone out." Yardley did not glance up at Emily, her attention focused on straightening the ink, quills, and papers on the writing desk. "The duke is at the Lords, and the duchess is paying calls on Lady St. James and Lady Agnes Sinclair."

She took another sip. "And my brother?"

"Lord Thomas received a message from His Grace to visit Strathmore House."

Hmm... that was odd. Thomas had been on his way back from the Westovers' home when he was shot, and both Edward and Kate seemed keenly aware of her brother's agitation toward visiting at this time in the afternoon, because it invariably meant he'd be traveling home at sunset, that time of day when the footpad assaulted him. Perhaps the request for him to visit meant they thought he was healed, and not just physically. Or perhaps... perhaps it meant...

Goodness, she wasn't certain what it meant! Her head was suddenly groggy, making thinking difficult.

A nap. That was it—she needed the nap she'd grown used to taking in the afternoons. She'd just finish her tea, then lie down. But her hand shook as she raised the cup to her lips, and she blinked hard to keep her eyelids from drooping shut.

As confusion and sleepiness fell over her like a cloud, Emily watched as Yardley sat down at the desk and dipped the quill into the ink, then scratched out a note on a piece of stationery, one with the gold-embossed *EMC* imprinted across the top.

Emily stared at her, her swirling mind suddenly unable to focus. Why was Yardley sitting at her desk, using her stationery? "What are..." Her lips grew thick, barely able to form words. "What are you..."

Yardley blotted the ink and shook her head regretfully. "Why couldn't you have gone to Glasgow as we'd planned? I would have gotten the money, and no one else would have been hurt." Swiping the back of her hand against her eyes, she carefully folded the note and rose. "You'd have been safe then. There would've been no need for any of this."

She set the note on the fireplace mantel. When she finally glanced over her shoulder at Emily, tears streaked down the older woman's cheeks.

"I would have taken care of you, just as if you were my

own daughter. But I need the money, you see. For my sister. She's terribly sick and can't afford medical care, can't keep up her dress business...We could have helped her with all of that, you and I. If only you'd listened to me."

Emily shook her head as the chair began to tilt beneath her. Something was wrong, *very* wrong. "The tea," her tingling lips forced out in a garbled mumble. "You...the tea..."

Her body numbed. Her breathing came labored and hard as she fought to keep her eyes open. The teacup and saucer fell from her deadened hands and spilled across the floor.

"But you had to let that man into our house," Yardley scolded angrily. "When he arrived, you forgot all about leaving, didn't you? Now we've no choice but to do it this way."

Emily's head swirled so thick with dizziness that her stomach rumbled nauseously, and for a moment, she thought she might cast up the poisonous tea. Her hands groped numbly for the chair arms as black spots flashed before her eyes in time to her pounding heart, her vision growing darker and darker.

With every ounce of strength, she levered herself up from the chair, opened her mouth to scream. But no sound came—

She sagged slowly toward the tea-stained rug.

Yardley caught her.

"There now, don't you worry, my lady." Putting Emily's limp arm over her shoulders, Yardley led her toward the door. "It'll all be over soon, and as painless as possible, I promise you that."

* * *

Emily blinked rapidly. The room around her came slowly into focus as the fog lifted from her eyes. Her head pounded with sharp pains as she tried to remember who she was, where she was, what had happened...

"She's waking up." A familiar voice cut through the blurriness inside her head, and Emily was just able to make out Yardley's concerned face in front of her in the dim lamplight.

"Finally." A man's voice came from the darkness behind her, this one unrecognizable. "You put too much of that damned powder in the tea."

"I had to make certain she was asleep. I couldn't very well have her screaming for help while I was carrying her out of the house, now could I?"

Her fuzzy mind slowly registered what they were saying. She'd been drugged—that was why the tea tasted like licorice, why she'd gotten so tired, so suddenly.

And Yardley had done it to her.

"You..." The word was thick on her tongue as she struggled her mind and form words. "You..."

The haze lifted fully from her eyes now, but she had no idea where she was. Empty except for pieces of trash and debris strewn across the plank-board floor, the room must have been inside an abandoned building, an old warehouse or office still inside the noisy city. And near the river, judging by the stench of fish rot pinching at her nose. The last reds of the sunset seeped in through the holes in the roof over their heads, and the sound of rumbling wagons and horses drifted up from below through the broken windows. A rat scurried along the far wall.

She sat on a wooden chair in the middle of the room, her wrists tied to the chair arms. Her feet were free, but her legs were still too weak from the drug to function. Even if she'd been able to stand, she would have fallen to the floor.

"Yardley." Her lips tingled as the feeling slowly returned

to them, and she concentrated on the woman before her, willing herself to find clarity and regain control of her body. "What...what's happening?"

Her maid shook her head, distress pinching her face. "I tried to help you when we were back at Snowden Hall. I tried to make you understand that you had to convince those men to leave," Yardley told her quietly, "but you wouldn't listen."

Ice water ran through her, and fear stole her breath away. "The fire...you set the fire?"

"I had no choice. It was only a matter of time until they found out about the baby and—"

"Shut up!"

The man who was with her shoved Yardley aside and leered down into Emily's face. Her eyes widened in recognition—Harold Crenshaw, the bored young man who came to her house for tea with his father.

"*You*...it was you all along," Emily whispered fearfully, knowing she was looking into the eyes of a murderer. "You killed Andrew."

"Of course, I did," he admitted arrogantly with a sneer at his thin lips. "You think I'd let anyone stand between me and my fortune? Now, with you and your bastard gone, my father becomes a marquess, and when he dies, it all becomes mine...the estates, the title, every last pound and penny. *Mine*."

His eyes flickered coldly in the lamplight. She realized with sinking terror that there was absolutely no mercy in him, no empathy. He'd pitilessly murdered Andrew and tried to do the same to her—and he was still planning on killing her and her baby. If she couldn't find a way to escape.

"I wasn't able to make you have an accident like your husband, although God knows we tried, didn't we, Yardley? The fire, the phaeton..."

The maid shifted silently from foot to foot, clearly uncomfortable beneath his attentions, as if she didn't trust him not to come after her as well.

"Fortunately," he murmured as he trailed his knuckles down her cheek, and she shuddered with revulsion, "there are other ways."

Emily swallowed hard, the swirling fear making her shake. "You don't have to kill me." She prayed she could talk him out of this, or stall him just long enough to get away. "If the baby is a girl—"

"Then she'll take part of my inheritance in that damned allowance and dowry my father promised her." He laughed bitterly. "But I can't take the chance that it won't come out a boy and take everything. Besides, once it's born, if it has an accident then, I'll be blamed, and I'll swing at the gallows. Better to stop it now, I think."

"I don't think you really want to hurt an innocent baby." She tried again to make him see reason. "If you'd wanted to kill me, you would have done it by now, while I was still unconscious."

A slow, wicked smile spread across his face. He tsked his tongue with a shake of his head. "Where's the fun in that?"

Panic swelled inside her, the metallic taste of fear sickening in her mouth. *Fun*... An abhorrent shudder sped through her—he was enjoying this.

He put his hands over her bound wrists, pinching her arms painfully against the chair until she winced, and leaned in closer with a low chuckle.

"Of course I want to kill you, bitch. But if I'd done it while you were in Chatham House, someone might have interrupted us. And in the carriage it wouldn't have looked like an accident."

Her mouth went dry. "Why does it have to be an accident?"

She didn't care—*dear God*, she didn't care how he planned on killing her!—but if she could stall him a bit longer until her leg muscles worked again, she might have a chance of running away. Testing herself, she kept her eyes locked onto his but tried to wiggle her toes...and they moved. *They moved!*

Now, if only she could untie her hands and get herself free of the chair. She wouldn't have to run far to escape, only down to the street and into traffic, screaming for help, causing a scene—

He shrugged. "Accident, suicide...no matter as long as you're dead and no one suspects me."

Her heartbeat thundered in her ears. "No one will believe I killed myself."

"You were horribly unhappy recently, everyone could see that. Yardley will testify to it, too, won't you?"

Yardley folded her arms nervously across her chest and nodded stiffly, looking down at the floor and guiltily avoiding Emily's eyes.

"In fact, she's already written the note you left behind before you took your life and placed it in your bedroom for your family to find." He shook his head with a mocking look of grief. "You poor dear...you were inconsolable over the loss of your husband, whom you loved deeply, and the thought of having to raise this child by yourself was overwhelming. You just couldn't live with the constant reminder in your child of your dead husband."

"No one will believe that." Not Thomas, and especially not Grey. Despite the terror rising inside her, she took comfort in that—Grey wouldn't believe the note, and he wouldn't stop until he'd hunted down Harold and saw him hanged.

"Oh, you stupid chit!" He sighed with aggravation,

rolling his eyes. "They don't have to *believe* it. It just has to be good enough that they can't place blame on me."

"How?" she demanded, feeling anger stir inside her and slowly replace the fear. He thought she was weak and passive. Someone he could easily control and manipulate. Yet she refused to die without a fight. "How are you going to kill me?"

"You were so distraught that you took a knife from the kitchen at Chatham House, hired a hack to bring you here, and slit your wrists."

Oh God...

"In the morning, a rag-and-bone man will come inside this building, looking for scraps to sell, where he'll find your dead body." He laughed with grisly amusement. "Let's just hope he's better at reporting dead bodies than he is at driving phaetons."

He'd meant to frighten her but only infuriated her. "Slit a lady's tied wrists," she echoed, unconsciously clenching her hands even as they remained bound to the chair. "Spineless coward!"

Baring his teeth with a growl, he drew back his hand to strike her—then stopped at the last moment, just before he hit her face.

Enraged, he forced down his hand. "You almost had me. If I'd hit you, there would have been a bruise on your body, evidence that someone forced you into this." He leaned over her menacingly, his voice chilling. "That's the only thing stopping me from beating you right now the way I've longed to do since I found out you'd been bred and ruined everything. Punching your face, kicking your belly..."

He paused to lick his lips, and she sickeningly realized that he was becoming sexually aroused at the thought of harming her.

"I bet you'd beg for mercy, wouldn't you? Soft little cries and pleas—"

"Stop it!" Yardley scolded him furiously. "Stop playing games! It's time now." She held out her trembling hand. "Give me the money you promised."

With a murderous glare, Harold took out a small bag from his jacket. The gold sovereigns inside clinked softly together. "If you breathe a word about any of this," he warned as he slapped the bag into the maid's hand, "they'll fish your dead body from the Thames."

Silently, Yardley slipped the bag into her skirt pocket and handed over the knife. Even in the dim lamplight, Emily saw the monogram etched into the handle identifying it as belonging to the household of the Duke of Chatham. A knife taken from the kitchen, just as he'd told her.

Harold carefully undid the ties at her wrists so as not to leave any suspicious marks on her skin. No bruises to identify that she'd been murdered, she thought with horror.

She swallowed hard, her heart pounding relentlessly. She had one chance to escape, only one chance...

The last of the bindings fell away. Emily kicked her knee between his legs as hard as she could. He howled in pain, doubling over.

She pushed up to her wobbly feet, shoving him aside and running toward the door as fast as she could, her hands holding desperately around her belly. The street! She only had to reach the street, and she'd be safe. She reached the door and flung it open—

A hand grabbed her shoulder and shoved her backward. Her back slammed against the wall with a painful jar that ricocheted through her and left her gasping for breath.

A forearm pressed against her throat, crushing at her windpipe. Her fingernails dug into the muscle beneath the jacket sleeve in an attempt to free herself, in one last desperate attempt to save her life. But Harold's face loomed over her savagely, his teeth bared like a lion's in attack. From the corner of her eye she saw him raise the knife over his shoulder to stab her—

The sound of a gunshot tore through the building, and the ball ripped into his arm as the knife plunged downward. With a scream, he staggered back. Cowering away, Emily glanced up to see Thomas standing in the doorway, a trail of smoke rising from his spent pistol, and Grey's large body hurling furiously toward Harold.

Grey hit him with such force that the two men propelled forward into the wooden chair, smashing it beneath them as they fell to the floor. He punched his fist into Harold's face and stomach as hard as he could, so hard that she heard him grunt from the exertion of each blow. Blood and spittle flew from Harold's cut and bruised face with each sickening thud of Grey's fists.

"Grey!" She started toward him, but strong arms went around her and held her back.

"Not yet," Edward Westover said calmly behind her, watching over her head as Grey continued to beat Harold.

Long, agonizing seconds passed until the ferocity of his punches weakened, until each jab came with great effort in swinging punches that seemed to take every ounce of energy inside him. When finally he couldn't lift his arm for another blow, he sank back on his heels and took deep, gasping breaths, the fury in him spent.

Edward released her.

She rushed forward and threw her arms around Grey's shoulders, burying her face against his neck. He shook from the exertion of beating Harold, who now lay in a moaning, bloody mess on the floor beside him, yet his arms raised heavily up her back to embrace her.

Closing her eyes, she held him tightly. She so fiercely focused on feeling his racing heartbeat and breathing, on reassuring herself that they were both alive and unhurt, that she paid no attention to the way he nodded over her shoulder or how Hedley and another one of Grey's men gathered up Harold and carried him from the room.

"Brat," he whispered hoarsely, shifting to sit back and pull her across his lap. "Are you all right?"

She nodded against his shoulder.

"If that bastard hurt you—"

"He didn't." She cupped his face in her hands and leaned up to kiss him, not caring that Thomas and Edward were in the room and watching them. All that mattered was that she was in his embrace and the nightmare was over. "Because of you."

His arms tightened around her, and she never wanted him to let go.

"How did you find me?" Her fingertips traced over his lips. She couldn't stop touching him and reassuring herself that he was really there with her and that they were both safe.

"My men have been watching you." He turned his head to kiss her palm. "Hedley saw Yardley bring you out of the house. He followed you and sent for me."

Her eyes blurred hot at the betrayal. "Yardley drugged me. I couldn't stop her—"

"I know, love." He smiled reassuringly at her. "But I told you that I would always protect you, now and for the rest of my life. And I meant it."

She knew he meant more than protecting her from Harold and Yardley. "But your work—" she choked out. "It's important to you."

"It is," he agreed solemnly. "But you're even more important to me, Emily. I will find a way to make my career work once we're married, in whatever way I have to in order to keep our family safe."

Our family. A soft thrill of joy pulsed through her at the possibility.

"But I won't live without you, brat." The strength of his determination and love seeped into her. "I simply won't."

She nodded through her tears, knowing now the depth of his love for her, of his resolve to never leave her. And her heart blossomed. "I love you, Grey," she whispered and leaned up to kiss him again. "I've loved you since that first kiss—"

A sharp pain pierced through her, and she cried out. The muscles in her belly contracted into a sudden and severe cramp so harsh that it ripped away her breath.

He grabbed for her shoulders to steady her. "Emily!" Concern instantly flashed across his face. "Are you hurt?"

"I think—" The blood drained from her face as she reached for her belly. "I think the baby's coming."

His eyes widened. "*Now?*"

"Oh God," she whispered, the terror of a fresh hell sweeping over her. "The baby isn't due for another month. It's too early!"

"It'll be all right," he reassured her as he climbed to his feet and lifted her into his arms. "I'll get you home, and everything will be just fine."

But as he carried her from the building and she buried her face against his shoulder, she couldn't find comfort in his assurances. Because something was wrong. Terribly wrong.

Chapter Sixteen

"If you keep pacing like that," Thomas drawled as his eyes followed Grey on his path across the billiards room, "you'll have to replace the rug."

Grey glared at him but never slowed his long strides as he once again traced the length of the room.

"Leave him alone," Edward admonished quietly as he grabbed the crystal decanter of cognac that Thomas had liberated from his father's study two hours ago and refilled everyone's glass.

Stopping in mid-stride, Grey turned toward his former colonel and nodded with appreciation. Thomas had been teasing him mercilessly all night, and it was nice to finally be defended. "Thank you—"

"After all," Edward continued sardonically, his face deadpan, "he's about to become a father."

"Go to hell," he growled at their taunting, shooting both of them a murderous look, and began to pace again.

Tonight, he had no patience for their antics.

Five hours. It had been five hours since they'd rescued Emily and brought her back to Chatham House. Five hours since her mother and Kate Westover rushed her into a guest room that would serve as the birthing room and sent for the midwife, and Thomas and Edward took him into the billiards room to wait. And wait.

And wait.

While Grey spent every moment on his feet pacing, with Thomas and Edward tormenting him relentlessly in their own brotherly way of attempting to distract him, Emily had been confined in the other wing of the house. Only periodic updates from Kate Westover assuring the three men that all was going as well as could be expected eased his nervousness. The wait was maddening.

At some point during the evening—he'd lost track of the time—Dr. Brandon arrived at Edward's personal request. The old physician's distaste at being called out for something as unclean as female matters was apparent, but not even the illustrious Dr. Brandon would refuse a summons by the Duke of Strathmore, so he spent the evening discussing hunting and politics with Emily's father downstairs in his study while the midwife and the duchess tended to Emily. Her mother paced her own vigil in the hall.

Hedley had sent word that Harold Crenshaw had been sewn up by the surgeon and delivered to Newgate to await trial. In the confusion, Yardley had gotten away, but his men found her fleeing north toward Scotland and brought her back to London, putting her into the same prison as Crenshaw.

Emily and her baby were finally safe.

If all went well with the delivery. Despite the young duchess's optimism, Grey had clearly seen concern in her eyes during the reports she'd given them, the last one nearly two hours ago. The baby was early, and with Emily being so thin, carrying so small ...

He paused in his pacing to briefly close his eyes. *Not the baby—please, God, not the baby!* If anything happened to the baby, he didn't know how Emily would ever be able to bear it.

"Cognac." Edward held out a glass to him. The single word was not a question. Only the colonel was capable of making the offering of a drink into an order.

Mumbling his thanks, he took the glass and watched as Thomas circled to the far end of the billiards table to take his shot. He and Edward had kept up a running game of billiards all night between their barbs at Grey's expense. But apparently, despite all their teasing and outer appearance of bravado, they were just as preoccupied over Emily as he was because Grey could count on one hand the number of balls either of them had successfully sunk all evening.

"Worried?" Edward asked, cutting into his thoughts.

"No." He frowned into his cognac. "Terrified."

"You should be." There was no teasing in his former colonel's voice now, no sarcasm. "You're about to gain a family."

As he watched Thomas lean across the billiards table to take a second shot, Grey felt his throat tighten with emotion. He'd dreamt about having this since he was a boy but never truly thought he ever would. To be part of a family with a wife, brother, child—although he wasn't the father, in his gut he felt as if the baby were his, already loving it as much as any father could. *Good God*, he shook from the enormity of it all.

"If you're worried about Chatham and the duchess, you should know that they're coming around," Edward confided in a voice low enough so Thomas couldn't hear that they were talking about his parents.

Grey glanced at him over the rim of his glass. "Is that so?"

Edward nodded. "Her father no longer wants to kill you."

"Well." He took another swallow and answered wryly, "That's something, I suppose."

"Makes for less interesting family dinners, however." Edward clapped his shoulder. "He won't stand in your way now."

Nothing stood in his way now. He would see to that. He would marry Emily and have a family with her.

And yet...

"I know she was lying before, the reason she gave for refusing my proposal, but damnation, Edward, she's not wrong," he admitted quietly, staring down into his brandy. "My past can only cause problems for her and the baby."

"That's not true."

"She's the daughter of a duke—"

"A widow," Edward reminded him.

"Who might be delivering the next Marquess of Dunwich as we speak," Grey countered grimly. "And I'm a former army officer and son of no one, with a well-honed reputation for being a rake."

"You're a major. That counts for a lot."

He grimaced. "Not enough, not when that's all I am. If I had a family name to go with rank, if I were the second or third son of a peer or a landed gentleman..."

He ran a frustrated hand through his hair. There was no point in contemplating what could never be. Viscountess Henley was right—he'd made a fine life for himself, a far better one than he ever should have had, and he had no right wishing for more. But what he found himself wishing for more than anything was to make Emily happy, and he wanted to prove to her that he deserved her. In every way.

But his chest burned with the impossibility of it. A man

couldn't change his past. God knew he'd spent his entire life trying to do just that.

"You're more than you think. A major with enough money to keep her in comfort, the hero who saved her life—"

"An orphan," he admitted grudgingly. "I lied about being a blacksmith's son."

A dark flicker of surprise registered on Edward's face. Only for a moment, but in that beat, when his friend's eyes narrowed on him, Grey saw betrayal.

"I had no choice." He glanced away toward Thomas on the far side of the room, avoiding the accusation he knew he'd see on Edward's face. "I had to lie to you, to Thomas— to everyone—because it was the only way to make a life for myself. I never would have gotten into the Dragoons as an orphan."

"It would have made no difference to me, you know that. Or to our friendship."

He shook his head. "I would never have made it to Spain in the first place if I'd told the truth." He'd still be a groom in the Henley stables. No—he'd have been dead on the street before he reached fifteen. "Thomas doesn't know."

"Does Emily?"

He gave a small nod and couldn't help the smile tugging at his lips. "She knows exactly who I am, but the brat loves me anyway. Can you believe it?" And *that*, more than any other reason, was why he loved her.

"Then that is all you need." Edward gave him a knowing look and tapped his glass against Grey's.

Thomas sauntered across the room toward them. "What are you two talking about?"

"I was in the middle of calling Grey out for being a damned liar," Edward informed him matter-of-factly.

"I see." Resting the cue against his thigh, Thomas leaned

back against the arm of one of the red leather chairs lining the wall and waved his hand commandingly. "Then by all means, continue."

With a growl, Grey rolled his eyes. "If you two don't stop—"

A scream cut through the house. A high-pitched and pain-filled female cry.

Grey's blood turned to ice, and he started toward the door.

Thomas shot out the cue stick, blocking his path and stopping him. "No," he said simply but forcefully.

Angrily, he knocked the cue away. "Get out of my—"

"No." Thomas stood, pulling to his full height and reminding Grey of the headstrong, reckless cavalry officer he knew in Spain. Right before he threw himself into a bar fight. "You're staying right here."

Grey's dark gaze slid between the two men, noticing how Edward had also shifted to place himself between him and the door. So *that* was why they'd insisted he join them in the billiards room five hours ago. It wasn't just to keep him distracted; it was also to keep him from bursting into the birthing room. By physical restraint, if necessary.

"Grey," Edward said with incredible calmness, exchanging his still-full glass of cognac for Grey's empty one, "why don't you pace some more?"

He flinched as another scream sounded, then nodded faintly as the blood drained from his face. He'd pace—yes, that was exactly what he'd do. But his legs shook with each stride he took, and the damned room wasn't long enough for a proper pace, forcing him to slow in frustration with each turn.

As the agonizing minutes dragged past, he ran a hand through his hair and considered charging the door anyway. But Thomas and Edward had moved to stand near it, like two sentinels flanking either side, and with those two men keeping guard, he wouldn't stand a chance of getting to Emily.

How on earth could women bear going through this? He couldn't remember a single time in battle when he'd been more on edge, more terrified, his heart pounding more fiercely than it was right now. *Never.* He never wanted to go through this again. He didn't think he'd be able to survive it a second time.

Then the town house fell quiet. He stopped, freezing in mid-stride, and the terrible silence and stillness that followed turned even more terrifying than her screams. He held his breath, straining to catch any sound, sense any movement in the house around them—

And then it came, so soft and faint that he almost couldn't comprehend what he was hearing…*A baby.* Its cries grew in volume and intensity until there was no mistaking its new presence in the world.

Thomas patted him on the back and grinned. "Congratulations, Grey," he said with affection. "You're a father."

Collapsing into a nearby chair, he took a deep breath and stared down at his hands, only to discover that he was shaking harder now than he had before he heard the cries. *Good God.* A baby. Emily's baby.

He truly *was* a father.

Kate Westover appeared in the doorway, her face tired and drawn. Glancing around the room, she spotted her husband, and the look of love that passed between them made Grey catch his breath. It was the same look Emily gave him in quiet moments when she thought no one was watching. Without a word, Edward went to her side and affectionately squeezed her hand.

Then the exhaustion on the duchess's face melted into a

soft smile as she gazed up at her husband. "The baby is small but healthy," she told them. "He's going to be just fine."

He... Emily gave birth to a son after all. But the thought barely registered before Grey's chest tightened with worry. He shot out of the chair and hurried toward her. "How's Emily?" he asked.

"Exhausted." Facing him, Kate furrowed her brows slightly with worry, and Edward's hand tightened around hers. "There were some complications."

Oh God. If anything happened to Emily . . . "What kind of complications?" Grey demanded.

Not releasing Edward's fingers, she rested her free hand gently on Grey's arm. "Emily is small, and it was her first child," she said gently in a calming voice. "It was a hard birth for her, but she's going to be fine."

Grey blew out a deep breath, his shoulders sagging with relief. Emily was going to be fine—Emily and the baby were both going to be fine. *Thank God.*

His chest swelled with love, and he longed to hold her. He started past Kate for the hallway, but her fingers tightened around his shirtsleeve, his jacket long ago shed in one of the first rounds of pacing. She stopped him.

"Give Emily time to rest." She gave him a reassuring smile. "When she's ready, I'm certain she'll want to see you."

He hesitated, glancing down the hall. He didn't want to wait any longer, not when he'd already been waiting over five hours.

"You stay here, *all* of you." Her eyebrow arched in warning, expressing how well she knew the three men gathered around her and how much trouble they could cause. Especially when they were together. "I'll come for you when she's ready."

With an affectionate squeeze to his arm, Kate left to return to Emily.

Edward placed his hand on Grey's shoulder and drew him back into the room. "A small celebration is in order." He withdrew cigars from his jacket breast pocket and passed them to Thomas and Grey.

Thomas grabbed the cutter from the fireplace mantel and snipped off the end of his cigar. "It'll soon be your turn to be a nervous father, Colonel, pacing at the birth." He tossed the cutter.

Edward caught it one-handed. "I'll damn well handle it better than Grey, certainly."

Distracted, Grey let the jab pass without comment. They would continue the game of taking shots at him all night, he knew. Just as he knew he was due each barb for how publicly he'd eschewed domesticity in the past, how mercilessly he'd teased Edward when he fell in love with Kate, and how he'd teased him even more when he discovered that they were expecting their first child. But his thoughts were with Emily.

He absently lit his cigar in the lamp and watched the tip glow red. The delivery was over, and she'd given birth to a marquess. Nothing would ever be the same for her. Her life could no longer be her own. Now she was responsible not only for her son but also for his title, his estates, his fortune... and all three hundred years of family history and social expectation accompanying it. And she didn't deserve to have that responsibility made harder by shadows of his past.

"Do you plan on smoking that cigar, Grey, or are you just going to stand there and watch it burn to ash?"

He glanced up and found Thomas grinning at his expense, so he popped the cheroot between his teeth. His chest warmed at the thought that Thomas would truly be his brother once he married Emily. "For the life of me, I can't figure out why Emily tolerates you."

"Ironically," her brother returned the volley with a teasing smile as he leaned back against the wall, "I was just thinking the same about you."

Grey's teeth sank into the cigar. Unwittingly, Thomas had no idea how much his teasing jab cut to the quick. What could a former cavalry officer and War Office agent offer her that she'd need or want now? Emily claimed she loved him just as he was, but she deserved more.

And damnation, he was going to give it to her. Flinging his cigar into the fireplace, he stalked toward the door.

Thomas straightened, puzzled. "Where are you going?"

"Out," he answered shortly. "There's someone I have to find."

"Tonight? At this hour?"

"Yes." He glanced backward at his two best friends as he strode from the room. "And tell Emily that I'm not going anywhere."

* * *

Grey pounded his fist against the front door of the dark town house.

"Mind your manners!" The old butler opened the front door and scowled out at him in the light of a small candle. Obviously not expecting visitors at this hour, the man had made a halfhearted attempt to dress in his uniform jacket but still wore his nightshirt and slippers beneath. "You're waking the dead, blast it!"

"I need to speak to the viscountess," Grey demanded.

"It's past midnight." The man furrowed his bushy gray brows together, peeved at having been woken from his sleep, and began to close the door. "Come back in the morning at a proper hour!"

"I need to see her *now*." Slapping his hand against the door to hold it open, Grey glared down at the butler. "Tell her Major Nathaniel Grey is here. I am certain she will want to see me."

The butler hesitated. Grey knew the man was weighing in his mind the decision of whether to send him away until morning, fearing he might be there for an important reason, or go upstairs and wake the dowager. Neither choice was appealing at half past midnight.

"Her ladyship is abed," the butler protested. "If this can wait until morning—"

"It cannot." He strode past the old butler into the marble foyer. "Send her maid up to wake her. I'll wait here."

"Sir, I insist! You must return in the morning."

"Grimsby," a female voice called out from the landing, "who is it?"

Grey turned to look up the curving staircase at Lady Henley. Even in the middle of the night, even wearing a dressing robe, the dowager exuded an imperialness that would have awed half the *ton*. And undoubtedly had at some point in her eighty years of life.

Odd, then, that Grey was most likely one of the few people in London whom the old woman could not intimidate. "I need to speak with you."

"It is the middle of the night." She tightened the belt cinched around her waist. "Must we do this now?"

"Yes."

She arched an elegant brow. "A proper gentleman would call at a reasonable hour."

"I'm not a proper gentleman, though, am I?" He pinned her with a hard gaze. "Unless I am after all."

With a slight hesitation, understanding the full meaning behind his cryptic words, she pursed her lips and nodded curtly. "You can wait in the drawing room. I shall be down in a moment."

She disappeared back into the shadows of the first floor, Grey assumed to dress properly before heading into the battle that awaited her.

"This way, sir."

He followed Grimsby into the drawing room and waited while the old butler lit the candles, then stirred up the fire. It was clear from every grudging move the man made that he disliked being woken in the middle of the night.

"Thank you," Grey said quietly when the butler straightened away from the hearth and then shuffled out of the room, presumably to hurry back to his quarters before her ladyship could send for tea and biscuits.

But there was a decanter of scotch on the side table, and that would do far better than tea for what was to come tonight. Without waiting for an invitation, he poured himself a glass.

"Pour me one as well," the viscountess ordered as she walked regally into the room. It hadn't taken her long to don a morning dress and pull up her silver-gray hair.

He obliged and poured scotch into a second glass, then held it out to her. "You know why I'm here, then?"

"Why else would you pound on my door at midnight, Nathaniel?" She eyed him cautiously over the rim of her glass. "I heard what you did this evening, by the way, how you saved Emily Matteson's life. The rumors are already circling through Mayfair."

That didn't surprise him, knowing how much the society hens loved juicy bits of gossip. "She had the baby." With a faint smile, he swirled the scotch. "A boy."

"Well, then, here's to the new marquess." She lifted her glass slightly in a toast, then took a large swallow. The tough old woman could handle her liquor better than most men he knew. "Lady Emily is well, I assume?"

"Yes."

"Hmm." She gave him a long, assessing look, then turned to sit on one of the chairs before the fire, gesturing for him to take the other. "They will promote you, you know. For saving her life and the life of the littlest marquess." Then she emphasized, "*Colonel* Grey."

"No, they won't. I'm leaving the War Office," he informed her.

"They will," she corrected with firm certainty. "And a nice position in London for you as well."

The way she said that pricked at him, and he clenched his teeth. "Because of your doing, then."

"Don't be foolish, my boy. You're far too intelligent for such nonsense." She pointed a finger at the chair in a silent command and scowled when he didn't obey. "Of course, it was my doing. As soon as I'd heard what you'd done, I contacted Lord Bathurst to make certain he knew how valuable an agent you are."

"What else has been your doing over the years?" His jaw tightened. "The position offer in Spain, my rank in the cavalry, being assigned to the First Dragoons...or did it start even before then with my very first job as a stable boy?"

"You were always an excellent horseman and a dedicated soldier. I merely put in a good word for you along the way. There's no sin in that."

"Not in that," he challenged. Finally, he sat, and the two of them stared at each other like two enemies sizing up each other before battle. "But there was sin before that, wasn't there?"

She said nothing, but when she raised the glass to her lips, he saw her hand tremble.

He leaned forward. "Tell me," he ordered.

"You've made a fine life for yourself," she commented, and he noted that she didn't deny the accusation. "Why does the past matter now?"

"Don't be foolish," he echoed her words. "You're far too intelligent for such nonsense."

Her eyes flickered at that, making him think she was pleased at the way he challenged her. But whatever he'd seen on her face disappeared quickly. "All these years, I've kept watch on you, and not once did you try to learn the truth from me. The one person who would have known, the one person who knew everything that happened in Trovesbury Village...not the vicar, not the constable."

She reached into the pocket of her pelisse and withdrew two letters, then tossed them onto the floor between them. His eyes followed—the letters he'd written to the parish vicar and county constable inquiring about his birth. The hairs on his nape bristled.

"You could have come to me at any time, Nathaniel, but you never did. Until tonight."

"It never mattered before," he answered honestly.

Her lips pulled into a slow, knowing smile. "So you've set your sights on Lady Emily, have you?"

Despite the tightening of his gut, he stared at her stoically, years of gambling and spying teaching him to hide all emotion from his opponent. "Aren't you going to tell me that I'm overreaching my station, being too ambitious for a former groom who mucked out your stables? For a soldier to dare aspire to marry a duke's daughter?"

She scoffed at that. "Of course not."

"Why not? Everyone else in your social circle would." He

leaned forward, elbows on his knees, and fixed his gaze hard on her. "Yet you know I'm even worse than that, don't you? You know I was an orphan. You've known from the moment I arrived at Henley Park."

"Yes." Her gaze never wavered from his.

"Yet you, a woman who shouldn't have deigned to even glance in my direction, think so highly of me." His eyes flickered as they studied her. "I could never figure out why you would pay any attention to me at all—the urchin for whom you arranged an education equal to that of your own grandsons, whom you got commissioned into the First Dragoons."

"You achieved success yourself, Nathaniel. I only made certain the right people noticed."

"Yet I was nothing to you." He paused significantly. "Unless I wasn't. Unless you knew something that held you in debt to me." He leaned back in the chair and swirled the scotch in his glass. "Are you going to tell me now, or should I start guessing?"

"Something tells me your first guess would be correct," she murmured.

Keeping his silence, and trying to ignore the sudden nervous pounding of his heart, he stared at her and waited. *He knew.* Something inside him had known for years but denied it, had known but never pressed for the truth. Because knowing the truth would not have made any difference.

Until Emily.

"Boys showed up all the time at Henley to ask for work in the stables or gardens." She stared down into her glass, her voice distant and reaching far back into herself. "But there was one…The first time I spotted that boy, I knew who he was. I recognized my son Charles in him as clearly as if he were once again standing before me himself as a child. So

I made certain the boy was given work in the stables, an education, and later, an army commission. It was the same career he would have gotten had he been publicly recognized as my grandson."

Grey felt the words swirl down his spine, as clearly as if she'd shouted it—*Viscount Henley was his father*.

"But now," she continued as she looked up at him, "that boy wants to marry the daughter of a duke, and all that he has accomplished is still not enough, is it?"

"No," he admitted quietly, setting the unwanted scotch aside. This fight with the dowager had been a long time in coming, but it was still far from over. "You know what I need from you," he told her quietly. "Why I came here."

"I told you before, Nathaniel. I will do anything I can to make your way easier—I owe you that. But I will not let you nor anyone else hurt the Henley name." She shook her head. "Your legitimacy will irrevocably damage the reputation of my family, and I cannot allow that."

"You've freely given me everything else." A warning edged low in his voice. "Do you really want me to take this by force?"

Her lips pressed together. "You have no proof."

"I don't need proof. All I need is rumor, helped along by the fact that I look just enough like Charles Henley to fan the gossip." He shrugged, hoping she understood that he was not bluffing in this. "I already possess the reputation of a rake. I have nothing to lose."

But *she* did. Her family's reputation could be ruined by the scandal, and from the troubled frown on her wrinkled brow, she knew it, too.

She stared at him, as if trying to determine if he would truly destroy her family if she refused, if he would take his pursuit of recognition as a Henley through blood and battle.

But he could have saved her the trouble of wondering; he would certainly do just that, if necessary. Recognition of his legitimacy was all that now stood between him and complete happiness with Emily, and he refused to give up the fight.

"I don't want to disparage your family, Lady Henley, but I swear to you I will if I have to. You know the man I am." He locked his gaze with hers. "You know I will do exactly that if left no other choice."

For a moment, she didn't move. Then he saw her shoulders sag, and he knew he'd won.

Nodding slowly as she exhaled a shaking sigh, she rose from her chair, and Grey stood, affording her the respect she deserved as a lady. And as his grandmother. Her old body was stiff and moved slowly as she crossed the room to the small desk beneath the window, but the woman was still formidable despite her age, still intimidating enough that few would dare defy her.

She sat with a grace that hinted at the delicate beauty she had once possessed in her younger days and pulled open the drawer to reach for the pen set and paper within.

"I have no idea who your mother was, and I am certain that even Charles did not know he'd gotten a child on the woman." She scratched the quill across the paper, pausing in her missive to glance pointedly across the room at him. "My son may not be faithful, but he is always careful. I assume that in this situation with you he shall be no different. Be careful in turn with him, then, Nathaniel."

"I will." He took the warning to heart, not imagining that the viscount would take well a forced recognition of his bastard son nearly thirty years after the fact. But the man would simply have to learn to live with it.

"I suppose I put off this moment as long as I did because it never would have made a difference before," she admitted grudgingly, "except to hurt the family. And there *will* be scandal and gossip, be assured of that. All I can do is help control the damage."

"Be assured that I never wanted to hurt your family."

Her only acknowledgment of his comment was a small nod of her head and a tight pursing of her lips. It would cause scandal for the Henleys, yet illegitimate children were common among the *ton*. The news would be replaced by some other juicy scandal by year's end, and by then, everyone would have stopped caring about his connection to them.

And God willing, by then, Emily would finally be his wife.

She carefully blotted her signature, then folded the letter and held it out to him. "There—my statement of legitimacy, officially recognizing you as my grandson."

Giving her the courtesy of not reading it, he slipped it into his jacket pocket. "Thank you."

Her tired eyes met his with an air of inevitability, as if she'd been expecting this moment for a very long time. And truly, he'd noticed that she'd not struggled with a single word in her written statement, most likely having rehearsed it in her mind for years.

"To avoid as much scandal as possible," she explained, "we will take the initiative. Charles will quietly recognize you as his son within the next fortnight."

"How can you be certain of that?"

"I shall *make* certain of it. If he wants to inherit my dower when I die, then he'll have no choice." She looked at him incredulously, as if he were mad to ever doubt her ability to obtain exactly what she wanted. In this life or the next. "I regret the circumstances of tonight and wish there had been another way. But I do not regret helping you become the man you are. You have done well for yourself, Nathaniel, as successfully as if you had been recognized from the beginning. Better than his other sons, in fact." She paused, and in the dim light, he thought he could see her eyes glistening. "I wish you and Lady Emily well."

Standing regally, she reached to take his hand, and he let her. A very small but first step in reconciliation and forgiveness, for both of them.

* * *

Emily sat back in her bed, propped up by half a dozen pillows piled behind her, and held her sleeping son in her arms. The love and happiness swelling inside her nearly overwhelmed her.

A baby...she had a baby now, and she could barely believe it. A little wriggling mass of pink flesh and a dusting of dark hair, a tiny upturned nose and full lips beneath long lashes closed in sleep. Blue eyes, like hers. Ten fingers, ten toes—she knew because she'd counted them at least a dozen times since the midwife first placed him in her arms. He was a tiny miracle, and she lowered her lips to gently kiss his forehead and breathe in deep the sweet scent of him. She supposed she should put him back into the bassinet drawn up beside her bed so both of them could get a few hours of sleep, but she couldn't bring herself to let go of him. Not yet. They had been through too much together to part so quickly, even just to lay him down for a nap.

Beyond her bedroom windows, dawn arrived over the city, the dark night fading away into muted blues and pinks beneath the growing light as the sun inched higher. She couldn't help but feel as if the whole world was holding its breath, waiting for the new day to break, and that a new part of her life was dawning along with the morning.

A knock sounded softly at her door, but her gaze never left her baby's sleeping face. She smiled as he stirred in his sleep, his little fist lifting to his mouth to suck on his fingers.

"Emily." Heat swirled down her spine at the sound of her name, spoken in a deep, reverent tone.

She glanced up to find Grey standing in the doorway, his chocolate eyes warm as he took in the sight of her and the baby in the morning light.

"Dear God," he breathed hoarsely, a softly stricken expression on his handsome face, "you are so lovely."

She knew she looked a fright, wearing only her dressing gown and a fresh night rail she'd tugged on after her bath, with her hair pulled back into a loose chignon at her neck to keep it out of her way. And she was certain her face appeared just as tired as she felt.

"I'm a mess," she corrected, flushing with embarrassment.

"Not to me. To me, you're the most beautiful woman in the world."

Her throat tightened with emotion. Smiling at him, her eyes gleaming, she lifted the sleeping bundle in her arms. "Look what I have," she teased, wonder audible in her voice. "It's a baby."

His lips tugged upward. "So I heard."

"Would you like to meet him?"

His eyes flickered warmly over the baby as he stared at the little bundle in her arms. "Very much."

Slowly, Grey came forward and sat on the edge of her bed. She turned slightly to bring her son between them. Carefully, he pulled down the baby's soft blanket with his forefinger and stared in astonishment.

"So small, yet so perfect," he whispered. He drew his fingertip along the curve of the baby's chin. When he touched the pink lips, the baby opened his mouth and instinctively tried to suckle his finger.

She heard him catch his breath, saw the mix of love, pride, and utter amazement flash across his face. Her heart melted with overwhelming love, that something this small, this helpless and vulnerable, could stir such emotion in him.

He blinked hard and cleared his throat. "Have you given him a name?"

"Stephen."

"Stephen," he repeated quietly. "Edward Westover had an older brother named Stephen."

"Kate told me. Do you think Edward will mind?"

"Not at all. Stephen was a good man, and he deserves to be remembered. It's a fine name…Hello, Stephen."

The baby's tiny hand clasped around Grey's finger, and he made a soft mewling sound in his sleep.

Grey chuckled. "I think he likes it."

"Good." She nodded, adjusting a tiny bootie on the baby's foot. "Family is important."

"Yes, it is," he agreed in a soft murmur, an odd tone to his voice she couldn't quite place.

"He has Thomas for an uncle, and I would like Edward and Kate Westover to be his godparents."

"They'll be honored," he assured her.

She paused in her fussing with the bootie to flick her gaze up to his for only a beat before returning to her son. "When I said surrounded by family, I did not necessarily mean my parents, you understand."

He laughed and shifted to slip his arm behind her, finding a way to hold both of them in his arms. He placed a soft kiss at her temple.

"As for the baptism, I'm certain my mother will insist it

be held in St. Paul's, but I know she won't understand when the bishop calls out Stephen's name. Family is important," she repeated for emphasis, "and so he is being named after his family." She whispered, finally raising her eyes to his. "Stephen *Nathaniel* Crenshaw."

His lips parted in stunned surprise. "Emily—"

"I thought that I could let you go, that letting you go to Spain was the best choice for you," she rushed out quickly, "but I was wrong. When I asked for you last night after the baby was born and you weren't here—I couldn't bear it, Grey." She reached for his hand as it rested on the mattress beside her, her trembling fingers lacing through his. "I need you, Stephen needs you . . . and you need us."

She leaned forward to touch her lips to his, closing her eyes as she willed with every ounce of strength left inside her for him to realize how much she loved him, how much she and her son needed him. How she couldn't tolerate the thought that the sun might rise tomorrow to find him far away from her.

For a moment, he didn't move, and then his lips began to gently caress hers. His mouth slid along her jaw to her ear before he shifted away from her.

"I didn't mean to upset you last night." He looked down at the baby and ran his hand over Stephen's smooth head. "I wanted to be here, but there was a woman I had to find."

"Oh." *A woman.* A hollow pain panged in her chest. She gave a soft sniff and tried to hide the jealousy that flashed white-hot through her.

He grinned. "My grandmother."

Her heart skipped, not understanding. "Grandmother?"

With a firm nod, he withdrew a folded paper from his jacket pocket and held it out to her.

She stared at the note, barely able to breathe from the

stunned surprise cascading through her in waves. "What is that?" she whispered.

"A birthday gift for you and Stephen." He looked deeply into her eyes. "Read it."

With trembling fingers, sensing the enormity of the moment, she took the note and read the elegant handwriting. A single sentence with a signature beneath... A gasp tore from her throat. This was *impossible*!

Her eyes flew up to his, her fingers tightening against the note so hard she wrinkled the paper. She fixed her gaze on his face, on trying to find sense in what he was showing her.

"Viscount Henley?" she breathed.

"Yes."

"No!" With a fierce shake of her head, she shoved the note back at him. "I love *you*, Grey. I don't care who your family is or is not—it holds no importance for me. I don't need that declaration to build a future with you."

"I know," he told her softly. "But it will make that future easier, if you still want me."

Tears gathered on her lashes as she admitted, "I've wanted you since I was sixteen, from the first time I laid eyes on you."

He reached into his pocket again, this time to withdraw the engagement ring he'd offered her three months ago. The tiny ring of diamonds and sapphires shined in the morning sunlight as he tenderly slipped it onto her left hand and raised it to his lips to kiss it.

"I love you," she whispered past the knot of emotion in her throat.

"You'd better." With a wolfish grin, he murmured, "Because now that I've got you, I am never letting you go."

Smiling through her tears, she lifted the baby toward him. "Hold your son, Nathaniel."

As she placed Stephen into his arms, his chocolate-brown eyes found hers. In their warm depths she saw their future stretching out across all the years before them. Together. "I love you, Emily."

"You'd better," she purred his words back to him, leaning in to kiss him over their sleeping son, "because I am never letting you go."

Thomas Matteson vows to capture the highwayman who has been lifting the *ton*'s purses. But when the thief turns out to be the most beautiful, fascinating woman he has ever seen, Thomas may be the one in danger of having his heart stolen...

Please see the next page for a preview of

HOW I MARRIED A MARQUESS.

CHAPTER ONE

Mayfair, London
October 1817

*L*ord Chesney?" Jensen's voice cut through the midmorning stillness of the stables behind Chatham House. "Are you here, sir?"

Inside the end stall box, Thomas Matteson, Marquess of Chesney, stilled, hoping the butler would simply leave and not interrupt his morning. The same morning he'd so carefully arranged by giving the grooms time off to attend Tattersall's. He let the silence of the stables answer for him, interrupted only by the restless shifting of horses in their stalls and a pawing of hooves. One of them snorted in reply.

But Jensen persisted in ruining his morning. "Sir?"

Stifling a curse, Thomas stepped into the aisle and closed the door firmly behind him. He brushed the straw from the sleeves of his maroon riding jacket. "What is it, Jensen?"

"A visitor, sir." The portly butler hurried forward, silver salver in hand.

Thomas fought not to roll his eyes at Jensen's formality. An employee of the Matteson household for nearly twenty years, the man took his position seriously, even during times like these when the duke and duchess were at their country estate and Thomas was the only family member in residence.

And he was in residence precisely *because* his mother and father were not, turning Chatham House into bachelor's quarters until they returned in January. Yet Jensen and the rest of the London staff continued to serve with the precision of a military regiment, taking pride in their positions in a duke's household even while the duke was away.

And while the old lord was away, the young lord would play...or at least that had been his plan. But it was deuced hard to do when the staff followed his every move. For heaven's sake! Yesterday morning he caught Cook spying on him to make certain he ate breakfast.

Most likely, their close attention came upon orders from his mother. He would have found her concern endearing if it didn't aggravate the hell out of him. And it was damned grating that nearly everyone he interacted with these days— including the household staff, apparently—still thought of him as fragile. As still not fully recovered. As *broken*.

"My lord." Jensen presented the card with as much flourish as if he stood in the gilded front hall of Stonewall Abbey rather than in a stable with his shoes dangerously close to a pile of manure.

"Better watch your step, Jensen," Thomas warned as he took the card. "This isn't the foyer."

He watched with amusement as the proud butler slowly took a step backward.

Then he read the embossed name on the card. "The Earl Royston?" *Odd.* Why the devil was that man here?

"I've put him in the drawing room, sir." Jensen hesitated and cleared his throat as if dreading telling him, "And Lady Emily is taking tea in the morning room."

His lips curled grimly. Yet another person set on ruining his morning, apparently. "My sister is, is she?"

"Yes, sir."

"Tell Royston I'll join him in a moment." He arched a brow. "And please tell my sister that she has her own London town house and should bloody well stop haunting mine."

"Yes, sir." Despite the curt nod of his head, Thomas knew the portly butler had no intention of passing along *that* message.

Straw rustled inside the stall behind him, and Jensen furrowed his bushy brows. "Should I call for one of the footmen to help you with your horse, sir?"

"No need." He waved off the offer. At the sound of more rustling, he added, "Just a filly I've been attempting to break."

With a shallow bow, and careful to miss the manure, Jensen turned smartly on his heel and retreated toward the house.

Thomas waited until the butler was out of sight before opening the stall door. Folding his arms across his chest, he leaned against the post and looked at the woman standing inside.

"Just a filly you've been attempting to break, am I?" Helene Humphrey, the young widow of the late Charles Humphrey, pouted with mock peevishness as she brushed at the straw clinging to her riding habit. The same habit that just moments ago had been pulled down to her waist and bunched up around her hips as she'd straddled him in the hay. "How positively uncomplimentary of you, Chesney."

He shrugged. "You're the one visiting my stables, Helene."

"And where else am I supposed to take such a fine morning ride?" She turned her back to him so he could fasten up her dress.

He did as she wanted and fastened her up—of course he did. He was a gentleman, after all, and a gentleman always helped his lover freshen her appearance after a tryst, even if she made assignations with half of London society and had just ridden him off six feet from a pile of horse shit. Having settled into wealthy widowhood with all the restraint of an opera diva, Helene thrilled at indulging in a string of dalliances, including those she'd risked before Humphrey died.

That was why he enjoyed bedding her. With Helene, a man got exactly what he saw...no secrets, no surprises. Just a beautiful and eager woman with a hot mouth and a cold heart.

"One of these mornings, we really should put you onto a horse." As he fastened the last button, he lowered his head to brush his mouth against the side of her neck. "I've got a new gelding you might like."

With a wicked smile, she turned in his arms and reached down to cup his cock. "Why would I want a gelding," she purred, "when I've got a stallion?"

Her fingers caressed him through his riding breeches, more in possession than desire. Drawing a breath through clenched teeth, he reached down to grasp her wrist and pull her hand away. He didn't like to think of himself as providing nothing more than stud service. Even if the implication were true.

"At least your guests have good timing." She stepped back and tugged at her gloves. As with the hat, she'd kept her gloves and boots on the entire time he'd been inside her.

Mercifully, she'd discarded the riding crop. "Ten minutes earlier, and I would have been extremely put out."

Ten minutes earlier. He would have been annoyed, but would he have truly cared?

His chest tightened with disquiet. Good Lord, had his life really come to this? Pre-appointed tumbles in a horse stall with a woman he didn't even like, done more to release the acute uneasiness that pounded relentlessly at him than for physical pleasure?

Just one year ago, his life still possessed meaning. He'd felt alive then, and he never would have sought out a woman like Helene. In public, he had moved at the center of society, taking advantage of all the benefits that life within the peerage afforded, concerned with nothing more than fast horses, faster women, and the odds in the book at White's. But in private, he'd served as a War Office operative, his skills highly valued and his work important, and his life was filled with purpose.

Until everything had gone so horribly wrong. Right in Mayfair, of all places. That was the evening when he learned the difference between being alive and truly living.

And his life had become a living hell. Unconsciously, his hand reached for his side, for that spot just above his hip where the bullet hole still hideously pocked his skin.

"Next Thursday morning, then, for our usual ride?" She trailed the end of her riding crop suggestively along his shoulder as she stepped past him into the aisle to leave. "Although, I have *so* been wanting to try riding bareback."

He grabbed her around the waist and pulled her back against him. He'd found release with her just minutes ago, but he was still restless, still oddly unsatisfied, and recklessly sought one last moment of distraction with her. "When it comes to being bareback, Helene," he murmured as he nipped at her earlobe, "I suspect there's nothing you haven't already tried."

He drew a soft moan from her as his hand fondled her breast through her riding habit, and his cock flexed. Did he have time to take her again? Nothing more than a quick, desperate diversion, certainly, yet one that would keep at bay the rising anxiety for a little while longer.

Giving a throaty laugh, she slipped out of his arms. "Insatiable!" she scolded with a teasing smile and smacked him playfully on the shoulder with the riding crop. "But I'm due for breakfast, and you have guests waiting."

Then she sauntered away, shooting him a parting look of a heated promise for their next morning ride. Her hips sashayed wide with every step from the stables and down the narrow back alley to her waiting carriage.

Blowing out a harsh breath, he stalked toward the house with hands clenched in frustration. Not over Helene. Frustration over— Christ! *Everything.*

However much he knew he should be grateful for still breathing and moving, the long and painful recovery, coupled with the public exposure of being shot, left him nervous, desperate, anxious. An unexpected movement or shadow could send his heart racing and his breath panting, and the rush of adrenaline through his body would rattle him beyond control.

He ran his fingers through his black hair, cursing them for shaking. The War Office wouldn't give him another field assignment now. He'd become too conspicuous for espionage work. Too *wounded.* And both because of the shooting and his position as the duke's heir, the military refused him any sort of commission. Even the damned admiralty rejected him, for God's sake.

Apparently, he wasn't even good enough to drown.

Yet he couldn't bear the thought of returning to the life he'd led before he joined the War Office, when he had nothing to do but wait for his father to die so he could become a duke. After fighting against Napoleon on the Peninsula as part of the Scarlet Scoundrels of the First Dragoons, he found little meaning in being a society gentleman. In the past few months, he'd worked his way through all the pursuits enjoyed by the quality...horses, gambling, women. Until nothing was left. But he felt just as empty as before.

No wonder so many men gambled away their fortunes, became drunks, or turned into rakes who sported in ruining young women—they were bored out of their blasted minds.

When he thought about what little that life held for him and the darkness now edging his existence, he doubted he could survive. He'd managed to hang on to his sanity during the past year only by clinging to the hope that he had connections in the government who could help him get back into fieldwork.

Jensen opened the front door as he bounded up the steps and strode inside the town house. He paused at the foyer table to sort quickly through the morning mail, searching for one particular message, one specific—

He saw the letter, and his heart skipped.

Earl Bathurst.

With a nervous breath, he broke the wax seal to scan the message from the Secretary of State for War and the Colonies, the man responsible for overseeing the War Office and his last chance at returning to the field. But each sentence caused the uneasiness to grasp out for him again, to clutch and strangle at him with its claws, and his heartbeat sped sickeningly as the blackness crept in around him.

Bathurst had refused his request for another assignment.

He remained unconvinced that Thomas had recovered enough to continue his work.

As the ghost pain pierced him, he covered his side with his hand, even knowing that the wound was completely healed by now. He pressed his eyes closed to concentrate on his breathing. Slow, steady, controlled—

"Anything I can help you with, sir?" Jensen was at his side.

Opening his eyes, he covered his humiliation with a shake of his head. "Just put all this in the study, will you?"

He tossed the unwanted letter onto the pile and turned away. He would deal with it later, once he was alone and could fully absorb the refusal of this last desperate attempt for life. But now the Earl Royston waited upstairs in the drawing room for him, and he had to appear to be normal in front of his father's acquaintance from the Lords, no matter how painful the engulfing blackness in his chest.

Taking a moment to gather himself, he paused to lean his shoulder against the doorway of the downstairs morning room and looked in at his sister as she sat on the sofa, her feet curled up beneath her, an open book on her lap. He'd brought her such worry over the past year, and the guilt of the hell he'd put her through only added to the tightening that clenched at his gut.

But for now, she was relaxed, happily humming softly to herself, and absolutely glowing. He smiled at the sight of her.

"Do you have a valid reason for being here, Mrs. Grey," he drawled, hoping his voice sounded more steady than he actually felt, "or are you simply spying on me again?"

"The latter, of course." Emily returned his smile as she set the book aside and reached toward the tray on the low table to pour a cup of tea. His sister moved with an inherent gracefulness that turned women green with envy, and the sharpness of her mind only served to distinguish her even more from the other society ladies. "I know you have a visitor waiting for you—Royston wished me good morning when he arrived—but when you're finished with him, I expect you to join me for tea."

Not a request, he'd noticed. "You know, officially, I outrank you."

"Only on paper, brother dear." She took a thoughtful sip. "Although, it wouldn't hurt to put your title to good use and consider calling on some of the young ladies who—"

"No."

She shot him a peevish glare over the rim of her teacup, which he ignored. He would have to marry someday and produce an heir, but there was no hurry. No need to punish some poor girl unduly by bringing her into the madness of the Matteson family sooner than necessary.

"You came to check on me again," he accused gently, although in truth, he was glad to see her.

"I came because I had the day to myself for once, and I wanted to spend time with my loving brother." Despite that obvious lie, she scolded lightly, "Shame on you for insinuating otherwise."

He arched a blatantly disbelieving brow. Emily was beautiful, charming, elegant...and an absolute pain in the ass whenever she meddled in his business, which was most of the time. But he loved her, and he would gladly lay down his life for her—when he wasn't set on throttling her himself. "Where has Grey gone off to, then?"

"He and the colonel went to Tattersall's to look at a hunter that Jackson Shaw has up for auction," she answered far too smoothly, clearly having practiced her response in anticipation of the question. She never could lie well, not even as a child. "Kate and the twins are away at Brambly

House. And I couldn't bear the thought of being all alone at home, so I came here."

"You couldn't bear the thought of *me* being all alone, you mean," he countered, knowing full well that she had her son, his nanny, and a dozen servants to keep her company. "So you came here to torture me."

With a shrug, she lifted the teacup to her lips. "If you can't torture family, well, then who can you torture?"

"And that," he pointed out earnestly, "sums up every Matteson family dinner since we were five."

She choked on her tea. Laughing, she cleared her throat. "Go on, then, see to Royston. I'll be here when you return."

"Dear God," he grumbled painfully, "truly?"

He saw the devilish smile she tried to hide behind the teacup, then turned into the hallway.

"And give my regards to Lady Humphrey the next time you...*see* her."

He froze. *Damnation.*

Rolling his eyes, he glared at her over his shoulder. "You've become as much of a spy as that husband of yours."

With a wave of her hand, she dismissed him. "Torture, spying—it's all Matteson family business."

Yes, he conceded lamentably as he took the stairs three at a time, he supposed it was. Except for him. Not any longer.

Pushing the black thoughts from his mind, he strode into the drawing room. "Lord Royston."

"Chesney." Simon Royston, Earl Royston, warmly clasped his hand. "Good to see you again."

He smiled shortly at the earl, the warmth of the man's greeting assuming a familiarity much closer than the two men actually shared. Royston was his father's acquaintance. Except for passing greetings at social events, Thomas had rarely spoken to the man.

In comparison to the Matteson family, with its title going back nine generations, the Roystons were recently titled, the current earl only the third of the line. But the earl's grandfather had been well admired among his peers, and Simon Royston carried on that reputation. Because of the man's acquaintance with his father—and more so due to a niggling curiosity about what brought the earl to Chatham House during the off-season, a curiosity that just might distract him for the remainder of the morning—Thomas was willing to receive him.

He gestured to the liquor cabinet. "Whiskey?" Not yet noon, the hour was early for a stiff drink, but Thomas noticed the tension in the older man's body, the dark circles beneath his eyes indicating lack of sleep. The earl could use a drink. And if truth be told, so could he.

Royston nodded. "Please."

Thomas poured two glasses and handed one over, then motioned for the man to sit. He settled into his chair and watched as the earl tossed back nearly half the whiskey in a single swallow.

"I have to admit," Thomas said as he studied him over the rim of his untouched glass, "this is a surprise. Of course, as a friend of my father's, you're always welcome here, but surely, you know that Chatham is in the country for the hunting season." As should be every other man of landed property who had the good sense to avoid London this time of year. Including Royston.

"I came looking for you, actually." The earl paused. "May we speak in confidence?"

He nodded, holding back a puzzled frown. Whatever could Royston want with him?

The man leaned forward, elbows on his knees, and rolled the crystal tumbler between his palms. "There's been trouble at Blackwood Hall."

Thomas had never been to the country estate, but he knew of the place, which had been in the earl's family for as long as the title. Situated in the heart of Lincolnshire, the estate was two days' hard ride from London under the best of conditions; at this time of year, with the increasing cold and fall rains, a coach would be lucky to reach the estate in four. So whatever sent the man scurrying to London must have been serious. "What kind of trouble?"

He answered glumly, "Highwaymen."

"Highwaymen," Thomas repeated and carefully kept his face stoic, not letting his disappointment register at the mundane answer.

Royston grimaced. "I know what you're thinking—where is there a road in the Lincolnshire countryside that doesn't have highwaymen?"

He had been thinking exactly that but instead offered, "Actually, I was wondering why you didn't go to the constabulary."

"I have, but to no avail." He finished off his whiskey. "It's a puzzle, that's what it is. A damnable mystery."

With his interest pricked at that comment, Thomas stood to refill the empty glass. "How so?"

"There appears to be no pattern, except that there is." When Thomas frowned at his enigmatic choice of words, he continued. "The only robberies in the area have been guests returning home from Blackwood Hall, and then, not all the guests and not all the time." He grimaced. "We're being targeted. My guests. *Me.*"

"I wouldn't go that far." He tried to keep the patronizing tone from his voice, but truly, the description of the robberies struck him as simple paranoia. "You're a landowner in Lincolnshire. Highwaymen rob wealthy travelers, so more of your guests than—"

He shook his head. "*Only* my guests, Chesney. No one else."

Well, that was odd. Still... "It doesn't mean you're being targeted."

"When the carriages are stopped, only the men are asked to hand over their valuables. And one man in each coach, no matter how many other men are inside, and never anything from the women. Not even when openly displaying diamonds and pearls."

A highwayman who robbed only one man per coach and left jewels? Finally, Thomas was intrigued. He leaned forward. "How long has this been happening?"

"On and off for the past two years."

He arched a brow. "You're just now noticing the pattern?"

"I've noticed, I'm ashamed to say." Royston glanced down at the whiskey in his glass. "But it never needed to be addressed until now."

"What's changed?"

"I have hopes for the Lords next session. Some important positions will be opening, and I want to make my mark. You of all people should understand that."

Thomas stared at him inscrutably, wondering exactly how much the earl thought he knew about him, then lied, "I'm afraid I don't." He set his whiskey aside. "Besides, I'm not involved in anything of importance in the government." *Not anymore.* "So why did you seek me out?"

Royston leveled his gaze on him, and his face took on a hard expression. "I know things about you," he answered quietly. "I have connections in the War Office who have vouched for your... special skills."

Thomas remained silent, unwilling to either deny or validate the earl's assumptions about him. Those special skills they'd assured Royston he possessed were the same ones they no longer wanted.

"I want you to come to Blackwood Hall and investigate this." Asking for help from someone twenty years his junior was clearly difficult for the proud earl, but judging from the exasperated look in his eyes, he'd found no other solution. "I want this stopped, no matter the cost." His gaze dropped unassumingly back to his drink. "And if it goes well, I see no reason why I shouldn't put in a good word for you with Lord Bathurst, assuring him that you have my full support and confidence."

Bathurst. Thomas froze even as a shot of adrenaline jolted through him. This could very well be the opportunity he'd been seeking. Royston wasn't wrong—he possessed a set of finely honed talents that had served him well as an agent, and he ached to use them again, even for something as small as this. Something that could bring purpose back to his life.

"Do we have an agreement, then, Chesney?"

Thomas nodded slowly, outwardly calm despite his racing heart.

"I'm hosting a party next week." Royston set aside his glass and stood. "A fortnight at Blackwood Hall and a chance for a group of peers to gather to break up the boredom of the country season. An irresistible target for the highwayman, I presume."

Nodding, Thomas rose to his feet. "Make certain the guest list is common knowledge to your household staff."

Royston hesitated, incredulity flashing over his face. "You think it could be someone within my own house?"

"I think it could be anyone." Thomas slapped him on the shoulder and walked him downstairs. "See you next week, then."

He took his hat and gloves from Jensen and left the house. "My thanks, Chesney."

And mine to you. More than the earl would ever know, because this might just prove to be his opportunity to show the War Office that he was not only fully healed and ready for another field assignment but that he was just as sharp and vital as ever. If not more.

His body pulsed with excitement and the first real hope he'd had in a year. Arresting a highwayman in Lincolnshire certainly wasn't on par with the spying he'd done before, but it might just get him noticed. And at this point, with all other avenues blocked, he would claim whatever small victories he could.

Small victory? He laughed at himself. Who was he trying to fool? He knew the truth, no matter how reluctant he was to admit it.

Two weeks at a boring Lincolnshire party might just save his life.

"Business concluded, then?" Emily looked up from her book as he sauntered into the morning room and slumped down heavily next to her on the sofa.

"Not business." He grinned, feeling like the cat who'd gotten into the cream. "Pleasure."

Her lips twitched. "And here I'd thought Lady Humphrey had already departed."

He shot her an icy look that made grown men quake in their boots but only seemed to amuse her. *Brat.* "Royston invited me to a party he's throwing next week at Blackwood Hall."

"Oh?" Her bewildered expression spoke volumes, incredulous that her brother would so eagerly gallop off to a party certain to be filled with dull dandies and old gossips.

He dissembled, "Apparently, the earl has political aspirations and wants counsel on some recent matters that have been troubling him."

"And he picked *you*?" Astonishment rang in her voice. "He wants to succeed at these aspirations, does he not?"

He grimaced at the teasing insult. She was needling him, trying in her own fashion to get the truth from him, but he would keep this investigation to himself. Emily was one of the few people who truly knew of the hell he'd gone through—was *still* going through—and he didn't want to concern her. If the trip to Lincolnshire went as well as he hoped, he would tell her afterward when all was set to rights again.

And if not...well, there would be little she could do to help fight back the anxiety he knew would come, the clawing blackness that would eventually devour him whole.

"You know, getting away from London might do you good," she added thoughtfully. "You might be introduced to a whole new group of potential wives."

Stifling an exasperated groan, he kicked his boots onto the tea table. "You know, brat, when you were a child, I sold you to the Gypsies," he told her bluntly. "I'm still waiting for them to take you away."

Emily laughed, her brilliant blue eyes shining with affection, and offered him a cup of tea.

Fall in Love with Forever Romance

KISS ME IN CHRISTMAS
by Debbie Mason

Back in little Christmas, Colorado, Hollywood star Chloe O'Connor is still remembered as a shy, awkward schoolgirl. And there's no one she dreads (and secretly wants) to see more than her high school crush. While Easton McBride enjoys the flirtation with this new bold and beautiful Chloe, he can't help but wonder whether a kiss could have the power to bring back the small-town girl he first fell in love with.

Fall in Love with Forever Romance

PLAY TO WIN
by Tiffany Snow

In the third book of bestselling author Tiffany Snow's Risky Business series, it's finally time for Sage to decide between two brothers-in-arms: Parker, the clean-cut, filthy-rich business magnate . . . or Ryker, the tough-as-nails undercover detective.

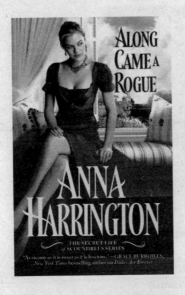

Fall in Love with Forever Romance

NECESSARY RISK
by Tara Wyatt

The first book in a hot new action-packed series from debut author Tara Wyatt, which will appeal to fans of Suzanne Brockmann, Pamela Clare, and Julie Ann Walker.

SEE YOU AT SUNSET
by V.K. Sykes

The newest novel from *USA Today* bestselling author V.K. Sykes! Deputy Sheriff Micah Lancaster has wanted Holly Tyler for as long as he can remember. Now she's back in Seashell Bay, and the attraction still flickers between them, a promise of something *more*. Their desire is stronger than any undertow...and once it pulls them under, it won't let go.